Country Library

THE PHASIAN BIRD

Chee-Kai, the 'phasian bird' or pheasant, is the central character of this novel set in the Norfolk countryside, an affectionate portrait of the world in which Henry Williamson lived before the Second World War. He depicts its wild life with all the skill that went into *Tarka the Otter*, and there are shrewdly observed human characters as well, the stockman and teamsman of the farm, the stranger who buys the holding (and whose life seems mysteriously bound up with that of Chee-Kai), and the men of the nearby village. Williamson conveys the loyalty of man to master and the distrust of outsiders that bound such a community together, and sets beside this small human world the greater community of the natural world.

THE PHASIAN BIRD

Henry Williamson

THE BOYDELL PRESS

First published 1948
First published in COUNTRY LIBRARY 1984
by The Boydell Press
an imprint of Boydell and Brewer Ltd
PO Box 9, Woodbridge, Suffolk, IP12 3DF

ISBN 0 85115 238 4

Printed in Great Britain by
St Edmundsbury Press, Bury St Edmunds, Suffolk

NOTE

The author hereby acknowledges his indebtedness to a writer, whose anonymity has been preserved, for the description of Jago the gamecock contained within these pages.

PART ONE

Chapter One

———❦———

At the western end of the meadow there was a wood called the Carr. It was a narrow plantation of larch, pine, willow, elm, and sycamore, with wildling bushes of white and black thorn striving to grow under the canopy of the taller trees. Originally the Carr had been planted as covert for game birds, when the meadow was reclaimed from sea-marsh in a past century, in the time when the power and strength of England was in the land, before the cities and the factories had absorbed both and taken control and so had begun the slow decadence of the land and of the people sprung from the land.

In those days before the general use of coal, before the idea of the steam engine, the power was vested in the great lords of land, and there was unity of life upon their estates. The beauty of the English countryside arose out of this unity. Woods were planted, land reclaimed from the sea, village design and rural craftsmanship were paramount, for gold was mastered by the few, and had not become the master of the many. There was in the great estate, embracing villages and farms and manors and seacoast, but one voice, and therefore one direction of life; not, as when the strength and the power were absorbed by the industrialists of the towns, many conflicting voices and a multi-headed misdirection of life which in the end caused the near-ruin of the English country, its woods and fields and villages and farms and manors and sea-coast, and its peasants and farmers and squires who had made its ordered beauty and design; and which caused also the dereliction of the urban industries and the towns which had made the factories and the ugliness of England. This is the story of a game bird, a hybrid pheasant, in the period of change that came upon the countryside, and these facts are set down as part of the background to the bird's life: for all background in England at this time was man-made, or man-mismade.

There was an ivy-clad pine tree growing at the northern end of the Carr, where the wood came to a point on the riverbank, and beside the meadow. Where other conifers, planted as shelter for pheasants, had died in the soil which was only a couple of feet above the water level, the pine at the end of the wood had lived because it stood out of a mound that had been thrown up by the cutting of a drain or dyke. Its surface roots had turned away from the low-lying swamp where willows leaned and grew in a jungle of their own crooked limbs, and had thrust along the dryer earth of rich maritime clay and darker silt, laid there by the spades of the dyke diggers. Thus the pine lived, its surface roots drawing nourishment from the compost of dead leaves and decayed twigs that lay upon the mounded earth; and round its copper-scaled trunk were twisted heavy thongs of ivy, whose dark leaves had reached and spread nearly to the crest of the pine.

The wind, that ever seeks song, drew from the pine tree with every wandering air a sibilance, or a humming, or a roar as the gale passed rudely onwards. Already the high winds of the equinox had passed through the Carr, and the leaves of sycamore, beech, elm, and ash had fallen on the woodland floor, on the drift or path beyond the river, and in the water swilling along slowly through the meadows to the sea. When the leaves had fallen the beaters had gone through the Carr, striking bole of tree and branch with sticks, and uttering low cries to drive the birds to the line of men with guns spaced on the far meadow. Three weeks later the beaters had entered the wood again, and once more the shots had echoed from the distant hillsides, and spent pellets had rattled on the twigs and branches of the trees in the Carr.

At dusk there were no pheasants in the wood, which was to the owls and the mice and the cries of water-fowl. The game birds which had survived the upward smacks of whistling shot were afraid to return to their roosts in the Carr; but as the days followed in absence of men and dogs in the fields, they forgot their terrors, and returned to the roosting trees, and once more the cocks crowed one to another in the distant woods of the farm.

At the time of the winter solstice there began to move over the western hemisphere the long thrust of Siberian air which drove down every winter from the Pole, discolouring land and water until, pouring through the passes of mountain ranges on its way to the Equator, its impulse was expended in the rebuffets of the sun upon deep blue ocean set with coral isle and palm.

This dreaded wind of northern Asia lisped by the thin stubbles of the acid soils of the scald and breck lands, by the broken field-gates and the thistles and docks and ragwort stems of the thin pastures, it blenched the tips of the reeds growing thickly in the dykes where teal and mallard flighted, dropped down, and splashed to feed in the pallor of first darkness; the wind screamed faintly by the rusty barbs of wire that threaded the overgrown hedges, and poured in chilling jets through the broken tiled roofs of stable, hovel, and barn. What colour of fields had not been drained in the dereliction upon farming was rasped away by the multitudinous and invisible tongues of the dry wind from the east.

The plowman in his layers of thin coats cried to his horses drawing the plow turning seven-inch furrows across the field from headland to headland while yet the soil was unfrozen. The thin and unmatched horses, fed on poor hay and few oats, their fetlocks shaggy with the grease of neglect, paused in the furrow to rest, unable to pull at the chains wrapped with strips of old sacking against the galling of their flanks: for their harness did not fit, being bought at auction for a few shillings—broken collars, worm-eaten sails, and uneven swingle-trees. Fed on bread of white flour from which the golden skin of the wheat had been sifted after grinding as "offal", spread with margarine made in part of the fat of whales and jam of pea-straw and mangold-pulp coloured and sweetened chemically, and refreshed by cold, near-milkless tea from a bottle once holding chemical fruit-drink, the teamsman holding the long lines to the rusty bits was nearly as languid as his horses.

The door of his stable, of crumbling brick and flint walling, had fallen off its wooden post, and sacks were nailed in the space against the dreaded wind. Outside the dislodged and rotten threshold of the doorway was a pit of mud deep to the knees of the horses, whose legs were seldom dried with straw when they were taken to the stable after the day's work. For the farmer's capital was gone in debt to the bank, and the only money he made from working his farm of nearly three hundred acres was from the syndicate of urban sportsmen who had the shooting; and that sum did not cover the tithe on the land, which had to be paid every year to the Church of England.

The woods were pitted and scoured by the diggings of rabbits, and the counter-diggings of trappers and ferreters; the timber trees had been thrown nearly a quarter of a century since, during an industrial war; and the woods, once the pride of the landowner, were, save for a few old beeches and oaks of irregular shape, wildernesses of self-sown growth of elderberry and sycamore, of creeping sucker of elm and unwanted horse-chestnut, and bird-sown ash.

On the adjoining field, a sticky brown clay was being turned up in strips, hiding sparse barley stubble, by an old Fordson tractor with cleated wheels. The tractor owner-driver, the pores of his skin dark with paraffin, and clad in oil-stained clothes, as his machine trundled before its three-furrow plows beat his scarred hands upon his thighs, and stayed his impulse to go home; but he had a wife and children, and he plowed by contract for nine shillings an acre, which paid little more than his running costs. He passed a hare crouching, bulbous-eyed and angular, in its shallow form, and reflected that it was worth but a shilling at the back door of the village dealer, who covertly bought the game (for which he had no licence) which in those days hardly paid for the getting. The wind nipped the nails of his fingers, and spitting away the flattened and wet fag-end upon his lip, he blew through his clenched hands, and set himself to endure another hour, for another six shillings. His machine trundled on, compressing the acid pan over the subsoil the tighter, and long after the horses had been taken down the hill it was moving darkly through the dusk.

The single-furrow horse-plow remained where it had been left on the headland, the unpainted swingle-trees from which the worn chains had been unhooked hanging to its beam, for in the morning ice lay in brittle patterns upon the mud before the stable doors. Towards noon the wind lifted and a duller cold settled in the valley, though the air was warmer. It was the dullness of moisture weighting the air, and soon the heaviness was visible, straying as small specks of snow about the vacant landscape. The grey specks crossed each other aimlessly in the light airs of the dull sky as men went home to their tea.

With the darkness the snow fell thicker, touching the faces of men walking to the village pubs, settling on their eyelashes with wet touch. When they went home again after closing-time the street was white, and so were the roofs of cottages, while their footfalls were muffled. In the morning it was still snowing, and while they waited in the stable at seven o'clock, by the light of a candle, the labourers wondered what work they would be set that day, or would they be stood off, and thus lose a day's pay of six shillings. When the farmer came he said there was no work for them, and without word, without grudge, they walked slowly to their cottages again in the snow. There were over two million men without work in Britain: some had never worked since leaving school many years before.

The snow drifted to the earth, each flake a unique pattern, varying with angle and form of line. The snowflakes were of frozen water, and clear as water, but the diversity of angle and facet reflected rays of light as infinite as the designs of leaf and frond of green nature. Thus the white light was returned to the sky, and men said the snow was white.

Again the wind was drifting as the spirit of ice over water and land, the snow streaming as spectral smoke with the moving airs. Drifts increased under the eddies of the wind, where flakes rested tranquil in the hollows of movement. Brambles that during the years had overgrown fallen gates and posts, in tangled over-arching from uncut hedges, were filled with snow. The horseplow on the headland was smoothed of its framed purpose, becoming as a hulk of snow with broken spars, ensculped and emblanched above the frozen waves of furrows. Each tree trunk in the Carr was moulded oval by the snow clinging to windward, as the clear air poured in from the north-east.

On the white bank of the river beyond the pointed end of the wood were pressed the marks of a heron's feet, where the bird had stalked, anxious and watchful, to the water-edge, to strike a roach and lift out the red-finned fish between the mandibles of its sharp beak. On the snow lay the big scales of the fish, which had been too large for the heron to gulp head-first down its throat. The bird had banged the roach on the snow to break it, but the silver-scaled fish had slid about; the bird had picked it up and shaken it, and tried to prise it open for the eggs which it knew were not formed within the fish, for the heron was many years old, and accustomed to eat the roe of roach before spawning time in late May. The lanky grey bird, its playful mood over, had flown away to the marsh, where beside the fast-flowing waters of the river in the gut below the sea-wall sluice the small flat-fish it fed upon in winter were to be taken. After the heron had gone, an otter had come out of the willow-jungle and amused itself by sliding down the snowy bank, pushing the stiffened fish with its nose, as the bright plow-point precedes the share. The otter made three shoving slides down the bank, its ear on the fish, then lost interest and galloped through the Carr on the scent of a hare. It was a young otter, playful with its first smell and touch of snow.

After it had gone, a dark bird with mincing steps that flipped its black and white tail walked out of the dyke where the reeds were bent with snow and pecked at the fish with its yellow and red beak. The bird did not want to eat the fish, but only to peck it, lest it be alive. Losing

17

interest, the water-bird went away. Soon the silver fish was frosted and stiff.

A sound as of hounds' baying came from on high: a clamant, near-musical sound, from where geese, spread half across the sky, were flying in from the sea, talking among themselves of the clover leys, the meadow grazing, and the brown arable of the fields spread below them.

From the north-east, from across the dirty grey waves of the shallow sea breaking on long ridges of sand wherein timbers of wrecked wooden ships were buried, the wind blew spume and rift upon the sandhills of the low coast, upon the smoothed hillocks bound by the long spines of the marram grass which faintly screamed as the sharp air whipped them. Into one hillock at dusk, as the moon rose up beyond Spitzbergen, a short-eared owl flopped spread-winged amidst the littered crab-claws and curlew-feathers of an old springtide-line. Another owl fell near the firstcomer, then darkly another, and another, falling softly dark and still. The owls had flown across the sea from Norway, to feed on the mice and voles of Britain during the hard weather. Upon the back of one owl so to arrive slept the tiniest bird, a goldcrest, migrant like the owl, but unable on its moth-like wings to sustain the long estranging flight. Falling tired, it had chanced to drop upon the back of the owl, had clenched its feet upon soft feathers, and sunk to sleep, while the larger bird beat long and hollow wings in slow soft journey over the fretted wave-tops. There in its warm roost the goldcrest slept till sunrise, when with a minute cry of alarm it saw the yellow-ringed eyes of the owl, in the head turned sharply to stare down its own back, fixed upon it. With a feeble cry it flitted away, and hid in the grasses, while the owl flapped into the air and flew on hollow, sedge-sere wings in quest of mice in the fields beyond the marshes.

With the owls across the North Sea had come wood-cock, in many numbers to drop upon the bushy growths of sea-blite, wormwood, and sea-lavender, so tired that their long bills had stabbed the brown clay where they had pitched. Before the rising of the morning star, and as the moon declined to the west they flapped inland, and settled to rest in hedge-bottom, under bramble-bush, and by the bases of trees in the woods upon the slopes and crests of the low hills.

A fresh woodcock rises before spaniel or beater with the noise almost of clicking wings; a tired bird moves away in slow flapping flight, fluttering darkly against the snow to pitch but a score of yards distant, breast and beak-tip touching the ground, its dark-sherry coloured eye glowing with the most gentle stare, as of a spirit innocent and beyond fear. In an age of chivalry, or before the age of profit-first, the fowler with wheel- or flint-lock, were he also lord of his land and therefore assured of his place and living, would not pursue such sorry game; but in the time of our chronicle, the theme of living among most men was profit, and the biggest profit, for any outlay of money.

By mid-morning snow-flattened reports of twelve-bore guns made the cock pheasants scratching in the heaps of cavings beside straw-stacks hold erect their heads. The hen pheasants continued to feed on the weed-seeds and broken barley kernels picked out from among the yellow, snow-stuck clots of cavings, for they knew that they were no longer shot at in flight, but only the cocks, since it was near the end of the season of pheasant shooting.

The reports sounded flat across the snow as double-barrel guns were fired rapidly at the brown, leaf-mottled birds with the long slender bills. The shooting of the farm had been rented for half a crown an acre—less than the sum of the tithe upon the land, which was seven shillings an acre—a take-it-or-leave-it offer having been made to the farmer, who for some years had been losing money by farming, and was therefore much in debt to the bank. Most owner-occupiers looked to their sporting rights to pay the tithes on their land. The "guns" of the syndicate with a couple of dogs walked in line over the meadows and down the tall sprawling thorn-hedges which with brambles and briars had choked the ditches undug since the war. Every woodcock seen was shot at. The dogs picked up some birds which had not risen, but which remained crouching, through exhaustion, on the ground darkened only by feathered bodies and the dead leaves of the hedge-bottoms. Gun barrels became too hot to touch. One sportsman, wearing a black office suit with leather leggings from ankle to knee, was swearing to himself, irritated by the thought that he had not brought enough cartridges; the worry of the thought made him shoot wildly, and one flapping bird after another rising darkly out of the snow was missed, until he was calling them all bastards. He was the principal sportsman of the syndicate; it was he who had taken the shooting at half a crown an acre and sub-let it at seven shillings and six-pence to the syndicate, thereby getting his shooting free, as well as a cash profit.

Suddenly he shouted angrily as one of the guns fired at a hen pheasant put up by a dog from a bramble bush, to be followed by another hastily emptying two barrels when the first had missed the bird. Several breast feathers, grey and brown, fluttered to the snow. Mollified by the sight of the bird flying on across the meadow towards the Carr, the man who had shouted explained to the others, in a voice suddenly conciliatory and plausible, that only the day before he had arranged to rent the shooting for another year, and so it was to their advantage not to shoot any more hen pheasants that season. "It'll pay, old man," he said; and he repeated the phrase again, ruefully, when regarding fifty-seven woodcock laid in line on the snow at the end of the day's shooting. "Think what we missed, by not bringing more cartridges, old man. We were damned fools not to have brought twice as many. It would have paid, you know, old man, it would have paid."

Chapter Two

The hen pheasant which had been shot at four times while flying above the straggling line of guns was a young bird, whose toe-horn was still soft. She had been living for several days in what used to be called the Willow Plot. This was an area of about half an acre at the end of the Home Meadow which originally had been fenced off from cattle, and willow-slips had been planted, for the growing of osiers used for basket-making. But since the decline of craftsmanship in the villages and country towns, the Willow Plot had not been cultivated. The best of the osiers, the straightest rods, were still cut just before the rising of the sap at Easter, by a man who made hurdles as wind shields and view screens for gardens; but the rest were left, to grow as they would. So the Willow Plot was now an overgrown wilderness enclosed by rotten posts and rusty barbed wire, where in winter winds the overgrown osiers rattled together and swayed against grey driven clouds. Otters, following up the dykes, knew it, and sometimes in dry weather slept in the clumps of rough sedge-grass. In early summer the meadow-sweet put forth its creamy blossoms around its verge, giving cover to pheasants, who sought the Plot for the security it gave them. Hares knew it, too, and quatted dreaming in their forms among the tussock grasses by day, while moorfowl moved discreetly by the scaly stubs of the willows, to seek tadpoles in the rusty water of its central hollow. In the old days water had flowed through the Willow Plot, from the dyke under the Long Wood, carrying fresh water from the springs bubbling out of the chalk underlying the hilly fields; but now the ditch leading to the Plot was trodden by cattle to a flat course green with water-grass lying under ice and snow.

A wandering dog, a brindled lurcher kept like all other long-legged cur-dogs in the village for taking rabbits and hares and quatting partridges at night, had followed the sportsmen and their black labradors that morning, and in the old odours of their passing had quested for its pleasure. It belonged to a village butcher, a man whose portly and rubicund appearance was due to a habit, based on economic necessity, of eating a large portion of the unsold meat of the beasts he slew. The lurcher dog helped his master in this, for a pastime. Constant friendly attendance of this animal in the slaughter-house yard for scraps and lumps had dulled the dog's speed and sense of smell, even as excessive eating of meat had dulled the wits of the butcher. The lurcher's eyesight was therefore keener than its nose. It was an amiable creature, and regarded as a pet by his children. Sometimes it went to school with them, but was invariably expelled, and on such occasions was to be seen standing outside in the street, its ears at half-cock, as though it wondered what to do. When after harvest and in winter the corn-stacks were threshed upon the small farms of the neighbourhood, and the valley echoed with trundling, chuffing noises from the fifteen-ton engine on ponderous straked wheels drawing drum and elevator, Little Bingo, as the lanky dog was called, soon found its way to the familiar scene, where it enjoyed blowing into straw, prancing with bright eyes and cock-ears to snap and chop mice, and the pouncing-upon and shaking of rats while men on the lowered corn-stack prodded and struck with their two-tined forks.

And following behind the shooters after woodcock that white morning of Saturday, Little Bingo had pranced and trotted to its secret hunting, ears angular and tongue pink-flacking over teeth as it leapt among the tussock-grasses of the Willow Plot, to behold anything in movement. The hen pheasant, crouching under brambles, had risen in alarm, and flown to her base in the Carr, passing over dark figures of men with pink or grey faces looking upwards with staring eyes from which issued the flash-thwacks that were the most terrible noises upon her consciousness.

Reaching the wood, the bird fell to the ground, scrambled to her feet, fell over, paused a moment to listen with neck extended, then hobbled and flapped away in the snow. She stopped, her gape wide in shock and fear, under the pine tree; and by a fallen branch she crouched, the hue of her plumage resembling the hue of the barkless limb and the sere grasses fringing it. There she quatted, her beak still half open, on snow pressed to a cavity by the warmth of her body. Below the cavity a hole, made by the stump of one leg broken at the knee by a No. 5 pellet, slowly turned red, as, trembling, the bird listened to the reports of guns in the wood above the sloping field. Only when they had ceased by several minutes did she shift her position to settle more easily on the snow. Her beak closed, her eyes shut, to open again and remain awhile half open, before gradually closing in sleep.

Her eyes opened once more at the sounds of stealthy steps in the snow. The bird with the jerking white tail, which had pecked the dead roach on the river bank, was approaching the pheasant. It was an experienced and cunning moorcock, and its name was Gallinule. Seeing it peering at her, and feeling menace in its attitude, for

24

the moorcock was poised to peck her on the back of the head, the hen pheasant stood up, only to fall sideways. Immediately with dark wings dropped Gallinule ran in and struck with its beak at her forehead. She uttered a squeak of fear, and Gallinule struck again. She tried to stand up, to match the poising and weaving of the bird beak to beak, but she fell sideways on her broken leg, and at once her enemy struck her on the skull, pulling away in the slightly curved tip of its beak two small feathers. The next blow was aimed at the eye, but the hen pheasant shifted, so that the moorcock's beak-tip broke the naked papillated skin around the orbit. Pain and fear made the hen cry out, and the cry awoke a bird which, with feathers ruffed out to hold warm air around its body, had been sleeping, beak sunken on its breast, in the top of the pine tree. The bird, a hoody crow, rose up on the branch where it was perching, checked a desire to stretch its wings, and silently looked down upon the scene below with a view to profit itself. For it was Harra the Denchman.

Harra the Denchman is the name given by wildfowlers, shell-fishers and others of mud-flat and salt-marsh of the coast, to the grey crows which every winter fly across the North Sea from the forests of Denmark and Norway. The name Harra is said to be a corruption of Harrild, the Danishman, leader of an invasion about a thousand years ago, one of many raids of the North folk which crossed the sea in galleys to raid farms and to return with cattle and grain. Sometimes after fighting and killing the inhabitants the North folk settled to farm the land, living for safety in camps set with stockades and sunken ways. Blue-eyed men with fair or reddish hair, broad of jowl and loud of voice, becoming fat towards middle-life, live in the villages and the little towns built around the decaying ports of the coast to this day, being descendants of those who had invaded the lands of the South folk—smaller, darker men of a type still living and working upon the heavy lands of the interior, called Suffolk.

Sunken under rush-clump and coarse poa-grass of the meadow—in the lows or hollows of which lie water-plashes for six months of the year, feeding ground of snipe but useless for cattle—was the skeleton of a wooden ship which had sailed up on the tide, bearing the pennant of the raven at its prow, nine hundred years before—the last invading galley of the Nor' folk: and every winter when grey crows have flighted across the waves of the shallow sea, to seek what living they might find, men of that coast have said one to another, Harra the Denchman has come again.

The grey crow peered sideways down its long black beak, past its sharp point, and the irides of its ice-blue eyes expanded and contracted with the featherlets on its pate. Knowing itself to be superior to both birds, it was stimulated to strike and kill. Unclasping its feet, Harra the Denchman jumped off the branch and slipped down head-first with wings open, partly crooked; with a throaty *kaa-r!* it opened its wings as a brake, and pitched on the snow to examine swiftly what it saw. Gallinule, perceiving the crow, immediately lowered its head and ran into the willow jungle, flapping its wings for added speed; while with a screech of fear the hen pheasant leapt up from the dark apparition and flew with rapid beats of her short wings through the bare branches of the trees.

Her pinion feathers struck some twigs of an ash tree, and a powder of snow strayed in the swirled air of her passing. Alarmed by the urgency of her flying, a ring-dove resting in the thick ivy stifling the head of a syca-more clapped its wings over its back with a loud smacking

26

noise as it flew across the river, away from the narrow wood. The sound caused the hen to strike the tip of one wing on a tree branch, and so to dishevel the ends of the primary feathers. Gliding through the thorns growing at the edge of the dyke which divided wood and meadow, the line of her flight was straight but uneven, the stricken wing dipping and the bird rocking to recover, only to wobble again. Clear of the trees, however, the thick pectoral muscles threw in forward and backward sweep the short wings, while the tail feathers expanded and quivered with the thrusts of the wing-bones linked by sinew to the prow-shaped breastbone.

A brown falcon soaring on a current of air rising above a sun-patch on the snow of the field beyond the meadow—four hundred yards away—fixed momentarily its gaze upon the black object dangling under the flying pheasant, as it might observe a mouse hanging from the foot of its mate. So sharp was the vision of the little falcon that it knew at once that neither small bird nor mouse was being borne by the familiar sight of a pheasant climbing to fly over the wood on the steep side of the hill above the meadow. Instantly the kestrel's gaze returned below, to where with head bent to focus the stereoscopic sight of its full liquid eyes, it had been observing red and green and blue flashes in the snow. The little mouse-hawk was not hungry, and as it leaned breast and wings to poise itself on the thermals or rising air currents, the refractions of sunlight from the snow crystals held its life force momentarily in thrall.

The hen pheasant thrust herself over the tops of trees growing up the steep side of the hill, and throwing up and over the highest beech of the crest, paused with hollow wings to rest and glide, as she saw below her a sight that made her turn and glide lower until with depressed tail feathers and elbows turned backwards for secondary wing-feathers to brake forward movement, she alighted and ran to walking pace, but to fall over, and to stop herself on her elbows. Thereupon she moved forward irregularly, keeping balance by wing-tip touches on snow, to lose her fear among others of her kind scratching in the heaps of cavings left by the barley-stack which recently had been threshed out by the fifteen-ton steam engine. The cavings lay in a heap, beside the snow-filled tracks of wheels of the heavy engine which had drawn away the tackle after the day's work. The heaps were composed of fragments of straw broken within the whirling drum and shaken out of the sieves below the box. Once the custom had been to cart the cavings into the woods, to be tipped in heaps to hold the native pheasants from straying beyond the boundaries, perhaps near sheaves of unthreshed corn tied round the base of a small tree, the corn-heads downwards to hide the grain from sight of pigeon, rook, and jackdaw. The custom was still used on farms whose occupants held the copyholds of their lands, and therefore owned the sporting rights, which gave them a direct interest in maintaining the stock of game birds upon their fields and in their coverts; but on the farm of our chronicle, such customs had, in a local phrase, been let-go.

The farmer was in a bad way, dulled by care; and thus his heaps of cavings were never cleared up or burned, but left to rot in the fields, and to spread the weeds of crab-grass, dock, thistle, charlock, and goosefoot.

The time of the beginning of the story of the Phasian bird is towards the end of the fourth decade of the twentieth century, when the majority of the arable fields of Britain were weedy or "tumbledown" to indifferent grazing; when sheep did not pay, bullock fattening was uneconomic, grain growing was hazardous, so was chicken

28

and egg farming: only milk paid its way. Farm gates were rotten on their hinges, if indeed those wrought iron hooks were not fallen out of their square holes in the decaying posts. Rural cottages were very much as they were one, two, even three centuries ago. So much cheap foreign food was imported into England, as interest on loans to backward countries, that it scarcely paid a man to go poaching any more. On that afternoon of early January over a score of wild birds were feeding on the site of the threshed stack, scratching in the heaps of weed-seeds and cavings; nobody disturbed them; and the hen with the broken leg fed the more easily because a cock pheasant, stimulated by sight of her, scratched by her, walking round her, dropping a wing beside her, and uttering a low gubbling sound as he bent his neck as if to pick up a barley kernel, as he pretended to follow her movement when he was not making display around her.

Chapter Three

The frost did not grip the snow long enough for the green woodpeckers, which dwelled in the woods and fed mainly on ants, to starve and die. The sea was warmer than the land, and a thawing fog hung in silence over the coastal farms. New growths of nettles arose above the dark mould of the Carr, glinting with pale stings, hollow and pointed, protecting delicate stem and leaf with acid. Voles and mice moved out of their ball nests of leaf and bark fibre in cracks and holes of trees; woodcock flapped their last dusk-flights through the woods, and returned over the sea to northern lands. Owls with feather-horned heads flew among them, dark in the green light of the small moon. The bittern which had stalked among the reeds of the dykes, striped brown and yellow as reeds made feather, beat away to the east, to Holland across the waves, whither before him teal and widgeon had sped, eager with zest of vernal creation. Spiders, exploring the cracks of tree-bark with silken rope of security—as roped men climb mountain crags—moved to the warmth of the sun; treecreepers, wrens, and tomtits sought them, trilling, piping, whistling as their bodies were nourished for the joys of mating and nesting. Dipping in undulation of heavy straight flight across field and meadow from grub-bored bark of elm to anthill, from anthill to dying beech tree or scoriated ash, the green-and-yellow woodpecker cried his colours in laughing strokes of sound—*yaffle-yaffle-yaffle*—and the plowman following his horses felt easement in his work, and stopped to roll and light a cigarette, to indraw a few puffs of smoke in satisfaction. Already his plow-breast was scoring better, the rust nearly worn off the iron, so that the furrow was crumbling nicely as it flopped over. At midday as he sat on two sacks in the hedge-bottom, eating his dinner, he noted happily that the furrow-shine was gone off the morning's work, the warmth was making the soil faintly to steam, while his horses munched their armful of over-year'd hay contentedly. The sky was pale blue, with high clouds scarcely moving from one hour to another.

When once more he arose to his feet, paper wrapping of food left by the hedge, to take a double swig from his bottle of cold tea, to roll a fag and light it, the gulls standing about the field, awaiting further furrow-turning, looked up from their midday doze. Soon they were screaming and jostling behind the walking figure guiding the plow by the iron handles, speaking to the horses, crying *coop-yer-hold!* at the higher headland for the pair to turn to the left, and at the lower end of the field, again *whee-eest!* for the slow turn to the right.

Halfway across the field the horses stopped for a rest and at once the spiralling swirl of gulls, which had been flying and flapping and alighting to within six inches of the plowman's heels, drifted away in silence, flying wide and high as individual birds in the pale sky. The hen pheasant feeding discreetly in the furrow a dozen yards from the plow crouched low until the horses began to pull, and she heard again the whisper of iron in the gravelly patches coming through the ground. She had no fear of plowman or horses; yet she crouched, scarcely knowing that she did so.

31

Unknown millennia of Asiatic living, during which human cultures or civilizations arose in cities becoming petrofact and finally ruinous upon the soil which had been forgotten as the only true begetter of life, with another two thousand years of northern living since the Romans had brought to Britain the coloured birds of the swamps of Phasis, a river in Colchis—every moment of living thrilled with the need of perpetual concealment, of readiness to run to keep life—were stored as impressions within her blood which thereby held to its own purpose, as a spirit behind the local perceptions of her brain. So she crouched at the innocent passing of man and horses, as the noise of iron share lifting stones and sand came as a rustle, as a whisper, through the expanding pores of the warming earth. She heard, too, the murmur of worms in their galleries; the stir of soil by beetle and wireworm; and she heard the trip of mice feet as two short-tailed voles, flung out of their nest in the rearing furrow, hurried away before the white and screaming descents of gulls. The voles, fat with beech-mast, were dazed by the light; for when their world abruptly had been turned inside out, they had been flung from a sleep of more than a fortnight in their nest of bitten dry grasses, wherein, curled and warm, they had lain clasping one another round the neck with their forepaws. Now as they scurried and tumbled over old frost-smoothed furrows a herring gull large among his smaller black-headed brethren perceived them and on long and narrow wings swept down, and upturning those wings as brakes, dipped to seize first one vole in yellow beak with its crimson spot and predatory tip, to gulp it down its throat, and then, running to the other vole crouching in the shadow of a frost-split flint, to strike, crush, and swallow it likewise. Thereupon the gull, white of breast and grey of folded wings, stood on the crumbling furrow and uttered a wailing, yakker-

32

ing cry, as though of complaint that its aloneness was penetrated: the call for mating, for it was not paired.

The hen pheasant, lifting her head, saw the cold yellow eye of the statuesque bird of prey upon her, and liking it not, she leapt up and flew away to the meadow below, gliding over the tall and ragged hedge which grew by the choked ditch which had not felt a spade for over a quarter of a century, ever since the ending of a war arising out of a way of living which had despoiled both soil and peasantry of the mother country.

The hen pheasant soon forgot the former use of her leg, and ceased to notice the dangling and withered foot which dragged as she hopped, sometimes stumbling, to her feeding. She was wary, but not fearful, of the horses and implements which came to work down the furrows of the field whereon she fed with other hens and the cock which never ceased to look around, with raised head, as they moved quietly over the soil levelled and made friable by strokes of harrows and the clanking cylinder of sheet-iron drawn by a bow-bellied chestnut horse. All living things were content in the warmth of the March sun and the windless day. The boy guiding the horse with long lines of rope as he walked behind the one-horse roll whistled and sang for pleasure on the seed-bed. He had just left school, and this was his first job; and to be entrusted with a horse and roll made him feel fine. He followed, up and down the field, the teamsman with two horses pulling two baulks of rank harrows—two heavy frames of iron set with long curved iron teeth for bringing clods to the top of the seed-bed. The light cylindrical roll pressed the clods to a fine mould.

Leaving the aged Suffolk standing gratefully in the shafts of the roll, the boy went to get a drink from his tea-bottle by his side-bag lying with his coat under the hedge; and the pheasants which had been walking on the soft, worked soil disappeared among the rising nettles above the old ditch, waiting in the tangle of the overgrown hedge until their territory was clear once more. They had been selecting from the fine soil of the seed-bed sharp flinty grit for their gizzards, which ground their food to a fine fluid after it had passed from their crops. When enough grit had been taken by each bird, it walked to the dyke by the Carr to sip water; afterwards to pluck the tips of young blades of ryegrass growing on the mounds of the meadow above the lows where shrinking plashes of water lay, stagnant and warm in the sunshine. With the grass-tips the pheasants ate roots of silver-weed and buttercup, which they found by scratching at the edges of new mole-heaps lying black upon the dry areas.

At evening horses and men went home, the teamsman riding on the half-bred Percheron mare and leading the old black gelding, while the boy followed on the curved back of the aged Suffolk Punch which had patiently drawn the roll. When they had gone the birds walked more freely about the field, seeking beetles which with the cooling of the soil had burrowed under the surface.

When the dwarf owl began to waul like a cat from the Carr, and its mate to reply like a peacock, the cock pheasant arose and flew down the field, calling his hens to follow. His roost was in the thick dark-green mass of branches and ivy at the top of the pine, but the hens roosted in the lower branches of different trees. As a white mist began to spread in layers over the meadow, the cock rose up on his perching branch and cucketted—crowing two hoarse notes in rapid succession—a raucous noise followed immediately by the clapping of wings. Distantly from other coverts came the challenging cuckets of sentinel cocks. Westwards the sun had gone down small and red in the dry atmosphere, and the evening star hung upon the clear twilight with the thin talon of the new moon. The dwarf owls ceased to waul and wail; the hollow notes of a tawny owl came from the dark mass of the wood on the top of the hill; and the stars of night shone upon the earth.

Morning came into a clear sky, and the glancing rays of the orient sun charged the mist on the meadow, so that a yellow lake seemed to drown all the low land between the tops of the thorn-bushes on the river-bank and the horse-roll standing at the bottom of the field. To his men waiting by the broken stable door the farmer gave the order to load the two-hundredweight sacks of Spratt-Archer seed-barley, standing on the asphalt floor of the Corn Barn, and to drill the field with twelve pecks an acre. "No, make it thirteen," he added. "One for the birds." Then he went home to breakfast, breathing the keen air with satisfaction; but turned in his track across the dewy grass to the premises, saying he had forgotten to order the rate of artificial to be broadcast from the seedlip. He was in plenty of time to catch the men, although twenty minutes had elapsed since he had first left them at the premises, for the horses were only at the point of leaving the stable when he returned. Ignoring the time wasted, he said, "Put it on four hundredweight per acre, and try and spread it even, for a uniform sample." Relieved, he turned away.

When the tumbrils, drawn by the horses, appeared by the broken gateway of the field to be dressed and sown, the pheasants had crossed the field, feeding on small beetles which were already active in the flattened topsoil, and were resting in the Long Wood. There were five hens with the cock, and all were content. Leaves of dog's mercury and sweet-violet were rising green among old leaves and twigs scattered on the woodland floor, and

35

nettles were high enough to conceal the birds when they crouched. Ring-doves were croodling in the ivy-thick heads of some of the sycamore saplings, where the females were making their nests of pleached dark twigs. The sun cast long shadows in the wood and across the field, for it was yet three hours to noon. With a piercing silver note as straight as its flight the kingfisher crossed the meadow to its nest in a tunnel pecked in the loamy top of a disused quarry, among the exposed roots of beech trees growing in the wood above.

An observer unacquainted with farming methods in that period of depression might have been excused for attributing some of the causes of the depression to the human happenings that now occurred, thus substituting effect for cause. The gateway to the field was above a slope, which led to the lower part of the field from an area of rough grazing separated from the meadow by a reed-choked dyke. The two tumbrils, one loaded with one-and-a-half-hundredweight sacks of fertilizer, the other with two-hundredweight sacks of barley seed, were halted on the rutted track below the slope. The cartload of fertilizer had been drawn from the premises, distant by three-quarters of a mile, along the track under the Long Wood by two horses, one in the shafts and the other a trace-horse pulling by chains attached to hooks fixed to the shafts. This was the heavier load, being twenty sacks weighing thirty hundredweight. The men at the premises, after the farmer's departure, had argued about this weight, one declaring that the wooden wheels of the tumbril would not carry so much, that the stub-axles would break away from the half-rotten ends of the wooden axle. The teamsman, unable to feed his horses on the proper ration of crushed oats, but forced to feed them on damp sugar-beet pulp and unpalatable woody hay—

spoiled at the haysel because bleached too long in the sun, owing to lack of labour, and cut over-ripe for bulk—said that his horses could not haul a ton and a half up the sloping field. As for the third horse, the aged Suffolk Punch with the curved spine and dropped belly, he would have to pull the eleven sacks of seed-corn, weighing twenty-two hundredweight. Then who would draw the seed-drill to the field? There it stood in the hovel or cart-shed, its hopper still half-filled with wheat-seed which had lain there since it had been brought home from wheat-drilling in November, four months before. Mice had lived in the hopper off and on during the winter, and what wheat remained uneaten was rotten with their urine. As for the axles of the tumbrils, they had not been greased for years, and the sapwood of the ash-shaft or pole had long been abandoned by the death-watch beetle. So the men had argued what was best to do, and their argument had continued for some minutes after the farmer had left a second time. They were not deliberately wasting time; they were concerned with what would be the best method to get fertilizer, seed, drill, and light zig-zag seed-harrows to the field, and then to finish the field by knocking-off time at 4.30 p.m. The teamsman was nominally in charge, since he received four shillings a week more than the others, but he did not want to accept responsibility since he was paid nothing beyond his 36s. 6d. a week as teamsman, and the other two men (one of whom was his father, the yardsman, who looked after the cattle, and milked the cow kept for the farmer's household milk, and kept an eye on the eggs of the hens laying wild about the premises) had no intention of regarding him as foreman. Also, they had different ideas of how the job should be done, and expressed these ideas not in action, but in argument.

Now a second discussion was taking place on the rough grass below the steep slope or causeway leading up to the field called the Breck. The teamsman wanted to draw the load of fertilizer up the field, and set out the sacks, so that the second man could begin to broadcast the grey chemicals from his seed-lip, or tray lying across his stomach and slung from a piece of old rope over his shoulders. While he was broadcasting the artificials, the teamsman would return to the premises with the Suffolk horse to fetch in the empty tumbril the second and final load of fertilizer, which must be set out upon the seed-bed before the barley could be drilled. To this the man with the seed-lip objected: he would have the dirty job of casting the powdered grey manure, which got on clothes and hair and in eyes and nostrils and ears, while the teamsman was walking beside the tumbril during a couple of hours. The third man then asked about the drill: how was that to come to the field? That stilled the arguing voices, and all three looked at the hollow-backed chestnut horse standing at rest, head and belly sagging, between the shafts. "What do you think, father?" asked the teamsman.

The older man, the stockman, continued to fill his charred pipe, its cracked bowl bound by two turns of copper wire, and the split mouthpiece bound by adhesive rubber tape. "Got a match, 'bor?" he asked. Then deliberately lighting it and puffing rank smoke, and packing down the dark shag tobacco with a splayed forefinger set with a yellow nail like a crushed acorn, he looked up, and gazing at the treetops where a hoody crow had just alighted, said contentedly, "Ah, that's the first smoke since half-past five, and I'll be going home to breakfast now. He knows!"—pointing to the silent, watching form of the grey crow—"Harra the Denchman knows the carn is goin' in to-day!" As though in reply, the crow dipped towards the group of men and carts, and cried, *Kaa! Kaa!*

"Howsomedever, we must cop on with the job," said the stockman, suddenly active. "I'll fust gi'e yew a hand settin' out the 'fishals, then yew take back the tumbril and me and him"—pointing with pipe-stem to the younger man who wore an ancient buttonless mackintosh coat, tied round the middle by binder-twine in preparation for broadcasting the fertilizer—"will set out the seed on the headland, then ah'll bring the tumbril back with me an' two 'osses, and yew bring the 'fishals back and leave Smiler"—the Suffolk horse—"in the stables, and ah'll lead him back with the drill."

"Don't forget the seed-harrows," remarked the labourer in the stained mackintosh coat. He had been waiting for six years to get married: waiting for a cottage in the village to fall empty.

"Moreover than that," said the teamsman, pleasantly. "Ah'll bring 'em atop the bags o' fishals. We won't be in no muddle. Harcourt's got half his barley in, and most of his oats, so they say down to Cross." Harcourt was the christian name of a neighbouring farmer—all labourers referred among themselves to farmers by their first names—and Cross was the village meeting-place of men after the day's work, where the main or Church Street was joined by another road crossing the river by the brick bridge. "We shan't be in no muddle," he repeated, and turned to call to the horses which had been standing, occasionally stamping their hind feet because of the irritation of mites in the skin of their fetlocks, before the tumbril filled with sacks of chemical manure. The plan of work known, the men moved off easily; the stockman preceding the tumbril to pace out and mark the places where the sacks should be dumped for convenience of filling the seed-lip and also of giving to the broadcaster an idea of the amount to be flung out by hand for an even scattering upon the seed-bed; and the others following, one leading the horses and the other pulling off the sacks at intervals and letting them fall upon the soft earth. The boy was told to gather sticks for a midday fire by the hedge, for the wind suddenly was chill.

By mid-afternoon the top-soil of the Breck had been faintly dusted white, and four of its acres drilled with barley an inch and a half under the surface. Behind labouring horses dark with sweat the old drill moved up and down the field, the cogs within its hopper revolving over holes adjusted to permit thirteen pecks of yellow corn to trickle into every acre of earth, dropping down eleven seed-spouts. The iron shoes of the spouts parted the fine soil, stroking away the white dusting of salts of nitrogen, phosphorus, and potassium that lay upon its surface. The drill had been made in the United States of America and exported thence in 1910; it had been in constant seasonal use upon five farms, and sold by auction at Michaelmas or Ladyday, on four of them when the farmers had died, gone bankrupt, or otherwise been defeated. Helped by the boy, the teamsman filled the hopper from the heavy jute sacks standing at intervals along the bottom hedge of the field. This hedge, of wildly writhen and overgrown white-thorns, was tunnelled by rabbits. During the past two decades many a bushel of seed, left unsown owing to miscalculation, had at the end of the drilling of a field been poured down one or another of the deep hedgerow rabbit burrows about the farm, and the hole covered with soil slurred by iron-shod boot.

By knocking-off time, which was about twenty minutes before the actual hour of quitting work—since the men reckoned that by the time they got to the premises it would be half-past four—only half the field was drilled. The man who had broadcast the fertilizer considered that his day's work had ended with the job, and at half-past three had gone to the hedge to collect his side-bag. The teamsman called to him asking if he wasn't a'going to cover the drills with the seed-harrows—the Suffolk horse had been standing idle ever since the sacks of seed-corn had been set out in the morning—but the other replied he had had enough. His eyelids were inflamed by the chemicals; and he wanted to take his lurcher dog on the sheep-walk by the marshes, in the hope of picking up a rabbit. Well, take Smiler home, called the teamsman. So, sitting on the side of the tumbril, the other departed. At 4.10 p.m. the teamsman left the drill by the hedge, un-hooked the pair of horses from the long pole and swingle-tree, and throwing up the boy on one horse, he clambered upon the back of the other. One behind the other, they went home under the Long Wood as the pheasants, which had spent the day on the meadows and in the coarse yel-low tussocks of the Willow Plot, crept out of the wood by gaps in the rusty and torn sheep-netting of a previous farm-tenant, and filled their crops with Spratt-Archer barley. It was a fattening food, a warming food, and it stimulated the cock to display in semicircles around his hens in order to induce them to crouch and to accept the tread, which was all he desired of them.

Chapter Four

━━━━━━●◆●━━━━━━

When Harra the Denchman had dipped and cawed in the treetop, his gesture had nothing to do with the corn-sowing as a means of easy feeding; for the impulse that moved sap and blood and seed was moving all life of the hemisphere. Harra the Denchman had delayed when other hoodies had gone because he was attracted by a female carrion crow in the High Wood, who had played with him but left him the moment she saw a male crow like herself; and now on a warm and lifting wind crossing England from the west the grey crow flapped across the sea to his northern forest.

The vernal impulse came from the sun, lord of all physical living. In tender throaty voice the carrion crow articulated to his mate as she smoothed the inside of her nest hidden in the dense ivy atop a sycamore tree. Glinting low over the river, following its curves under the Carr, the kingfisher scintillated at a sudden rising turn and shot into the wood, flying down a pale green tunnel of branch and twig to his fishing perch over the dyke beyond. His keen whistle pierced the sunlit quiet of the wood, and hearing it Dufa the ring-dove perching in an ash tree flew out of the Carr, clapped his wings over his head as he climbed to stalling point, and dived in a curve to climb again, to dive and climb a third time before flying back to the tree. Joy had uncurled like a spring within the smoke-grey breast of Dufa, urging display unto his mate. The green woodpecker, pushing himself up the bole of a withered tree by the strong pointed feathers of his tail, while grappling the bark with his horned toes, threw back his red head, and cried his yallery-green notes. The skylark, climbing the turquoise air upon a thin chain of song, heard the cry, so did the boy harrowing over-whart with five zig-zag harrows the drills of barley on the Breck. The chains on the swingle-trees jingled; the iron tines of the harrows struck deeper notes from the flints. The work was light, the horse was easy, the day was warm.

Over the central slope of the field the lapwing cleft and swept the air black-winged, crying *pii–wit—pii-o-wit!* while his mate walked in mild distraction twenty yards from her eggs laid in a hollow lined with four fragments of frost-burst couch-grass—a weed dreaded by the farmer, the foul or creeping grass whose white pointed cadets drive even through potatoes in their advance for new territory. The grass fragments had been picked up in her beak and laid there that morning, around the four eggs blotched in black and brown. Several times the site of her nest had been altered: when the cultivator had gone down the weathered furrows, to break them into lump and mould; again when the long recurved tines of the harrows had drawn through the broken furrows, tumbling the lumps, breaking some and working others to the surface, while causing particles of soil to trickle into air-spaces below; when the cast-iron cylinders of the two-horse roll, revolving clankily within the ash-wood frame, in their squeezing angle of curve had crumbled the lumps into loose soil; when the lighter harrows had stroked up and down the field, pulling on top the smaller lumps; again as the light one-horse roll of thin sheet-iron had smoothed

43

the seed-bed; and when the drill had dropped twenty-two hundredweight of seed-barley into the fourteen acres.

Yet the lapwing's four brindled eggs had remained unbroken during the passing of seven implements, ending with the zig-zag harrows pulled by the two old horses called, in many an auctioneer's catalogue, Blossom and Smiler. Each time before iron of hoof or shoe or tool had passed by, a human hand had picked up the eggs, set them aside; and after passing, a human figure had troubled to kneel upon the ground, to scoop a hollow, and to set within it, pointed ends to centre, four eggs like small pears blotched by canker; and after each occasion the mother-bird had, with hesitant pauses to pick up small stones and drop them again in her nervousness, walked to her eggs, gazed at them, touched them with her beak to put them closer together, and then squatted upon them, working her thighs between them to hold them against the warmth of her body within the overlapping feathers. The head of the syndicate shoot had offered the stockman a shilling a dozen for any plovers' eggs he brought to him, provided they were fresh, but none of the labourers, though poor, would take the eggs from the birds, which for centuries had been known, to those who worked upon the land, as friends of the farmer.

Now the boy was "crossing the work" with the delicate seed-harrows, light-tined not to disturb the seed or to bury it deeper than the one-and-a-half-inch depth of sowing. His fragile seed-harrows left thin lines athwart the drills of corn in order to deceive the rooks, some of whom were already prospecting in those areas of the field most distant from the working implement. The rooks had not come for barley, but for the wireworms which swarmed in the soil. Even so, they knew how to dig for seed corn when they wanted it; they were in the habit of digging overwhart the lines of the final harrow-

44

ing—"crossing the work" indeed!—in order to uncover a row or drill of seed, thereupon to follow it up straightly until their crops were filled. Not all the art and mystery of farming was hidden from those birds of immemorial husbandry, the rooks!

While the boy was sitting in the hedge and eating his dinner and drinking from his bottle of cold tea flavoured with tinned milk from which the cream had been extracted (the tin sold in the village shop labelled *Not for Infants*) he heard the cry of the male lapwing as the bird swished down at the rooks approaching his mate upon the nest. Swallowing his mouthful, the boy arose with waving arms of a human scarecrow and yelled *Garr-rrt ye!* at the black birds. The rooks, knowing the noise to be harmless, took no heed, but walked as before in search of wireworms. But the hen pheasant, wary and nervous with but two millennia of European living in her blood, crouched at the far edge of the field where she was feeding on seed-barley.

Sown at the new moon, the seed chitted soon; and within the second week thin lines of points up and down the field cast a pale green mist upon the soil of the Breck made lighter in hue by the drying east winds, which traditionally were said to be worth a king's ransom because they enabled the work of seed-bed preparation and drilling of corn to go forward without check. April-sown corn in that country of small rainfall rarely established a good plant before the waterless periods of May and early June, which meant loss of the full ear in due season.

The forehead of the cock pheasant was a deep green, and the naked skin around his eyes and sides of his face was scarlet. The feathers of his neck and throat were green, sometimes glowing with purple. The feathers of his breast, plump with good feeding, were a rich rufous hue, shot with purple sheens, and edged with black. His flank feathers were buff, tipped with violet. The eighteen feathers of his tail were dispread and tilted as he strutted beside the hen and dipped to display the gloss of colours upon wing and flank, the olive of tail fringed with shades of reddish-violet and crossed by black and rufous bars. The cock bird shone and glowed with colour as he showed his power and beauty to the near-colourless hens, whose plumage was drab as sere leaves and dry nettle stalks. He jockled as he strutted and ran in curves about and about her. The vermilion skin around the eyes lost its scaly appearance and became smoother and wider as the heat of the blood swelled the envelope of the body, until every feather seemed to be iridescent, and the tufts of feathers above the ear-cavities became as aigrettes. To the resurgent feeling of the hen was lured the power of the cock; she ran, she paused, she quatted; triumphant, he trod her, neck extended to peck and hold the featherlets of her crown; triumphant while she received his seed. Afterwards he stood beside her a moment, ruffling his feathers and shaking his wings, a mere bird without purpose, dishevelled momentarily; then, assuming his normal indifference, he raised his head to listen and to peer, and walked to his own ways within the thicket of the hedgerow. The hen walked in another direction, towards the Carr.

The same cock pheasant served five hens which roosted in the Carr, and had chosen their nesting places within or near it. The hen with one leg—the other now was withered, hanging by twisted sinew to a healed stump—had scratched a hollow in dark leaf-litter among nettles rising to enclose the fallen branch of the pine tree. She picked up lengths of dead nettle-stalk in her beak and laid them in the hollow, with a few yellow leaves of an old year's growth of ivy. And there her first egg, pale olive green, was laid as the barley points began to open to the blade.

Sand-martins, which a month since had come from Africa to the northern spring with willow wrens and chiffchaffs, flitted over the meadows, thinking of their nesting holes pecked in the face of a sandpit upon the farm. The woodpecker and his mate had spent happy hours striking and prising with their beaks a round hole in the tall trunk of a living beech tree within the High Wood, and digging downwards to enlarge a cavern wherein the glossy white eggs would lie. The king-fisher had laid her seven white eggs upon the bones and scales of roach, minnows, and water-beetles on the floor of the chamber at the end of her chalkpit tunnel. In the cradle of stick and sheepswool at the top of the ivy-dark sycamore lay the carrion crow's hatchlings, later to be fed on the young of small birds taken from their nests.

Every morning the hen pheasant crept quietly to the nest hidden by tall growing nettles, and laid an egg beside the others. Once as she was about to fly to it from the verge of the meadow, she saw Gallinule the moorcock staring at her: she ran at him and sent him scuttling back to the river. Gallinule knew well the taste of pheasant-eggs; he likewise knew the richer, orange-coloured yoke of moorhen's eggs, for all was food to Gallinule.

When ten eggs lay coldly under the dead leaves with which the hen covered them as she crept off the nest, a man stopped his car on the road above the river, and crossing a plank bridge to the meadow, approached the pine tree. Parting the nettles with a stick, he peered down and found the nest; and removing the leaves carefully with a twig, he took four of the pheasant's eggs and put them in one pocket. Then he withdrew four eggs from another pocket, and placed them in the nest. And having brushed back the leaves with the twig, he withdrew quietly the way he had come.

The day after the hen pheasant had laid all her thirteen eggs, she began to sit, whereupon the cock pheasant ceased to visit her; but he knew where she was, and where the other hens he had trod had their nests. He was the sentinel of the Carr, and not of any particular nest; he was a warning voice only, a grating double-cry among the trees; he was Kock-karr; he was king of the birds of Colchis.

While the hen was sitting, a change took place in her skin, which no longer gave out scent by which stoats, dogs, otters, and other enemies might have been led directly to the nest. The pheasant's scent was absorbed into the intestines, so that her droppings were odoriferous, and not her person. While she brooded the eggs, her blood grew hotter. Through lime-shell and inner skin, both porous, of the eggs, oxygen was drawn, to build upon the plan or spirit of life within, forming clots connected by veinous threads of blood to brain and gill and reptilian shape. Each egg carried the racial history of the Phasian bird, from its inception within the cooling vapours of creation, from amoeba to fish-form, thence to reptile that crawled from water to land and arose on hind-feet to run; and from running developed the sweeping flaps of skin upon its arms which increased to vanes and finally, taking to itself light and colour and reflection, breaking into feathered flight, triumph of celestial artistry which strove sempiternally with the sun against the forces of negation and darkness. Within each egg phases of racial history succeeded one another, moved by the heat of the bird sitting day after night and night upon day: millennia upon millennia swept in solar ghost and phantasma as

48

fossils in the rocks of Asia, in time measureless to man as sunlight glinting in the sands of Colchis; and so, in twenty-four days, to the final design—a feathered chick, with eyes, brain, heart, kidneys, liver, and belly that was the absorbed yoke-sac, tapping and chipping with the horny nib upon its upper mandible around the wider end of its shell for the final leap from darkness into light.

The hen covered the eggs, giving of her body's warmth, shifting uneasily as slight cheepings arose with little movements under her. She hearkened to the chipping within the shells, and settled closer with love and anxiety.

Of thirteen eggs, eleven hatched. The hatchlings broke their way out of confining shells, and lay, wet and fatigued, in the nest. All day the hen covered them, while they slept, and their featherlets dried.

The bird within the twelfth egg was smaller than the others, and had not the strength to force its way out when, towards noon of the following morning, the hen, clucking softly and tenderly, moved away with her nid of dappled, speckled chicks. So it slept, or languished, in the darkness of its cavern, and soon lost vital heat and ceased to cheep to itself, and its movements ended. By the thirteenth egg, which was infertile, the chipped egg lay, and the dews of evening settled on its coldness.

Chapter Five

⟫⟪⟫◈⟪⟫⟪

The Carr stood upon a strip of land which was the shape of half a bullock's hoofmark, narrow and curved. Along the inner curve of the wood moved the river; around its outer shape lay the dyke through the thick upstanding reeds of which water trickling in from the trodden ditches of the meadow, and from the springs under the Long Wood, moved sluggishly. At the two pointed ends of the Carr the dyke was only a few feet from the river bank, and thus only by two narrow tongues of land could the meadow be reached without going through water. The Carr stood upon a peninsula. The time came when the hen wanted to take her chicks upon the meadow.

She moved with quiet uneven movements akin to hopping, away from the nettle patch with eleven chicks speckled and barred in buff and brown, agile as shadow-light a-shake and a-slip on woodland floor under windy movement of the green treetops. As they moved they stopped to pick up small insects astir with the full pulse of spring, and to peck timorously at leaf and flower.

Small passerine birds trilled and warbled in the wood; rooks cawed afar. The hen looked around with every forward step of stealthy movement; every suspicion called forth a slight cluck, which changed hesitant chick-movement in swift slip to cover. Another cluck, low and reassuring, and scattered dappled running started forth from hiding. The hen was nervous, she was strange to action after the long bemusing brood upon the rest. Every sound and sight was violent to her; pigeon flying over and wing-struck branch rattling: rabbit rising on haunches, ears upright, brown eye staring; splash-strike-series of moorcocks' wings on the gliding unseen river, as they squabbled about their water tenements, with cronky-croaky-icicle cries: plapping sounds of dung a-drop from red bullock standing in the shade of the wood slanting upon the rising grass of the meadow. It was full spring; voices of cuckoos echoed in the valley; turtle doves and swifts were home across shimmering deserts and wavering dark oases of fronded palm on yellow Parthenopean shore: twin leverets were feeding loose from the hare in corn plants thick enough to take the first shining wind-wave of the season. A nightingale sang in a thorn bush growing on the bank of the river. A dace leapt for a fly in a pool by the roots of trees uncovered by winter floods. Here was quietness, here was peace.

Rest, my little ones, rest; all is not self, all is not fear. In an open space grown with dark ivy upon the wood-land floor the mother squatted, dropped her wings and called her chicks to push for warmth and safety into her loose feathers. Almost at once, tired after their first journey, their eyes were closed and they were asleep.

Over one of the naked roots of an ash tree growing on the river-bank was a round hole. Wet marks on the bank revealed where an otter had recently clambered after swimming for and catching roach. The red-finned fish, thick-scaled and hog-backed, usually moved in droves up and down the river, passing rare and solitary trout hiding under the bank; but now they were spawning, thrusting and splashing at a gravelly verge of the river to rid themselves of eggs and milt. There were few such spawning places, owing to mud and silt which poured in by the drains which were increasing with what was called progress. The river by the Carr was partly clear of silt, and where the water-crowfoot grew in long waving tresses the roach had gathered to spawn.

Just below the splashing, shoaling fish Gallinule had been quietly paddling, taking the berry-like eggs as they drifted down with the current. He had flown away with a croak, legs trailing and wingtips splashing, when the otter had swum up beside him, showing its pointed whiskered head and little jetty eyes directed horribly upon him before the animal had dived again, bubbles breaking upon the surface of the water in a chain revealing its passage upstream. The roach had moved away downstream, except one fish of two pounds—for they grew big in that chalk stream—which the otter chawed as he lay on his back in the water. Thereafter the animal with the coarse brown spiky hair had clambered noisily, with plomping strokes of hind feet and flacks of thick tail, upon the exposed ash-roots and squeezed itself into its holt under the tree. It was a dog-otter, and sometimes slept in the open, upon ledges of ivy-clad rotten boles of trees which had fallen aslant standing trees, and also among the twisted willows near the pine tree.

The hen pheasant heard the noises of the otter moving into its holt through the earth, which was a lacework of large and small roots lying under and upon the surface of the wood. As the otter scratched at the ticks upon its neck its claws struck a main root of the ash and the sounds were borne along a curving yellow root to where the bone of the bird's short leg rested upon its end. Had the otter listened, it would have heard the noise of the bird's heart, returning in beats of sound along the root. But the otter slept, secure in its own power and content with easy living. While it could get eels, roach, and an occasional trout from the river, it did not bother to hunt on land; but sometimes it ran through the Carr for a frolic.

Later that afternoon it felt such an impulse, and leaving its holt, after yawning and scratching and shaking itself, it rolled on the bank, pushing itself along on its neck; then rising on its four short legs, it sniffed, and quested about the air for interesting scents. Finding one, it set off along a path, passing with crackling of fallen spruce twigs within a yard of the hen once more brooding her chicks by the ivy-grown stump of a snapped larch; and when the bird leapt up, uttering a screeching, grating cry and with loud whirring of wings flew noisily away from the chicks which had scattered and run swiftly to crouch to invisibility, the otter merely checked, and rolled on its back, delighted with the noise and flurry.

Sometime later a series of low muted clucks drew the chicks to where the hen stood, anxious and trembling, among clumps of pink campion. She took them to another part of the Carr to sleep the night, while owls flew overhead, and pitching with talon-scratchings upon accustomed perches, peered down for movement, and saw nothing.

The otter was a young water-beast who lived alone, not yet mated, his dam and brother-cubs having departed in mid-April for the marshes and mud-guts of the seacoast. He was a playful animal, and often his thin cry or whistle was to be heard in the dykes and lower reaches of the river at night. The bullocks grazing on the meadow knew the cry, and often followed the low shape in curiosity as it lolloped about in the dusk, pushing itself against the domed heaps of moles' redoubts and the humps of anthills which studded the higher grazing levels above the guts of the original salting discernible in the straggling lows of the meadow. There was a scent sometimes lying in the Carr which the otter followed eagerly whenever he crossed it, remembering the grey animal which once he had chased through the grass and lost in the dry ditch overgrown by brambles where mead ended and arable began. The grey animal was a cat, which had taken to living wild in the wood. Once it been a kitten lapping milk with others of its litter in the unwashed cow-house of the farm premises: milk daily tipped into an old cracked cast-iron cooking crock, to hold the cats for the catching of mice and rats. When it was grown, the cat found that rabbits were more exciting to wait for and to kill than rodents in barn and stable; and being male, it lived for excitement and pleasure only. While leaner, slinking females took mice and rats and smaller rabbits for their kittens, the tom cats indulged their spare lusts upon rabbits, especially the larger bucks. At first the tom had brought home its kills for the stockman, laying rabbits by his oatmeal-bin, patched by tin of biscuit-box where rats had gnawn through its wooden sides, and greeting his patron with vertical twitching tail and plaintive mews as it rubbed against his leaky gum-boots, which he wore winter and summer; but as it grew more experienced in lust and fighting, it ceased to lug to the cowhouse bucks as big as itself, and took to living in the woods. Its head broadened, the bars on its grey fur became more pro-nounced, its eyes assumed the pale bright stare of a hawk, and it avoided man as an enemy, hiding and sleeping down rabbit-burrows. But one night its paw sprung to-gether the jaws of a gin set to catch a rabbit, and after much contortion and howling the animal tore itself loose, whereupon it ran wildly away, and never returned to the woods by the premises. It made its home in a hollow tree of the Long Wood, moving out to hunt only at night. Sometimes it travelled far, living rough until the particular courtship that had drawn it from its base in the Long Wood was ended.

On one of its journeys the tom walked through the Carr, and remained there, as the riverside wood was remote and unfrequented by man. Seeing the otter once or twice had shocked it with fright, but not with terror as being caught in the trap had; and in reaction to the fright, curiosity had helped to keep it in the Carr. It selected for itself a hide halfway up the slanting pole of a dead spruce tree, in the old nest of a sparrowhawk. There on a platform of knotted larch twigs, where old notched bones of birds were pressed, the cat was wont to rest, and gaze down upon movement below, as it digested its nightly gorgings upon flesh and fur.

One rainy morning, when leaves of the barley plants upon the Breck were grown enough to hide all but the heads of two partridges standing upright in the corn, the hen pheasant walking on the path in the Carr glanced up and saw fixed upon her the yellow eyes of the cat sitting in the hawk's nest. The cat had been watching the pheasant intently because of her shuffling progress. Feeling menace in the cat's stare, the hen gave the alarm to her chicks. They ran to cover, and crouched. The hen remained in the open space by the ivied tree-stump, watching the cat, and uttering urgent clucks. The cat blinked, and glanced away, for it did not like being looked at; but it was observing while its gaze was away. The hen stood unmoving, while clucking to the chicks to remain still. This continued during several minutes, until at last the cat sulkily removed its indirect glance.

At once with the easing of tension the hen's notes changed to a higher pitch. She was calling them, and they arose, and ran to her. Turning her back upon the cat, she hoppited away, talking to the chicks who paused and ran about her, between feeding and following, uttering low clucks to keep them by her. After a score of yards her pace slowed, but she had not forgotten the eyes behind her. She led the chicks to the northern end of the Carr—past the jungle of fallen and ingrown willows, whose drooping boughs had put out roots wherever they had touched the swampy ground—past the pine tree—past the thorns growing on the narrow tongue of land between river and dyke. Now that she was about to leave the shelter of the wood for the open land of the meadow, she hesitated, because never before had she ventured into the open with chicks, since she had been but a chick herself twelve months previously. So she stopped on the edge of the shade of the pine tree, standing on the bank of the river, where a patch of grass grew thick and dark upon a soil that had absorbed many carcasses of fish, with otter-spraints or droppings, because she heard the splashings and cronkings of waterfowl in the river below. She knew them as enemies; she had been frightened by them as a cheeper, and again when Gallinule had attacked her. So she hesitated. But also she was frightened by the face of the cat, which she saw in memory; and it was this memory —a short one, as with most active birds and mammals, including man—that made her, after hesitation, to walk down the raised grassy bank of the river and take to the meadow, in the full shine of the sun.

Soon she was easier, with the menace of the cat face receding, and as hope lightened her spirit. The grass was lush on the meadow, there were many thistles rising there, with rush-clumps, for cover. Calling the chicks, and with head held low, she walked cautiously forward, observed by a hen cuckoo on top of the fir tree.

The cuckoo soon returned to her watch of three pairs of titlarks flitting about the rush-clumps; for the bird was set upon laying an egg in each nest just before the female titlark, or meadow pipit, had finished laying her own set. She had done this for two past seasons, taking and eating a pipit's egg in exchange for the one she had laid in the nest. For the cuckoo was a bird which, like the human courtesan, accepted the delights of mating while avoiding the burdens of responsibility, which she put upon other birds. She was on the point of laying an egg when the hen pheasant left the Carr. Knowing the bird to be harmless, she launched herself from the fir top, gliding to her destination without wing-beat in order to be as inconspicuous as possible. And, gliding over the pheasant, the cuckoo, who had the shape of a hawk, scared the hen, who let out a sqwark as she dropped with half-spread wings upon the grass. The grey-blue shape glided on, towards a rush-clump in the middle of the meadow. The pheasant, whose chicks had scattered at the sqwark, rose up again, and saw Gallinule, drawn by her cry from the river-bank upon which he had chanced to climb, walking towards her.

Gallinule uttered grating little cries, and flapped his wings, his neck thrust forward, as he did when pursuing a rival. Two other moorcocks appeared on the top of the river-bank. The hen pheasant watched them, and as the leading bird came nearer, uttered a screaking cry.

At once the chicks, obeying the cry of fear and of warning, ran to crouch close under grasses into which they had thrust themselves. The hen, after moving with anxious uncertainty towards the leading attacker, who was Gallinule, began to hasten, hoppiting and wing-flapping, through the grass away from her young. But Gallinule, perceiving movement in a rush-clump, ran to a chick, which he struck with his beak several times, and pulled it out, feebly kicking as it lay on its side. By now the other two moorcocks had joined him, and were squabbling

57

over the inert chick. The hen pheasant returned, dragging a wing to simulate helplessness, using herself as a decoy. She screeched wildly, and dashing at Gallinule, drove him away, to return in desperation as she heard the cry of another chick being pecked by a water-bird.

Other moorfowl, drawn by the noise, were appearing over the raised bank of the river. Seeing them from the hawk's nest, the cat clawed its way down the bole, and ran along the otter-path to the edge of the Carr. After intent scrutiny, crouched low and tail-tip switching, the cat moved forward, and was halfway to where the hen was fighting with several dark birds before one of them saw it, and gave the alarm as it ran for the river. Others followed. The last to leave rose in flight, but the dazed pheasant was unable to get away before a paw-stroke of the cat knocked a bunch of feathers from between her shoulders, and then she was beneath its weight, as it bit through her neck; and dispread upon the grass with staring eye and gaping beak, she uttered a final cry.

It was the habit of the stockman to go down to the meadow every morning to count his grazing beasts, and to see if they were "doing". The bullocks did not belong to the farmer; they were the property of the cattle-dealer who would sell them the following Michaelmas to some farmer or other who still farmed in the old-fashioned way that lost money: that is, the farmer would buy bullocks to fatten them for beef, with turnips, hay, and ground-nut cake, the beasts meanwhile treading barley straw spread in yard or box, to make the muck to grow the roots and corn of the old-fashioned Norfolk four-course shift which maintained the soil's fertility. The cost of buying the beasts off grass, and of fattening them during five or six months, would be greater than the money he would get for them when fat; but how else was he to obtain the muck to keep his land in heart? So the old-fashioned farmer who cared for his land became every year nearer to bankruptcy.

The cattle dealer paid the farmer two shillings a head a week while his beasts grazed the meadow, and the stockman went down every morning to see that they were "doing". When he reached the plank over the dyke farthest from the Carr, he stood still and gazed under his hand at the peculiar behaviour of the sixteen bullocks near the river-bank. They were moving, between walk and trot, with heads extended in curiosity, towards something in the grass which he could not discern. As he stared, he heard the startled howl of a cat and watched the bullocks kicking their heels in the air, before breaking into a canter.

To his surprise he saw a cat running with the greatest speed, followed by what appeared to be a dark brown dog very low on its legs. Behind the animal were the bullocks, one or two of them bellowing. The cat was running towards him. He stood still. When it was about a gunshot away, the cat saw him, and stopped abruptly. Then it jumped round, saw the otter, its hair stood up, its tail fluffed out; it let out the loudest howl he had ever heard from a cat, and raced at right angles towards the river-bank, while the otter, after a momentary stare at him, ran in the opposite direction, towards the Breck, and disappeared into the reeds of the dyke.

The stockman, pleasantly stirred by the sight, removed his cap, scratched his head, and said aloud, "That's a rum 'un!"

The bullocks came to a stop, and began to blare at him. He walked towards them, counted them by their heads, then set off towards the Breck, crossing the dyke by a plank, and so up over the barley of the Breck to a higher field, where the other men were singling sugar-beet plants, each man on his own plot, which he hoed by contract: thus all worked hard and continuously.

As the stockman passed over the barley, with its pale green leaves shining in the sun, he was watched by two partridges in the corn near the lower hedge—Pertris and Pertrisel, whose chicks, scarcely larger than bumblebees, had hatched that morning.

Chapter Six

———⊰⊷⊶⟡⊷⊶⊱———

When the otter had crossed the scent of the cat, it had followed it from curiosity to the end of the wood and the open meadow. Seeing the low rippling form approaching, the cat had sprung back from the sight as though repelled by an electrical charge that lifted every hair of its body. Its momentary paralysis of action was accompanied by a prolonged yowl; and by the yowl its terror was discharged, whereupon it turned and fled, pursued by the otter. The bullocks had lifted their heads and snorted on hearing the loud cry of the cat, the skin of their shoulders twitching, for they had felt, in their lethargic way, an effect of the cat's shock. In release they lolloped after the brown object galloping through the grass; they followed because they were disturbed and it was running away from them. When it disappeared, they trotted around, slowed up, and stood about, blowing and sniffing in cautious bewilderment. After a while they began to graze in line across the meadow, while the stock-man went slowly towards them.

When he had gone, they continued to pull at the grass with their tongues set with little rasps which held the blades in the curl of the tongue until the teeth gripped and pulled the bite into the mouth, to be swallowed, without chewing, into the first stomach. And so, moving

61

slowly and peacefully, they drew towards the end of the Carr, where, some lying down, others standing, they composed themselves to bring up cuds of grass to be chewed, and swallowed within another sac or stomach.

As they rested there, the moorfowl reappeared over the river-bank, which stood well above the level of the meadow. The birds walked cautiously, flipping their tails, and pausing to look around. Perceiving no danger, and reassured by the tranquillity of the bullocks, of which they had no fear since the beasts never interfered with them, they walked directly to where the pheasant lay dead upon the grass. A light breeze was blowing from the bullocks to the scene of the slaying, otherwise the bullocks would have spent some minutes sniffing at the smells in the grass, and their cloven feet might then have killed those chicks which remained alive, occasionally cheeping faintly to the mother who did not call them.

The moorfowl fluttered and squabbled over the carcass until the crop was picked open; then Gallinule, an ex-perienced feeder upon wounded and dead game birds not picked up after a shoot, drove away the others, to gulp large beakfuls of its crop until his own was crammed, when he lost interest, and returned to the river, to creep under a cluster of grasses overhanging a little inlet where he might sleep unmolested. When the other moorfowl had picked all they wanted of the flesh off the bones, they too returned to the river.

At noon, when the bullocks had risen, stretched them-selves, dropped their loose dung, licked the hair of their flanks in contentment, and ambled away to drink at a bay in the bank of the dyke trodden by the feet of bul-locks in the past—long ago the flints and chalk-lumps spread there in an age of careful husbandry had gone under the pug—the pair of partridges on the Breck took their chicks, now dry and active, to a broken bridge which led on to the meadow. The bridge had been made of pitch-pine baulks, from an old wooden ship, laid on brick-walling built up each bank of the dyke, and then covered with chalk. The resin of the baulks had resisted rot for a quarter of a century, but now there were gaps where tindered wood had fallen and holes showed in the chalk covering.

Usually the partridges, when crossing the bridge over the dyke, had, after a scrutiny to left and right and skywards, run along one narrow side which was without holes; but now, with their young, they made of the crossing a most cautious business. With an authoritative note to his mate and chicks, telling them to remain still, Pertris moved through the strip of rough grazing below the Breck and came to the bank above the dyke. There he stood for several moments, listening, standing with head held high, the retinae of his keen eyes sensitive to any movement that might be of danger. Seeing and hearing no danger, he called Pertrisel, and she began to bring the chicks carefully through the grasses, while Pertris continued to stand upon the bank, his head raised. When they came near he ran down to them, and the chicks quatted to rest, the parent birds upright and watchful beside them.

After a while, Pertris, with low clucks, moved through the grass, stopped, and again stood up sentinel. The chicks ran to him, and thus by advancing, pausing, and ever watching, Pertris brought his little covey to the bridge.

Here he showed again the same caution. He walked over the chalky surface, grown with thin grasses and set with flints, with some hesitation, constantly stopping to utter notes telling them to remain crouched, while he looked around. But all was well, and called by low clucks,

63

the chicks crossed the open way which was hot to their feet after the grass, and so came to cover again on the meadow. Pertrisel walked behind them, while Pertris led them to a colony of rye-grasses and white clover which grew in a patch above the dyke.

There, while Pertris stood at watch, Pertrisel plucked at the tips of tender leaves, and the immature seeds forming with the pollen on the rye-grass stems, talking softly to the nimble chicks as she pecked. Already these bee-like birdlings, speckled and striped in pale brown and buff, were nipping the ends of low grass-blades for themselves, taking minute green and yellow insects which rested there.

As they hurried hither and thither within their small scope, Pertris stood observant and upright. His plumage was coloured with the hues of leaves fallen from trees of wood and hedge in the autumn of the English year—pale buff of oak, brown of hawthorn, rufous of horse-chestnut—and of ash of wood-fires made in winter and early spring by men eating their dinners in the lee of hedges—the hedges between fields of arable along which, seeking berries and seeds, partridges fed in the bleak months of the year. There was a band of dark feathers, coloured and shaped like a rusty bullock-shoe turned up by plough or harrow, around his lower breast; but already the dark colouring of it was beginning to fade. The great party after the turn of the year, when new feathers of clearest colours were assumed for the jousting and claiming of territory and love, was long over; colours had faded in a workaday season, with the dust-baths and crouching and running and flinging up of feathered wings in flight.

Unlike the gaudy Asiatic—the bird of the White Necklace—with his harem of dun hens left to fend for their families, the cock partridge was loyal, meticulous, and brave in care and defence of his mate and young. His watchfulness was never relaxed, and he shared with his mate the brooding, or comforting, of the chicks. When they had fed, and were standing sleepy-eyed, Pertrisel called them softly to her, and they moved to her warm body, pushing into her loosened feathers and under her dropped wings; and Pertris squatted beside her, but with his head by her tail. Thus one parent bird watched from east to west, while the other surveyed the air and line of land from west to east: both birds ready, at any instant, to spring apart and to make noisy diversion at any hostile intrusion. The chicks slept, while the shadows of the partridges moved perceptibly with the sun.

The cuckoo flew to the top of the pine tree standing at the corner of the Carr, and sat among the dark green needles rising over the mantle of ivy, watching the movements of small birds about the rush-clumps. She had laid an egg in the nest of a titlark that morning, while holding in her bill one of the dark mottled eggs she had lifted from the nest. A few moments afterwards she had flown to an elm in the Long Wood, and perching on a branch, had crushed and swallowed the titlark's egg. After a rest, she had flown to the top of the elm, one of three vantage points from which she overlooked her territory.

The cuckoo had several mates, which she called by a prolonged bubbling cry. Flying to her, the rivals often became incoherent, shouting *cuck-cuck-cuck-oo*, in notes of differing keys, or uttering but a single sqwarky *cuck* followed by cursing noises. Likewise the hen cuckoo had the power to stimulate and upset the smaller male birds of the nests she visited. The cuckoo watched the nests of her dupes, timing the laying of her egg in each one so that when it hatched the nestling cuckoo should not be at any disadvantage in its labours of heaving out the other eggs or nestlings. She visited the nests while the female titlarks

65

were in course of laying their eggs, before they began to sit on them; and always when she appeared at a nest, the male titlark would jitter before her, quivering and fluttering his wings before the great courtesan. When she flew away, he would follow for a while, vainly twittering, to return again to his mate and to find her shivering her wings and, with open beak, behaving like a nestling. So he would seek food to feed her, as sometimes he fed the cuckoo on her visits. His mate took the beakfuls of insects with a feeling that contented him; but the cuckoo never gave him restfulness.

The cuckoo sat in the top of the pine tree, among the needles humming with the south wind. She had fed herself on caterpillars eating the leaves of willows in the Plot. She drowsed in the warmth of the gentle air, uninterested for the moment in the voices of male cuckoos calling about the woods. By instinct all small-bird movement attracted her, and a stir upon the ground rising slightly in the centre of the meadow made her eyes open wide. Clumps of rushes grew sparsely there, among the uneven mounds of the ant-hills. Staring at the movement, the cuckoo saw that it was not that of titlark, and her sight unfocused from it.

The movement had been made by a pheasant chick, which had wandered there, uttering feeble cries. It was cold and languid, having so little energy that its occasional cheeping was nearly inaudible. It was the only survivor of the nid from under the pine tree, for after the hen's death the other chicks had been hunted down and eaten by the moorfowl, which had returned to the carcass in the afternoon. One chick, which had moved farthest from the others—being a little swifter and warier—had escaped. Now its movements were slow and trembling, and after moving about all ways, it settled, with fallen head and closed eyes, in a cavity made by a cloven hoof.

The sun's radiant rim rested upon the uneven billowing line of green tops of the trees of the Long Wood. The calls of a partridge, like a rusty key turning in the wooden lock of the great tarred doors of the Corn Barn, sounded across the meadow.

Pertris stood upon the terrace of ant-hills, calling Pertrisel and the chicks. Watching alertly from a mound, he saw the heron flying upriver, to one of the shallows where roach were spawning; he saw the moorfowl stalking one another and feeding on river-bank and meadow by the wood; he saw the barn owl flying down the open ride in the High Wood, watched it fluttering at the edge of the barley, to drop suddenly, then rise again and fly along the top of the Breck. *Per-tris, per-tris, per-tris*, in a wheezy, key-scraping voice, and at the sound Pertrisel, the chicks running about her, moved forward confidently.

So they came among the ant-hills, where the soil was drier than the rest of the meadow, and where Pertris had scratched several dusting troughs, for like most partridges, he suffered from parasitic insects. Safely home, the parent birds scuffled their breasts and bellies in the dusting hollows, while the chicks ran about and picked up specks of cockle-shell and sand, flapping their wing-stumps to run the faster. The sun was now moving down behind the distant woods on the line of the hills, and the air over the meadow was beginning to stir the grasses. The two partridges stood up to stretch wing and leg, to ruffle feathers and shake off the dust, before settling to preen flight-quill and tail feathers.

Afterwards Pertrisel looked about for a roosting place for the night. Finding a dry hollow, open all round for a clear view, she squatted there, beside a hoof-print in the clay—it had been made when the soil was damp, but now was set hard—dropped her wings, and called the chicks to her.

Pertris walked to her side, and sat down, his head to her tail. He settled gently, feeling slight movement under the edge of a wing, and hearing with pleasure a faint chirping as one of his chicks pressed itself against him. He spoke to Pertrisel, and she answered him: a soft, throbbing sound in the throat, uttered with beak closed, a sound of contentment and relaxation. She settled closer to the earth, now that the chicks were safe and still. Her eyes began to close. Pertris remained watchful.

After a few moments he shifted to ease the slightest of movements against one of his feet. He lifted the foot, but there was no further movement, and gently he lowered his leg until his foot again touched the ground; but his weight remained on the other leg, for spirit and body were fully in service to the young.

The movement had been made by the lifted head of the surviving pheasant chick, as its ebbing consciousness had dimly sought the warmth that was life. The movement, slight and feeble, exhausted almost the last of its strength. Had another bird chanced to roost there, even a hen pheasant, it is doubtful if it would have survived; in all probability it would have been pressed upon the clay.

The partridge was sensitive with the power and light of a hundred thousand years of wild living upon the soil from which his being was sprung. There was in his blood no tameness, or dependency on living through the efforts of another species, as there was in that of the immigrant bird of Asia. Pertris, without conscious thought, but by the beauty of pure racial thought which is behind instinct, held his leg sensitive to movement of which he was not sure; and after several minutes, the movement was felt again; and once more the leg was lifted, delicately, tenderly. Under him he heard the least noise, the cheeping of a chick that was scarcely audible; his thigh was touched; he moved it sideways. He felt the feathers of his belly stirred, and lifted his body to give freedom to the cold chick who, as the star of evening was glowing with full soft light over the dark woods, had so far recovered as to creep to the surest warmth between the thighs of the partridge. And as the evestar followed the sun below the horizon of the west, and the constellations gleamed in the pastures of the night, the eyes of Pertris closed, and he too fell asleep.

Chapter Seven

———◦◦◦◦◦◦◦◦◦———

Before the pearl-like star of morning was dissolved in the rose-pale wine of dawn and the first lark had flown up to greet the day, Pertris was awake, and listening. Soon other skylarks had arisen from the corn of the Breck and the fields around the meadows, singing as they climbed to points of light hung aloft the dimming night. He heard the under-twitter of swallows still in their nest beneath the broken timber-bridge over the dyke, the voices of wrens and warblers in the Carr, and from afar, the soft throaty mutter of waking carrion crows in the High Wood. Soon the meadow was crossed with birdsong and the watery cries of coot and moorfowl in the dykes, with noises of cattle rising and stretching themselves before moving off to graze.

Light flooded over the rim of ocean, the sun rose and cast thin green shadows amidst the gold-spiked grasses; gulls passed in formation, flying inland, under high clouds changing hue from pink to gold. From the distant Home Meadow came the thuds of hoofs as the farm-horses, seeing the teamsman approach with an old aluminium saucepan in one hand, and bridles across the other arm, lumbered away from a familiar trick. Smiler, Blossom, and Gilbert knew that the saucepan (which the teamsman had picked out of the river, which for many years had been regarded as sewer and rubbish-dump of the formless village) was empty; had they not upon other occasions trusted voice and gesture of the teamsman, and followed him off the meadow through the gate leading to the stables, only to find their happy anticipation of crushed oats was a mockery. But it was not altogether the teamsman's fault, for there had been no crushed oats in the stable. The farmer, pressed by his creditors, was economizing. He had urged to the teamsman that the work of drawing the horse-hoe between the ringes of sugar-beet was light work, and grass should be enough for the horses, and the teamsman could think of no other way to get them to stand for him to slip the bridles over their heads. Pertris heard his voice coaxing them by name, and then the noise of heavy feet pounding away.

He sat beside Pertrisel. Both had been fully awake for some time, but neither had moved, for the chicks were still sleeping. Cuckoos were calling, and in the Carr the wauling of dwarf owls broke out. Their nest was in a decayed ash tree, and the pair had six owlets in a hole of the tindered wood. Pertris knew that when the owls called one to another they were not hunting, yet his head was turned to the black shape of the wood. He watched a snipe overhead flying in a ragged circle, breaking its perimeter to climb steeply, to dive as steeply and brake with its tail, to make with the feathers a thrumming noise to its mate with her young among the rush-clumps.

Pertris stood up, and stretched his body to detach the chicks from his feathers. Faint cheeps came from under him, and he answered with soft clucks; but when one of them pushed unexpectedly from between his legs and thrust out its head from the brown-and-ash feathers, Pertris was startled into silence. He bent his head to look at it, for it was strange upon his sight, its head being several times the size he was accustomed to seeing below him. As he gazed, the chick cheeped several times, and the stiffening of the cock partridge relaxed. He answered,

71

and dropped his wings with the instinct to shelter. Thus the larger chick was adopted by Pertris, and accepted by Pertrisel as he ran among the tiny partridge chicks.

The sun's orb was now behind the trees of the Carr, whose shadows upon the Breck were being withdrawn across the barley. White sea-swallows flying over the gilded azure levels of the sea moving around the shingle tongue of the Point were gold-winged as they splashed into the water, opening crimson mouths to take silver sprat and sand-eel. As the high cirrus clouds faded of their gold with the full light of morning, the tips of the meadow grasses glinted blue and green and red. The chicks sipped the dew, and plucked the tender tips of clover-leaf and grass, while Pertris and Pertrisel scratched at the anthills, disturbing the brown insects, which their chicks peered at, but were afraid to take.

While Pertris was watching from a hillock, he noticed a moorcock stalking among the rush-clumps. This was Gallinule, seeking a more tasty food than the roots of river-plants. Gallinule saw the partridge, but continued as before, approaching indirectly, moving this way and that, as though he were uninterested in the sight of the partridge with raised head, standing on the terrace of the anthills. As a young water-bird, Gallinule's chief food had been part of the tender, pithy stems of river-plants and weeds, kernels of sprouting barley, snails and shrimps, the eggs and fry of fish and frogs, and occasional potato peelings and guts of fowls and rabbits which had drifted down the river, from the garbage pails of the villagers above; but he preferred the taste of flesh, and from feeding upon cold and carrion flesh he had grown a taste for blood. If he could find a nestful of young titlarks or upon the arable after rain a partridge chick cheeping plaintively by itself, exhausted after struggling behind the others, weighed down by a pat of sticky soil upon the hind-toe

72

of each foot, and left behind, Gallinule's eyes would flick with eagerness. Pertris remembered the moorcock from his own chick-hood, when Gallinule, feeding with others of his kind upon winged ants, had run through the grass clumps of the terrace to strike him in the neck; and on that occasion the cock partridge his sire had behaved as now Pertris acted: he ran at Gallinule, screaking like the iron key being turned violently both ways in ancient wood-and-iron lock, so violently that corroded iron and beetle-bored beechwood frame broke ... which was Pertris dashing at the pied yellow-beaked water-crow with the stilty legs. A feathered fury broke upon Gallinule with strike of wing, beak, and foot; and promptly the moorcock turned tail and flapped away, reassuming upon the distant river-bank his melancholy, water-weed eating, surprised vegetarian appearance. After him with clocking whirr of wings flew Pertris, screeching as Gallinule fell backwards into the water over the bank, and dived downstream. Thereupon the partridge wheeled over the adjacent field, beat his wings and glided over the dyke, and braking abruptly, pitched upon the stamped chalk of the approach to the broken bridge; and after cocking one eye then another eye at the sky, called *per-tris, per-tris, per-tris*, for Pertrisel to bring the chicks to a more settled place. And after scrutinizing land and sky once more, he ran over the bridge, and along his path through the grass, a wandering path resembling the run of a rabbit, but narrower, and not so defined, to join his family.

By the end of the day Pertris had led the bee-like chicks across the Breck, through a ragged hedge of wind-shaped thorns, and down a slope of thin grey grass between the upper edge of the Long Wood and the lower edge of the High Wood. Here were many small insects that the chicks might take from the grasses.

The slope of grass was only about three acres, and beyond this area the field extended steeply to the south in a series of rolling ridges. This field was known as Steep Piece, and its loamy soil, overlaying chalk, was both laborious and tricky to cultivate. The grey loam when wet was dour and claggy; it stuck to the boots of men, the feet of horses, and the iron wheels of tractors; and to attempt to work the land in that condition was to spoil it for a season. But if it were too sticky to work one day, almost by the next it might be too dry. The field, owing to the steep slope and porous chalk beneath its thin skin, dried out rapidly: to plow with horses up and down the slopes was to wear them out prematurely, if not to break their hearts; and plowing with wheeled tractors of the conventional design, the lumbering machines were liable to dig themselves in or to rear up their front wheels precipitantly and turn over backwards with their drivers. So the field was left to itself, and a miniature forest of thistle, dock, ragwort, and thorn-apple had risen out of a mat of couch-grass: a place much sought for its cover and food by pheasants, partridges, and an occasional corn-crake and quail. It was threaded by wandering runways of rabbit, hare, and rat.

Extending along the upper edge of this incult field (it had last been plowed by teams of shod bullocks, in regular rotation of the Norfolk Four Course Shift introduced by "Turnip" Townshend from the Flanders war) was the lynchet or bank tunnelled by rabbits and grown with elderberry and other tree-weeds sown by birds. Beyond the lynchet lay an upland field which was in cultivation, bearing what were known as "small seeds"— of clover, ryegrass, alsike, and cowgrass grown for fodder. The small seeds, as was the local custom, had been drilled across the lines of two-inch-tall barley-plants during the previous spring, and the rising barley had acted as nurse to the tiny plants until the corn was cut at harvest, when they had the light and soil for themselves. Enduring the winter they grew strongly in the following spring, as a hay crop. Now as the sun approached its highest curve of midsummer, the windwave was on the grasses and clovers. It was a field whose fertility had not yet been entirely sucked; and the hay was thick, though docks and thistles, wild radish and other weeds were frequent. The scents of the flowers of white, pink, and red clover, of tall moon-daisy, campion, and scabious, with the pollen adrift from flower and awn, helped to overlay the scents of the birds; and so, upon this higher field several hen pheasants and partridges had brought their families, while hares had their forms there; and thither came rats, stoats, and weasels, and the wild cat which had returned to its rabbit hole in the HighWood, and a solitary dog-fox that had wandered in from the sandy plains, set with forests of conifers, of the interior known as the Brecklands. The dog-fox, who was old and slow, with infirm teeth, lived almost entirely upon slugs, mice, and beetles, with an occasional young rabbit.

In fields adjacent to the clover layer, men were standing with bent backs, hoeing their plots of sugar-beet plants, which were now in the four-leaved stage. Each man was intent as he moved slowly down his row, pushing with hoe-blade, nicking, striking, scraping away all plants save one left every ten inches or so. Each man on every acre would strike away more than a million plants of sugar-beet, together with weeds of dock, thistle, charlock, pimpernel, speedwell, crab-grass, and eyebright; each man, with a thin steel blade, eight inches wide, riveted to a swan-neck of iron fixed to a handle five feet in length, would leave between thirty and forty thousand plants to the acre, each about an inch high, with leaves growing on a thread of stalk scarcely thicker than one-thirtieth of

75

an inch. Sometimes the corner of the hoe would hesitate momentarily while the keen eye above directed the edge of the blade to the stalk of a plant growing beside another plant selected for leaving: the least moment for decision, and the unwanted plant was pushed off its roots. For double, or twin, beet growing in and by one another, in a twist and tangle of the yellow-white roots, was undesirable: a crop was desired of one plant every ten inches in the ringes or rows, with a root fifteen inches long growing to a taper from a crown in maturity perhaps six inches in diameter to its point or base no thicker than a pig's tail: a clean tapered root which would hold little or no dirt when knocked. A good man hoeing might earn, by his intense and sustained scrutiny and skill—akin to the care and energy of Pertris and Pertrisel guarding the covey— half as much again as his usual weekly wage. Standing with bent neck and rounded shoulders ten hours a day for five and a half days in the sunshine, moving slowly sideways across the field, a good man took home on Friday forty-two shillings.

In the clear, quiet hours of morning, before the hoers came to their work, and in the evening after they had gone, Pertris and Pertrisel led their chicks upon the sugar-beet field. Here was good feeding, in the wilted heads of the weeds which had been scraped from the rows whereon the little plants stood singled and solitary. Here, too, the partridge chicks could run and dry themselves after wetting their plumage in the dewfall upon the clover field. Their feathers were now more distinctly striped: at ten days they were strong, and could lift themselves off the ground with rapid circular motion of arms now sprouting wing-feathers from grey quills. The larger chick ran with them, yet always near Pertris; for of danger to its living it seemed ever to be expectant. It cowered at the least strange noise; and once, when it had lost Pertris temporarily—the partridge was dusting himself a few yards out in the beet field—it ran to and fro, uttering a high thin plaintive cry, unlike that of other pheasant chicks. Pertrisel did not heed it, nor did it run to her; she had never taken notice of it. Pertris clucked, and the chick ran so fast that it flew. Beside the cock partridge once again it was happy, and contentedly preened its feathers while Pertris settled into his dust bath.

Usually at the time of the hoers coming to work in the sugar-beet field, hen pheasants and partridges with their young withdrew into the northern hedge, and then, leading the chicks down the slope of the bank, entered the tall grasses of the layer. Here was shelter from eye of hawk and crow, while seldom the weasels, and an occasional stoat that hunted along the hedge-bottoms, entered the thick green growth of grass and clover. But one morning, after they had moved down from the higher field, an unusual sound in the air made every mother-bird draw her chicks close to her, to crouch low and to listen. It was a sound like the call of the quail, a rare visitor to the uplands of the farm, but uttered more frequently, and with a harsher quality. Afterwards there was a swishing sound, continued regularly as it moved down one side of the field, and simultaneously up the other side. The scent of tobacco came strongly, in wafts with the moving air. Voices of men. Then came a more menacing noise: the rasp of a file on metal teeth. The mowers had come to the field.

When a lane had been cleared by the two scythe-men, the cutter, drawn by two horses guided by the teamsman sitting on the iron seat, began to clacker round the field. The fearful noises of the mild steel teeth on the cutter-bar

77

shaking sideways between cast-iron fingers lifting the green grasses for the shear filled the birds with terror. They led their chicks deeper into the field, away from the noises which, as they were not harmful, were soon accepted with less anxiety. Nevertheless, they remained uneasy, and only relaxed when at noon the noises ceased. The men were sitting on old sacks in the hedge, eating their dinners, while the horses, the bits still in their mouths, ate from two heaps of dark green clover and lighter ryegrass lifted in armfuls from the wilting swathe. Work was resumed fifty minutes later; they were allowed half an hour for their midday meal.

The two scythe-men kept the corner of the standing rectangle of grass rounded, so that the cutter could continue without check at the turns. Even so, the cutter frequently stopped, while the teamsman got off the sack covering the iron seat, and with a heavy iron tool, called by him a screw-hammer, he knocked, wrenched, tapped, and bashed. All the moving parts of the cutter were worn, loose, or ill-adjusted. He heaved and tugged, and poured upon them from a bottle a black liquid given him by a tractor-driver in the village, of old engine-sump oil; he wiped his hands, with their bleeding, broken skin, first on the cut hay, then on his trousers, before uttering a familiar local incantation, *We won't get in no muddle*; and with this blend of lubrication and faith, the machine was somehow induced to cut again. The knives, sharpened on a wooden form by a three-sided file, were changed after every acre of cutting; small stones and protruding flints (for the layer had not been rolled after the winter frost had lifted the surface) gave the steel teeth jagged dents and dulled edges.

The cutting of the hay proceeded as it had in former years upon the farm—the cutter, nearly thirty years old, had been bought at auction for three pounds, from its seventh owner—and in the late afternoon only a small triangular area of standing grasses remained. Boys let out of school appeared with sticks, and Little Bingo the butcher's dog pranced with them. The farmer arrived with a gun, to shoot the rabbits as they ran out, for the men to take home.

While he was standing there, the farmer heard faint cheeping sounds in the uncut grass. Somewhere within the last two acres a hen bird was hiding with her chicks. The ryegrass was nearly two feet tall, the red clover was thick, and he knew from experience that a search for the birds would be in vain. How could they be got out safely? He wanted to finish cutting that day, for he was behindhand with the hoeing; the yellow weeds of charlock were choking the lines of beet-plants, and the men were complaining that they were not making their money, the going was so slow. There might be several hens with chicks in the uncut triangle of grass, and they would lead them away safely later in the evening if the cutting were stopped. Yet the hay should be cut, while the weather lasted. Moved by contrary impulses, the farmer stood there, outwardly placid, but inwardly irresolute. For he did not really mind if the hay were cut or not; he was past caring, or rather worrying; he was a worn-out man, an automatic man, with few selfish impulses left in his nature. He had accepted old age, and the fact of his almost total failure as a farmer. Yet he did care that things should be done properly, but only with the ghost of his former self.

The clattering cutter came down the field again, and when it was near the farmer a cock partridge flew up, with loud demonstrative whirr of wings and squealing, grating cries, to flop almost at once among the swathes of fallen grass a few yards away, and to squat there, its eyes bright upon them. The farmer could feel upon himself the bubbling of the bird's heart. He took the pipe from his mouth, and held up the stem.

The cutter stopped, the driver dismounted, and together they searched and peered among the standing grasses at the apex of the triangle. Boys came near, with sticks grasped tightly in their hands. In a mild voice the farmer asked them to stand back. The boys shifted their feet, yet remained as before, but with the sticks held loosely. Little Bingo leapt around. The partridge flew up before the dog, squealing, flopped again, and ran with trailing wings in an arc. "Keep your dog back, Billy," said the farmer kindly, after the bird had flown up, to fall fifty yards away, and stand, head upright, looking at the dog. "You shouldn't bring a dog at this time, you know," in a gentle, impersonal voice. "He come by himself," replied the boy. The farmer patted the boy's shoulder. The boy held on to Little Bingo by the loose scruff of its neck, while the half-hearted search for the chicks continued.

At first there was no sound, then the two men heard a faint squeaking. A tall grass of cock's-foot trembled: the faintest touch at its base sent a puff of pollen flying from the seed-head. The farmer peered down, and his fingers closed on a chick. After staring at it intently, he put it in the pocket of his coat.

The sky had an orange tint spreading from the western hills and woods. The work must finish; the men wanted to get home to their tea. "You don't want to bring the dog until corn cutting," murmured the farmer, to the waiting boys. After a few moments, the boys went away, leading Little Bingo by string round his neck. The cutter rattled on.

Small hares dashed out, leverets which had recently left their dams. They ran down the swathes; paused in bewilderment, pressed themselves down. They sat up again and lolloped on, aimlessly around the field, not knowing where to go or what to do. Three ran back into the triangle of standing grasses. The cutter passed down the other side.

Silent gulls flew in formation overhead, flying darkly for the shingle tongue of the Point where they roosted at night. The clacking noise of the cutter came down the field again. The chick in the farmer's pocket was cheeping faintly, as its eyes closed. They opened at the slightest sounds: rook cawing from the pines of the High Wood: lorry driving along the distant road above the river: sniff of farmer: cluck of Pertrisel among the grasses.

The cutter came near, clacking its iron nerves; it passed, and the farmer, an old infantry soldier, saw the shrapnel-like puffs in the grass-heads, and smelt the scent of the hay, with that of the rank shag tobacco smoked by the stockman as he swung his scythe.

A pipit flew out of the narrowing grasses, circled hesitantly, and dropped down again. At least the skylarks would have reared their young, and be safe, he thought. He peered again into the green island of grass, trying to find the chicks. The cutter stopped again. Pertrisel crouched still in the thick bottom of trefoil and clover. Only when the noise of the cutter continued, did she move and speak to her chicks.

The farmer laid down his gun. He had been one of the best shots in that county of famous shooters; but for some years he had ceased to shoot. In the pride of his farming, upon nearly two thousand acres, before the first industrial war in which he had served for four years, after which in the depression of the 'twenties, his ewe-flock was sold—the beginning of slow decline—he had been known to kill two birds with a left-and-right of his Purdey gun, reload with two cartridges held between the fingers of

81

his extended left arm, and kill two more birds—four partridges of the same covey fleeing over his stand. Years of farming at a loss, due partly to an inability to adapt himself to changed conditions, had sapped his desire to shoot; while the great landlords who had invited him to their coverts had been compelled by taxation and the depression to let their sportings to syndicates of rich townsmen.

The gun laid beside him, the farmer squatted on his heels, and watched the cock partridge running nearer, stopping to call with head raised. He hoped the hen would respond, and lead the chicks into the swathes, and away; but he knew the dread of a hen with chicks for unfamiliar, open ground. There was just a hope the cock would lead her out: it was a bold bird, running back again and again close to him, showing itself as a lure, while it called to her in the grasses. Trying to lessen the bird's anxiety, the man remained as still as he could. But Pertris saw the figure swaying, and the churring call—the rusty key turning in the wooden lock of the Corn Barn—changed to a harsh and reedy warning. The cheeping ceased, with the trembling of the tall stalks within the diminishing area of standing grass.

The cutter came nearer. It was nearly nine o'clock, British Summer Time; both men and horses had had a long day. The cutter went on, up and down the centre of the field. It came to the last two cuts in the narrow tongue of grass. More hares ran out. There was no further movement. The farmer was puzzled. Where was the hen pheasant and the rest of her nid? And the hen partridge, with her chicks?

"Raise your cutter-bar," he said, in the hope that it would pass over the chicks. The cutter passed up the field, turned round, and came down again. The farmer could see nothing, even when all the grasses lay in swathe.

82

He walked back along the last swathe and saw a patch of brown feathers in the grass. It was the back of the hen-bird. One small chick peeped out from her wing. He bent down to touch her and saw that her head had been struck off, as it had been raised in watchfulness to protect her young. "Pity," he said, to the teamsman. "I looked as best I could," said the teamsman, rolling himself a cigarette from tobacco in a worn tin box. The farmer lifted up the body. "One chick under her. Well, the cock may look after it, and there may be others. Want it?" he said, holding the body, warm and limp, in his hand. "No use to me," said the teamsman, licking along the edge of the cigarette paper. The farmer tossed it away, and it fell loose-winged on to a swathe.

Then standing upright again, he took the pheasant chick from his pocket, and holding it at arm's length examined the markings of its feathers. He put it back into the pocket, while taking from the other pocket of his jacket a case of steel-framed spectacles, which he put on his nose before bringing out the bird once more, and, holding it closer, examining its plumage with a knowledgeable eye. The stockman, who had come up silently, stood beside him.

Looking over his spectacles at the stockman, the farmer said, "Where's the hen of this bird? I didn't see any chicks fly out, did you?" And examining the chick again he said, "This is one of the four I planted in that nest down by the Carr, no doubt of it. See the difference in the markings?" The stockman peered. "The Chinese call the bird Chee-kai, which means 'arrow-bird'." As though in reply, a thin piping note came from the chick. "There, you see he knows his name!" the farmer added, smiling. "He'll find his way to the hen, I expect, when we're gone."

He put Chee-kai on the ground, near the body of Pertrisel. The other men were already going down the field, homewards; and saying good night to the stockman, the farmer picked up his gun and walked away.

That night Pertris, after calling in vain for Pertrisel, roosted in the sugar-beet field, with two chicks warm and sleeping under his feathers. The name of the partridge chick was Perdix.

PART TWO

Chapter Eight

In the time of these happenings the soil of Britain was most neglected by the town-mind, which considered it to be the worst investment for its money; thus many farmers who put their land first, before the idea of profit-at-any-price, were enslaved to the banks, thus figures increasing in red ink within a ledger held for some the power of death over life. One morning when Pertris was dusting himself in the dry and loose soil of the anthills on the meadow, Chee-kai and Perdix imitating him, the unhappy farmer, confronted by an ultimatum from his bank manager, took his gun and walked by the overgrown hedge of the lower Breck, and after standing in the shadow of a hawthorn whose trunk was rubbed smooth by the flanks of bullocks, put the muzzle of the gun between his teeth, cried silently to the vacant sky, and jerked the trigger against a thin branch-stump projecting from the bottom of the trunk.

Pertris was shocked by the report; he jumped from the hollow of his dust-bath. The two chicks responded to the shock of the adult bird. They crouched, ready to spring to run or flight. Tensed, the three awaited, their heartbeats slowing. After about half a minute Pertris relaxed; he settled; the eyes of Chee-kai and Perdix began to close once again in the noonday heat upon the terrace of the anthills.

The bullocks stood in the shade of the tall and bushy thorns, seeking relief from warble-flies shooting crisp-winged through the glare upon the hardening earth. Cuckoos called no more; their voices had faltered and broken. Songbirds too were silent; their young had gone from the nests. The sun burned in great brilliance over the High Wood, casting the most sparse shade of midsummer. The bullocks were awaiting the coolth of the breezes usually drawn across the meadow about noon by the massifs of heated air arising from the arable fields lying beyond the wooded horizon. The air was yet in balance, and still; and in the stillness, above the high summer hum of insects, only the plaintive voice of Dufa the native wood pigeon was heard from the woods.

The bullocks stood among the blackthorns which grew in a brake beside the overgrown hedge. These black-thorns had crept out upon the meadow as suckers, unchecked during the years following the industrial war, and the suckers had arisen and strengthened until the dense dark bushes were twice the height of a man. Paths had been trodden through the stiff spines and branches of the brake, wherein stems of the wild rose, dark, thick, and set with talons, arose to bear their blooms beyond the tops of bushes; and about the paths stood the bullocks, afraid of the bright buzzing lines of warble-flies which, in the sun, had been lighting on their legs and depositing thin yellow eggs upon the hair of the shuddering skin. Before thrusting themselves in terror into the brake, the bullocks had galloped around the meadow, tails held stiffly in extension of their spinal cords. The eggs of the warble-flies would hatch into grubs which would bore through the skin, and feeding on tissue covering the flesh for ten or eleven months, would grow in size until they were half the length, but all of the thickness, of the stockman's little finger. These grubs would lie in their cells showing as humps on the skin on the back, each hump pierced by a breathing hole, through which, distended and white, they would gnaw their way, to fall upon the ground where, if not taken by heron, jackdaw, crow, or pheasant, they would secrete themselves and pupate; and breaking a way out of the brown cylinder within a few weeks, would crawl forth as heavy flies, to uncrease and to dry their wings, to await from the sun the glister of crisp vanes for swift flight of mating, after which the females would seek a host for their eggs.

In dread of the warbles, whose coarse wing-note was vibrant upon the radiant noon heat of the meadow, the bullocks had pushed themselves into the shade of the thick-spined blackthorns and the talon'd briars, there to stand inert, in dread of the whirr and glister of brown-and-black flies, hairy of body, and with wings laced with black.

The master-bullock had thrust itself deepest into the blackthorn brake. Gradually it composed itself, feeling cooler in the shade. It ceased to flick the tuft upon its tail. And standing there, it began to breathe deeply of a strange and disturbing smell, which drew it forward in blowing curiosity until its head and shoulders were thrust through the hedge. It stood under an ash-tree whose trunk was hollow, the bark of which had enclosed seven separate threads of barbed wire, with the staples nailing them, during the past half century, when British capital, based on sweated factory labour congesting the towns in flight from the countryside and seeking a greater profit in usury, had been transferred abroad, to the detriment of both Empire and Home market.

With staring eye and snuffling nostril the bullock was

pointing its muzzle at an object lying crumpled, with shattered faceless head, in the nettles growing out of the slope of the choked ditch of the Breck. Two rusty strands of wire prevented the bullock from getting near the body of the farmer, but such was the beast's uneasy curiosity that it pressed against the barbs in order to smell with greater certainty what it feared.

Waves of wind were beginning to move across the meadow, billows of cooler breezes rolling in from the sea to replace the heated air rising off the inland fields, roads, and roofs. The leaves of the ash-tree shook; the sappy yielding barley stems were pressed open by the sea wind drawing susurrations from awn and leaf and, as the breezes eddied onwards, purple heads of the thistles standing stiffer than the corn. After the first turbulent charging of the gusts the sea-wind steadied, moving less unevenly; the pale brown beards of the barley heads drew lisps from the air; the leaves of the ash rustled with myriad small tapping noises. While across its muzzle flowed the coolth of the water-wind, the master-bullock forgot the fear and fascination of glazing blood; and as the odours of growing grass increased in its nostrils, it backed away from the wire fence and pushed sideways to the path trodden through the brake. Other bullocks began to stir, and soon they were walking slowly to their grazing, to spread out fan-shape and to feed in line of heads to wind. They passed by the terrace of the anthills, heedless of and unheeded by Pertris sitting there, a chick under each wing, sheltered from the glare of the sun.

When the bullocks had passed, taking a step forward for every half-dozen tongue-twists of grass pulled, Pertris stood up and looked around. After a scrutiny he began to walk through the grasses, plucking at seeds; the chicks did likewise. They took the fibrous seeds of meadow foxtail and crested dogstail, of timothy and fescue, the small black nodules of white clover with those of the soft brome grass. And crossing by the broken bridge to the common, Pertris led them to earth-castings recently thrown up by moles questing for worms along their galleries through the roots of the grasses. On the warm earth were to be found two-winged flies and beetles, and grasshoppers and wolf-spiders among the stalks and bents of the rough grasses.

As the land was cooled by the exploring sea-winds so the ascent of hot spirals of air lessened, and gradually a balance or steadiness came about; the reams as of shot-silk, purple and green, rippled smaller upon the barley of the Breck; the heat of the sun replaced the pourings of the wind; the dry leaves of the ash ceased to move upon its grey twigs and branches. Pertris walked up the steep bank to the hedge above, for seeds of the goose-grass whose bines twined among the nettles and the clumps of coarse cock's-foot stems. There was shade on the top of the bank, where the partridge rested on one wing, lying sideways, and extending the other wing. Perdix the partridge chick settled to preen his feathers, sitting beside the larger Chee-kai. A small black fly passed by his head and Perdix snapped at it, and missed it. The fly returned, weaving around, and after several little jumps at it, Perdix climbed upon the back of Chee-kai, the better to get the fly. With satisfaction he caught it between the mandibles of his beak, swallowed it, and squatted where he had been standing. Soon his eyelids drew over his eyes, and he slept. Pertris began to draw his flight quills through his beak, pausing to glance around after every few digs of his beak into his plumage.

They were resting there, near a warm heap of black and white flints thrown into the hedge by boys paid a penny an hour to collect them off the Breck many years before, when the bullocks began to walk in file towards the drinking place trodden wide in the bank of the dyke. The leader walked first, through the pug of chalk and clay, then bent its head to drink. Others followed, standing on the flints of the dyke bottom, swishing their tails. The under-bullock—the weakest animal—stood on the turf above, afraid to go among the others of the herd until they had drunk and cooled their feet; for usually it was shoved away, butted, and generally bullied for being weaker than the others. In the yard of the premises during winter it had "shrunk", being afraid to compete for the feed of sugar-beet pulp and chopped barley-straw in the manger, until the stockman had put it to feed and rest by itself in a box.

While the under-bullock stood unhappily on the bank, a warble-fly whizzed past its left ear and it gave a snort of fear. The fear passed at once to the beast next to it; and when the under-bullock uttered a short bellow, the herd quivered. Dashing among them with stiff tail, the under-bullock started a panic. Other warble-flies, drawn by the warm milky smell of the red beasts, were now streaking and buzzing about them. The master-bullock snorted, and plunged across the dyke, bearing down the single thread of wire, which had been twisted round some leaning stakes of willow thrust there by the stockman (no craftsman) to keep them from crossing to the common on the other side. Thus the herd clambered up the broken bank, and started to run over the coarse grass, tails outheld stiffly behind them.

They ran up and down the common, pursued by the warble-flies blowing their eggs upon the warm red hairs of the legs and flanks. Maddened by fear, the master-bullock crashed into the broken gate tied by binder-twine to the tottering posts in the gateway, bore the stockman's contraption down, and ran into the Breck barley. Others followed it, while the under-bullock, stuck in the mud of the churned bottom of the dyke, remained behind—free of the presence of the swarm of warble-flies, which had followed with furious zest the stampeding drove.

When the stockman walked down to count his bullocks he saw the lone animal standing over its fetlocks among the churned mud and broken lines of water-cress in the dyke, and the other bullocks clustered together at the top of the Breck, near the wire fence that shut off the field from the pines and oaks and ash-trees of the High Wood. He stood and stared at it, wondering what he should do. After removing his greasy, shapeless cap, and scratching his scalp with the broad and split nails of his left hand, he crossed the dyke by a plank, upon the end of which was nailed an old iron pail, laid on its side and crushed oval, its rusty bottom removed, to make a sort of tunnel. Within the tunnel was set a gin-trap, to catch any stoat or weasel passing that way.

The stockman's idea was to walk up the lower side of the Breck, and get the bullocks down by the side of the High Wood, and so to avoid a stampede through the middle of the field, which would lay the barley. He worried, knowing that his master was hard put to it, but to what extent he did not know. He did know, however, that the pig-meal merchant had been pressing him for the money he owed.

The worries of a master affect his men directly by their concern for their own jobs, and their living therefrom; and indirectly by lack of leadership, and of clear direction of their work, which they do not like to think will be wasted. So the stockman worried as he trudged up the lower side of the sloping field, his rubber knee-length boots flapping against his calves, his feet bound with rags within the wet canvas interiors which, in all weathers, effectively held in the sweat. The stockman wore the rubber boots all the year round, as his father had died painfully of rheumatism, which he thought was caused by damp feet.

Walking inside the sea-wind-writhen thorn hedge at the bottom of the Breck, the stockman flushed a partridge which sprang up before him screaking *Per-dix! Per-dix!* as it dropped a yard or two away into the corn. A pheasant chick and a small partridge chick then arose and fell near it. The stockman stopped, thinking that he recognized the cock-bird who had persistently called during the cutting of the hay, and also the squeaker that his master had handled.

The stockman's son, horse-hoeing between the ringes of sugar-beet, had told him of a partridge he had seen there, nursing one large and one small chick; and here they were, dropping into the barley. He thought to remember to tell master next time he saw him. Master had called the li'l ole totty bard sump'n, what wor it, now? Arrow bard, thet's it. And thet cock partriss wor' a kind bird, a-motherin' a stranger like thet. Ah, there's truth in a dumb beast, he mused to himself, as he had many times before, of the animals he had tended and the birds he had seen during the fifty years he had worked, boy and man, on the land which was his life.

He trudged onwards, walking on the edge of the barley, above the holl or slope on which grew a mass of rank weeds—thorn-apple, burdock, hemlock, nettle, monkshood, and tall spear-thistle. Abruptly he stopped, seeing with a start the body of his master, lying by the purple and yellow blooms of woody nightshade. There was the gun lying askew, the grey hair clotted with blood, the arms dispread, the body lying in the sunshine.

The stockman felt himself quivering, he drew a deep breath. His sight became unfixed from reality, as though

94

seeking beyond the void which had confronted him almost with a physical blow. Then, as a tear broke down his cheek, he pulled off his cap, and fingering it uncertainly, looked down at the woeful sight, understanding all, and therefore uttering no words. After a while he gathered within the circle of his arm, within the ragged sleeve of the coat master had given him, some corn-stalks which he pulled up by the roots, placing them over the shattered head; and then continued simply upon his way, to get the bullocks down from the top of the field by way of the Long Wood, to save laying the corn. Having got them on the common, he tied up the rickety gate as best he could, using loops of rusty barbed wire which tore the skin of his hands already thickened and calloused by his life's work. He stared awhile as he watched the bullocks walking down to the drinking shallow, where the under-bullock yet stood in the mud; sighed, turned abruptly, and walked up the way he had come, to the field where the hay, having been turned several days to dry after rain had spoiled it, and sun bleached away most of its virtue, was being put into rows by two men and a boy with two-tined forks, and the rows being swept into heaps by a horse-drawn toppler and wooden prongs. The teamsman was holding the curved ashwood arms of the toppler, and throwing off the heaps of hay collected on the great wooden prongs. Later the heaps would be built into cocks, which would stand in the field an indefinite time before being carted to the stack.

The stockman told his son, in a quiet voice, what he had found. "Oh", said the teamsman, thus expressing his deep concern. Amidst the sere stalks of the ryegrass on the toppler lay the remains of a partridge. The stockman picked up the flattened frame of bone and feather, and held it on the palm of one hand. It was dry and light; all flesh was gone, removed by ants; but the seeds of the open crop were still to be seen in the bony cavity beside the breastbone.

The son looked at the father, and the deep look of the older man's eyes went into him. The son felt in his pocket for tobacco tin and cigarette paper. Carefully he rolled a cigarette, and without a word held the loose and uneven cylinder for his father, who took it and tucked it behind his ear. "I'll tell the constable," said the stockman, "better let master bide until he sees him." "What about us?" said the teamsman, rolling a cigarette for himself. There was much unemployment in the district. "They'll hev to keep us on, there's the beet, and we'll have the harvest," replied the stockman. The teamsman lit his cigarette, and took several short puffs of the dark shag tobacco. "Had I better fetch a tumbril, father?" he said. "And a bargain of straw?" The stockman nodded. "And bring a waggon rope, we'll hev to pull out the bullock from the grupp first." The teamsman thought. "I'll tell Billy and Fred to keep on cocking," he said. "We'll need them to lift up master." He puffed at his cigarette, inhaled deeply. "He was a good master," he said. "Ah," replied the stockman. "That's the bird master held up the cutting for, isn't it, father?" "You've a-got it," said the stockman, staring at the wind-stirred frame of Pertrisel lying so lightly in his hand. His eyes were clear and gentle. "He was kind," he said, wondering who would take the farm, and telling himself that he would not want to stay there under a new master.

Tossing the feathered skeleton on the hay, the stockman went down the field, just as Pertris, followed by Chee-kai and Perdix, ran out of the fringe of the barley, and entered the hayfield. With a low cluck Pertris bade them be still, although he was not afraid of the figure of the stockman, which he observed many times a day, knowing it to be harmless.

Chapter Nine

Chee-kai grew familiar with the ways of the partridges upon their territory. Wild and shy by nature, he had inherited from his splendid ancestors a wariness greater than that of the ordinary hybrid pheasant, and a stronger frame for running and flying; and by imitation he grew to the habits of Pertris. Every day the three birds went the same rounds, after waking in one or another of their roosting places upon olland (hay aftermath), terrace of ant-hills, or wild grassy space between the High and Long woods called the Pightle. They fed along the raised banks of the dykes, made of mud and decomposed reeds pulled from the water in past years, among docks and nettles; along the hedge and sloping bank above the narrow common, and in the grass of the common itself: they had their runs through the Breck, and the olland where thin stems of ryegrass and stalks of clover were arising tremulous and green upon yellow patches whence the haycocks had been carried to the stack at one corner of the field. The eastern acres of the sugar-beet field were theirs, together with the strip of mustard sown there—in the stockman's words—to "hold the bards".

One morning when the three were walking down between two ringes of sugar-beet, picking off insects from the leaves whose edges were turning yellow and brittle with leaf-scorch, Pertris saw a rat coming towards him. Immediately he uttered the harsh alarm—staccato like an old wooden police rattle once used by crow-starving boys upon the farm to drive rooks from Michael-mas-sown wheat—and ran at the rat, a deadly enemy. It was a big buck-rat, which had sucked many a pheasant's egg and eaten chicks when it could get them. Usually the partridge would not get close to a rat, with its curved yellow teeth capable of ripping and slashing flesh, but something in the rat's demeanour made the bird fearless. With beak and claw and wing he buffeted it—and the rat sat up and grizzled, making no attempt to bite and hold the partridge.

During the sudden encounter Chee-kai and Perdix had run a dozen yards, and were crouching motionless, each in the shadow of beet-leaves. The rat turned away sullenly from the furious attack by Pertris, and moved, as though dragging itself against an invisible inertia, to a patch of yellow-clay soil where the sowing of the beet had failed. The ground was hard, and little cracks wandered through the pan of sun-baked earth. Nothing ever grew there, except thistles and dwarfed charlock, or wild mustard, for there was no humus or plant-food in the biscuit-dry soil, which lacked also salts of magnesium and boron. It was a rutting place of rabbits which had their burrows in the High Wood; and when barley or oats were sown upon the field, in the rotation or shift of the cropping, the corn seldom reached higher than the heads of the amorous animals, whose teeth cut the thin stalks and whose drop-pings soured the soil. Therefore it was bare, year after year, a trodden playground of the verminous and promi-scuous quadrupeds, the old bucks among which, out of jealousy and sexual appetite, regularly dug out the litters of the does and ate their naked young, in order the sooner to enjoy the pleasures of the rut.

Upon the infertile earth of the rabbits' playground the sun shone bright and hard, and exposed to its pitiless logic, the rat uttered a thin, puling scream. Its will-power seemed to be sucked from it: it moved slower and with lesser movement until, with dragging tail, it stopped, sat up, and grizzled. At the first cry of the rat Pertris had paused, as though the impulse to confuse the enemy had been removed by an invisible power. This, indeed, had occurred; and the bird stood half a dozen yards away from the rat, almost quiescent, but with raised head uneasily expectant.

The condition of the rat had not been caused by the attack of Pertris, and the bird knew it by the thread of fear that vibrated within it. Soon the cause was apparent. Following its trail from the wood, through the mustard and then through the area of panned soil, rippled a small sand-coloured animal with low legs, flat whiskered head set with stubby ears, and a tag of a tail. It rippled over the hot pan of clay, and seeing the rat crouching there —in bulk thrice as large as itself—the weasel tumbled on its back and rolled over and over. Its rolling ended in a somersault that stood it upon its hind legs; and after instant scrutiny, it moved as though in glee over the ground to the rat. Whereupon the rat opened its mouth and squealed with impotent rage and the helplessness of bound fear. The weasel's bright little eyes seemed not to see the rat; it ran shadowless around the humped animal with a light-hearted trip of speed that seemed to be binding its quarry with unbreakable threads. Having enjoyed itself thus for a while, the weasel moved closer to the rat, stopped a moment to lick its shoulder with swift licks of a pink tongue, then as the rat let out a gibber of despair, it jumped on its back and bit into the main artery behind the ear. Swift movement was over, and the spell: the weasel sat there drinking the blood of the unresisting rat which, had it the will to fight, could have killed the smaller animal with its sharp chisel teeth. But the weasel had been created with more sun-fury than most animals; it had naturally a more concentrated power of lust, which by its very nature had drawn the life-will from the rat's spirit before withdrawing from its body the vital power or blood. So far Pertris had stood there, unable to move; but as the rat's head drooped with glazed eyes, Pertris with a shriek flung himself into the air and called Perdix and Chee-kai to follow him. Thus the stockman, walking over the aftermath to determine whether it was grown enough for bullock-bite—the flies on the meadow were tormenting the beasts, and he wanted to give them both respite and a change of feed—saw Pertris dipping, curve-winged, over the hedge, saw it swerve away from him, swing round and drop to grass; followed a moment afterwards by Chee-kai and Perdix, flutter and curve of miniature wings—the rusty-lock cry, and they dropped down, and were invisible.

Pertris dusting himself beside his charges one morning on the terrace of the ant-hills saw Gallinule approaching; he ran with head held low towards him, and drove him off. But Gallinule had come this time for hatching crane-flies: long-legged insects struggling out of their cases upthrust among the roots of the grasses. Pertris saw one, seized it, ate it, and called Chee-kai and Perdix to the feast. Soon several pheasants had come from the hedges and arable fields and woods, to eat the luscious daddy-long-legs. Jackdaws flew and floated down from the blue sky above the High Wood; a heron throwing wide grey wings over the river, seeing the birds feeding there, wheeled and sideslipped and alighted on tall thin legs. Chee-kai and Perdix soon tired of shaking their heads to break up fly after fly, and sat themselves down by a rush-clump, where a large rusty brown bird with hawk-like appearance but mild eyes was squatting on what once had been a titlark's nest. Around the nest, hidden, and nearly absorbed by the soil, were the fragments of the titlark nestlings which the young cuckoo, at the age of two days, had heaved out of the nest. The cuckoo's foster parents came with beakfuls of crushed flies, which the cuckoo swallowed, ever opening its beak for more. Old cuckoos had already left the meadows and fields, moving south day by day on their return journey to Africa, whither in a week or two the young cuckoos would follow, impelled by an inner voice-sense.

After resting upon the terrace of ant-hills, the three birds went into the barley field as the sun was moving into the south-west, and walked through the standing corn to the hayfield. Pertris had a favourite lie on top of the clay bank rising above the Pightle at the edge of the High Wood. The bank was grown with brittly stems of blackthorn which creaked as they rubbed against one another in windy weather. The westering sun shone upon the bank, which in early spring was fragrant with wild sweet violets; and now at high summer the little black seeds were in the pods. The Pightle sloped down from one end of the High Wood to the flank of the Long Wood across a narrow area of uncultivated land about a gunshot wide.

A branch of a dead thorn had blown into the centre of the Pightle during the winter, and grasses had bound it, making a wispy shelter wherein a hare sometimes quatted. The hare fed on beet, clover leaves and sugar from the knot-joints of green barley which the thin teeth cut slantingly as the hare held a stalk between its paws. It was a peaceful place, resounding with the cooing of doves and sometimes the di-syllabic, fervourless, off-season cucket of a cock pheasant—*kok-kack!* followed by the short and rapid wing-whurr.

The Pightle was slumbrous and quiet upon a midsummer afternoon, echoing with the distant plaints of doves, the twitter of a passing finch, and the humming undertone of bees and flies.

It was a peaceful hollow, and Pertris had worn a track diagonally up the bank to his sitting place, while a more pronounced track revealed where Chee-kai had scrambled, followed by Perdix. The stockman passed by sometimes, pretending not to see them, not wanting to upset the cock-bird; while Pertris knew his figure, and his custom of moving about harmlessly.

When the stockman passed by that afternoon, however, on his way from counting the bullocks on the meadow, taking a short cut to the premises, he saw at once that something was amiss with the birds. Pertris was running on the short grey wire-grass as though he had been struck on the head, and had lost both sight and sense of balance. Hearing strangled squeaks, the stockman looked about the bank, and perceived the partridge chick standing there with open beak and dropped wings, shivering and gaping. Walking quietly closer to the bank, puzzled by its behaviour, he saw suddenly that the bird was staring at the head of a snake which, with tongue darting to and fro to measure bulk and distance, was coiling itself in preparation for striking. The stockman knew that a viper had in its mouth a hollow fang under which was a purse of poison, and when it bit, the poison was squirted into the wound.

Feeling himself twitching, and the hair of his neck prickling, the stockman with a growl strode forward and struck at the viper. It curled round the end of his ashplant, and the impetus of the swing flung it into the air, to fall near the thorn branch where the hare was crouched. At once the hare bounded forth with ears laid back and doubling thrusts of its long hind legs, while the stockman said aloud, "Timid Wat! Wisht I'd a dog!" in admiration of the bounding speed. Then he turned to the adder, and broke it several times with blows of his ash-plant. "Blast," he said to the dead snake, mackerel-marked along the length of its underparts. "Yew med not frit that li'l ol' totty poult like that, it ain't justice." And after turning it over with the end of his stick, the stockman strode away to his tea, thinking of a man he had met on the meadows, who had questioned him closely about the farm, although he did not look or talk like a farmer. Others, standing on the village cross-roads of an evening, had previously told of seeing a foreigner walking over the farm, sometimes studying a map he carried, and making notes in a book, but this was the first time the stockman had encountered him.

When he had gone, the hollow of the Pightle was calm and still in the westering shine of the sun. Chee-kai and the partridges had run through the High Wood into the mustard, thence to the sugar-beet field, where they sought for insects.

The leaves of beet plants, from turning yellow, were now in July curling dry and brown. For many years now the field had been robbed of nearly all its moisture-holding humus, and the chemical plant food broadcast from the bags of fertilizers could not be absorbed by the fine surface-feeding rootlets of the beet without moisture. The field was drying out; there was nothing in the earth to hold the water; nothing to bring up by capillary attraction during the season of growth the six hundred tons of water needed to bring an acre of sugar-beet to maturity. Worms, by whose patient tunnelling and digestion of dead and dying leaf tissue the soil is renewed and made gracious, were nearly extinct on the top-soil; rapid plowing by the multiple mouldboards of tractors had exposed, during the early springtimes and back-ends of the years, the worm population of the field to the flocks of black-headed gulls which swirled behind the plowings; chemicals in the soil had killed their eggs.

No muck had been carted to and spread over the field during the 'twenties and 'thirties of the century; it did not pay to keep bullocks as of olden time to tread straw into muck in the yards during the five months of autumn and winter. Sheep, once declared to be walking dung-carts on hoofs of gold when folded on swede turnips brought from the Flanders wars by "Turnip" Townshend—the sheep whose wool had made the prosperity of England before coal made the dark, satanic mills wherein the rosy-faced countryman's children had become the pallid introverts of the slums—had limped lead-footed, since frozen mutton from abroad sold in the chain shops of metropolitan finance had broken up the native ewe flocks. Cracks now opened in the field, which upon a time had grown one of the best samples of fine-ale barley in East Anglia.

The farming business was being carried on by the trustee of the dead farmer's creditors, an official of a bank, until Old Michaelmas Day, when the farm, which had been announced for sale, would fall vacant. The farmer had died insolvent. The land bore first and second mortgages. His debts came to several thousands of pounds; the assets were his household furniture, his clothes, the livestock on the farm, and what was called the dead stock—machines, implements, ladders, etc.; the covenants—hay, straw, muck, and standing crops; and the sporting rights. Since partridge shooting began on the first day of September, and pheasant shooting began on the first of October, while Old Michaelmas Day fell on the eleventh day of October, the syndicate of sportsmen made a bargain with the trustee to take the shooting for the ten days of October. Owing to the dry spring there had been good conditions for the rearing of birds, and the stockman had reported a lot of pheasants in the woods and by the river. The syndicate had got the ten days' shooting for a few pounds, and they were determined to shoot every fine day, and every wet day if need be. Why leave anything behind for anyone else, they argued, declaring that it was a matter of business.

Meanwhile the corn harvest was not far off. In the early mornings of July mist lay upon the meadows, and as the sun rose up from beyond Asia a haze of heat lay upon the wilting fields of roots and the still stalks of the corn beginning to blench with the passing of the summer solstice. The hum of insects was declining, with the seeding of flowers; linnets were beginning to flock again; wings of hive-bees were frayed; edges of leaves of trees and plants, by which they breathed, were worn, sapless, edge-withered. Bubbles of decay arose from the warm and sluggish waters of the river moving down to the sluice gates of the sea-wall, through weeds which choked and raised the flow. The meadows were eaten bare by the bullocks, grey with thistle floss, strewn with dry dung amidst turf turned brown by urine. Upon the pantiles of shed and barn clumps of moss became black and brittle in the heat. At evening the river-banks and the meadows were dotted black and white with moorfowl. Trout, enfeebled by lack of oxygen in the water, rolled over and died, covered by the grey mucus of asphyxiation. As they hung upside down in the inert bines of water-crowfoot and river-parsley, Gallinule and other waterfowl picked the flesh from their bones.

The stranger—the "foreigner" of the stockman—walking along the headland of the sugar-beet field one afternoon, perceived something that checked him abruptly in his walking. He stopped, and remained still for nearly a minute, for he had come upon what to him appeared to be a most extraordinary sight. Upon the brown earth, a bare patch in the sugar-beet, a partridge was crouching. Beside it was a bird of drab plumage, upon whose shoulders was sitting a little chick of some sort. They did not see him, for he had approached out of the sun and up wind: a cold air moving in from the North Sea was shaking and rustling the yellow-brown leaves of the beet, while his outline was dissolved by the westering sun not yet low enough to throw a long warning shadow before him. Thus, immobile, he was able to stare at the strange trio a dozen yards away from him. By the curved umber-brown marking upon the breast of the partridge, the bird was a male: but was the other bird, apparently its mate, with the solitary chick sitting contentedly on her shoulders, also a partridge? Surely not: the beak and head were of a different structure, while the markings of the plumage were distinctly not those of a hen partridge. Slowly, with smooth motion, he felt for the leather case of the Zeiss monocular glass slung on his back, opened the case carefully and quietly, withdrew the lens, slid it up the side of his jacket to avoid any extension of his silhouette, and set it to his eyes, focusing the glass upon the group. The clearer view made him more puzzled than before, for the female bird appeared to be some sort of landrail. Yet how could it be a rail, with a tail coming almost to a point? Its forehead, chin, and cheek patch below the eye were white, while the crown of its head was quite dark, like its lower face and ear-covers. Its lower neck was a reddish-brown, unevenly marked with black, in a broad stripe. The mantle and scapular feathers were grey, spotted with black through the centre of which a white streak ran. The lower breast seemed to be a creamy white.

He had studied wild birds in various European countries during many years; but he had never seen a bird like the one sitting there, with a partridge chick between its shoulders. Were birds of different species beginning to make friendships? After the conflicting emotions which had assailed him as he walked over the farm, arising from ideas which had attached themselves to him like the round burrs of burdock clinging in masses to his tweed trousers and jacket, the mystery and strangeness of the sight added to his feeling that physical or material living was but the illusion—and often the distortion of the illusion—of truth.

Not wanting to disturb the birds, he retreated gradually into the haze of the sun, and only when he was well out of sight did he turn and walk rapidly along the way he had come, hoping to see again the old fellow who lived about the cowsheds, to whom he had spoken a week or so ago on the meadow, and received reluctant, if not evasive, answers to his questions.

Chapter Ten

U pon the scald patches of the fields the barley had withered in the heat before it was ripe; the grains in the ears were shrunken and fibrous. A motley collection of sheep, un-thrifty lambs with old crones that limped with foot-rot, were accommodated for a small cattle dealer, until he could sell them, upon the fungus-ringed upper grazing of the hills around the premises. They lay panting in the glare of day, amidst the black pellets of their own dung. The stockman, standing in the shade of the chalk pit by the cartshed, hand over eyes to regard the brassy sky, muttered that a tempest was coming. The coppery heat under lurdan clouds was a weight upon his being. Pulling off his shapeless cap, clutched like a rag in a root-like hand, he wiped the sweat from his face, dark brown below a forehead unexpectedly white. "Blast," he said, to the foreigner, who had just walked down the hill, "it's what yew call hot. Look you at that roger's-blast thar!" He pointed to a sudden spout of wind whirling over the grass and tearing at the leaves of the beech-trees.

"Tempest—roger's-blast," replied the other half to himself, "I suppose those phrases were being used long before Shakespeare was born. By the way, I saw a strange sight in your sugar-beet field. There was a cock partridge, mated, apparently, to a bird I could not identify. There was a partridge chick on its back."

"Ah," remarked the stockman non-committally, a light nevertheless coming into his eyes. "I reckon that the roblet's hen wor killed by that li'l ole wild cat wot live in the Carr, and he excaped and j'ined up wi' the partrisses. Our boss"—he spoke softly—"thought arter the hen partriss wor killed by the cutter, the cock might tek to a chick or two, being lonely like. I've a-seen that roblet with that cock partriss several times, up by th' pightle and the bad lands."

"Roblet? What is that?"

"A squeaker."

"A young pheasant?"

"Thet's it."

"And that cock partridge has adopted it?"

"You've a-got it."

The foreigner stared at him. "Tempest—pightle—bad lands—roblet—roger's blast—yes, this is Shakespeare's England." He fell into thought a moment, and then looking up sharply, said, "What are the 'bad lands'?"

The stockman did not answer. He did not know what to answer. The best fields of the farm, lying away from the valleys, had long ago been sold, leaving only the "bad lands" around the Elizabethan premises of massive flint and brick walls—now tunnelled by rats. The stockman had spent his life upon the "bad lands"; he had watched more than one farmer going wrong on them; he had seen his late master come to his death because of them—the fields of steep and sticky loam, that "wore up" men and horses —"hungry lands" that were little good without sheep— and after sheep the barley was likely to go down, when it had to be cut by hand. The "bad lands" cost too much to work; they did not pay.

The stranger stared at the stockman, then he said, "I like this place. I'm going to try and buy the farm. I'm going to learn to be a farmer. I want to work with my body, in order to think naturally. Everyone I know says farming is finished in England. Their ideas are finished, but they don't know it—yet."

The stockman gave him a steady look. Then cryptically, out of the corner of his mouth while looking at nothing, and as though addressing no-one, he murmured, "Mind they don't do yer, they all spit in one pot." He would say no more, but strode away, a bottle of disinfectant under his arm, to kill the maggots of blowflies eating into the claggy, rattling rumps of the sheep upon the hills.

Squatting on the neck of Chee-kai, Perdix looked about him contentedly. He climbed there by habit, to watch and snap flies, of small sizes, that came within the sharp focus of his eyes. When one passed near, he caught it, crushed it in beak, and swallowed it. High in the air many winged ants were flying. Gulls swerved and checked and fluttered among them, taking the black insects. It was the wedding flight and migration. Upon spiralling wafts of warm rising air the winged swirl was borne, upwards to a livid cloud that was slowly detaching itself from darker vapour masses seemingly petrified under a lime-white hardness of sky. In the west spokes of light stuck out from behind swarthy clouds that seemed to be choking the light of day. A furious pallor was spreading over the earth.

As the thunder-heads moved overhead silently in their ponderous masses, twilight descended upon the woods and fields. Pertris arose, shook his wings, and started to walk to a roosting-place upon a bare patch in the beet where sometimes the birds slept. The feathers of his breast were ruffled as he walked, for a wind was moving snake-cold upon the landscape. The pines in the High Wood were humming; leaves of deciduous trees were shivering their pale undersides. The chilly gusts coiled as with many serpents' tongues over the fields, hissing in the hedges, sweeping fiercer through the pines with the sound of surf breaking upon the shore. Leaves whirled away like spume. The under-pallor of the thunder-heads made all objects wryly sharp in their windy dishevelment. An azure flash of lightning hissed from a massive copper cloud and one of the tallest pines of the High Wood appeared to crack with violet flame.

In the rebound of the thunder cock pheasants were heard crowing from their ivy-mantled roosts in the tall trees. Pertris raised his head and cried twice, while his wings dropped to cover the frightened young. The sun-spokes from behind the cloud were marred in falling blackness. The surface of the earth was a-leap with driven sheets of spray. Hailstones shrieked upon the rotten sugar-beet leaves, which broke and were torn shapeless. Rain jumped from the hard pan of earth. The feathers of the crouching Pertris were beaten out of shape and colour. Again and again the lightning struck instant-bright, turn-ing all things standing out of the earth to grey stone. There was no earth; the beet-field was a wrinkled shallow sea of silver, growing grey mock-thistles of water above the leaning weeds. Water-plashes advanced creamily before the wind. From them jets of stones, leaf stalks, and sand were dashed up to fall upon Pertris. Pertris was clotted with soil one moment; the next it was washed off his streaked feathers. A cold cruelty of hail succeeded the rain; sharp fragments of ice beat upon his head, neck, and back so hard that some of his feathers were broken, others were gouged from the exposed skin. Still Pertris tried to crouch, his wings dropped to protect the young. His beak was open with pain and exhaustion.

Rain now swept so swift before the tempest that as it struck upon the watery field in flashing streaks it was carried into the air again as white smoke pouring onwards. Still Pertris struggled to keep his stance in the muddy streams of water beginning to pour down the slope of the field, while two woeful heads, bare like his own, looked forth shivering from the bedragglement of his wing-stumps. But the muddy streams increased, rattling down the slope with stones and roots, to cascade through the hedge and away down the slope of the lower hayfield. Pertris was swept away, the chicks were lost to him.

The tempest travelled a circular course, and expended its elemental torment upon the sea. A clear primrose light opened in the western horizon under mild cumulus. As these serene ranges of summer vapour moved to the eastern zenith the sun's rays descended upon the fields and woods again and laved them with mellow light.

Afar over the sea hung the black bombards of nimbus, shot with flashes about the hanging haze of grey and resounding with the grumblings of the storm. The wings of gulls flying to the sandhills of the Point of Terns were shining white against the blue of sky seen beyond the high strata of cirrus which had looked down remotely upon the local storms below. It was a calm summer evening. Already the gulleys cut by streams pouring down slopes of the beet field, and the muddy deltas at the bottom of the hay field, were settling from upon loose softness.

Thinking that this was an occasion in which to observe the effect of soil erosion upon what the stockman had called the "bad lands", the stranger left the cartshed where he had sheltered during the tempest, and set forth with an ash plant he had cut from the hedge, to walk once more upon the uplands. Coming to the "bad lands", he found that the clay stuck to his shoes, making him a clodhopper. He kicked hard, but the clay-pattens would not loosen; he had to claw them off with his fingers. That sticky soil, the stockman said, would clog mould-board and breast of plow if you went on it at the wrong time. "Yew hev to ketch the Bad Lands right."

He looked at the crop of sugar-beet. Many of the leaves had holes torn in them as though by shrapnel. A mush of melting hail lay in some of the slight hollows of the field. Continuing his laborious plodding he came to where the rows of beet ended and the mustard began. Down the hollow most of the surface water had run away, cutting a gulley nearly two feet wide in the hard pan of the subsoil. Following down beside the gulley, he came to the exposed roots of the thorn-hedge through which the water-course had been cut, and stooped down to observe the sand and gravel left in the ragged bottom. The plant food in the silt had been washed down over the clover field, and lay in a streaky delta where the ground became level by the edge of the Long Wood. Regarding this area of several tons of fine mud he saw a woeful bird trying to walk away through the thin stalks of clover, and knew it to be the bird he could not identify earlier. He ran to it, and picked it up, while it kicked feebly and made a thin high cry through its open beak. He dried it as best he could with his handkerchief, and put it inside his shirt, against his ribs, to warm it.

While he stood there, a partridge, which had been quatting in the aftermath, poked up its head and uttered a wheezy cry like *perdix*. It looked to be a wet and ragged bird. At once the stranger thought that the smallest bird was likely to have been washed down the gulley as well, and being light, would have been carried somewhere upon the delta of mud below. Thither he went, to examine the area of soft silt methodically, beginning at one flank and walking down, searching every square foot in a section about a yard wide and fifteen yards long. At the bottom he turned round, and walked up again, searching the next yard-wide section. So he came upon something held in the mud, with only an eye, a winglet, and a brown-yellow foot exposed. With two fingers crooked he dug out and held the sorry object within the cup of his hands, breathing warmly upon it, before slipping it against his ribs beside the other.

The partridge sat in the clover and watched him. The man, suddenly tired, crouched on his heels, waiting for movement against his ribs. He was hungry, and depressed by the mental weight of what he had undertaken. Despite superficial impatience with the mental slowness of others, once he was set on a thing he would not relax until it was accomplished. He sat there for over an hour, watched by the partridge, while the beams of the sun warmed him, and he felt that in some way the bird trusted him: for its wings were spread, also to be warmed by the sun. What a queer beginning, he thought, stroking the head of the "roblet" with a finger, and making with pursed lips soft, flute-like notes to reassure it, as he held it warm against his flesh; and standing there, he wondered how it would all end. Strangely he could not see any future; and by this, he thought, the beginning was indeed inevitable.

The stockman, passing by the High Wood on his way from the meadow the next afternoon, saw the three birds in their usual place upon the bank, the smallest one upon the back of the middle bird, and was glad to know they had come safely through the tempest which, within his knowledge, had killed several birds.

Chapter Eleven

In August the barley of the Breck stood still and blanched, the awned heads bending upon thin necks; but only when the heads hung limp and touching their parent stalks, all life gone and sap out, did teamsman and stockman "sarvin' the interests of the farm", walk into the Breck to see if the corn was fit to cut. The multitudinous flossy and grey heads of the thistles did not wait for the cutter; they were fit a few days before the barley. Conscious of the responsibility put upon them by the trustee, father and son solemnly walked into the corn, like two farmers come to make a decision, and snatched at odd corn-heads, rubbed them between their palms to break off the awns, and, after scrutiny, tested the quality of the kernels by biting several into halves to see if the interiors were flour-soft or hard-grey. Whether mellow or steely, nothing they could do now would alter the sample; only rain and the dews and the mists of the sea could do that; but they were testing the sample. "That's rotten-ripe," said the stockman, and the teamsman agreed. "We aught to open of it up tomorrer. If the wind comes to blow, thet'll shill out."

Their passage set adrift the shining thistle seeds, which floated away in warm currents of air to settle far and wide. Finches with crimson faces and yellow-slashed wings—

birds of the heaths, the royal-coloured King Harrys of the East Angles—came in twittering flocks to the Breck, for thistle seeds were one of their favourite foods.

In the morning, the field was "opened-up". First, scythes, some worn thin and near-useless—the labourers had to provide their own tools, according to the custom of the country—swept a way round the field for the reaper-and-binder, a rattling machine imported from the United States of America more than a quarter of a century before. It was pulled by a hired Fordson tractor, while the teamsman sat on the iron seat in the rear of the contraption and banged a stick on a sheet of metal covering a portion of the working parts whenever those parts ceased to work, which was frequently. The thwacking and banging was a sign to the driver of the tractor to stop. To rectify the stoppages the screw-hammer was always ready in the box, with sundry old bolts and nuts; but the chief tool used to apply direct action to stoppages to the reaper was the teamsman's shut-knife. With the open blade of the shut-knife the teamsman jabbed and poked and picked at the iron jaws of the knotter, to remove that which had stopped the outfit—a barley kernel. The crushed grain pushed out, the cutting continued, and for a while the machine consented to tie the knot of the twine around the sheaves just before they were flung off upon the stubbles.

So the harvest of the corn in the fields of the farm was begun and continued. About half of every day was spent in motion around the rectangles of standing corn; the other half was passed in immobility, and mechanical problems to be solved by either screw-hammer or shut-knife. The sheaves were picked up by men following round the field, and set in stooks of eight, to allow the rain to drain away should the weather change.

The weather did change. Clouds moved over from the south-west, from the Atlantic beating upon the western cliffs of Cornwall and crossing the island to the east. The creditors' trustee welcomed the wet spell, for the rain would soak the grain, which, drying in the winds, would be the more mellow, and thereby its condition for malting would be improved. But the men grumbled; they were paid a lump sum to get the harvest in, and wanted to finish in the shortest time possible. During wet weather they would earn nothing, but stand by to start work again when stalk and sheaf were dry once more.

Again the horse-binder jattered round the area of standing hollow cornstalks, drawn by the massive iron tractor compressing harder the pan under the top-soil; again the stick banged on the dented cover of sheet iron for the acrid monster to stop amidst its own fumes of part-burnt kerosene; again the shut-knife prodded, dug, thrust, and stabbed at a seed lodged in the iron teeth of the knotter. But what had happened? As though in revolt with the barley against vile man the binder spewed forth stalks without knotting the encircling twine, so that they fell loose; more banging, more blue acrid smoke, more jabbing, more muttered incantation, *We won't be in no muddle, 'tes nature to stop now and agen*; further prodding of valiant solitary kernel and jerk of string, clacking rotation of handle; on the seat again, forwards! Thereupon the binder, as though in remorse for past shiftlessness, and determined to make up for lost time, began to tie furiously so many knots that soon it was tangled in its own stringy fervours. *Bang! Thump! Bang!* Screw-hammer to the rescue! Three olive-green fighter aircraft suddenly dipped over the pines of the High Wood and roared low over the field, beating up the harvesters, and startling Pertris and his two charges who some time before had run out of the corn, and were sunning themselves, their crops

117

filled with barley, in the hedge. "H'm," said the stock-man, gazing after the swiftly diminishing fighter aircraft, seen for the first time over those fields, "thar's allus money fer thet".

We won't be in no muddle. But the incantation, or prayer, to the god of machinery was without avail. The binder started to throw off strings of sheaves, linked together like some of the sausages turned out of the machine, on Fridays, of the rubicund butcher who bought, usually late, and always reluctantly, and only after a friendly visit from the constable, an annual licence for Little Bingo. Inefficient, yes; but the stranger, obser-ving local ways, and ever on the watch for the partridge and its charges with whom he longed to share friendship and trust, felt a human kindness and tolerance of the human scene. What form would a painting of that scene take? The clanging heat of the harvest sky—the clukker-ing, clattering, wood-sail-turning, thistly-sheaf-ejecting contraption proceeding between two and three miles an hour—ritual of "shet-knife" and "screw-hammer"—rab-bits dashing out of standing corn into bright and un-familiar stubble space—boys with sticks running, striking, shouting—throwing themselves upon sheaves under which grey coneys crouched terror-still—Little Bingo, springing forward into uncut corn, bounding through it head high the better to view grey ears scuttling—"Little Bingo, Little Bingo, come you here!"—long-tailed brindled lurcher dashing before and around boys, some-times tumbling over as pursued rabbit stopped suddenly, to dash overwhart its former line—shouts, cheers, *thwack bump bang!* more shouts, dry jatter of machine stopping —sudden squeaking slow climbing flight of callow late-hatched pheasant poults rising flutter-winged out of near-white stalks with down-hanging bleached-prawn heads—dark brown ragged spires of docks, worn green

118

thistles—hot stir of air in motion with despoiling fumes of kerosene—nearly gone forever the old English harvest scene, the Constable immortality of everlasting England. Here was the last of individuality, the last of inefficiency, the interval between the old that was nearly dead and the new that lay beyond an agony of mud and blood and maggot, unless, unless. . . . The newcomer closed his sketch-book, and joined the others setting up sheaves under the unthinkable brilliance of the sun. Onwards, knock it down—set it up—carry the corn and be done with it—no hats thrown into air as the last sheaf was pitched on to the waggon—no horkey or harvest supper, no squire, no tradition, no ideal of service—all eaten hollow by the golden tapeworm—no dancing in the barn, no revel, no Corn Dollies made of the first-cut stalks of wheat. Thresh it out, cash it out: the creditors want their money.

Now of a morning, upon stubbles where the last rows left by the jangling horse-rake had been carted, and the threads of a myriad migrating gossamer-spiders stretching from stalk to stalk made a golden tunnel to the sun, it was possible to learn what had been generally hidden in the four months since the rising of the corn: the numbers of game birds upon the level lands of Norfolk. A casual walk of an unknowledgeable man upon the farm in June would have given the impression that pheasants were uncommon there; but now, when the stacks were made—some leaning but kept from falling over by long poles thrust into slanting sides—when feed was plentiful and rich in dropped grain and tender clover leaf spreading in layer across the stubbles, any number between a dozen and two score of adult and three-quarter grown birds might be seen quietly walking near any wood or thorn-grown marl pit of the arable fields. And since no human enemies appeared, the birds grew in confidence with so many of their own kind feeding in view. The pheasants were watchful; but the partridges were wary, having a swifter wildness of life.

Chapter Twelve

October the first, when the season of pheasant shooting began legally in Great Britain, fell on a Friday of that year. The syndicate which, it will be recalled, had acquired for a few pounds the sporting rights over the farm for ten days until Old Michaelmas Day, when the tenancy lapsed, drove up in their cars, on the morning of that day, leaving them on the grass before the Corn Barn. They were determined to waste no time. The season lasted until the last day of January, and normally there would be four, or at the most five, shoots over the farm, with beaters, stops, and seven or eight guns, with perhaps a couple of by-days walking after cocks when Christmas had passed; and no regular sportsman would think of shooting until after the birds of that years's hatching had got their mature plumage. They would not shoot them while they were what was called squeakers.

Not that the members of the syndicate were ignorant of the local custom. Why, they reassured one another, leave anything for anyone else? If they didn't shoot all they could, they would be fools. And they were not fools; they were business men. So they were determined to shoot as long as any game were left, within the limit of their ten days.

The originator of the syndicate had started his career as

a clerk in a bookmakers' office, but after a few years he had gone into partnership with a clerk in another concern as moneylenders. This profession, depending on a condition of social decline for its success, had shown good profits. He had other irons in the fire, among them a property investment company which bought and sold small shops, cottages, and houses. He was a red-haired fleshy man in the late thirties. The hard eyes in his round pink face never smiled when he grinned, for nearly all of his thinking was in terms of what could be made use of, or turned to a profit. He had brought with him in his car—a cream-coloured saloon of rakish-luxury appearance, built of cut-price material in order to imitate speedy makes of repute at one-third the cost of the hand-made motor-cars—a guest whom he knew to be a wealthy man, and a first-class shot: he felt this guest would add tone to his shoot, and also be a useful man to keep in with.

The guest might have been any age between thirty-five and fifty. He was an ex-alcoholic who had been chemically treated in order to make negative a craving for drink and drugs. Cause or cure, perhaps both, had given this man a sagging face, grey-yellow and expressionless, a dull wit, and an indifference to anything except the moment's occupation, since his inner life or consciousness, which formerly had taunted him with its self-contradictions, was now deadened. He was bored by living; and he tried to escape boredom by playing cards, by betting on horses he seldom saw, by speculation on the Stock Exchange, and by shooting. During the past month he had been seen upon the sand-flats of the sea-shore at low tide, practising shooting at dotterel, greenshank, and other wading birds, in order "to get his eye in", as he put it. He had shot scores of birds, and had not bothered to pick up the bodies. His income came from a share in a factory in the industrial North, which his grandfather had created, his father had continued, and the grandson had avoided. Never having done any real work in his life, his will-to-live had lost concentration; he took to drink, which made him sexually impotent; then to drugs, of which he had been "cured". Now he lived an automatic life. He was a coldly efficient shot with his single-trigger double-barrel 16-bore Westley-Richards gun, with its chasing of gold inlay and engraved heraldic crest which he had, not being armigerous, filched from another family of the same name. His hand-palms sweated coldly, and the acids had in places minutely prickled with rust the blueing of the gun barrels.

The other "guns" were a partner in a football pools promotion concern, an artificial-fertilizer salesman, a cattle-dealer ("Reckon he ruined our boss", the teamsman more than once had muttered out of the corner of his mouth, to his father, the stockman), a cosmetic-salesman, a retired actor of sorts, and a businessman from Liverpool who had settled in the district.

Soon after ten o'clock with half a dozen beaters, including the boy and two of the farm-workers, hired at four shillings each, the eight guns left the premises to walk to the first stand below the High Wood.

Like most countrymen who worked with their bodies and thereby were single-minded, the stockman was loyal to the idea of a master. Therefore, as he stood by the cart-shed he was perturbed. His loyalty was to the master who paid his wages: the trustee of the creditors of the dead farmer. He was paid six shillings a day, and an extra two shillings a week for looking after the stock on Sunday. The trustee came in his car every Friday after work to pay the men outside the Corn Barn, and so, unless someone told him, he would not know that the men were taking the day off to act as beaters, when they were supposed to be squaring-up the muck in the yards for valuation. This idea had been put into the stockman's mind by the leader of the syndicate drawing him aside as soon as he had arrived in his car, and out of the corner of his mouth—after casting his eyes around, in the convention of secrecy of his class—suggesting that nobody need know about the time taken off for beating: he would get his wage-packet as usual, and half-a-crown from each of the guns as head-man. To this the stockman had said nothing, feeling it was not justice. Always at the back of his mind was the fear of being out of a job; and this fear was complicated by a belief that all masters stuck together to keep the working man down, despite his knowledge of what paid in farming, and what did not pay. They all spit in one pot. Huh, an' some'm'r out fer the biggest penny, he thought, with disgrunt, watching the moneylender going to the cream-coloured car for cartridges. He watched him breaking the cartons, tumbling the red shells into a leather bag, and dropping the broken cardboard boxes beside his car.

The idea, common to all shooting owners or tenants in East Anglia, was to hold within the boundaries of their land those game-birds which were hatched and reared there. Many extended the idea by luring over their boundaries what birds they might, by various devices, entice into their coverts and fields. A usual, and obvious way was to grow belts of mustard, or perhaps buckwheat, along a boundary, particularly where it adjoined thicket or carr belonging to a neighbour. After corn-harvest, in the calm days of September, gamekeepers might be observed walking along the boundary hedgerows scattering tail-corn of wheat and barley, to accustom the neighbouring birds to walk there, and feed. After a while a few raisins dropped from the keeper's pocket with a slight string of tail-corn as he walked towards distant marl-pit or coppice would teach the birds to stray off their native fields; for of all foods raisins are perhaps the most exciting to pheasants.

In olden days of wheel-lock with smouldering fusee, and later with muzzle-loader and percussion cap, it was the custom to walk up the birds, to drive them from covert with spaniel setters and pointers, to shoot over the dogs as the quarry arose to seek safety away, away, away: to fire a little above the tails of birds as they climbed with powerful beats of short wings seeking safety. To reload with charge of black powder from the horn, to ram home the wad with ground ash-rod, to pour in a measure of leaden shot from the flask, and hold it there by pressing another wad into the barrel—while the hands trembled with eagerness, blue smoke filled the nostrils, and the rocketing of wings sounded with the trisyllabic screech of cock after cock—patience, patience!—to place copper cap upon iron nipple which was hollow to lead the flash to the detonating chamber—such was the sport before it was discovered that birds would fly some distance to their feeding grounds, and, on being alarmed by discreet tapping in covert, would run and crouch, run and hide, and on being approached by a line of besmocked men brushing through the wood, would arise in flight and then glide and beat their wings, glide and fly strongly to their roosting places, or homes, in straight and often high flight. So a new technique came into practice, and shooters began to use the expression *high pheasants*. Spinneys of conifer, sweet chestnut, hazel, cobnut, and other trees were planted; shrubs of snowberry, broom, box, rhododendron (were the soil not chalky or alkaline) and berberis were set in the woods for cover; quick-set hedges, sometimes called bull-fences or bullfinches, were trained and trimmed to a height of six or seven feet, to conceal from view the line of shooters, or "guns" as they came to be called, from partridges and pheasants which were driven before the line of beaters moving through fields of swede-turnip, rape, and mangold-wurzel, and across stubbles green with clover, sainfoin, ryegrass, or lucerne, and so to the concealed guns. Where the arable sloped steeply to a low valley and rose as steeply again to other fields, therein was an excellent stand: for the birds crossed the sky flying high and strong against cloud and blue space, to fall one after another into cones of shot spreading up from barrels which, as it were, stroked them in silhouette out of the sky, after automatic allowance for height, speed, and deflection. Indeed, the speed of stroking or overtaking, with the muzzle of balanced gun, of the bird along its line of flight, was automatic to the crack shot. No aim was taken deliberately, no conscious thought preceded the swinging throw of the gun which pulled the trigger. The muzzle of the gun stroked, as with the sure stroke of a painter's brush, the line of flight: the image of the flying bird in the eye of the shooter was over-taken and covered by the muzzles of the twin barrels: the cone of leaden pellets was thrown out of the thin cylinder —of old-fashioned hand-beaten damascene or modern rolled-steel—upon the empty air into which the bird was flying to meet the pattern; and the bird, stricken by sudden hissing blow of shot, lost its life.

Standing near the Willow Plot, his feet covered by rubber boots which laced up the front and fitted to the shape of his legs, the guest of the syndicate swung his sixteen-bore forward to left and then to right: two birds fell. With one hand he gave the empty gun to the loader standing behind him, while receiving his second gun with the other—raised it and swung and pulled the trigger, swung again and fired: birds crumpled and dropped wing-loose. Pinned to the soft meadow by a burnished-steel pin with ring holding the swivel of the leash, his golden Labrador bitch sat and waited obediently on her haunches, among the tall rusting growths of meadow-sweet and persicaria. Cock pheasants in screeching terror arose off the floor of the Long Wood, flew up through the tall beeches, oaks, and sycamores; slimmer hen-birds broke covert with them, flying straight for the Danish Wood on the hill beyond meadow and river, where was sanctuary among brambles and thorns. The Danish Wood was of great interest to archaeologists and those who cared for the history of their county; also it was in use as a rubbish tip for village garbage by the Parish Council. Squeakers, young birds which had not yet moulted, slender birdlings weighing scarcely more than a pound, callow and soft of feather, fluttered among them. Guns cracked, rapid reports echoed around the green valley. Heavy, gleaming cocks, thick of breast muscle and flying with great strength, hurtled down the sky and thudded almost violently into the weedy pasture. Dun-coloured hens flopped slew-winged. Immature birds fell softly, lightly, around the standing men. Hares ran through the wood, to pause wry-eared, long nostrils working, amber eyes back-staring; to spring round to run a few paces before stopping again: to set off at a lope, changing to a gallop along the line whither panic pressed them.

Timid Wat, startled from his form in the grasses of the Pightle, leapt the dyke under the Long Wood, and while over the fresh water green with star-wort his head was knocked back by a cone of shot fired from ten yards distant that broke teeth and pierced eyeballs, ears, skull, forefeet, chest. The bleeding punctured carcase fell into the water.

The man who had shot it was dressed in a golfing suit of imitation hand-woven Harris tweed made in a Leeds factory by machinery. He was the retired vaudeville actor, the next gun to the sallow-faced expert. He had fired out of a feeling of exasperated inferiority because the expert had killed most of the birds passing over his head before he himself had had a fair chance to point his non-ejector at them. The expert had wiped his eye again and again, in fact, in contempt of the other's sporting pretensions.

The hare-smasher glanced around before reloading with quivering hands. A pheasant flew low out of the woodland foliage, to his right; he threw up his gun and pressed the trigger before he could take aim, and the shot clapped over the head of the expert, who glared at him, and muttered "Don't shoot down the line, damn your eyes!" "Sorry, old man," he called out, with forced geniality. "It was your bird, I'll admit. Sorry. I fired instinctively!" The other disregarded him, beyond muttering for the loader to hear, "Instinctively! I suppose you were born with a gun in your hands." He was already depressed by the company, which he felt to have drained his energy. He lowered his gun, in sudden distaste of them all.

As he opened the breech of his gun, to let it rest upon the crook of his right arm, two partridges and a young pheasant following them flew thirty yards above his head. The pheasant flew strongly, catching the partridges over the meadow before they came to the river. The tweed-clad sportsman was too abashed, momentarily, to take aim, while pretending that a shell was jammed in the breech of one barrel. Pitching in the Danish Wood, the birds reached neutral ground, for the boundary of the farm was at the river.

"I left them for you, you know, old man," the retired actor called out, with a forced laugh. "You're the star turn of this outfit," he added. Thus mollified, the expert casually knocked over a couple of moorfowl which were inexperienced enough to take to the air, when they could have run safely through the tall meadow weeds to the river: the ex-actor was momentarily too abashed to have fired at anything more running on the ground.

The day's bag was brought before the Corn Barn in a decrepit cart called a hermaphrodite, with the mud of several winters upon the spokes, hubs, and axles of its loose wheels, to be laid out on the grass for all to behold: seventy pheasants, including forty-nine squeakers, nine partridges, three wood-pigeons, nine hares, fifteen rabbits, two snipe, seven moorhens, and a sparrowhawk.

Next day, a Saturday, the syndicate shot again, as well as on the following Monday, Tuesday, Wednesday, Thursday, Friday, and Saturday, all of them fine, sunny days of St. Luke's Little Summer. The last bag was thirteen squeakers, one hare, one wood-pigeon, two dwarf owls, twenty-nine moorfowl, two teal, a mallard, and a golden plover. The moorfowl were shot in the afternoon, when they drew the meadows and the river-side. The shooters saw several times the number of water-birds they shot, but the majority of them refused to fly. One bird gave them quite a lot of trouble, and even some fun. This was Gallinule, who crept under a black-thorn bush on the bank and climbed among the thick dark spines, where he sat looking at them, refusing to be prodded and shush'd out into the air. The moneylender swore at him, peering at Gallinule through the thick mass of spines a few feet away from the bird's narrow peering head, and even spat at him, but Gallinule, who had met shooters before, continued to perch there moving only its eyelids. "The bloody nerve of it!" said the sportsman genially, one among other faces. He would have blown the damned bird to rags, he declared, but for the danger of a blow-back from twigs and branches bursting the barrel in his hand. "G'art'v'it, fly, you blue funk!" he jeered. Gallinule blinked, but did not shift. At last the exasperated sportsman tried to thrust his hand into the black twigs and spines—and received a peck on his index-finger that made him cry out angrily, and suck a thorn-scratch on the back of his hand. "Did you see that?" he cried indignantly to his cronies. Then he laughed with them. "Well, the sod deserves to live," he decided in sudden generosity, as Gallinule squatted there, quiet as a gowned old lawyer. He got down carefully, step by step, from his place only when the reports of guns had gone far away up the valley.

As the moneylender divided the bag, in consultation with the stockman by the bodies lying on the grass before the Corn Barn, the shooters agreed among themselves that the golden plover gave the finest sport of the shoot, fitting end to a wonderful week. After each man had taken a treble gulp of whisky from the gallon earthen-ware jar, he began to tell his neighbour his part in this final shot. They had come nearly to the premises when a solitary bird, calling its hoarse sweet cry, had flown over the Home Meadow from the direction of the sea. They all crouched on one knee. One of the sportsmen—the ex-actor—prided himself that he could imitate many wild birds' call-notes, and piercing notes, sweet and wild, came from between his front teeth. The bird swung round, hesitated, cried its short social notes of quest and greeting, and flew in a circle. Meanwhile seven men had hastily been seeking cartridges and pushing them into the breeches of guns. The plover was fifty yards high, out of range, but fourteen reports came from fourteen up-pointed barrels. At the last report the flier seemed to hesi-tate, and uttered a frail cry. Fourteen eyes watched it faltering, watched its wings beating without progress, watched it falling. Cries of exultation, as from boys, greeted the sight: they told each other that it had been a grand ending to a very sporting day.

Pertris, with Chee-kai and Perdix, heard the shots as they crouched in the clover layer of a field beyond the heap of rusty cans and other garbage dumped beyond the Danish Wood Camp. They had escaped when, for a moment, the guest had sulked by the Willow Plot on the first day; and Pertris had remained on the new territory with his charges while reports had continued to sound over the river. Two days later, on Old Michaelmas Day, all being quiet, they flew across the river and returned home.

Chapter Thirteen

———⟡———

The sugar-beet field was not used as a roosting place again, since with the losing light of the afternoon dews made heavy and wet the stalky leaves of the plants, and by dusk they were dripping with moisture. Nor were the roots dry and warm again until the sun had plowed a third of its shining furrow from the sea in the east to the distant pinewoods behind the sandhills of the west.

Chee-kai was now growing out of the callow, slender appearance of the roblet, protected by the hues of earth and undergrowth. His new appearance was immediately arresting for its difference from that of other young cocks which were beginning to crow weakly about the woods. Grains of corn, berries of shrubs and plants, caterpillars hurrying over the ground to seek pupation, acorns falling from oaks, keys from sycamore and ash, and brown mast from the beech, made rapid growth of muscle that smoothed the angularity of breast-bone and thigh, and pushed from blue-grey quills the glossy coloured feathers of a plumage the thicker to hold warm air the closer to his skin. In his growing awareness of startling colours he stood up to regard movement and sound about him, where before he would have crouched without spirit or curiosity. Once, hearing a sound that disturbed him he drew himself up and uttered a high, penetrating, metallic cry. In reply an old cock pheasant in the High Wood let out its double grating screech followed by short tattoo-like beat of wings. The cucket had not the challenge of the vernal solstice; it was more a cry of companionship, for the old cocks were beginning to gather and feed together in the fields, and the young cocks to walk together near them.

These young cocks, in moult, were beginning to show colours upon breast, back, neck, head, and tail: colours of the sun's vibrations, repeated from Asiatic patterns of prehistoric millennia, which all the centuries of European living had scarcely modified in hue and sheen of purple, green, and red. Their new and long tail feathers were of an olive colour, fringed with varying shades of violet, and barred by black bands: for their plumage was a variation of the markings of the birds of the valleys of Caucasia and far Colchis. They were crosses between the black-necked, or so-called Old English pheasant, and the Ring-Neck called Shan-chi, mountain chicken, by the Chinese. These Shan-chi, white-collar'd pheasants of Jehol and Korea brought to Britain by traders of the East India Company, were bold birds, rising in steep and direct flight whither their minds drove them to a vision of safety, the energy stored in their breast muscles rippling visibly with each thrust of the paired wings along the extended feathers of the tail, which were eighteen in number. The vitality of these wild pheasants was great; but greater powers of flight, of wariness, and sense of safety were developing within the nerve-ganglions of Chee-kai—the solitary Chee-kai, the Arrow Fowl—an impulse which was to surpass even that of Pertris, the speedy and evasive brown bird of the heaths of Angle-land.

As he grew in size, Chee-kai became more alert for himself, where before he had crouched and skulked under

133

the eye and voice of Pertris. His life was ruled by his sight, in lesser scope by his hearing, and within the nervous carefulness of sight and hearing his smaller senses of taste and smell directed his movements. Always he moved from a base of security to which he returned at the slightest sight or sound of danger, seldom rising in flight. He ran in zig-zag, he hid. A vole tripping past him as he fed on acorns under one of the oaks of the Long Wood, or a mouse appearing unexpectedly, would cause him to jump; and even the movement upon cob-webbed tinder-wood within the hollow ash on the meadow, standing above the choked ditch below the Breck—movement of a red goat-moth caterpillar about to seek the earth wherein to pupate—made him run with great speed across the barley stubble to where Pertris and Perdix were watching anxiously for the cause of alarm.

Gradually the intense shock the birds had felt when the syndicate had been shooting all they could while yet (as they termed it) the going was good, was allayed by the silence that fell upon the farm. The new farmer was apparently too busy to think about shooting. There were no bullocks upon the farm now, all had been sold at the auction. Instead of pail-feeding calves with milk, inducing them to suck with his finger as substitute for teat, the stockman fed the large circular and revolving iron mouth of the concrete-mixer. Squeals of lorry brakes bringing loads of gravel to relay the roads echoed from the chalk quarry instead of the squeals of hungry pigs. Coveys of partridges, reduced to three or four, flew from adjoining farms to the quiet stubbles and deserted sugar-beet acres, finding sanctuary from lines of beaters with flanking white and red flags, with sticks that loudly struck hedge-stub and tree-branch, kale-leaf and sugar-beet stem to drive forth the birds to the line of guns at the various stands. Pheasants, running over the boundaries, remained a day or two before returning to their familiar homelands. Hares, fleeing from the extended lines of beaters walking slowly across leys and stubbles, ran into the woods, and finding easy feeding in clover-field and among the roots, remained to rest and sleep under the trees, sheltered from the winds.

But the established farmers on the boundaries of the farm with the steep fields and woods planted for covert shooting a century and more agone had not sown mustard on their boundaries in vain. The massed plants, pale green of leaf and stem and crowned by sulphur flowers, holding upon their small and numerous leaves but few raindrops after a shower, offered a closer security than the woods, and easy passage. The birds might move rapidly through the soft stalks in any direction, and not be seen from air or earth; and to the mustard they went.

In the old times of wealth limited to the few, called the quality, no landed proprietor would consider any practice that drew his neighbour's game-birds into the coverts or carrs or heaths of his estate; but with the passing of the power, or the money, of the quality to the quantity through the industrial revolution, the manners of the gentleman might be imitated, but not always the matter, of his living. Competition for money involved different standards of conduct; and when the wealth had been gathered within the towns and taken from the land, the standards of the towns were adopted by many country-men who only thereby could hold their own.

Honest yeomen, serving their land first, became poor; the smaller squires likewise. So the Game Syndicate arose dominantly upon the countryside of East Anglia—where a low rainfall upon lands generally light and medium of soil and farthest from Atlantic clouds enabled a large number of chicks to survive in the tender early weeks of their lives—and farmers who managed them were concerned to show their patrons good heads of game.

They were not concerned with the standards of sportsmanship of a former age. The idea was to draw all the birds they could by offering food and shelter. Were there many oaks in the adjoining woodlands, and thereby many acorns? Pheasants soon filled their crops with the glossy, ovoid seeds, that pattered through the rugged branches, some eaten near-hollow by grubs of oak-moths; and the tannin in the kernels ground within the bird's crops made them thirsty, whereby they needed to drink. Were no river or pond near, the birds would walk to drink, even to troughs placed beyond the boundary, where a few raisins, scattered by the keeper, taught them the pleasures of wandering farther away from their birth-place. Many acorns, too, made the search for food easy, when the bird would stray for interest and even from curiosity. Crops of cabbage, kale, swede, beet, and other roots grown centrally in farms tended to draw the birds thither, but no guns must be fired in the vicinity, no dogs seen: the nervous, speculating pheasants must be reassured, lulled to a feeling of security, and, on the morning of the shoot, having gone there for feeding, they must be held there, by men posted soon after dawn with flags on sticks, until the beaters came in line to drive them over the first stand of concealed guns.

An alarmed and agitated pheasant, discovered suddenly in its crouching place, arises with burst of power through muscles to wings, and rockets away to its home or base, climbing as it flies fast over the hedge where the guns have been placed at intervals sixty or seventy yards apart, each concealed behind an upright and rectangular screen of branches left to grow along its extent when the hedge was pared in the winter. "First things first": only when the roots had been lifted, when the muck had been carted from the dungsteads and "spreed", well-rotted and "black as butter", upon the ollands before plowing for wheat in the four-course shift of hay, wheat, roots, barley, which traditionally maintained the fertility of the land, were the hedges trimmed.

"Thet's what yew'd call several bards on the farm, guv'nor. Y'arter injoy yarself sometimes, 'bor. Yer all wire." All wire—all nervous tension to get so many things done at once. "All them bards," mused the stockman, "Ain't yew goin' to hev a shoot, guv'nor?"

The stockman and the new farmer were standing by the concrete mixer, during the dinner half-hour. Nowadays there was much talk about the goings-on of the farm. "More money than sense," suggested some on the village Cross of an evening. "Come to teach us how to farm land? He'll larn!" These remarks were caused by the way money was being spent on the place.

An artesian well was being sunk at the base of the chalk quarry, with heavy pounding of hollow steel borer slung under and dropped from a steel tripod by a stuttering two-stroke engine. Wood shuttering for concrete lay about the premises, with stacks of new red pantiles, rafters, battens, joists, and pipes for draining yards and cowsheds; heaps of flints and piles of bricks for repairing crumbling and cracked walls; a dozen five-barred field-gates, with clapping and hanging posts, had arrived only that morning. There were galvanized iron pipes and tanks; farm implements bought at auctions and brought home on a lorry; and talk of cutting a new road up the steep hillside to the uplands, and making concrete bridges over the dykes between the meadows.

"Thet's enough work to last an orn'ary man a lifetime," said the stockman. "And ya don't eat narthin', guv'nor."

Up the street cottages, condemned for darkness, dampness, and rottenness, which had stood empty for many years, were being broken down for rebuilding. The new farmer was his own architect, surveyor and builder. Scores of tons of concrete were to be laid in slabs upon flints tipped into the mud-pits about the premises, while only that morning the new farmer had announced that two thousand tons of gravel and flints must be dug before Christmas from the pit he had hired, to remake the pot-holed roads.

Where was all the money coming from, the teamsman asked his father, by their cottage fire in the evening. And what about the work on the farm? The autumn plowing? The sugar-beet, ten acres of it, that needed plowing out, knocking and topping and carting to the dump for the lorry to take to the factory before the frosts came? And when was the valuation muck to be carted out of the yards? The rain would wash it all away down the new drains unless something were done to shift it—nearly two hundred tons of it. And the new man was a-doing-of the cottages himself, having had no experience of building; and meanwhile living in the broken-down chaff-barn that had no windows to it, only splayed ventilation holes that let in the cold east winds beginning to drive across the sea and the land. And there at night he sat, by an oil-stove, wrapped in blankets, making sketches on great white sheets of paper. What was going to be the end of all this work that had suddenly come upon the farm? Why was the new man a-doing of it all? The teamsman, whose horses stood and stamped all day in the stables (they had been bought at the Sale) had asked his father to sound him on the matter of the neglected sugar-beet. For, he said, we don't want to see a new man wrong, else they'll be saying down to Cross that we aren't earning our master money.

The newcomer was fully aware of the neglect of the

138

sugar-beet, and the other seasonal farming jobs. If he allowed himself to think too much about them, the thoughts would tear away his resistance. The truth was he had taken on too many things at once, including the feeding of himself, while he was getting a home ready for his wife and child. While he stood beside the stockman, during the dinner interval, his thoughts were away; he was thinking that he ought to be away, attending every local Michaelmas auction of live and dead farming stock, to buy implements and beasts. His capital was low; but he regarded his power of work as his main capital. Even as he worried about absence from the auctions, he knew that his idea, which the teamsman did not think much of, was the right idea: to leave the farm alone—to have no croppings for the first year—to buy a hydraulic Ferguson tractor when the reconstruction work was done, and plow all the arable and keep it bare-fallowed all the following season. Thus by cultivations and, if need be, by cross-plowing they would get rid of weeds as well as expose the tired soil to the benefit of sun and air.

"What about the beet, guv'nor? Thet's sp'iling, and time's a-gettin' on." "Yes, we'll have to get the roots off. We'll start as soon as the two new rubber-tyred tumbrils arrive. Now I must go and look at the cottages. We're running out of bricks. They only told me this morning, and I can't get a load for at least three days. That's what comes of having no foreman. The carpenters can't put the roof on until the bricklayers have built the walls. And I must get window-frames, I've forgotten them. Can you start the concrete-mixer if I go away now? Remember what I told you about opening the air-intake when once the engine is running. It will get indigestion badly if you don't, and blow pessimistic black smoke in your faces. I'll see you later." He hurried away, while the stockman stared after the nervous, hurrying figure. Then he went to fetch his side-bag, and sitting down, opened his big shut-knife, and cutting off a long slice of cheese, thrust it into his mouth by way of the blade. A slice of bread followed, and then a slice of onion; and thus, at intervals and in this order, he consumed his dinner, washed down by draughts of cold tea out of his bottle.

On the sugar-beet field, on the dry depression where the roots were small, in the warm sunshine of the late November day, Chee-kai and his two companions, now much smaller than himself, crouched contentedly, relaxed, dozing. Reports of guns came from over the boundary, where birds as they flew before beaters crossing a neighbouring field of savoy cabbages came over the fire of the last stand before the luncheon interval.

Harra the Denchman, the grey crow from over the water, was back again to the riverside Carr. His raucous voice was heard in the High and Long woods, and upon the marsh as he perched on the railings of the sheep bridge crossing a tidal gut. Aslant the wind blowing up the North Sea from east of south-east the woodcock came, as dead leaves animate and covered by shadow under the moon's pale flames casting the waves into bronze. Teal flying low over the sea from the poldered dykes of Holland slept by day upon the shallow waters between cockle-holed levels of mud and the great barriers of sand, holding here and there the timbers of wrecked ships, which made the coast so perilous for vessels trading between the little ports which for centuries had been silting up with the drift of tides. At twilight, with mallard and widgeon, the teal flew to their immemorial feeding places on stony ridges where sea-grasses grew, and in the fresh waters of the meadows behind the sea-wall. Gales stripped the leaves from the trees, revealing in moonlit and starry night the dark shapes of wood-owls perching on branches as, their throats swelling, they uttered the soft throbbing notes in pleasure of tawny-glowing orb of eye and mottle of soft feather-pattern in brown, black, and white—the soft, tremulous flute-like cries of new love and of old love re-affirmed. Glittering low in the south-eastern sky the great constellation of Orion shook its gemmeous fires upon the air, while from under silver-edged clouds came the trumpetings of geese which had flown down from far Spitzbergen.

PART THREE

Chapter Fourteen

The sugar-beet was got off the higher field, but not before frost following rain had joined some of the fanged yellow roots, lying topped in close circles where the men had flung them, to the soil. The tumbrils had not arrived, so the farmer had bought two old ones from a small local farmer who also did a bit of dealing. The carts came lurching down the steep slopes, sideways in deep ruts, to the dump at the far end of the premises—shake, sway, and shudder of the old and half-rotten, dung-crusted tumbrils. This was not farming, the newcomer declared again and again, as though to reassure himself. He had not yet started; this was merely getting rid of the remnants of sloth and decay. The weeds, the neglected horses and implements, the general dereliction of the place were but manifestations of inferior human thought, of fatigue in the body politic; these visible thoughts in decay had to pass away, to be succeeded by those of resurgence, this old disorder had to be replaced by new order. He was determined to have no compromise with the old, lest it confuse the new: no crops should be grown on the farm until after the bare-fallows had cleared the land, until the roads were re-newed, until the cottages were reconditioned with wide windows, electric light, and drains, until the woodland yard was rebuilt, until the cowhouse was redesigned to take a milking machine, with cooler, sterilizer, weight-recording of yields of each cow, and a two-way drainage system to lead the liquid manure to a special tank, thereby helping to build up the lost fertility of the fields; the stables and other buildings to be repaired, and a new cut made in the side of the hill where now iron-shod wooden wheels were almost wrenched from their iron stub-axles, and shafts seemed likely to tear the leather-covered straw collars off the necks of the horses. In imagination arose the beauty of new plantations of spruce and larch, lined with silver birch, new orchards of apple and pear trees, and a press for making cider and perry; the trout stream set with elm-boards at intervals aslant the bed of the stream and half-way across its width, to quicken the cur-rent and swirl the water about, and so to scour the filth overlaying its bed of chalk and gravel, and to create hides for trout and spawning beds for their eggs. He dreamed of a new village of skilled and happy people, of dances and harvest suppers, of laughter and the strength of harmoni-ous living, of a true balance between country and town.

There was an area of rough grass growing with bird-sown thorns, land too steep to cultivate, above the rutted track along the side of the hill. Tall ragged hedges grew against the sky at the top of the slope, which made a shelter against the east winds. Here the would-be restorer sat with his men, on old sacks, resting and eating, in the midday warmth of the low sun; and here, too, when men and tumbrils had moved away up or down the hill came Pertris and Chee-kai with Perdix to rest in the mellow beams of the sun. When the laden tumbrils jolted and swayed down the tracks, shaking off yellow roots, the birds crept into the hedge and remained still, watching men and horses away beyond the tall thorn hedges ruddy with clusters of haws, and the brighter hips of wild roses among the bare thorns. Now that few insects or grains of corn were to be found on unploughed stubble and olland, they sought their food along the hedgerows and the edges of the woods.

It was the third week of January before the carting of the beet was finished, and the tumbrils ceased to move up empty into the fog-red fire rising upon the upland field, to return with last loads through evening's dusk made purple by the solar embers dying frostily beyond the woods of the west. Horses and men were glad to end the day's work and return to stable and cottage; the three birds crouched together for warmth upon the grassy Pightle at the northern end of the steep field. Beside the thorn branch where once Timid Wat the hare had quatted at rest, they settled to sleep.

Other pheasants were at roost in the sycamores of the High Wood above them, and in the branches of chestnut and beech of the Long Wood below them. The cocks perched near the tops of the trees, among the dark mantles of ivy that were more massive than some of the slender trees to which the climbing plants clung; the hens perched below them, also hidden by the thickness of leaves. Some of the mantling ivies were so heavy that in the gales of past winters the trees which supported them had fallen, top heavy, to lie aslant other trees yet upright in the woods. As ivy to trees, so mortgage to farm, thought the new farmer, hastening in twilight to the group of corn-stacks by the High Wood, which were to be threshed during the coming week. A cock cucketted as he walked among the frozen tops of the beet scattered upon the field, another replied from the Carr, a third from the distant end of the Long Wood.

The threshing tackle, pride and perfection of the Age of Steam, ponderous with vast straked iron wheels and

147

black cylindrical body, moved its fifteen tons of steel upon the farm. Digging its twin-tracked way up the steep slope, it paused on the crest, while from its iron belly three men dragged forth a steel cable to which was bound a great iron hook. They hauled the cable to the bottom, where the hook was fixed to the tow-bar of the massive wooden box enclosing the threshing drum. This patent, as the teamsman called it, together with the lank wooden straw elevator linked to it, was slowly hauled up the hill by the stationary engine above, chuffing and shaking as the fly-wheel whirled its polished black circles. It was dark when the driver and his mate had manœuvred engine and drum in position by the first stack, and, having covered the furnace fire with slack, crossed the field below the Pightle by starlight, and under the Long Wood to their bicycles left by the farm premises. Owls were hooting in the woods; rabbits fled from their voices; mallard flew up, from the dykes below, softly crying *quazz-quazz-quazz* as they circled over the meadows dim with the silver dust of stars across the sky. As they approached the premises, they heard the horses stamping on the cobbled floor of the stables; and passing by the hay barn door, saw a figure within sitting at a table, on which stood a hurricane lamp. They paused a moment; he appeared to be drawing something on paper pinned to a drawing board; and then, coming to their bicycles in the hovel, they mounted and rode away, thinking no more about it.

There were so many weeds in the corn-stack that before the first hour of threshing was over, the toothless but energetic octogenarian called Old Charley, forking away from the side of the box the pyramids of chaff and broken bits of straw and weed-leaf, called caulder, was covered as by grey mould, and then by grey fluffy feathers: for thistles were the dominant weeds of the fields. From the shaking sieves under the box fell showers of black hard shot-like seeds, forming into pyramids like miniature slag heaps by a coal mine: these were charlock or wild mustard, seeds which rolled down worm-holes and lay dormant during centuries away from the light. With the charlock dropped brown, softer seeds of dock, which had to be shovelled away lest the heaps choked the outfall from the sieves. At the far end of the box the stockman, standing by the trickles of corn coming from the spouts into the open mouths of sacks, remarked to the farmer that during the war, which had ended twenty years ago, such weed seeds, for caged birds, made a bigger price in the market than barley. "Blast, carlick seed wor close on a hunner pound the ton. Come war, yar'll be a'right, master."

It was a dull, cloudy day; but in the afternoon a weak sunshine filtered through, before the sky grew grey again, and a dull half-light settled on the fields and woods. Steam was blown ragged from the tall funnel of the engine as the first snowflakes of the winter drifted upon the figures of working men. Carting a ton load of two-hundredweight corn sacks down the hill was even more perilous than the carting of beet, for owing to the thaw the thin iron-banded wheels of the lower side of the tumbrils were sunken in ruts almost to the hubs; the weight of the tilted carts pressed on the lower wheels, so that the teamsman expected any moment to hear the breaking of the axle and to see the tumbril lurching over, perhaps throwing over the shaft-horse with it. But they got down somehow, the horses straining to pull to the gateway up the slight slope out of the hollow. The bringing up of water was a problem, too; the engine required four hundred gallons a day, as well as half a ton of coal. The watercart was a rusty coffin-like tank on wobbly iron wheels whose axles were only six inches from the ground.

The wheels sunk in the slippery clay to the axles; whereupon the three horses had to pull the solid, slopping coffin as a plow through the stubbles. They arrived at the engine dark with sweat, and feeble, while more than half of the water had been lost. "Ah," remarked Old Charley, the chaff-and-caulder man covered with grey fluff, and moving, sack tied round waist, and two-pronged fork in thickened, cracked hand, to the farmer, "yew can't beat bullocks fer draw'n wa'er fer trosh'n, wi' all yer will, 'bo'!" and with this advice, the ancient man moved back to his place of work. There was laughter at what he had said, and the remark was repeated later at the Cross, and elsewhere; and with it a nickname was given to the newcomer: a name by which he was always known afterwards—Wilbo.

Despite snow, the 'trosh'n' of corn-stacks continued during the following days, until all were threshed, and straw-stacks stood near their former sites, with great heaps of caulder and weed seeds. The straw-stacks were at the edge of the High Wood by the ruinous bullock-yard, and thither pheasants came to scratch in the caulder and pick up barley kernels left thickly around where the threshing drum had stood. The snow lay lightly on the ground and among the straws of the stacks, not thick enough to discomfort the birds. Partridges came too, Pertris and Perdix among them. One bird with red legs, and coloured more brightly than Pertris, ran at him and leapt to spur him, but Pertris was a bold bird too, and met the French partridge in the air, beak to beak and claw to claw. They leapt and fluttered and struck five times in three seconds, and then broke away one from the other. It was not a serious attack, as it would have been a month later; the "Frenchman" was a quarrelsome bird, and merely challenging upon the feeding grounds of his covey; there was enough grain for all, and after the challenge, both birds avoided each other.

When Chee-kai walked out of the wood, a sight already known to the other pheasants of the farm, no bird challenged him, as he fed quietly beside the two partridges. Dufa the ring-dove, with other native wood pigeons, flew there to feed, with stock-doves which had come over the sea in great numbers from Scandinavia. Harra the Denchman and other hoodies flapped, with rooks and jackdaws, to the quiet place sheltered from the winds and seldom molested by man. For now that the crops were off the land, the work was going forward with pick, shovel, and concrete mixer; earthenware drainpipes were being laid and sumps made; galvanized tanks and pipes being fixed, while roofs were relaid with creosoted rafters and battens to be hung with new red tiles; load after load of gravel was dug from the rented pit, and spread on the roads. The men grumbled at the variety of the work, and at the pace set by Wilbo, who seemed, for some reason, to be a man working against time.

Standing among yellowing reeds that filled the dykes from bank to bank the yellow-striped bittern made a noise like the brittle roar of a bull with paper lungs; and the larger grey heron, his cousin, answered *krar-r-k!* as on wide vanes he glided down to fish for roach under the river-bank. At dusk—"cock-shut" light of dead and gone buskin'd fowlers peering with long-barrelled flintlock, woodcock flapped up and down their rides through the trees, but no ruddy upward stabbings blasted their joy in brown silent flight above a white and black earth. Starlight reflected on the slow river was shaken by the angular ripples of the swimming otter who, crawling in the shallows where the horses went to drink morning and evening, stared at the light burning behind the window of the granary near the stables. The otter listened and sniffed, and in its own time, returned to the river, indifferent to the human figure with head bent over papers on a table, his eyes smarting with lack of sleep, his thoughts struggling against that which declined in the shadow of its own inertia, perhaps to be as compost under the new growth arising whence the icy wind was beginning to thrust across the hemisphere.

Discoloured and bleak were meadow and upland field while the cold airs poured from over the stained waves of the sea: the dreaded frost winds from the east. What sap was left in stalk and leaf was crystallized, bursting cell and breaking fibre, part of the annihilating sweep from tundra and steppe. Standing at the open granary·door long after the otter had gone down the river and under the sluice-doors of the sea-wall to the marshes, the human figure stared for momentary companionship at the Dogstar blazing its running fires above the High Wood; and lifting his eyes to follow the winding star-stream of the Galaxy, he saw Boötes the Herdsman treading the black pastures of the night, and the Bull, red of eye, sniffing the Pleiades, lying before its feet like the luminous shell-fragments of a partridge's nest soon to dissolve in the springing meadows of the dawn. Turning away from his phantasies, he closed the door, took off his boots and lay down upon a camp-bed, drawing a rug over himself, for brief sleep before another day.

In their courses the stars moved westward over the sun-less dusk of the western hemisphere. Far away in the windy woods owls were calling, their soft feathers shaken and pressed upon their bodies. Rats rustled inside the flint walls, moving along chill runs that were centuries old. The wind sought and found every fracture of the masonry built in the jocund Elizabethan heyday. In the stable the two old horses stood still, their heads hanging; each had drawn up a hind leg to stand the easier, while dozing before broken mangers where rats regularly ate about one-fifth of the evening feed of crushed oats and chaffed hay. Under the pantiles, on the fragile-rotten battens crossing the rafters of the cartshed, sparrows perched, heads in neck feathers for warmth and oblivion; secure within an old nest of moss and oak leaf set in a great crack of the wall of the Corn Barn, the russet wren lodged, above a pair of tomtits roosting side by side, headless, motionless save for slight shivers in moments of the persistent wind.

Upon an upland field, in the lee of the High Wood, among the stubbles of barley and thistle where the wind sighed, Pertris crouched with Chee-kai beside him, head to tail by habit; and on the back of Chee-kai, Perdix sat asleep.

Snow drifted with the wind from the east, hiding the stars before dawn; the rising of the sun gave only a blank opaqueness of light to the wan landscape. Snow fled over the stubble field, tapping the grey hollow stalks of the dead corn plants, coming to rest by broken flint and rust-thickened bullock shoe which the plow had turned and returned many times since the Crimean War, whither the ox's flesh, salted in barrel, had gone, to feed homeless soldiery. Snow in dry whorl and fleck hung and hovered in pockets of the air, eddying and sweeping before the invisible death of the wind. And as light made less indistinct the black boughs of trees and the hissing stacks of straw near the High Wood, Gyr the white falcon swept in from the sea, cutting sharp-winged down the blizzard, swinging up to hang watching, cutting short circles before sweeping down again, to turn once more and stare below for movement. Remote over the High Wood the white falcon hung sharp in the grey streaming wind, flickering as he watched, as he rose upon the gusts without falter: then, his full brown eyes filled as with pulse of sharpest light, he climbed upwind, to turn a thousand feet east of the place where Perdix awake was stretching himself on the back of Chee-kai—there was a screaming hiss, a craking cry from Pertris who seemed to burst upwards in feathers, another as talons struck the young partridge, a flurry of small feathers whirling away with the snow, and a sharp-winged shape flinging up over the treetops, one weighted foot hanging darkly below.

Chapter Fifteen

⸺⟨◈⟩⸺

Chee-kai remained crouching on the ground, shocked momentarily beyond movement. Terror alone had not abashed him, but the blow which had killed Perdix, breaking the bones of one wing and stripping feathers and skin of the back, had made numb and inert the nerve ganglions connected with the brain. He lay on the ground, the vision of the falcon's eye and curved beak fixed before his sight. As he recovered, as his blood was stimulated to action by glandular discharge, he scrambled to get his feet under him, and throwing himself into the air, flew over the beeches of the High Wood and, still climbing, came to an apex above the meadow, his wings making a keen whistling sound, his long tail held straight behind him, an arrow-bird sped into a strange new world, by the twanging bow of terror. Then above him he saw the falcon, and with a small plaintive cry he dropped one wing and, pivoting upon it, slewed round, and with tail feathers dispread as brake, rushed head first to earth. He saw the dark green needles of a pine-tree, enclosed in ivy, below him, and crashed upon it, to lie there quivering, resting on the tips of his wings until, his senses reassembling within his being, he grasped a branch, flapped upright, and looked about him.

After a while his sharp eye perceived the form of a bird

sitting quietly in the tree below him, but the grey and black plumage and black beak were familiar and harmless —for the bird was Harra the Denchman. Reassured by the quiet appearance of the crow, Chee-kai shook himself, ruffing out his neck feathers, and stretching his wings to feel their length and throw. The light of confidence came in his eyes, for he could see all about him from a height for the first time—never before had he been perched in a tree. Suddenly he lifted his head and listened to the cucket of a pheasant in the High Wood—a reassuring sound, for it was not the urgent treble screech of alarm. Elated by his vision, and by the feeling of security that he could see all about him, Chee-kai uttered, through closed beak, a trilling, soft note of high pitch, resembling the muted song of a hedge-sparrow. Hearing it, Harra the Denchman cocked an eye upwards, curious that such a sound had come from a bird of a size and appearance it had never seen before.

Thus Chee-kai came to the tree under which, nearly nine months before, he had tapped and chipped his way out of a shell.

There were other pheasants in the Carr, and when the hard weather had softened into mist and rain, to be followed by the sun ashine through windless days, there was much crowing among the trees at morning and evening. The shooting season had ended with January, though wildfowl could be shot legally for two more weeks. Sometimes reports of twelve- and ten-bore guns came at twilight from the meadows below the Carr, where men standing within hogshead barrels, sunken level with the ground, shot at the dark outlines of mallard, teal, and other duck flighting up the river to their feeding places in dyke, decoy, and pond. From his roosting place near the top of the pine-tree, Chee-kai could see the ruddy flashes that came from the lower darkness; pheasants in the High Wood remained silent, and from the Long Wood also, as though by agreement, there was no cucketting.

Nettles, dog's mercury, wild arums, and ground elder began to arise among the dead leaves on the woodland floor, among the smaller leaves of sweet violets, and celandines. Chee-kai sought his food in the Carr, and also on the meadow, picking apart old bullock pats and frost-sered clumps of horse dung, for the beetles and worms that lay beneath; scratching up roots of silver-weed, and seeking wireworms which were active among the clumps of decaying grasses. Other cock pheasants sought their food in the wood and on the meadow, but always they kept apart from his strangeness. Once Chee-kai found a slow-worm stirring from its hibernation in a heap of white flints by one of the ruinous bridges over the dyke, and after breaking it by blows of his beak, swallowed it; another time, he caught a mouse, and ate it. So far Chee-kai had not been molested by any other pheasant, but one morning as he was scratching at the tuberous roots of creeping buttercup on the bank above the dyke near the base of the pine-tree, he looked up at a noise and there was Koch-Karr, veteran survivor of three shooting seasons, the bases of its sharp and long spurs stuck with dried blood and featherlets, running at him with green-tufted head held low and a fury of killing in its eyes. Chee-kai stood still in surprise. The old cock flung itself at him, its wings pressed back, and struck at his head with the horny daggers behind its scaly legs. Chee-kai jumped high in the air: the jump saved him from being pierced in the neck, such was the rage of the attacker. Nevertheless, that bird received a shock, for Chee-kai, as he descended, struck at him with his spurs, and the

157

weight of his heavier body was behind his strike. The old cock sqwarked and fled. It ran down the path through the wood, made by wandering bullocks of past seasons when they had broken through the wire fence at the northern apex of the Carr, pursued by Chee-kai. Another cock sqwarked as it saw him, and such was its surprise and fear that it plunged into the reeds below the wood, and found itself in the water of the dyke. It swam to the meadow-bank, and scrambled out, while a third cock, seeing it, crowed and flapped its wings in challenge. But perceiving Chee-kai, the third pheasant ran away across the meadow and concealed itself in the dry ditch below the Breck.

From the distance came another sound—the noise of the key turning in the wooden lock of the Corn Barn door. When the cock pheasant moved out of the ditch on to the meadow again, where in the hollows lay water-plashes fringed with bright green floating leaves of the poa grass, a red-legged partridge ran from him: this was Kakkabis, a young unmated hen who had been listening to the sound of *Per-tris, per-tris, per-tris* in the distance. She ran upon the unploughed barley stubble of the Breck, whence the call had come.

Chee-kai, standing still inside the Carr, heard the cry at the same moment, and hastened towards it.

The green woodpecker crossed in heavy loping flight from the Carr to the beeches of the High Wood, uttering the volant cry of spring. Almost the gay-coloured bird might have been the herald of tourney, for soon the Carr and the meadow, the overhanging High Wood and the hedge below the Breck were a-stir with the pitter patter of running feet, the cucket and buffet of combat. Ever since the open weather of early January, cockbirds had been pursuing hens feeding quietly, running in semicircles about them, displaying with dropped nearside wing and spread tail, as though to catch them in individual nets of gleaming colours; and occasionally one cockbird would run, with head held low, at another, to be met by a like crouching stance, which, however, had usually been broken off as though by mutual agreement.

But now, with the approach of St. Valentine's Day, when the woods and meadows were a-chirp and a-twitter, a-whistle and a-caw, the cucketting wing-whurrs of cock pheasants became more raucously frequent as the birds began to fight for territory upon which the hens went their discreet and, as it were, unregardant ways. A cock courting a hen would break off its luring display around her to dash at another cock coming upon its range. The hens had no choice: the tread they would accept in due season was for their young. To the cocks came a different sensation that was as an added weight to their frames, an extra strength to muscle of leg and wing; their eyes saw clearer and bolder, their power of movement became swifter; they clashed, and triumphed—or ran. With ear-tufts erected the old cock ran to one of its hens, sensation thickening on approach; spoke to her with low goppling clucks; the vermilion skin around eyes swelled with the pressure of blood; the feathers loosened upon the surgent body. Hearing a rustle in the thick clumps of tussock-grass, seeing a dark green head and white-collar'd neck upraised, it ran in turgid fury at it, prepared to leap and stab with spurs; but the head was withdrawn, and the cock swung again to the hen, pleasurable feelings within it extending with strength and colour of being. The hen would avoid looking directly, fearing to draw upon herself such power, yet knowing she was held to him; and he ran upon her closer, while the feeling in her drew down his wing and curved his neck and tail as though into her very being. The cock, gleaming with colours in vibration, was curved to the centre of her being as a sun-bow to the centre of the sun.

The old cock, seeing a white head by a bramble bush, a white head cowled in black, screeched—subsided—fled. But Chee-kai was only seeking Pertris.

Pertris led his new mate Kakkabis to where the clumps of old tussock-grass grew thickly on the drift beyond the Carr. The drift had not been used as a cart track, nor had it been grazed, for many years; it was overgrown with great tussocks, called bull-fronts by the stockman, which in early March were sere and rustling in the east wind. Here, too, lay other wrecked stalks of a past summer, of knapweed, wild carrot, wild parsnip, hemlock and hemp agrimony. The drift lay between two dykes; and at the end were the first trees of the High Wood, which grew on steep chalky slopes above the meadow. The drift here was sheltered from the east winds by a blackthorn brake, whose suckers were slowly crossing the old carriage way. Thin stem and dry grass rising two feet high made a sheltered nesting place; and hither, in the second week of April, when Harra the Denchman had crossed the sea to his dark spruce forests, when young bullocks were tearing eagerly the young grasses of the meadow, when the Carr resounded with the cooing of Dufa the ring-dove who loved bathing in the stony shallows of the bullocks' drinking place, when the new farmer sometimes sang as, sitting on a new tractor, he ploughed the sunlit slopes of the Breck—hither among new leaves and stems arising out of the old growths of the quiet drift crept Kakkabis the mate of Pertris to lay her small speckled eggs—and hither, of an early morning and sometimes of an evening, but never in the broad lights of day, came a bird of shimmering plumage like to gold on its back and deepest black on its lower chest and belly, carrying behind it an immensely long sweep of tail, of feathers grey and buff barred in chestnut and cinnamon —a bird matchless and therefore solitary, yet inspiring loyalty of so deep a quality that its frail cries drew to its side a small brown bird, near to which it fed in contentment.

"Blast, I what you call like that patent," observed the teamsman, watching the twin breasts of the plow, attached hydraulically to the rear of the new tractor, turning the stubble on the Breck. The teamsman's horses stood, hitched to their plow withdrawn from the furrow, to permit the machine to pass, before they would set-in again and follow down the field, which was being plowed on the round. "Ah, thet I do, an' all!" he added, as he watched critically the furrow-slices rearing up, to flop over, cracked and loose. Even so, he thought, with a slight impelling anxiety, you can't beat horse plowing. The movement of the old single-furrow plow, attached to the long stilts, shook the slice as it came up and left it looser than the more rigid slices of the conventional tractor plows. But looking again, he saw that the new type of tractor did not plow rigidly: the plow had a springiness about it, that was like that of his single furrow. "Thet's a good patent, innit tho!" he repeated, in a serious voice. "Yew wasn't sucked in when you bought thet." And then, "But I won't hev it that tractors 'll beat hosses, thet I won't!"

Even so, he was a little afraid; for the new patent could turn over four acres a day while his horses could plow but one acre. Would Wilbo get rid of the horses? He didn't seem to like them, saying they stamped too much; whereas horses always stamped. He said they stamped because of mites in their legs, but he, a teamsman, wouldn't have that. In all his fourteen years with horses, and father's forty years, he had never heard spoken of mites on horses' legs. It was nature that they stamped. Mites in cheese, maybe; he didn't know about that; but horses!—it was out of books Wilbo read—"theory"!

Thus reassured by his thoughts, the teamsman, who was keen to serve the new man well, cried to his horses, jerked the long lines of rope to their bits, pressed on the wooden handles of the stilts, and set the wheel in the furrow, to follow the tractor. They were plowing on the round—going round the field as a needle plows the furrows of a gramophone record, but in reverse, working from the outsides to the centre—thus to plow down the steep slopes on the eastern side and up the lesser incline of the western side by the Long Wood.

It was kind weather, the air soft and the wind like a waft of the sun from the south: a morning of gossamers drifting over the furrows, and sudden glints of rainbow colours momentarily visible to the plowman's eye as, his shadow before him, he went down the field of new-broken earth. Man, beast, bird, and insect were buoyant in gracious air.

Swimming in the river, Gallinule the moorfowl flipped his pied tail, while his mate sat on her seven buff eggs, speckled with reddish-brown, laid within a nest of buff flag-reeds woven upon a ledge of the bank. Oenas the stock-dove, the water-bibber, clad in the hues of ripening grapes and vine leaves, bluish grey, glossy purple, coral red of legs and feet, sat near his mate on her nest in a hole of a great willow growing by the river, cooing happily before gliding to splash in the shallows where the bullocks drank; for all doves love water and bathing therein.

His journey across the sand plains and hillocks of Parthenopia and over the blue middle sea to Europe and the isle of Britain being ended, Crex the corncrake dropped on weary wings into the cowslips rising yellow among the meadow lands of his forefathers; from Africa, too, had flown Quaquila the quail, from whom at evening upon the far end of the meadow came the cry of *Wet my lips—Wet my lips*, in liquid undertone as the bird called his mate ever to be near him. As the moon arose out of the sea and shone through the vapours of the marsh the cry of Crex joined the cry of Quaquila, a harsher sound, like wood drawn down a toothcomb— *crake, crake, crake*, as the bird pushed through a silver haze upon the dewy grasses, moving its head side to side, thus seeming to throw its voice from different places.

Sitting beside his father before a coal fire in the cracked iron grate set in the wide brick hearth built for the burning of wood, within a damp and decayed cottage raised on a bit of wasteland two centuries before by an industrious labourer, the teamsman wondered whatever the stranger called Wilbo was about. He was disturbed by all the semi-scornful remarks that he heard at the Cross, and wondered if he ought to stick working for a master of whom it was continually being said that he did silly things. What was the sense of plowing all the arable when the season was too late for the sowing of corn and root? All the grass fields, too, were to be plowed. And when that was done, all the plowed work was to be chalked, ten tons to the acre to be carted, spread, and left to lie on top. Someone had asked him that evening what Wilbo was a-drilling on the fields beside air. There was no sense to it; they might as well be farming in order to sow air and reap wind. It was all pay, pay, pay, and nothing coming in for the wages, let alone the cost of the tractor, and a new 500-gallon tank for petrol to be sunk under the shed. Where was it all leading to? The new man said his money was nearly gone, and yet he was doing all this, and not

163

one seed going into the ground. "It's pay, pay, pay, Father," he repeated unhappily. "There's narthin comin' back, except a few shillin' a week for the ajoisted beasts." The agisted beasts were the bullocks, being grazed for the dealer who owned them, for two shillings a head per week. "Fourteen bullocks don't bring in enough even to pay yar wages, Father."

Removing the pipe from his mouth, the stockman replied, "Thar's'm sense tew it, if he ken holt out. Cultiwatin' of th' arable will put paid to the rubbage." He relapsed into pipe-puffing meditation, before speaking again. "A sack o' wheat they reckon tew pay a man's wages, but wi' the price to-day, it takes four sacks. Wheat ain't no good. Barley's scarce worth the drilling, a'most. And crushed oats fer hosses ken be bought cheaper'n'y be grown. Can 'a holt out, that's the question. He's done good to the yards now! All thet mud gone, yew could eat your dinner off the concrete slabs we've laid down." The teamsman thought before replying. "Ah," he said, rolling himself a cigarette, "if there's any dinner to eat, Father. What's it all for? It's pay, pay, pay all the time, and narthin' comin' back." "Yew wait," replied the older man. "Next yar, Wilbo say to me to-day, will come the crisis. After next yar's harvest, Wilbo say." "Next year's a long way ahead," replied the teamsman. "What'll we do meanwhile?" "Same as us'v done up tew now," replied his father. "Don't yew a-worry, son." And picking up a sheet of paper, the stockman turned to his favourite relaxation, football pools. "We might win forty thousand pun by then!" "I keep my money in my pocket," said the stockman. "Well, I'll tek a turn down to the stables, to see the hosses are all right. I suppose I'll see his light a-goin' in the granary, he's allus a-studyin' of books." "Theory!" ejaculated the stockman, as he puzzled over forecasts for next Saturday's wins and

164

losings. "Yar right, 'bor, theory won't get a man narthin," as he scratched his head over the problems of theoretical football.

Not everything was theory, however. Sometimes the farmer would stop the tractor, having steered it out of the furrow, and switching off the engine, would leap off the seat and walk away, giving himself the excuse that he must look at the bullocks, or the meadow grasses, or consider the method of rebuilding the broken culverts over the dykes. He certainly looked at the bullocks and stared at the grass, but his real motive in leaving his work was to escape the burden of it for a few minutes, to be free in the spring air, to renew the spirit. One such morning, having crossed the plank over the dyke to the drift he saw, just before his feet, the close-pressed plumage of a red-legged partridge covering her eggs. He watched intently, but without tension lest his thoughts perturb the bird, before returning quietly along the drift and so across the meadow to his plowing.

Chapter Sixteen

—◦◦◦◦◦◦◦◦◦◦◦—

During the early summer days the tractor moved at a rate varying between one, and two and a half miles an hour, up and down all the fields of the farm, plowing under weeds and poor grasses alike. The roads had already been made up with nearly two thousand tons of gravel and flints dug in the winter months. The artesian bore had been completed, a pump installed, tank and pipes laid in the cowhouse. New gates and posts stood where before had been gaps; roofs had been retimbered and retiled; service cottages rebuilt. All this had been, and still was, the subject of local speculation and gossip. The chief puzzlement was, What was Wilbo doing it for? And where was the money coming from? And how could he ever hope to see it return? Was there no end to all the fancy work? For massive concrete slabs having been laid about the yards, now there was talk of heavy concrete bridges, to take ten tons he was reported to have said, being built across all the dykes, leading from one meadow to another. Where was the sense of that? For a few bullocks to cross by, why make bridges strong enough to take the heaviest loaded beet lorry? If, as some said, it was all being done for a hobby, why did he always look so wire-drawn, why was he always in a hurry, rushing here, rushing there, digging first in the gravel pit for the roads, and now carting hundreds of tons of chalk on to the fields? And then his line of talk, uttered during rare visits to the Horn and Corn and the Turnip Arms, puzzled most listeners. He said that under the existing System an increase of soil-erosion was inevitable, with the pollution of rivers by sewage, and the silting of estuaries; while the same System produced the piling-up of unsold goods for export, with consequent increasing unemployment, leading to the inevitability of war. The golden tapeworm had enfeebled the body politic; only if all in Britain saw this, only if all worked for the idea of People and Soil, together with the Empire in service to the ideal of building a great new civilisation, could war with anti-Money resurgent nations, leading to the extinction of Europe, be avoided.

The older labourers listened in silence; but when he had gone, one of three occasional visitors to the pub, the moneylender accompanied by two of his syndicate pals, asked aloud, Who was the foreigner trying to suck in by such squit? And who was paying him to talk like that? The old country was all right, and if the foreigner didn't like it, if it wasn't good enough for him, then let him clear off and live where he considered things were better. No one asked him to come; no one was asking him to stay. Landlord, drinks all round!

The moneylender, who perhaps was prejudiced because he deemed himself to be done out of his shooting without sufficient justification went on to declare, in a quieter voice, holding a confidential note, that the new-comer was a crank, with neither sense nor money, and would soon go bust, as he deserved to, chucking away money like that when everyone else knew that even real farmers found it hard to make farming pay. But it was always the stranger who held the cockpit; they came along to teach others what was wrong, but how long did'm last? Cheerio, everyone.

The moneylender paid regular visits to the inn, to see the small dealer called The Flockmaster, who was one of his several agents collecting gold sovereigns.

Meanwhile the new rubber-tyred tumbrils continued to pull out of the chalk quarry by the cartshed, followed by the lorry, with loads of chalk. The chalk was set out in small heaps in line up and down the fields, at the rate of ten tons to the acre. The teamsman said flatly one day he didn't like doing work that led nowhere, and could not pay; to which the reply was made that the soil of each field had been analysed, whereby it was found that the lime content of some was low, while others were definitely acid. And since the government had offered to pay half the cost of digging and carting the chalk, why not take advantage of the offer. Likewise there was a grant of two pounds an acre for plowing old tired grassland, and putting it either in the arable rotation, or re-seeding on the up-turned sod with new leafy grass strains and clovers. "Then we're doin'-of all this with the taxpayers' money?" asked the teamsman. "Partly." "Why?" asked the puzzled stockman. "Because the industrial towns must be fed when they have their war." "Oh," said the teamsman, unconvinced.

The feeling that he was taking part in something silly still remained with him. To his father he said he could not see the sense of first plowing the land, then pressing it down again with the wheels of loaded vehicles and the feet of horses. And as the days and weeks went on, and he saw, with a kind of hopelessness, that the weeds, especially thistle and charlock, were growing the more luxuriantly for the plowings, he felt like chucking up; but when, after the chalk heaps had been spread evenly over one field, the tractor had gone upon it, a new implement behind it, the teamsman changed his opinion, and once again a reluctant, "Blast—I like that patent!" came from him. For the new implement was a cultivator with seven arms of curved steel drawing through the soil seven shining tines, each shaped like the wings of a dove recurved in gentle dive. By the movement of the lever which controlled the oil pumps which in turn controlled the depth of the steel wings, the cultivator was lowered and the forward movement of the tractor drew seven bright cutting wings through the green furrows, cutting roots of thistle and dock, stirring and lifting the soil under surface-growing charlock, campion, and goose-foot, until all the luxuriant growth of weeds was disturbed, the hair-like rootlets drawing moisture were broken, and within half an hour of the implement's passing they were wilting in the summer sun. Up and down went the tractor, covering more than an acre in an hour, while burning less than a gallon of fuel. When the stockman walked by in the afternoon, he surveyed several acres of a field which that morning had been a foot high in greenery, and now revealed nicely broken furrows and leaning, dying stalks. "Yew know a thing or two," he conceded, happiness in his face. "And yew say yew harn't done no farmin' a'fore?" The other replied that it was all in books, but refrained from using the word "theory". "Now after rain a new lot of weeds will spring up—for the land is full of weed-seed—and then we'll cross-cultivate, overwhart, isn't that the word? and kill them. The extra cultivation will make the seed-bed finer, and more seeds will chit. Then we'll cultivate again. And get them all; while sun, rain and air will bring back fertility."

That night the stockman, making his weekly football forecast, which was sent in with a sixpenny postal order every Thursday, declared to his son that if only Wilbo

169

would put some of his brains into pools, he might win a lot of money.

A clipping machine was delivered on the farm, and fixing it up, the new farmer said they would trim the hair of the horses' legs. In vain the teamsman protested that when it rained, the wet would soak into the skin, and rot the horses' feet; for without hairs to let the water drip clear, the fetlocks would have no protection. The clipper clicked, the hair fell, the horses stood still, grateful for easement of itching. Afterwards, with pail of water and tablet of mercury soap, a white lather was rubbed on heels and fetlocks. That night neither horse stamped on the uneven cobbled floor of the stable. The teamsman could not understand it; but he remarked again that when it rained the skin would crack, having no protection by nature against the wet. To which the reply was made that a vigorous wisping with straw would always remove wet on legs when the horses were brought to the stable after the day's work. The teamsman retorted that no one else round about ever did that. "Then you have a wonderful opportunity to set a good example. And don't forget to repeat the washing in ten days' time, to kill any mites that have hatched meanwhile out of egg sacs."

That night, at tea in his cottage, the teamsman said that what Wilbo wanted was a racing stable, what with the new hay-racks, curry-combs and brushes, oil for harness, and even polish for the buckles and brow-brasses. "Nobody else hereabouts is nice like that," he remarked. "And to-day he tell of a milking machine, and bringing the electric to the premises, and boiling steam to clean the pipes of the milking machine, because of germs, he say. That will be your job, Father." The stockman looked alarmed, then grim. "Do you believe in germs, Father?" "Naow!" replied the stockman. "Whoever see a jarm?

It's book-squit—theory! He'll larn the difference, don't yew worry yourself, my boy!" Thus reassured a little the teamsman walked to the village shop to buy his weekly ounce of British Oak shag tobacco—his happy-making Friday evening ritual, after being paid. He never went to a dance or into a pub, preferring, as he said, to keep his money in his pocket, which meant the Post Office Savings Bank at two and a half per cent interest.

One morning Old Charley, the octogenarian, who also did things which were much discussed at the Cross— such as his recent proposal of marriage to a young woman of twenty—appeared on the uplands of the farm, striding along with flapping overcoat, and long stick in hand. He said in a loud voice that he had come to see how Wilbo was getting on. Declaiming like a Biblical prophet with the temperament of a clown, he cried out that in the days of "old and true", when farmers were farmers and not just slobberers after the biggest penny, marl was "spreed" on the land every thirty years. Bare fallows, too, in the shift wor the only way to get rids of th' ole rummage. "If you're lived and spared, 'bo'!" he cried, "you'll feel the benefit of all this, ah, thet you will, 'bo'!" He left with half a crown in his pocket, a wave of his stick in the air, and a cry of "Fare you well, 'bo'," to the delight of the men who thoroughly enjoyed the crude humour of the pun, mixed with envy at the way the ancient had got money out of the boss.

Above the river bordering the meadows lay a road from which a wide view upon rush-clumped grazing extending to the High Wood, the Breck, and the Long Wood was spread before the eye of the traveller. Often the Flockmaster, a diminutive man with wizened face and mittened hands, drove along the road in his dog-cart drawn by the shaggy pony, and when he came to a curve in the road, near a thorn bush growing out of the steep bank below, he drew into the side, and watched what was going on. The bush hid most of his vehicle, and for that reason he stopped there. Among other activities, he travelled to sales and auctions, buying in order to sell again. His usual method at a sale was to try and find a hesitant or shy bidder who wanted a certain item; to bid against him, but discreetly, and to secure the item; then to offer it to him deprecatingly, with the formula, "I'll take a profit," meaning the sum of the extra bid— half a crown, or maybe a crown. In addition to this "bit o' buyin' and sellin' ", the owner of the pony—which was grazed on bits of waste land by the road—collected rags, bones, and scrap metal; he bought used fertilizer and meal sacks, to resell, after sorting and grading, and sometimes washing, to millers and whelk fishermen of the coastal town; and rabbit skins, nailing them to wooden planks of all shapes and sizes standing in the flint-built shed adjoining his cottage, and selling to an agent who supplied them as material for felt hats to a factory built in the Brecklands—a brick structure, looking like something transported from industrial London, standing on the outskirts of a medieval town where the previous main industry had been the knapping of flints for guns and pistols.

Sometimes the Flockmaster was accompanied along the coastal road by Little Bingo, the butcher's dog; but the brindled lurcher usually turned back by the Carr, and followed the tracks of rabbits in the scalt fields adjoining the marsh. Little Bingo came because he had to fill up his time somehow, and at the rattling clop of the horse's feet up the village street he usually set out to run awhile ahead of his friend the horse; while that aged animal, whether blinker'd between shafts or standing pot-bellied with permanent curvature of spine due to inferior feeding on road verges, was always pleased to see his friend the dog.

The Flockmaster pulled into the raised bank between the road and the rough slope of thistle, burdock, wild rose, and dock leading steeply down to the river, and watched what was going on in the meadow. The Flockmaster found the newcomer's doings of intense interest; feelings of puzzlement, doubt, and derision arose within him whenever he saw or heard anything about him. Yet, meeting him face to face, the Flockmaster was always respectful, touching his cap. At the Cross, where men met at evening to talk and stand easy, and in the pubs, the Flockmaster was said to be two-faced: he would say one thing about a man one day, and another the next. An only child, he had never married, but lived with his mother, now ninety years of age.

That morning, sitting on the moth-eaten cushion on the wooden seat of his cart, he looked from behind the bush to the scene on the meadow. The teamsman was driving the cutter, while the stockman was wielding a scythe, to cut the rushes and weeds; but instead of leaving them to wilt, the other two men were forking them into heaps, and then treading on the heaps to flatten them. If thet wor' haymakin', thet wor' a rum'n! For doin' of it thet way'd make that cut-stuff grow mouldy! Whatever was the foreigner a-doin' of? His men ought to know better'n 'at!

Sucking his dark brown clay pipe, with its stem broken off near the bowl, so that the rank smoke of thick twist gave a pleasant rasp to his nostrils, the Flockmaster peered, and muttered to himself. It's a rum'n, he repeated, and jerking the cracked reins through the brass rings long since darkened by a complete indifference to polish, he spoke to the horse which, waiting to tear as large a mouthful of grass as possible, in its own time lifted its head, and moved on along the road.

The Flockmaster was going to the sale of a bankrupt poultry farmer, in the hope of buying some old hens for a shilling or fourteen pence apiece. He would judge their age and condition by holding them upside down, blowing the feathers clear of the vent, and also by pinching their angular breasts. He carried in his cart a hen crate, rat gnawn and stuck with ancient feathered droppings, into which his purchases would be thrust.

Later in the week he drove along the road again, on his way to a furniture sale in the next village, to buy old brass candlesticks, china dogs, and such knicknacks which, placed on the high mantelpiece of his cottage, and on the window ledges within, would attract one or another of the occasional visitors who came to the village in August and September. He had sold several such pieces to townsfolk in previous years, as having belonged to his grandfather; and if he made sixpence over the price he had paid for each article, he was satisfied—and if a shilling, he had done well. For a shilling bought three pints of beer, which was the quantity that pleased his guts best at night in the Horn and Corn.

The Flockmaster lived with his mother in a cottage of three rooms, two up and one downstairs, in the village. His father had died sixty years before, when he had been four years old. His mother still went cockling on the mud flats beyond the marshes, barefoot and clad in layer upon layer of bodices and skirts against the cold winds of the sea, bringing back her pailful of succulent "blues", letting them stand in salty water to clean themselves before boiling them on the kitchen range. The surface of the yard before their cottage was thick with many hundreds of thousands of paired ribbed shells trodden into fragments by passing feet.

A fortnight had elapsed when the Flockmaster

again drove along the road, and pulled into the half-shade and part concealment of the thorn bush; and while his horse sniffed to discover what new growth had come there since the last pull-up to graze, he sat and took the pipe from between the three remaining teeth in his front gums, for sump'n pretty rum was happening on the meadow. He had twitted the stockman at the Cross about what was happening; but the stockman had told him nothing, beyond a significant, "See'ng's believ'n, harn't et? Then shouldn't wonder ya'll see, 'bor."

A machine a couple of hundred yards away was making a puffing, chuffing noise, while the men round it, led by the foreigner, were busy with pail, shovel, and wheelbarrow. What could it be? Was Wilbo digging of a well, out there in the lows, where all the water in Noah's kingdom lay a few inches under the surface? He had already digged a hartifeesian well, so 'twas said, by the premises, although the river ran only a yard or two away, and that harti-feesian well was said to be nigh on seventy feet deep! Stry-goodly clack-box, muttered the Flockmaster, and with this reference to a wasteful, glib-tongued person-ality (phrases that his mother had used often to him in the past, when he had shown little inclination for regular work), he pulled contemptuously at the reins, squirted nicotine juice out of the corner of his mouth, and drove on. It was a swelking hot day, and he was driving to the Melton July Lamb Sale, which he had attended out of bravado every year for a quarter of a century: for in that time he had bought but one lot only, seven unthrifty lambs which had had almost more ticks on their bodies than flesh. He had bid for them after taking too much beer, in order to show off before the big men. He had got rid of them, to another small dealer, but only after taking a loss of a shilling a lamb, a thing which he had never for-gotten, or been allowed to forget: hence his nickname.

Indeed, he did not want to forget it; he was proud of it; and every Melton July Lamb Sale he set out along the twelve-mile journey with the feeling that he might do a bit of dealing if he fancied, and to receive the quips of a few there who would have missed the shabby little figure, who acknowledged their attention with grins and knowing winks of the eye.

When next he passed that way in his trap, the Flockmaster stopped as usual to view what was happening. The occasion was his annual drive along the road with his mother, to see how the barleys were ripening; for he felt himself to be a man of knowledge, who, if only he had been given a chance to make a start, would have shown up most of the so-called farmers of the district—slobberers he called them—who had let-go their land by selling their ewe flocks—"and yew can't farm scalt' [light] land wi'out a yaw flock." He recalled the barleys of his boyhood, when he had been crow-keeping for a shilling a week, every day except Sundays, when a field that now yielded only a nine-yard stack, little more than half a day's threshing, would hold two, perhaps three, eleven-yard stacks. Now, as he stopped by the thorn bush, he told his mother that the clack-box foreigner was carrying his harvest . . . of mud holled out of the grupps and mouldy hay that was fit only for the muck'p!

Leaning forward and muttering, his old mother nearly asleep beside him, the Flockmaster was hardly able to restrain himself from calling out, "Yew whybibbling slobberers, yew all arter be put away!" as the lorry backed, and turned to cross by what now he realized was a new concrete bridge over the dyke. All that money wasted, when a few lengths of oak covered with chalk—the proper way—would have lasted half a lifetime or longer. More money than sense—and yet he had no money, he was all bluff, else why did he have to work like any labouring man? Money—fough!—he, the Flockmaster, could have bought him up, if he hadn't been kept down by others out for themselves at his expense all his life.

That evening at the Cross, by the brick river bridge which bore the scalloped marks of many toes and heels of boys sitting on the parapet, he spoke with the teamsman; but the teamsman, not so much loyal to his master as resenting the attitude of the dealer ("If yew put grease on yer hair he'd smell it and come to lick it off") replied laconically, before walking on to the shop to buy his weekly ounce of tobacco. The teamsman thought it was a waste of money, carting all that stuff to the High Wood and throwing it off in a heap as though it were good bullock muck, but he was not going to admit it before the chaps at the Cross, and be laughed at, working for a master who did silly things.

Systematically all was being loaded into lorry and tumbril, carried over the new concrete bridge to the gateway of the field, and on the track made by wheels up the Breck, through a ride in the High Wood, and to the clearing behind the woodland yard, where the level and growing heaps stood in line, each about five feet high and a dozen yards square. "Here is our harvest," said Wilbo, when all the yellow-green litter of rush, thistle, and rank grass had been spread in layers between the damp mud and rotting reed. "Here, in these hundreds of tons of compost, lie our yields of corn in the coming years." The teamsman regarded them stolidly. "Will yew thresh all that through the drum, then?" he asked, as though seriously. The other man laughed. "Yes, and it will come out of the spout good and corny, you'll see, if you're 'lived and spared', 'bor!" The teamsman then remarked that if the heaps were spread on the arable, it

177

would be putting back all the weeds that had been killed by the bare fallowing. "Nao!" cried the stockman, "the heat will kill them." "That mud heat, Father?" replied his son, when they were alone. "It ain't likely. He'll never see his money back on what he ordered us to do. It's dead. That mud is full of seeds of nettles and docks. You'll see I'm right. I'm not sucked in by this compass patent. It's all pay, pay, pay on this farm, and narthin' comin' back. I'm sick of it all—the Cross must think we're daft, that's what Flock said last Friday when I went down to buy my ounce of 'British Oak'."

However, the following Friday, the teamsman returned with some reassurance to his cottage, when he had deposited his weekly savings in the Post Office, and bought his weekly ounce of "British Oak" shag tobacco. Old Charley had been there, and he was always listened to as an authority; in his time he had been the best labourer for miles around. Old Charley had declared that "in the days of old and true", as he expressed it, the mud and reeds of the grupp pullings were always mixed in with chalk and "spreed" on the arable. "Yew niminipiminy macaroonies, whose belts never yet showed the frost at reapin', don't knaw narthin'," he had cried out, before striding off stick-tapping to his cottage in a village four miles distant. The 'frost' was sweat, salt-edged when it dried, penetrating the broad leather belts of reapers bending to cut corn with sickles in days of old. "Wilbo's the boy! He aint a lazy hoss, wot sweats ter see the chains, like all you modern boogers!" Roars of laughter had greeted his remarks. The teamsman said, as he sat on an upholstered leather motor seat that his father had bought from the Flockmaster for eighteen pence and which made two excellent chairs against the wall by the kitchen range, "Wilbo has his head screwed on right way in some things, I'll admit. I like that lil' old grey dicka"—the little

178

grey donkey as the village called the light hydraulic Ferguson tractor—"it's a good thing, that will pay for itself. Wilbo sometimes know what he's doin', I reckon." Then after a pause, the inevitable, "Where's it all leadin' to, thet's what I can't scheme out, Father."

A fortnight later, returning from buying his tobacco, he said, "They're saying at Cross that barley in Norwich Corn-hall has dropped to fifteen bob a coomb for best, and ten for orn'iary." A coomb was four bushels. "There'll be a lot of chaps on the dole this coming winter, they're saying. Wilbo has bought some axes, saws, and slashers, tew cut the hedges, so we'll be all right for work for a while, if he can keep on. How all the money's ter come back, that's what's worryin' me. And he don't even let the shooting, all them bards walkin' about, and crowin' their heads off in the woods. I saw Harcourt's keeper" (Harcourt was the Christian name of a neighbouring farmer) "goin' round the boundary to-day tossing out tail-corn, tew draw our bards. Why don't our boss have a shoot, Father? Fessans are fetchin' seven bob a pair, and thet would be suthin' comin' back." The stockman looked at his son knowingly. "Yew wait an' see," he remarked. "Wilbo know what a's dewin' of. Bards will fly a long way for raisins, won't 'm? An' reckon currants be good as raisins, don't yew, 'bor?" The teamsman showed interest. "Has he bin droppin' currants in the woods, Father?" "Maybe," replied the other. "To draw Harcourt's bards? That ain't like our boss. He ain't so nice as that." *Nice* meant an absence of give-and-take. "Naow!" replied the other, "to hold his own. Yew know that gaudy longtail what goes wi' the li'l ol' partriss? Flock see it yesterday fly up from the river bank, with the covey and he say Little Bingo nearly snapped it, but the dawg's overfed and silly. When I tell our boss that, he look anxious, saying that a' would'n want no harm tew come th' bard." The stockman puffed his pipe reflectively; then added significantly, "Maybe he think currants'll keep away poachers, tew." And so saying he went down to the Horn and Corn, where, the night before, someone had whispered something to him behind a hand. Acting on the information received, the stockman had taken his slasher with him to the upland fields during dinner time, and unknown to anyone else had struck the ends off a score or so of thorn branches in the hedges, leaving them lying where they fell. Later, after his tea, he had strolled there again, and gathering them together, had lifted them on a two-tined fork and carried them away.

Chapter Seventeen

⎯⎯⎯⎯⎯◦◦◦⟨◉⟩◦◦◦⎯⎯⎯⎯⎯

The previous night the stockman had heard that certain characters from the town, who were often to be found of an evening in the bar of the Norfolk Hero—a pub in the neighbouring village, named after the victor of Trafalgar—were planning to use a sweep net upon the upland fields of the farm. According to his informant, the characters were coming first to the Horn and Corn. The leader was a Cockney, a lorry driver who worked for a horse-slaughterer in the town.

In a yew-wood, wheel-back chair, much polished by hand, coat, and trouser-seat, the stockman sat and waited, his face easy and contented as he smoked shag tobacco and took pulls at his pint glass of dark fourpenny beer. The room was small, with several tables, at one of which sat some labourers playing whist. A fire burned in the grate. Upon the walls hung several relics of an age of opulence which had passed away: a large and heavy mirror emblazoned with the Royal Arms, advertising the brewers' own style and title as a limited liability company, together with their mark or badge; agricultural calendars which had turned dark brown in the smoke of more than half a century; the masks of two foxes, set with teeth a-snarl; a white pheasant in a glass case; a large ram's head; a leather collar of what was locally called a dicka—

little Dick the donkey. On a shelf were copper pans and beer-warmers, brass candlesticks beside dinted mortars and pestles, flasks for powder and shot; while laid on nails against the main oak beam which crossed the ceiling was an old flintlock goose gun. Hanging on the gun was a Corn Dolly, made of twisted straw with heabs of wheat in full ear. These things, together with the faces of those who had grown up with him since boyhood, formed part of the stockman's contentment as he sat loosely in the wheel-back chair, waiting to see if the characters would turn up.

When they did enter the low-beamed room, revealed in the open doorway by the light of the oil lamp hanging from a nail in the wall, his face at once assumed an expression of detachment as, avoiding to look at any one of them, he regarded his beer with an ingenuous stare. But soon the stockman was looking at them openly, aware that some on 'em had had sump'n to drink elsewhere.

The four men settled themselves noisily on the form against the further wall. The stockman thought to himself that they were no cop; young chaps who were likely to steal from anyone, while they were out for a bit of sport. Even so, he did not see why Wilbo should be robbed of his bards, even if he di'n't do no shu't'n.

"Bring four pints of sixpenny, guv!" said the Cockney, to the landlord, who stood and regarded their noisiness, while making no movement or sound himself.

After a pause, and stare, the landlord said, "What else?"

"That's all, guv!" retorted the Cockney, promptly. "What, ain't yer got nuffin but wallop?"

After a further pause, the landlord said, "I don't sell wallop. I sell beer, 'n I sell ale. And didn't yar mother teach you to say 'please'?"

"Blime, you're choosey, ain't you? Don't you under-

182

stand plain English? Four pints o' best beer—ale— please."

The landlord moved slowly towards the small adjoining room, with a low lean-to roof, where several barrels lay on trestles.

The stockman, with others who had done an honest day's work in the fields, listened with interested disapproval to what the characters were saying. The youngest of them, who was acting as though he had had too much beer, exclaimed:

"Too much bloo'y wind about ternight, thet's my opinion."

"Yar right, Billy."

"Nao!" The Cockney winked rapidly at the others, pretending to take the remark literally. He jerked his head, wearing a taxi-driver's peaked cap, at the back of the landlord. He had on a 'bus-driver's double-breasted jacket, with black leather on the sleeves. "Can't 'ave too much wind for this job, mate. The more wind the better. You ain't bin out with us before. 'Ope it blows a bleed'n gale. All you 'ave to remember, is to go upwind and upmoon. I seen bloody hundreds 's I was goin' to Scrivensett t' other evenin', and next day, comin' back with a norse from that bloke at Dallbrig I told yer abaht, I saw them in the sime plice, lookin' as vo they'd never'v shifted a bleed'n inch."

Here the stockman gave a slow wink to the man next to him. The next remark was made by the young man called Billy, who was the subject of joking among the four, since he had recently got married to a woman several years his senior.

"Won't th' wife be surprised when I turn out a sackful of partrisses for next Sunday's dinner!" To which the Cockney retorted, pushing his cap back on his head, and with a grin at the company, "Yuss mate, and won't you be surprised when you find you've set the old woman arterwards."

They remained there for the best part of an hour, in which time they drank four pints each, paying for the round in turn. Then, remarking that the moon would be up, the Cockney rose to his feet. "Let's get a move on. 'Ow about lettin' us 'ave some wallop in bot'les, cock?"

The landlord obviously had not yet taken to his guests. A burly man, his coat off and shirtsleeves rolled up, and smoking a pipe, he had moved during the evening quietly among his customers, taking their empty pint glasses to the barrel room, and returning to put them on the tables, collecting the money and slowly counting out the change in coppers. He worked a smallholding during the day-time, of four acres, growing corn and sugar-beet. Like most of the villagers who worked with their bodies rather than schemed with their heads, he was an honest man, forthright in speech when he spoke his mind—which was not often. Now he said slowly, "I told you I don't sell wallop. I sell ale, 'n I sell beer. An' I don't sell either in bo't'ols to your sort."

"Blime," said the Cockney, looking round with exaggerated surprise. "What's bit you ternight, guv? 'Ad a row wi' th' missus, or 'as the old pig gone off 'is feed?"

The burly smallholder advanced on him. "Get you out of this 'ouse," he said, slowly, unemotionally. "We don' wan' yer sort here. We ken dew wi'out yew. Get you gone."

The youths bundled to the door, the Cockney fighting a rearguard action with his wit. "What's the name of this boozer—'Orn and Corn don't they call it? You're the 'orn part all right, cock! That the old Dad up there?" He pointed to the stuffed ram's head, looking down from the wall with an expression not unlike that upon the land-lord's face. "'Ow long's 'e bin dead? Why don't yer bury

184

yer old man decent?" As the three others crushed through the door he uttered a loud "Baa-aa-aa!" then turned and vanished, while catcalls and laughter came from outside. The door slammed. Through the window the muffled barking of dogs in the village could be heard.

The innkeeper took a drink of his beer, and sat down quietly on a form. After a while he remarked as though disinterestedly, "Plenty of them sort travellin' 'bout nowadays," and relit his pipe.

"Blast!" said the stockman, quietly, to his neighbour, "I'd what you call like to see them-there characters come heads and holls the night, w'on I though!" He lifted his glass and swallowed the rest of his beer.

Outside, the characters were getting into a battered saloon car which had been bought off a dump for a pound. Unlicensed, it was hidden during the day in a shed behind a disused malting house near the quay of the nearby town —a little port which had been gradually silting and decaying since the Industrial Revolution—and used only at night, for pub-crawling, or for journeys to the Saturday Dirt-track Motorcycle Races.

Pertris had led Kakkabis and the covey of that season's rearing, followed by Chee-kai, through the hedge to the roosting field half an hour before owl-light. The birds had waited several minutes on the edge of the nettles growing under the hedge, watching unfamiliar low shapes on the field shaking in the wind. Reassured by the sameness of them, they had walked, with pauses for scrutiny, to the roosting place in the middle. The field, on the boundary of the farm, adjoined a road.

The partridges quatted on the ground, tail to tail with their heads outwards, thus enabling them to hear danger from any direction, while Chee-kai crouched in the middle of the circle. The shapes moving in the wind were now commonplace; the birds settled to rest, and soon were sleeping lightly on the soil. Little clots of black and white showed where they had roosted on previous nights.

An hour and a half before midnight, a yellow glow arose over the marshes lying to the east. As though pushed back by the wind moving over the land to the sea, the moon arose distended and red, to cast a luminous unreality upon field and cornstack, wood and wandering hedgerow. Soon upon the landscape another light appeared, wavering uncertainly with the curving of the lane; then it stopped, and its beam shone straight a moment, before going out.

The stockman, following up the hill, thought he would see some fun, and he was not disappointed. Standing by the hedge, he watched the car stop, and listened to the wild bellows of laughter as the characters got out. So prolonged was the merriment, the loud *Ho-ho's*, the noisy *Ha-ha-ha's*, as they staggered about doubled up with laughter, that he began to chuckle to himself. The noises subsided as they stood about, attending to the needs of nature, and he took advantage of it to move nearer to them, keeping hidden against the dark hedge.

The net was taken out of the car, and with subdued voices they moved down the drift, and so to the wide and level field, entering by the gateway, where were new oak posts and a gate which the stockman had helped to hang there.

He waited while they lined out behind the hedge, and set off across the field. The inexperienced youth called Billy was on the left; he seemed to have taken literally the Cockney's instructions, for after the net had been extended, he continued to walk down the hedge towards the moon, holding the end of the rope over his shoulder. Despite loud whispers, he trudged on, as though he were wading in the sea; whereupon the Cockney seized the rope and with an oath jerked it violently, pulling the other man off his feet backwards. There was a shout down the hedge; and immediately afterwards, a whirring of wings in the darkness.

At which the other man, on his feet once more, started to run, hauling rope and net towards the centre of the field, crying, "Come you on! I ken hear 'em. There's hunners in th' net! I ken hear 'em fluttering! Come you on! Keep you a-goin'!" He was running in an arc, collecting various thorn bushes in the net, and stopped only when he blundered into the others.

The Cockney was in a furious rage, and after some terse insults, some connected with Billy's recent marriage, he punched that youth on the jaw. Billy went down, but got up again, roaring that he wasn't going to hear the wife insulted by no man, and flung himself at the Cockney. They rolled on the ground, getting entangled in the net, and only stopped when the stockman strolled up, inquiring mildly what they were looking for. He pretended to be unaware of why they were there, and showed them the direction in which lay the road.

The next morning, revisiting the scene, he gathered up a torn net, once used for off-shore mackerel fishing, and after snapping several of its half-rotten meshes in his fingers to test its worth, he slung it over the gate, saying to himself that them as lost could find.

And going down to the meadows afterwards, to count his bullocks, he saw the two partridges and the longtail sunning themselves upon the terrace of the ant-hills.

Chapter Eighteen

Flocks of starlings flew across the sea, to feed on the milky kernels of the sprouting Michaelmas-sown wheat. Wagtails, pied, grey, and blue-headed, tripped over the waves after the starlings; the great grey shrike came with them, to perch in the blown thorn hedges dividing the first fields from the sheep walks and to clakker at kestrel and sparhawk wheeling overhead; woodcock followed in a night of yellow moon and on a north-east wind, the short-eared owls among them. Then came Harra the Denchman, with other of the grey-cloaked and hooded brethren, to pillage wood and hedgerow. They were slayers of small birds and rabbits, robbers of chicken runs, and killers of wounded game.

Behind the hydraulic tractor moving up and down the fields, flew many birds. After the summer bare-fallowing the arable was being plowed, to aerate the soil and to expose upon its furrows the largest area to the action of frost, and possibly, of snow. Glancing backwards at the swirl and scream of black-headed gulls following the bright breasts of the twin-plows reversing the surface of the earth, the impression given was of clamant and winged turbulence immediately behind resolving into a series of broken white spirals coiling off up-screwing furrows. Looking more particularly, the driver saw how each bird of many hundreds made its approach to the new-turned soil. Each gull as it alighted, with upheld tremulous wings and red mouth open to scream its excitement, ran along the furrow, jostling with others to pull at worm or grub only a few inches off the shine of travelling steel. The fortunate bird gulped rapidly, arose, flew to left or right of the line of plowing, gathered speed, and turned to sweep down again, perhaps to hang a moment, beating pearl-grey wings chalk-white underneath, a beak-thrust from the breaking earth.

The birds had no fear of the tractor or its driver, so long as the machine moved forward evenly and the driver remained a part of it. He sat on the iron seat, which was covered with a folded sack, and watched gulls hovering less than twelve inches from his face, feeling the tremulous excitement of life in the delicate soft shapes set with dark brown eyes, so different from the yellow-ringed, estranging sea-coldness within the eyes of larger herring gulls which never joined the sweeping, eddying throng of black-headed gulls. The herring gulls patrolled the seas and their living was of the wide grey turbulence of waves: they came on the land as rovers, alien and hostile; while the smaller gulls were of marsh and sand-bar, and gently ebbing creek, and the lands where the plow moved.

Sometimes the gulls flew away during the midday rest, and when the tractor started again the field was to the quieter pheasants, daws, and pigeons, all trustful of man and machine so long as it moved up and down the straight rectangles of the furrows. From the distance of a few yards the plowman could watch Oenas the wine-hued, Oenas the lover of summer days beside the river in the woodland's coolth, Oenas the stock-dove walking on coral-pink feet beside the spudded furrow-wheel trundling the brown earth. Oenas, shyest of birds, showed no fear of the machine whose engine-note beat against the smooth shear of the furrow as it turned over before breaking to fall loosely, so pleasantly to the eye of one in temper with the healing land . . . but if he so much as raised gloved hand to shapeless gull-splashed felt hat, or uttered a few notes of song, all wings would diminish as from a point of fear.

While plowing up and down a strip of land evernarrowing between the furrows the tractor passed a hare, crouching in its form scratched among a heap of clods. The hare remained there while the tractor roared away, and was still so crouching, as though hoping to escape detection, when it returned. The driver saw an animal entirely dominated by fear, its servant: not the smooth form of hare or rabbit seen in conventional pictures or behind the wire-netting of garden-hutch, but an uneven angularity or tensity of fear: long black-tipped ears pressed back: large pale resin-coloured eyes, set with staring black pupils, fixed ready to release with nervous fear-shock into the bloodstream a glandular fluid that would enable it to spring away with an acceleration abrupt and great—fleeing as the very spirit of fear, which was the major protective instinct of the hare, its tribal god. To the driver came the thought, Deprive such an animal of fear, and what did it become, in a cage of security?

When the sun shone, there was a feeling of exhilaration driving the light tractor that pressed upon the earth with half the weight of a horse's hoof, of optimism that the earth was being restored, that the diminished roots of the deeper-holding weeds—the capital or life-store of convolvulus, rest-harrow, creeping thistle, and couch-grass —would in the coming frosts, with the expansion of their sap, be burst, to shrivel and become humus, so helping to feed the soil for the orient and immortal corn which the town-mind despoiled of golden skin in its mills set above the slums of the half-lost, the dispossessed, the detonated flesh-fragments of Midas-wars. For as the sun went down, while a cold mist formed over the furrows, when gulls passed over in silence of successive flights to their roosting places in the marshes, and partridges began to call in the dusk, the spirit of the man on the machine began to droop with dark thoughts of what the future held. He knew that to work too long was to spoil the good effect of work, its reward in satisfaction; he had been plowing more than twelve hours, the body quiescent, the torso bent, the legs cold, the ears assailed by monotonous percussion. He was nerve-weary and dispirited, and feeling he could endure no more, he drove to the woodland yard. Feet were chilled, the very bones of the frame were cold.

The woodland yard had been built-up again, to hold in the coming years bullocks to tread the straw to make the muck to feed the land to grow the crops to nourish the people. Now it was empty; ready for the future. Its newness and tidiness were pleasing. He drained the radiator of water, tied down the canvas cover over the machine; then home across the Pightle between the High and Long woods—but quietly along the top, for in the middle of that sheltered area was the roosting circle of the partridge covey he had watched all the season, accompanied by the brilliant pheasant which his mind was beginning to regard as a symbol of resurgence and beauty.

Rain and wind threshed the trees and drove over the fields, stopping the plowing of the summer fallows. The tractor remained under cover in the woodland yard. The rains continued, splaying upon the clean buff metalling of the new roads the last of the fall's coloured leaves—brown of oak, hawthorn, and chestnut, yellow of willow and elm, black of sycamore, purple of guelder. With clouded water pouring from highway and field drain the river swilled ever higher, and the meadows were linked by wide plashes. The farmer went about with a worried look; he blamed himself for not working harder and longer before the weather broke; for like most subjective artists, once his mind was set on a thing, he could not rest until it was achieved. Both the teamsman and the stockman, genuinely concerned that he should succeed, tried to assure him that the plowing did not matter, that it could be done early in the year. The slight difference in the weathering of the unplowed section, they declared, would make no difference to the sample of barley. They could not understand why he declared that all he had done so far was nothing, nor why it was no consolation to him to be told that most of the other smallholders and farmers in the district still had the best part of their plowing to do. "Why, yar a year ahead on'm, master, arter all the wark'v cleanin' of it up! Don't ya ever injoy yarself, guv'nor? Why not hev a day'n knock over some of them fessaunts? If ya doan't, others will, I'm thinkin'."

The stockman had said nothing of the attempt to net the birds.

In a country district of heavy land, of dark clay overlying that most obdurate of all subsoils, the blue lias, old farmers used to say that to farm land properly, a man must go down on his knees to it. He must approach it with care, he must know when to go upon it, and above all, he must be sure to know when to keep off it; for if he plowed when heavy land was sodden with moisture, the furrows would turn up cold, claggy, and dour, and even the hardest frost following would not break up the wet slippery slabs into mounded rows of granulated tilth when, partly dried out by the ransoming winds of March, they would be ready for the first jubilant harrow-stroke of spring. To go upon heavy land when it was not fit was to compress it, to compound it, to puddle it as clay under

192

pressure of the potter's fingers, to kill it, so that no number of consequent cultivations, harrowings, rib-rollings, baulk-sladings, poundings, scratchings, stirrings, overwhart plowings would break down the lourdan texture to be as the castings of the shovel-paw'd mole—an animal lowly maybe, but one that, nevertheless, knew when to keep off heavy land.

The new farmer knew this; but his mind was driven, in revulsion against the complacency he saw everywhere about him, by the thought of action to counter the desperate brevity of time. One morning when weak sunshine was coming through a shining rift of low nimbus cloud, he uncovered the tractor, and re-entered the furrow where he had withdrawn the plow when the rains came. The field was upon the uplands, above the scalt coastal fields of sand and flint; it was a brown loam lying upon a yellow clay, and sticky when wet. The wind cut keenly across the field, with its steely winter view over meadows, marshes, sandhills, and sea.

Sometimes one or another of the twin steel revolving discs, the coulters cutting the ground for the lift of share and mouldboard, ceased to turn, being clogged with brown clay; whereupon the plows began, in the teamsman's phrase, to slade along the ground. Immediately the throttle was closed several thousand white birds, which had been jostling and screaming behind the twin brown slabs corkscrewing up behind the mild roar of the exhaust, took to silent flight.

For a moment only there was the peace of silence; then the white outward flight broke up and became individual birds anxiously waiting for the tractor to move forward. With clawed fingers heaving and pushing the shambled masses of clay, the plowman strove to clear the breasts, to turn the thin steel plates which were wedged by flints in their bearings; and when all was free again he put back the sack, which the wind had lifted off the seat, straddled his right leg over, and vaulted into position. Clutch out and gear in, lift of throttle lever, clutch in: machine roaring slowly forward again. A moment only, and the gulls were sweeping back, to dip screaming and to alight to pull at worm, to arise again to beat away into the wind, to swing round and down again, to hover and drop upon the breaking furrow-slice.

Once a bird, eager to get before the others, was caught by the falling earth and pinned beneath. The driver went on, until a sudden silence upon the departure of the flock made him look round. A white point was upheld out of the furrow a score of yards behind him. Walking back, he knelt to heave up the heavy slab, and uncovered a bird, which he held upon the palms of his hands, head to wind, until it recovered, and took off slowly and lightly into the air. While he was watching it wafting itself unevenly away, the sound of two shots came through the wind over his right shoulder, from the tall hedge which was the boundary of the farm. Looking across the level furrows, he saw a man standing beside the hedge, holding up a red flag on a stick. Only then, with a start, did he realize that he had not seen any pheasants walking upon the field while he had been plowing. Immediately he ran to the tractor and switched off the engine.

Away south, across fields invisible from where he was standing, a score of beaters were walking in line across two fields of sugar-beet, striking with sticks at the green and yellow tops of the plants as they did so. A man on horseback directed them, in the middle of the line. The beaters, as they moved methodically forward, were driving the game off the outlying root fields to the shooters waiting behind a tall hedge half a mile to the north. The man with the red flag had been placed there to stop any birds swinging downwind to the hollow beyond the boundary, and so off the land of his master.

More shots came from the south, where, among the advancing beaters, three of the guns were walking, to take any birds breaking away to the flanks or back over the line. The remaining six of the nine guns were spaced out at the stand behind the distant hedge towards which the pheasants, partridges, and hares which fed in the sugar-beet fields were being driven.

The labouring man holding the red cloth on the upheld stick fluttering in the wind was watching the "foreigner" through the leafless hedge. The "stop" stood upon a dark brown field, in one corner of which was a darker brown stack of sanfoin. It was a field favoured by partridges, for the aftermath of the sanfoin yielded many seeds. The soil there was clover-sick, so the coarse sanfoin was grown once every four years in rotation instead of the more usual small seeds mixture of ryegrass and clover. The pink flowers of the sanfoin had been murmurous with bees during the past June. Since the plowing of the adjoining fallow field, the partridges, with Chee-kai, had been roosting at night upon the sanfoin aftermath, and feeding by day in the sugar-beet and neighbouring fields.

The neighbouring farmer knew that; and therefore had ordered the stop to remain there until the beaters came level with him. The red flag would turn the birds driven from the roots from crossing the boundary to the safety of Pightle or High Wood: they would pitch in the sanfoin, and run to its centre, from where the beaters would bring them over the stand.

The man with the flag was a labourer who had worked, since leaving school a score of years before, on the yeoman's farm. He wore a woollen helmet over his head and ears, a long dark overcoat, and strips of sugar-beet pulp-bag were tied round his legs from the knees downwards, to protect them from the wet. He was smoking a fag, content with his easy day, for which he received pay at the full rate of six shillings, as well as a free lunch of bread, cheese, and beer. He was happy in his work, and regarded a day's beating as a holiday, and rest from muck-filling, a job he had been working on during the past fortnight: filling sixteen tumbrils a day with well-rotted bullock-muck, each load weighing approximately three-quarters of a ton—twelve tons a day, for six shillings.

The line of beaters was now coming across the second field of roots, at a slow but steady pace. The steward of the farm, on a bay cob, rode just behind the line. He was a red-faced man with sandy hair and eyebrows, and a wide grin, an amiable, all-weathers figure, reliable as the sun that rose red out of the east and set red in the west, a sturdy wide-bodied six-hundred acres man nicknamed Dick Turpin, who had lived through nearly seventy cycles of seasons with root and corn, hay and horn. The lives of the jovial steward's several sons were involved in the same seasons upon the land with him; one was the keeper, another a tractor-driver, a third a teamsman, the fourth a cowman. He bore the worries of his master and other problems of stewardship with a constant easy slowness which came from the settled knowledge that all things pass, yet come again.

Checked from their running through the green and yellow leaves of the matured roots by the hedge bordering the road, pheasants, both cocks and hens, began to rise up, flying strongly over the low line of thorn and holly, and coming to the summits of their flights over the sanfoin, beat strongly towards the shelter of a distant field of cabbages; and so they flew over the guns concealed behind a hedge halfway there, meeting the upward cracks and hissings of lead pellets. Now they were coming in threes and fours, in fives and sixes, boxed within the three sides of a rectangle of peril by shots behind and alarming red movements on either side. Fleeing over the sanfoin, with rocketing wings, impelled onwards by fear, and desire to reach the safety of the flatpoll field, many realized too late the mort-blast below them. They crumpled. Glossy cocks, of between three and four pounds in weight from feeding on barley, dropped to bounce thudding upon the stubbles. Partridges, crouching and running over the sanfoin, stopping with heads held up to watch, to listen, before running on again, obedient to their leader whose life was devoted in care and vigilance to the covey, sprang up at a call to fly forward with thropping of wings and crutchets of alarm. Strongly they flew onwards, skimming low over the hedge, while mature men who had shot driven birds since youth swung left upon a winged mark, and pulled; and almost before the bird had collapsed in the air, had swung right and fired the choked barrel, which bunched the pellets closer to strike upon the more distant mark; which fell.

One covey, which had run through the hedge, over the tarmac road, through the second hedge near a long yellow clamp of beet awaiting the ten-ton lorry, was moving over the sanfoin, now running, now pausing to look around and to listen. It reached left of centre of the brown field, where it stood still, the birds close together, a pheasant of unusual colouring and extraordinarily long tail accompanying them. Minute after minute the stopman with the flag watched the unusual sight. "Th' bard wor as yulla as a paigle," he said afterwards—its back yellow as a cowslip. As the beaters and the shooter on the flank came through the hedge and so to the sanfoin aftermath, he began pointing significantly with one mitten'd hand. The shooter held his gun before him, ready to lift it to his shoulder, but fifty yards away from the beaters

197

the covey flew up, appeared to hesitate, swerved sharply, and turned downwind. Despite shouts and the waggled red flag they flew on, low and fast to the boundary hedge. Two shots were fired after them, but the birds were out of range. The pellets scattered and were declining as they passed below and behind the covey which, with wings downcurved and shifting to ride the currents of air, glided steeply down the adjacent field to the hollow where the Long Wood came to an end. There they wheeled, and alighted on the plowed work.

The incident had been watched by the steward on horse-back with an expression of childlike wonder on his face. To the horse's upstanding ears the steward exclaimed, "T'at's a rum'n!" and in reply the animal made sounds like *wuf*, *wuf*, *wuf*. Both utterances seemed to annoy the yeoman farmer who, against his judgment, had fired the long shots at the strange pheasant, for he exclaimed, "Damned old grinner!" as though holding man and horse behind him to blame for the breaking-away of the birds.

After the shooting that day, two unusual incidents were discussed round the table in the farmhouse parlour where nearly a score of men and women sat at tea, during which a slip of paper was passed to the host, on which was written, in Dick Turpin's fist, the day's bag of pheasants, partridges, hares, woodcock, golden plover, snipe, and pigeons.

One was the sight of seven short-eared owls rising all together out of the rough ground of the Common, and, not being shot at, beating away from that place which lay in a groove of the hills between the farms. The second was the pheasant with the long tail flying faster than the covey of partridges, yet low as a partridge flies, avoiding rather than seeking height, a bird which had appeared to

198

lead the covey away from the line of guns at the second stand. It had flown on to the land of the newcomer whose presence in the neighbourhood was something of a mystery, and had not been seen again.

Chapter Nineteen

E ver since the summer Chee-kai had lived with the partridges a quiet and wary life interrupted only by minor shocks, as when a stoat seized one bird while they were resting at midday on the sunny side of the new-cut hedge along the hollow of the steep field; or when, a month before, during flight across the road, a partridge had struck the wires stretched between telegraph poles, and fallen with broken neck on the sugar-beet dump below. Chee-kai, following the covey, had seen the familiar curve-winged gliding flight of the partridge suddenly crumpling, but as no gunshot followed immediately, his consciousness had not been more than momentarily shattered; he had flown on more rapidly, skidding before the smaller brown birds, his long tail feathers making a whistling noise, to pitch in the centre of the field, under which the spread sugar-beet tops had been plowed. The shooting season had ended a couple of weeks back, when Harcourt the yeoman farmer, accompanied by his son and a couple of friends with their sons carrying 28-bores, and a keeper with a black Labrador dog, had taken a walk round his hedges and thorn-grown marlpits, to shoot all the cocks seen. Thereafter the fields and woods of late January and early February had been silent. No shot had sounded. Rabbits had been dug out, or bolted with purse-nets over their holes in the woods, with the aid of ferrets on lines; for owners of sportings wished the remaining stock of hen-birds to be at peace for the coming nestings. Those farmers whose lands adjoined the newcomer's were content that there had been no shooting there during the season, for their own stocks would be increased by straying birds. Even so, one grumbled that vermin would increase, and spread over his land: he was a man who habitually shot his birds closer than his neighbours, who were not unaware that their own stocks of hens would have to make up the difference: for pheasants stray, and spread themselves where there is food and no opposition.

It was a quiet time for arable farmers. The fields were sodden, unfit to go upon. The men carted muck from the yards, making square dungles to heat and rot weed-seeds inside fields of layer, ready for spreading upon the olland to plow under for wheat in the following October.

Meanwhile, the stewards awaited drying east winds of late February and early March to carry off the surface moisture within the frost-fretted furrows, when they would start the annual race to get the barley in.

Within the cowhouse of the premises the stockman had a rusty muzzle-loading, single-barrel gun. It was usually kept hidden within a wooden bin of crushed oats standing against the wall in the cow-house.

This wooden bin was dirty with marks of milk-greasy hands, bored by death-watch beetles, and gnawn by rats during the half-century of its existence. It was the stock-man's personal property, having been bought by him, with other firewood, for a shilling at the auction of his late master's effects. On the inside bottom of the bin, which had been clumsily patched with beaten biscuit-tin metal to cover the gnawn holes, was a blackish layer of ancient oats which was the home of weevils and moths: insects which periodically migrated to various buildings of the premises, to start other colonies feeding on meal, sacks, flannel linings of horse-collars, and old coats hung on wooden pegs in the stable.

Wilbo, observing all this decaying rubbish as he called it to himself, had wanted to bury it in his compost heaps, to burn the wooden bin with other wreckage of bullock and sheep troughs, ancient wooden axles and hubs of broken waggon wheels lying under the nettle patches, and so start anew, clear of these sad relics of the past; but he had seen that the stockman was attached to his oat-bin, as the teamsman demurred at the removal of old cob-webbed coats and mouldy horse-collars from his stable; and so the rubbish remained, with a feeling of frustration for the new man, who did not like to compel anyone except himself. He had seen the gun in the bin, and had wondered what it was doing there, as he had wondered about the net piled in another corner of the cowshed; but he had merely remarked that all wild birds were his friends, that he didn't like to see them shot at, and hoped that would be sufficient.

The fact was, the gun, for which the stockman had paid a crown, had been inside the box ever since his former master had given him permission to shoot pigeons from a hide in the Pine Wood during February and March.

Wilbo had bought some pedigree Rhode Island Red pullets and three new fold-units, and also some notebooks wherein he entered every day the number of eggs that were taken from the nesting boxes attached to the movable houses. The pullets were allowed to range freely, for their health's sake, since it had been decided that it was not practicable to fold them over the little paddock by the premises for the purpose of encouraging the clovers and finer grasses, with the fertility of the birds' droppings, to make a better grazing there; for the paddock, neglected for so many years, was but a wilderness of coarser weeds and rank plants. So the fold-units remained as houses, mere shelters for the night; while the birds roamed freely by day, picking up their food in the yards where recently bought Redpoll in-calf heifers, nucleus of a milking herd, trod straw spread as litter and bedding. Some of the hens made nests in the mangers, or bings as the stockman called them, and eggs were collected from these unofficial nests by the stockman, who had not told his master of their presence there, on the principle that what the eye can't see, the heart won't grieve over.

Intent on his vision of perfection, which included the laying of eggs in the correct places provided in the creo-soted fold-units, Wilbo, coming upon the stockman with eggs one morning clutched in his gnarled hands and also placed in the pockets of his ragged coat, had won-dered for a moment if his man were honest: for he con-fided freely and without reserve all particulars of the farm's business to the stockman, and hoped for a like frankness over details in return. He had often told his men that they could say anything they liked to say to him, declaring that the truth was as clear as sunshine, if only men would not conceal their real thoughts within the darkness of self. Now he waited for the stockman to speak, but all the old fellow said was " 'Tes nature," as he clutched a dozen clean buff oval eggs, saying to himself that the pullets were laying where they liked best to be, among the beasts in the yards. The stockman walked off in silence, and later handed in the eggs at the open granary door.

A week or so later, when he and his son had observed that certain jackdaws which flew about the premises, coming from the beech trees above the quarry and from holes and ledges of the chalk-face, were after the eggs, the stockman, to "sarve master's interests", determined to scare the black thieves with a charge of shot. And on the morning when Chee-kai was feeding within the fringe of the pine trees on the hillcrest with the partridges, the stockman surprised three jackdaws flying out of the yard, each with an egg in its beak; whereupon he got the gun out of the wooden bin, and after blowing into the barrel several times to remove moths, with spiders and blue-bottles hibernating there, and dusting his weapon stuck all over with weevil cases made of crushed-oats gummed together by the pupating grubs, he poured a charge of black powder from a metal flask kept on a shelf, rammed scraps of newspaper upon the powder with the ash ramrod, poured some shot from another flask, rammed more paper on the shot to keep it from trickling out, and waited in the hovel behind the new seed-drill, knowing that the daws would return for more. Which they did soon afterwards, excited by their thoughts of such fine food being provided for them after so long an absence of good husbandry upon their hereditary feeding grounds. BANG! went the old muzzle-loader; dust shot sighed upwards; blue smoke hung in the damp air; fragments of scorched paper floated down; the rocket of wings came from the pines above, as a golden arrow sped whistling eastward over the trees of the Long Wood.

It so happened that Wilbo was passing by the Corn Barn when the gun was fired; he heard also the whistling wings of Chee-kai. Hurrying round the corner of the long hovel, with its ten bays for tumbrils and implements separated by oak posts standing on stone feet, he came upon the stockman holding the gun in his hands, a quizzical expression of innocence in his simple brown eyes. On the ground near him lay a jackdaw, with a broken egg near it. "Hullo, what's this?" he enquired. "One of yar friends," replied the stockman, simply. Wilbo remembered, and smiled. "For a moment I thought you had fired at something else," he said; and passed on to his business of measuring the cow-house for installing a milking-machine. He was watched a few minutes later by the stockman who had followed him, and who regarded with disquiet what was being done. He was the more subdued, because he felt that in the matter of "the bards", he was not trusted.

Chee-kai had been feeding on ants, with Pertris and Kakkabis and the survivors of their covey, in the pine-wood that crested darkly the hill above the farm premises when the flat report, followed by a puffy blue smoke, made him crouch with fast-beating heart, before rising and flying away through the trees. He flew back again to the pine tree growing at the northern end of the Carr. After one uneasy night upon the ivy thick under its top-most branches, he resumed his former spring-time habit of walking and living by himself. As before, he sought food within the wood and upon the meadow and the Breck field rising up to the clustered trees of the High Wood. Clear days followed the passing of the frosts, when the cries of partridges were heard more frequently on the land; and always when he heard the familiar *chur-wick, chur-wick*, he held up his head to try and locate the calling bird, and a high, frail note would come from his closed beak. Once he saw a cock partridge running with another down a furrow near where he was searching for food, and moved to greet it; but the bird, not being Pertris, ran at him, to strike with wing, beak, and foot, whereupon Chee-kai turned away, and stood still, alone, as though undecided. Thereafter the cries at dusk and early morning, while always he paused alertly to listen to them, did not cause him to lift his head so high as with his former eagerness.

Once again through the peaceful countryside sounded the familiar and gladdening cry of the green woodpecker, ringing through woodland and field, *yaffle*, *yaffle*, *yaffle*, to be answered by the cries of titmice like the ringing of little bells. From over the grey serrated seascape came drying winds which stroked the dark plowlands, changing their hues until farmers or their stewards went upon the fields to kick the clods lightly with their boots, and observe how they broke to the movement. They drew their toecaps under the crust of furrows, and stared at the land, reckoning how long before it was fit.

In barns of old-fashioned farms men were set to work to dress the seed-corn which had lain all winter in rat-bedraggled pyramids upon the asphalt floors. Wooden dressing-machines, pride of mid-Victorian Agricultural Shows, were dragged out from dust and shadow; rusty sieves were put in place; oil was poured upon holes long since caked solid with ancient grease and dowst. While Dick or Tom scooped up bushel-measures of seed to pour between the wooden lips, Jim or Bob turned the crank which spun the wooden vanes which blew out the shrunken grains and shook the wire-sieves that sifted the tail-corn to the floor, while Ned or Joe shovelled the dressed corn into sacks of four-bushel content. On less old-fashioned farms the work was done by electricity, with but one man feeding corn and sacking seed; while modern farmers, having threshed out and cashed out all their barley, thereby suffering no loss by rats and mice, bought direct from seed-merchants in warehouses of market towns equipped with up-to-date machinery, Spratt Archer, Golden Archer, Plumage Archer, or small-strawed Danish barley already treated with mercuric powder against the spores of fungus diseases which might be lodged in crevices of the hard skins of the grain.

In the past season barley, the principal corn crop of the

country, had met a collapsed market, with prices dropping over 50 per cent below the prices of the previous harvest, since grain in many shiploads had been purchased by the City of London from Central Europe. Many farmers of East Anglia, unable to pay their debts by the meagre prices they received in the Corn Hall, went bankrupt, and were sold up.

Once again over a peaceful landscape moved teams of horses and mechanocades of tractors, to make the seed beds upon the light and medium and heavy lands, by drawing harrows, cultivators, rolls, chemical-manure distributors, seed drills, and seed harrows over the earth. Once again the cock pheasants, their fighting done and their territories held against rivals, stalked from the cover of coppice, marlpit, and hedgerow, and among their dun and complacent hens took the grains buried scratching-deep in the levelled brown soils. Farmers who held the copyholds of their lands, or whose rents included the sporting rights of depressed and absentee landlords, did not worry over the seed so taken; indeed, by custom, they included in the drilling an extra peck per acre for the birds, including rooks which knew how to discover the straight sowings even though the fields had been left harrowed overtwhart the drills. Black beaks preceding parchment-white faces of older birds—black hairs worn away by so much digging—uprooted the grain in the lines in which it had been dropped by the iron spouts, and while the mercuric powder caused a slight discomfort of indigestion, it served to rid livers and guts of parasites: an annual tonic.

Once again, as during all the centuries since the clearing of the forests—the history of man's husbandry upon the clearings, his settlements and departures, was to be read in the mud strata of the beds of dried meres and fens of the interior, which recorded in layers the varying and distinguishable pollen drifts of the forests and their clearings of grass and corn—men worked to grow food, in the hope that their labour would not be in vain, in the subconscious fear that their wives and families would suffer if they lost their occupations: not, as in previous ages, because there was not enough being produced, but because there was too much food and too many goods being made in the world, so that men lost their work and starved, or died in wars for export markets.

After the gathering of the following corn harvest the stockman said, "Yew ought to thank God yew had such fine carn this season, Guv'nor. Why, they're the best barleys in the district. And look at the price! More than double what it was last year, and narthin' started yet." He glanced into the serene blue sky. "I reckon yew ken count yarself lucky." But the Flockmaster, a man more of the market place, remarked down at the Cross, "Ah, Wilbo knew a thing or two, ah di'n'e? He knew what was comin', 'bor! An 'e knaw more than he would care to tell tew, ah, thet 'e du!"

Chapter Twenty

Out of a starless void, upon roads joining lightless villages and darkened market towns, upon lanes and drifts leading from sombre farm premises to the wide extent of arable fields divided by hedges and thickets and the darker masses of woods, snow·was falling, shrouding a landscape where all life was as though suspended. All the creatures of the day had gone to their homes, whether of hole in earth or tree, lee-side of hedge or building of flint, mortar, and wood, sheltering from the wet touch of flakes which fell sight-lessly about a soundless world; while the night creatures, unaccustomed to the change upon their senses, to the per-sistent, disturbing touch of snow on ball of eye, nose and hair-sensitive ear cavity, were reluctant to move into the grey unknown.

At first the snow melted on the warm surfaces of roads and lanes, which showed dark between the hedges, but as more flakes dropped in the thick air they merged into the fields reflecting the dim infiltrated pallor of the moon. Teamsmen feeling their way with outstretched hands to their stables found rest and meditation in the familiar ammoniacal darkness where, against wall or warm flank of horse, they smoked awhile before groping a return to their cottages through a silence that seemed to sigh as with the thoughts of poor people.

All night snow fell, and in the morning the sun rising out of the level sea of the south-east looked upon a new world. As the plangent beams glittered upon white fields and spread radiant through boles and branches of trees, Chee-kai, exhilarated by the scintillant gold, sat in the top of the pine, ensconced within a hollow of snow clogging the mat of needles, cones, and ivy leaves. The snow-crust level with the white collar around his neck gave shelter from the occasional winds that moved coldly through the branches. He sat warm in the brilliant light from the open southern sky, enjoying from on high the sparkle and spangle of a crystalline world. Throughout the morning he sat there in his eyrie, without desire to eat; the lightness of the air after foggy nights of frost, and misty noonday thawings, seemed to sustain him. When thirsty he pecked at the snow, which gave him a taste for the resinous needles; he snipped them with the sharp cutting edge of the upper mandible of his beak and swallowed, liking the flavour. The sun climbed on its low curve over the High Wood, and he sat within his shelter, sometimes drawing himself up to stretch a leg and wing, then another leg and wing, afterwards shaking his feathers, and settling to preen his flight quills.

For some weeks, whenever he could hurry away from his work, the farmer had walked about the edges of woods and down the hedges between fields, looking for Chee-kai, dreading that the bird had been shot. He had seen Pertris and Kakkabis, with four of their remaining covey, but the pheasant had not been with them.

On the afternoon following the night's snow he walked to the woodland yard, to see the beasts which had been there since coming off the meadows in mid-October. The stockman went to the yard twice a day, to feed twelve red-poll heifers and a bull on barley chaff and sugar-beet tops, mixed with crushed oats and decorticated ground nut cake, with long hay put in the racks for the beasts to pull. Two five-hundred-gallon tanks, holding rainwater from the gutters, stood on concrete platforms in the yard.

After looking at the contented beasts, the farmer went down through the wood to the top of the Breck, and leaning against a tree, took the glass from its case, and began methodically to examine the meadow and the Carr. His eye caught a flash of yellow on the top of the pine at the northern end of the wood, and focusing the glass upon it, he discovered where the bird was sheltering.

A man hidden in another part of the High Wood watched the figure standing, glass to eye, looking in the direction of the sea. At the sight, a feeling of exultation came upon the hidden man. He was a poacher, from the hamlet a couple of miles east along the coast road. A small-bore shotgun, folded, was hidden in a large pocket within the lining of his jacket. The feeling of exultation that he could advance himself in the eyes of his fellows by reporting a spy gave way to a steadier satisfaction in thinking that if he kept what he had seen to himself it would be a good excuse to explain his presence in the wood if ever he were found there. For now that war had come, the new farmer was the subject of much talk and suspicious regard in the locality.

Unknown to both men, patrols of soldiers had been out on the marshes night after night, with orders to arrest, and to shoot if arrest were resisted, anyone seen signalling out to sea. The soldiers had groused at the job, but the orders had come from Eastern Command, acting on information received from London.

In the February days that followed, frost hardened the snow lying upon fields of winter wheat, clover ley, cab-

bage, carrot, and other vegetables, and bound the waters
of the dykes. Harra the Denchman flew about the woods
and meadows, seeking small birds and rodents enfeebled
by lack of food, while flocks of wild pigeons assembled
from afar upon the fields of cabbage and kale. Some
farmers made hides among the snow-laden cabbages, to
shoot the hungry birds as they flew down: the flocks
flew up rapidly and away to other feeding places, and
circled widely, before coming down to perch in treetops
whence their sharp eyes could detect movement of the
enemy, man. Sometimes several thousand birds were seen
in the air at once, or in a great flock descending with
tumultuous clapping of wings. At a shot the roar of rising
birds shook the cabbage plants; the pigeons flew around
in lesser flocks which dropped down again to the vision
of greenery below—and the reports of guns. There were
not many farmers shooting pigeons that first winter of
the war, for the price paid by the dealers was but four-
pence a bird.

The red-polled heifers were warm and content with
their bull inside the rails and posts of the woodland yard;
for around the rails arose straw stacks, which had been
made there when the corn stacks had been threshed. The
tall yellow cliffs kept out the winds, and held in the
warmth. The beasts were, in the stockman's phrase,
"doin' ". The farmer went to the yard every day, sometimes with his wife or son, who now lived in a pair of
cottages converted into a farmhouse in the village. But
usually he went alone, taking his lunch with him. Hidden
in the straw on the top of the stack, he spent many hours
watching, sketchbook before him, and pencil held in
mitten'd hand.

The woodland yard was farthest from the village and
the damp, sunless yards and moss-grown premises under
the quarry and beech-wood, and always the thought that

the straw was being trodden into muck, right beside the fields where it was needed—no backbreaking haulage up the hill from the premises below—was pleasing. Sometimes he stood within the yard, near the beasts, sharing their contentment and warm-brown placidity.

There was little that could be done on the land; but the cutting of the hedges was proceeding, most of the limbs and trunks being piled for firewood for the open hearths of the farmhouse; the farmer would not burn any coal. Often after working with axe and slasher he walked to the yard, in order to think, or rather, to empty himself of thought, the glass in its case slung on his shoulder.

One afternoon, towards the end of February, after the heifers had eaten their feed, and were standing together near the empty hayracks, some with licked patches on their coats, others bending heads back to pass long rough tongues over the hair of ribs and hips, he was leaning on the rails as usual and watching them, feeling their deep and simple contentment, when he noticed a bird's head looking round one of the five-hundred-gallon tanks which collected water from the roof of the shed enclosing the north end of the yard. He kept still, and soon a cinnamon-coloured cockerel, with a smoke-grey mantle of feathers on its back, walked forth upon the straw. This was a wild bird, that lived about the yard. It had been the only chick to survive with a strayed hen who had laid in the woods and hatched forth a dozen eggs. Crows, weasels, rats, and the wild cat which had moved from the Carr to the High Wood, and which lived in a deep rabbit burrow, had taken the others. The solitary chick had grown up swift and wild, and whenever it had seen the figure of a man, it had run instantly into the corn. The hen, too, had become wild and quick, holding spread wings low and running with urgent noises in brief circles to draw pursuit from the hiding chick. But one morning she had been caught in a rabbit gin, and killed and without further ado put in a sack by the trapper, who had bought the right to trap rabbits on the farm during the winter, for ten pounds. Thereafter the cockerel, as the chick became when its tail feathers sprouted in a flaunting curve of smoke-grey and light brown, roosted by night on a rail of the yard, sheltered from the weather in a cavity where a heifer had pulled and eaten the palatable barley straw from the stack. But seeing the approach of a man, the cockerel would run into the woods and hide until it was quiet once more.

The heifers stood easily in the yard, their bellies filled, some licking their coats in satisfaction. The young bull stood in a corner, apart from them, without ambition and with little fire, for he had served his turn upon them all, and now was interested only in food, water, and peace. Standing motionless in an opposite corner, the farmer watched the cockerel as it walked across the litter, and flew up to one of the pressure-creosoted circular bins, wherein, after looking around for unusual movement, it hopped to pick up scraps of ground-nut cake and crushed oats. The farmer watched it, his eyes observing the sickle-like shape of its tail feathers quivering as it pecked.

The cockerel suddenly lifted its head to listen. From far away had come a whistle, followed by the noise of wood knocking against an iron pail. The whistling came again; but this time it was followed by bubbling, jockling cries from another direction, and the flapping of wings. The farmer's wife had come up from the premises with the afternoon pailful of mixed mash and tail-corn for the ten hen turkeys and two stag birds which lived in the wood. The turkeys ran over the snow to meet the woman, and followed her, with long striding steps, like animated old and tattered umbrellas, to the woodland yard.

Hearing their approach, the cockerel hopped to the

edge of the manger, drew itself up, flapped its wings, and crowed a challenge. For the cockerel claimed the yard and about an acre of woodland as its territory, which it shared only with its friends; and the turkeys were certainly not among its friends.

The farmer, immobile against the rails, was puzzled to know why the cockerel, apparently a lone bird, was so aggressive in its attitude towards the turkeys. When those deliberate, stalking birds, whose pink wattles so often turned pale blue as they uttered their broken-bottle cries in unison, had invaded one or another of the yards of the premises, the Rhode Island cock who watched over the hens of his area would usually attack them, and fight as he retreated before the slow, massed advance of the dark aliens; but in every case the cock was directly defending his hens, and their feeding grounds indirectly. Why then should an unmated and solitary cockerel fight the turkeys whenever they stalked near, or into, the isolated woodland yard? For birds, like men and other mammals, fought only for race and soil.

The bubble-jockle cries came nearer; and at last the rattle of the wooden spoon on the galvanized iron pail sounded by the five-barred gate, low and visible in the gap between two straw stacks. For protection against wind, faggots of brushwood had been laid upright against the gate. The farmer was standing to one side of the gate, keeping himself as still as he could, trying to move not so much as an eyelid. The cockerel was perched on the upright rim of the circular bullock bin, making slight clucking noises as though to itself; but a slight movement by the base of the water tank was observed by the farmer, and staring intently, he saw that a hen-pheasant was waiting there.

The next moment the cockerel flew down from the rim of the circular wooden trough, and muttering angrily to itself, ran to the water tank, and disappeared with the hen pheasant. Apparently it had gone to fight the turkeys, for almost immediately afterwards the jockling cries broke out in a chorus; the cockerel crowed raucously; then strutted, hackles raised, to run swiftly at the nearest intruder, to jump and strike at it with its spurs. The hen turkey went pale about the cheek pendules, and staggered backwards; but a stag bird advanced to lean down and deliver a sharp blow with its beak on the comb of the cockerel. The cockerel retreated, only to run in suddenly upon the stag bird and jump at it, while two other turkeys on either side of it advanced to lean and peck; the cockerel retreated just in time. So the umbelliferant cohort moved gradually forward, in a broken semicircle, while the smaller pale-feathered bird dashed in upon first one then another, only to retreat immediately afterwards.

The rearguard action continued round the corner of the shed, whereupon the farmer, climbing on the rails by the gate, pulled himself upon a shelf of the straw stack, which had been cut level by the big-bladed hay knife in course of littering the yard. From the shelf he slid down the outer straw to where his wife stood below, the handle of the empty feed bucket slung over the crook of one arm, and holding a small boy by the hand. While the dark eyes of the boy were fixed upon him, the farmer told them excitedly that the wild cockerel might mate, later on, with a hen pheasant.

Perched on the top of the pine-tree, Chee-kai heard the crowing of the cockerel in the High Wood, and the sound moved in him a desire to eat: for the woodland yard was one of the places he visited for food. Many a time had he scratched in the heaps of cavings which after the threshing of the barley stacks had been carted into the wood and left under the big chestnut tree that grew in that place

216

amidst oaks, elms, and self-sown elderberries. The heaps held barley kernels, and sometimes while scratching there Chee-kai had uncovered an object that he swallowed eagerly—a currant. The stacks, too, were good to visit, for the small mice which lived in the straw; while in the lean-to shed erected by the farmer were stored mangold roots and sacks of broken cattle-cake, fragments of which were often to be found on the floor of dried earth. Usually Chee-kai visited the yard in the early morning, before men were about, while the heifers were lying, their forelegs folded under them, chewing the cud of barley straw and long hay they had pulled from stack and rack during the night.

Chee-kai listened to the second crowing of the cockerel, to the faraway whistle and the rattle of the bucket; and at the familiar sounds he drew himself up, beat his wings together, and jumped into the air. He flew strongly over the meadow and the tall ragged hedge, and up the slope of the field, and so to the wood, where he glided between the pine-trees at its edge, to alight on the snow. He listened and peered, before walking in the direction of the yard.

A weasel ran fast over the snow near him, and he jumped with fear and alarm, crouching ready to spring into flight from the sight of the low rapid ripple that made him feel as though he were scattered out of his being, and half-helpless to get himself together again: but the weasel was hunting a rat by scent, and disappeared down a rabbit hole wherein the rat had crawled, already enfeebled by the imaginative blood-sweats of death which its will could not resist. From underground there came an impotent scream, which set Chee-kai free again, so that he ran away into the wood. A moment later he had forgotten the weasel.

Across the level field, tinged with the ruddy hues of the

sun descending behind the freezing vapours of the west, the farmer's wife and child were walking home. Chee-kai looked at them from the edge of the wood, and then at the shapes of turkeys swaying on the lower branches of an ivy-clad sycamore, as they prepared to jump and flap into the top of the tree, their usual roost at night.

A cry of *cher-wick churr-wick* came from the adjoining field. Hidden on the top of the straw stack, the farmer watched Chee-kai, until the bird disappeared along the edge of the wood, to walk past the gate with the faggots placed against it, and round the corner of the straw stack which towered above the rails of the yard. There, a few steps away in the open field, five partridges were scratching in the snow, seeking seeds and grains on the site where heaps of cavings had stood before being carted into the wood after the threshing. Near them stood the wild cockerel, and a hen pheasant feeding discreetly where it had scratched for her. The farmer saw the cockerel look up when Chee-kai appeared, but it lowered its head at once, recognizing the long-tailed bird as a familiar of the partridges near to which it had often fed with its hen-mother during the summer and autumn. Chee-kai began feeding with them.

Snow took on a purpurate hue as the sun sank lower; rooks flew silently across the sky; stray pigeons circled high, seeking shelter for the night; a star-point shone in blue-green space. The bull grumbled in the yard; the iron roof of the shed vibrated momentarily as it rubbed itself against one of the oak posts supporting the roof—familiar sights and sounds. Pheasants, cockerel, and partridges went on feeding.

A shot rang out in the wood. The bull stood still listening. So did the heifers. A pigeon flew out of a tree

over the yard. A moment later came a *pish-pash* of thin
clawed feet on snow, and a swishing sound as a long
feathered tail brushed the bole of a tree in rapid flight.
From the top of the stack came a low, fluting whistle; the
swishing sound stopped, before continuing again, but less
certainly. Stiff with cold, the watcher arose, and slid
down the side of the stack. The field was deserted; but
several dark blobs moving over snow in the far corner by
the hedge revealed the partridges.

Down at the eastern end of the High Wood, where it
descended steeply on a chalky spur to the meadow below,
the poacher with the small-bore gun stooped to pick up a
pheasant he had shot as it crouched on some leaves at the
base of a beech-tree. He folded it into the inside pocket
of his jacket pleasurably excited by what he had done.
Hearing the noise of someone running through the wood
above him, he too began to run. He descended rapidly the
slope of the wood, and came to the lower level ground.
Hastening on, he crossed over the snow upon the meadow,
coming to the end of the Carr, where was a plank over
the dyke. Ignoring the shouts of Wilbo following in
the dusk, he walked carefully upon the icy wood, and
came to the drift, and so to a wooden bridge over the
river. That was the boundary; and getting through a
hedge, he walked across a further field to the coastal road.
There, behind a hedge, his bicycle was hidden; he
mounted, and rode away.

That night the otter, after eating a wild duck it had
caught in the river, began to gallop over the meadow in
sheer exhilaration of living, and coming to the frozen
water of the dyke, jumped on the ice, galloped along it,
slipping but gathering speed, until, throwing itself over
on its neck, the beast slid along on its back until it stopped;
when it got on its low legs, ran to gather speed, and so to

slide again. The otter did this until it was hungry, when it went into the woods to hunt rabbits. On returning to the meadow once more, it crossed the tracks of the poacher, whose boots had been rubbed with lard against wetting by the snow, and checking abruptly, began to follow the tracks, sometimes rolling on them because of the smell of the fat. From the wooden plank it leapt upon the ice below, and continued its racing and sliding on the dyke until it came to the end of the Carr, where the pine stood. Chee-kai roosting in the top of the tree heard the fluting, wader-bird-like whistle of the otter on its way home, and settled more securely into his warm eyrie of snow.

Chapter Twenty-One

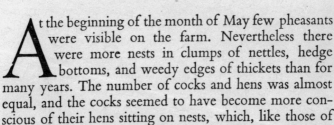

At the beginning of the month of May few pheasants were visible on the farm. Nevertheless there were more nests in clumps of nettles, hedge bottoms, and weedy edges of thickets than for many years. The number of cocks and hens was almost equal, and the cocks seemed to have become more conscious of their hens sitting on nests, which, like those of the partridges, were covered with dead leaves and other dry vegetation when the birds were off them. Here and there a cock pheasant was seen by the farmer to be sitting on a nest. He had observed earlier in the year that, while there had been some circular running and chasing of cock by cock, there had been little actual fighting.

He wondered if this changing behaviour of the cocks was due to the lessening of fear within them, caused by relaxation of the annual decimation of the species, and therefore to a partial allaying of the sexual instinct, which in the metropolitan human world during catastrophes, such as plagues or wars and the heightened death-feeling involved in those states, received exceptional stimulation, with consequent imbalance of paternal responsibility.

Brooding hen pheasants crept away from their nests by different ways, and after feeding, flew back to them direct, in order to avoid making tracks which might be followed through the grasses and other rising vegetation; for all wild animals followed paths or tracks through curiosity, and for ease of movement.

The clutches of eggs, after incubation of twenty-three days, hatched at the end of the first week of May, when Turtur the little dove from the Nile Valley was softly announcing his name among the blackthorns below the Breck. Pertris and Kakkabis, together for their third season, again made their nest in the tussocks of the drift. Once Pertris, now a seasoned bird, ran at Chee-kai when, walking down the drift, seeking beetles, he came near to the partridges' nest; but even as Pertris sprang into the air the menace went out of his address. Chee-kai had spoken to Pertris, in the little voice of his inner being like to a hedge sparrow's waking soliloquy; and jumping a ditch, had gone into the wood beyond the boundary.

By the time the pollen of the grasses had come to blow there was much excitement and fear upon the country-side. One morning when the tractor was travelling around the thick layer of Irish ryegrass, Dutch white clover, alsike, and red suckling of one of the steeper fields, draw-ing the cutting machine, black smuts began to settle upon the grey tank, and upon the bare arms, legs, and upper body of the driver. The smuts had drifted across the sea, from burning oil tanks.

It was the same field where Chee-kai, as a chick, had been sheltered by Pertris three years before. At the northern end of the field the land narrowed and rose between the High and Long Woods, to the three shel-tered acres of the Pightle. This area had not been plowed; the short, wiry grass remained, for the farmer wanted to see how, by folding poultry upon the sward, he could raise its fertility, a state which would be revealed by the increase of wild white clover among the grasses.

Upon an acre of the Pightle he had built a wire enclosure, and within were coops occupied by hen turkeys which had hatched their third and final clutches of the season. The two former layings of eggs, when found in the woods, had been taken away and put either in the incubator standing in the granary, or under broody hens. The idea was to cage the hens, and the poults when large enough, inside the wire enclosure erected on the Pightle, together with the stock birds sitting on their clutches in the coops, to protect them against stoats, weasels, and large rats which, the stockman had prophesied, would increase because the game birds had not been shot in due season. "Yew upsat thar balance of nature, Guv'nor, an' yew won't hev narthin' but pesky warmin."

The stockman was standing inside the wire enclosure with the farmer's wife and her small son, when he noticed smuts settling on her white blouse, and was remarking that there was a fire somewhere when he saw several men in city coats and hats walking through the gateway that led from the drift below the Long Wood to the field.

Of the five men, one remained behind by the gate, while the other four walked up the field to where the man and woman were standing with the child. The leader asked for the farmer by name, and on being told that he was cutting the hay at the other end of the field, and that the tractor would be coming along shortly, he thought a while and then in a quiet voice told one of his men to go to the edge of the High Wood, and to wait just inside it. Then he turned to the farmer's wife, and said, "You've got some nice turkeys here, I see. Are you troubled much with blackhead disease?" She replied that she did not know, as they were the first they had reared, but she thought her husband was going to inoculate the young birds soon.

The stockman regarded the strangers with sour face and offset manner, thinking to himself that they were nosey-

223

parkers from the War Agricultural Committee, come to tell them how to farm land; but when they walked, not together, but spread out, to the boss as the tractor came down the slope from the top of the field, and the boss stopped the machine and got off the seat, and was surrounded by them, fear and doubt entered into him. "What hev he done, M'am?" he said, while the little boy looked up at his face anxiously. "I can't think what they want," she replied, and after hesitation went with the child to meet the group now walking up to her.

The farmer told his wife that he was going away for a while, and asked her to tell the teamsman, whom he had taught to drive the tractor, to carry on with the cutting. "Don't let the cutting be delayed, the hay is now of such good quality," he said, as easily as he could, although his face under its deep burning by the sun was strained. To the stockman he said, "It mustn't be left in the swathe until it is bleached yellow and brittle, the chlorophyll and aromatic oils all gone. It should still have its green colour when you carry it, though it must be dry, of course. May I take my paints and canvases with me?" The last remark was addressed to the leading figure whose right hand was kept in the pocket of the light raincoat he wore. "Are you an artist, then?" "I try to be." "Have you done any sketching while you've been here?" "Yes." "For a living?" "Partly, yes." "What other reason have you, then?"

The question appeared to cause hesitation. After a pause, during which the five men stood attentive for a reply, the other said slowly, "Yes, I suppose I do paint to live, in the full sense of the term." "I see. You earn your living by selling, or trying to sell, what you paint and sketch?" The other nodded, whereupon the question was asked, almost casually, "Then why did you buy this land?"

Again there was hesitation, before the reply, "I wanted to help create a Greater Britain."

He was taken away in the midst of the five men.

The Pightle lay between the Breck in barley, and the steeper field of hay. Pertris, hearing the dreaded noise of the cutter, kept inside the barley, and Kakkabis with the chicks remained near him. The Breck sloped down beside the Long Wood, from which it was separated by a ragged thorn hedge, the trunks of which enclosed strands of barbed wire attached to rusty shreds of old hand-woven Scots sheep-netting, relic of an age before the golden hoof had turned to lead upon the countryman's consciousness.

Through a hole in the sheep-netting Chee-kai crept into the wood, to seek food in the leaf mould and ground herbage under the trees. He scratched up roots of wind-flower and common buttercup, plucked and swallowed yellow flowers of pilewort, and easily uprooting tender seedlings of sycamore, oak, and beech, he ate the root-sacs, together with worms, woodlice, and brown pupae of beetle and fly. At one place he began to peer and scratch with avidity, having smelt a strange smell upon the soil, where the farmer, during the past April, had with the stockman planted artichokes, an action approved by the old fellow because it would "hold the bards". These roots had already started to spread underground with the rising of the stalks set with pointed green leaves, and the farmer had intended to plant them along the entire south-eastern verge of the Long Wood, which was not in shadow until the late afternoon.

All day the cutter clattered round the steep and undulating field, while the teamsman sat on the tractor seat, and the swathes fell behind, to wilt in the sun. In the

225

afternoon heat Chee-kai crept from the Long Wood along the top of the Breck, and so to the High Wood where Pertris and Kakkabis and their chicks were dusting themselves on the raised bank at the edge of the trees where grew woodruff, thyme, and devil's-bit scabious. Kakkabis had led them up the bank, one after the other obedient to her low clucks, while Pertris had remained below, watching sky and field, with many glances at the turkeys in the cage below.

In the afternoon the farmer's wife, with her son close beside her, walked up the field to the turkeys' cage, their approach announced by a chorus of jockling cries. She carried the mash bucket in the crook of one arm, and held the boy by the hand, for he was frightened at what he had heard people saying, and expected any moment that terrible men would drop out of aeroplanes and kill his mother and himself. His father was something to do with the coming of the terrible men, and that was why he had been taken away in a large, black, shiny motor-car. And somehow, if the hay were not allowed to dry yellow in the sun, it would be all right; for the child had heard his father arguing with the teamsman about green hay and yellow hay, and he thought that it had to do with him being taken away. So, with gas mask in its metal container slung round his shoulder, the six-year-old child walked to the field with his mother, holding her hand tightly, relieved to see that the turkeys were still there.

In his free hand he carried a little painted bucket, bought the previous summer on a visit to the seaside, in which lay some tail barley scattered with currants—"to feed the faysan bird". For he had seen, on the easel in the small barn made into a studio, the painting of a bird that had given him a feeling of awe and wonder. And to know that it really lived on the farm, his father's favourite bird, and he might even see it now that he was to feed it every day, so that it would remain there until his father returned to the farm, filled him with such an emotion as he approached the Pightle that it was hardly to be borne, as the paling of cheeks, the momentary inability to speak, and the widening of his luminous dark eyes revealed.

There had been, until that morning, other pictures on the whitewashed flint walls of the studio: of the bird with down-curved wings and long tail extending behind it straight as the shaft of an arrow in flight over the meadow: of the bird, after throwing itself over backwards while in full flight and braking with wings and spread tail feathers bending backwards with the force of air, falling down the sky head first, with curve and sweep of spread tail above it, to alight upon the crest of a pine-tree—Chee-kai of the Chinese, the Arrow Bird, said by some to be the origin of the phoenix myth—a bird slightly larger than the common hybrid pheasant, but whose intensely yellow breast and back feathers were chequered with black and white and cinnamon, whose tail was six feet in length, whose flight, half as fast again as that of an ordinary cock bird, was as a golden rocket whistling horizontally over the tall pines until, curling down the sky head first to alight, it fell like a whisk of fire, like a comet made animate in grey, brown-barred smoke and flame, a prince of birds in chain mail of black and gold . . . upon the canvases in paint was held the imagination of the artist, by the plain seeing of truth.

When the farmer's wife had fed the old and young turkeys within the cage, she remembered the instructions for the curing of the hay; and telling her child that she would come back, she walked hurriedly down the field, to where the last acres were being cut in the distant hollow beyond the rising ridge or hump of the field. In her

227

worried state of mind she left the door of the cage open behind her.

Left alone, the boy stood by the gate of wood frame and wire netting at one corner of the cage, until his mother was out of sight. She had told him that he might scatter what he carried in his pail, where he had watched his father dropping corn and currants on former occasions. And when she had disappeared he turned round resolutely and walked uphill to the place.

He came to the top of the Pightle. Here the line of thorns leaned over from the winds of the sea. The boy's heart was beating fast, and when the sea came into view, in relief that all was there as before, he sat down beside a heap of white flints half overgrown by turf, between two twisted thorns, and breathed deeply, while with his fingertips he stroked the barley kernels in the pail. Looking backwards down the field to the cage, he saw that he was alone, and an impulse to cry came over him; but after a fluttering heave of breath, he calmed himself and found relief in touching the hot flints, as he had touched them before when he had sat there with his father. He pretended to find interest in an ant climbing over fronds of moss growing on one stone. He was putting off the act of scattering the corn as long as he could, because if he did it quickly, he would not know what to do until his mother came back. While he sat there he was striving within himself against terror: striving to make himself do what his father had once told him: "I am often frightened, but when I feel like that, I make myself go forward into danger, with my eyes wide open, trying not to think."

While he sat there he saw the familiar sight of the wild cockerel of the woodland yard walking along the edge of the Breck, on the cart track between green corn and the hedge below the tall pine-trees. The sight relieved him, for the cockerel, though wary and keeping to a distance,

228

was a friend he had often seen there, coming to be fed.

Getting to his feet, the boy began to drop grains of corn meticulously from between finger and thumb of his right hand, as he moved along slowly—now two grains, now three, now two, now a currant (he liked currants but would not eat one from the pail, as they were for the faysan bird), then three grains, then several more. He was doing what he had been told to do: not throwing it all out at once, but a little here, a little there, just as his father had done. He saw the cockerel walking towards him, and went on dropping the grains slightly faster, but not too fast, because if he did not make it last out until he saw his mother, there would be nothing to keep away fear. Then pursing his lips after wetting them with his tongue, he whistled short flute-like notes, as often he had heard his father whistle.

The watchful Pertris saw the cockerel walking behind the line of the twisted thorns, and with muted clucks to Kakkabis he led the chicks along the top of the raised bank, among the tussocks of light green grasses, bines of ivy, tall spear thistles, and thin stems of blackthorn. Chee-kai, who also knew the strings of food dropped there and down the eastern verge of the Long Wood, moved past the line of chicks led by Pertris, to the end of the bank, where he met the cool sea breezes susurrating in the first young reddish-brown beards of the season's barley. Out of the green corn another bird was moving, calling her variegated chicks to follow with soft cluckings—a hen pheasant who had hatched a clutch of eggs fertilized by the wild cockerel.

Strident noises vibrated upon the early summer airs—the cries of turkeys hastening out of the gate which had been left unfastened. The stag birds arrived first, striding

on black-grey scaly legs, the leading bird to be met by
Pertris who in fury burst in its face, striking with wing and
foot, before dropping down and running in a half circle
and exploding in the face of another stag bird. Meanwhile
with skreeping cries and wing trailings and prostrate
scutterings Kakkabis tried to divert the stalking attention
of the big black birds upon herself, and away from the
tiny running chicks. Although she dashed like a feathered
squib from one to another, she could not save two of the
chicks from being struck, each by a single deliberate beak
stroke of a hen turkey who was considered by the stockman to be a poor mother (for in the pen when rain fell
or evening came that gawping bird neglected her own
poults, and tried to push herself under the wing of another
hen turkey. Her bulk remained outside, but having in-
sinuated penduled head and upper part of neck into the
feathered warmth of a neighbour, she remained like that,
her eyes shut in an illusion of security, while her own
young cried their piping cries in vain. "Put thet tarkie i'
th'arv'n, m'am," the stockman had remarked mildly to
the farmer's wife, when five out of seven of her poults
had been found dead one dewy morning).

The other turkeys were now through the old slack wire
of the fence, between Breck and Pightle, eager to find the
grain. The hen pheasant with her brood had already disappeared into the barley; but the wild cockerel had dashed
out of the corn, drawn himself up, uttered a ringing challenge, and run at the nearest stag bird. The boy, standing
by the corner of the field, hidden behind the rising plants
of artichokes, watched the fight with thrilling excitement;
but when the other stag bird ran at the cockerel, and
jumped upon him from behind, treading him with its
weight of over twenty pounds, he felt distress, but stood
there, not knowing what to do. It was then that he saw
something that brought from him a cry of "Oh!", for

suddenly, as though materializing from the sun shining over the top of the trees of the High Wood, a bird of brilliant yellow-gold colouring, the cap of its head white and its face cowled in black, dashed into the fight, its long tail whisking and snaking about. The tail was enormously long, and smoke-grey, showing bars of dark brown as it sprang from its crouching run and struck a stag bird with its feet. The turkey fell back, recovered, and ran away; whereupon the golden bird leapt six feet into the air, its tail spread wide, and struck at another, which scuttled under the loose wire strand and followed the fleeing turkey. The two stag birds being defeated, with a chorus of dismayful cries the rest of the turkeys retreated. The boy shouted aloud in exultant relief; there was an instant black-and-white glance in his direction, as the victor stood still, showing a lilac and smoke-grey tail barred with dark brown marks, like peewits' wings in flight, along its great length: then with a whisk of feathers swishing against stalks of corn, it was gone.

When his mother returned, he told her excitedly that he had seen "the faysan bird", and showed her the two dead chicks placed side by side in the bottom of his pail, to be taken home for burial in his garden, an area of four square feet under an ivied wall where he had planted a potato, two beans, and some radish seeds. She was glad that he was happy, and they went home together, to find the farm premises being searched by several men, under the eye of the silent stockman. They asked about the concrete slabs, the underground petrol tank and pump, the reason of the concrete bridges that had been built over the dykes and the new road that had been cut along the hillside to the level higher ground. They visited the woodland yard, searching, and occasionally prodding the ground with a thin steel rod. Afterwards they came to the farmhouse and the studio, seeking in all cupboards and drawers for any maps or sketches of the locality; they read piles of correspondence; took the books from the shelves, methodically one after another, and shook them so that any papers between the pages would drop out. They stared at the paintings on the walls, and removed them one by one to examine them, both back and front; they tapped one, scratched the paint with a fingernail, then with the blade of a pocket knife; eventually they took them away, together with the sketch books and diaries, part of his correspondence, and all the sketches in a large folder. The pictures were photographed under the infra-red rays, and one was treated with chemicals, in an attempt to uncover beneath the paint any "cartographical matter likely to be of assistance to an enemy" in the words of the directive received from M.I.5.

PART FOUR

Chapter Twenty-Two

A nightingale sang in the silence of the moon by the Willow Plot, while a pearly whiteness of light filled the valley, and the worn tiles of cottage, barn, and stable roof glowed a deep red, as with warm, mysterious life. The reeling voice of a grasshopper warbler ran through the bright sheens of the meadow, arousing to excited song the sedge-warblers among the osiers. From the blackthorn thickets on the river bank near the Carr came the chattering of reed-sparrows. At midnight pale lunar fire glanced in gold upon the back of the bar-tailed pheasant, sleeping the more securely for the whistles of the otter playing in the river below the pine tree.

Partridges called in the dawn; morning brought colour to the valley; at noon the sea-cool waves of wind surged upon the green barley, under the hot and eddying airs of wood-edge and field. The sun of high summer burned over the land: hen pheasants sheltered with their nids content amidst the corn.

As the sun went down a land-cool flow of wind returned to the sea; rustling leaves of sycamore and beech made the only sounds until pheasants began to flap up into their roosting branches, and young owls called to their parents through a twilight lit only by stars and the green phosphoric flickers of shore-slanting waves.

Night fell, the wind ceased. No cocks crowed in the woods: no gunfire shivered dully over the sea: no bombers throbbed among the stars: and when the brief dawn came, no fighter aircraft tore the serene blue air of morning.

The sun of midsummer passed along the celestial shores, entering the sign of the Crab; and upon the earth, the prawn-like heads of the barley bowed beneath the blazing puissance of the day-star. So the days passed until the corn was ripe, under a sky whose silence in starlight and moonrise, from dawn to the setting of the sun, was apparent only to a very few within the island, themselves silenced by the most tragic paradox of western history.

Harvesters of corn, simple men without the complications of the market place, remarked the empty skies where only gulls blaked and the white sea swallows flickered above summer wavelets murmurous on level sands: while inland only the rattle of reapers and binders sounded with the jolt of loaded waggons and the cries of boys pursuing rabbits bewildered among unfamiliar sheaves.

After the harvest had been gathered in, men standing at night outside darkened windows and by flint walls in village street and local cross-ways, hearkened to one cock pheasant after another crowing in the woods, before they themselves heard the dull and rolling reverberations of bombs; the birds felt the distant vibrations which travelled through earth and trunks of trees to the branches clasped by their feet, before the air bore the blows to human ears.

To Chee-kai roosting in the pine-tree at the northern end of the Carr various other noises and sights became familiar and then commonplace as the weeks drew into autumn: waving beams of violet light that fumbled in the sky, giving a ghastly pallor-shadow to bush, field-gate, and bullock grazing on meadow: swift vermilion spots of light that fled down and across the darkness of the sky, meeting orange spots that arose from the earth, curving upwards at a slower pace, amidst sharp crackle and spasmodic rattle of Spandau and Lewis guns: the showers and scatterings of lights that burned in blue-white brilliance on hillside, stubble, and sometimes in the woods. But he never got used to an occasional instant-blue splitting of the night-sky, a colossal rent of light that revealed all as stone—river, road, church, wood, field—a moment before a shattering detonation seemed to disintegrate the tree. Earth and air rocked, as the landmine exploded on the hard chalky sub-soil of the uplands. In the clanging black silence that followed perhaps from the high remote sky would come a wooden stutter like that of the lesser-spotted woodpecker on a dead bough in the wood in spring, a repeated stutter, a double, a treble stutter, sometimes overborne by a final shuddering roar as the eight guns of a Spitfire ripped through east-flying Junkers or Heinkel . . . a slight smear of flame drew down from star to star, to fall as a trail of sparks, and be lost in darkness.

Yellow and black and brown, the leaves streamed through the trees with rainy gusts of wind that wrinkled the grey water-plashes on the meadows and rocked with scudding wavelets the darker, deeper flowings in the dykes. Leaves turned over in the river swilling to the cattle-trodden tops of its banks, a turbid flow fed by drains which discharged flushes of muddy water running down in gutter and ditch and rut of tumbril and tractor; while wheels of military trucks and the steel shoes of track-laying vehicles tore up the surfaces of lanes and drifts.

During the succeeding spring and summer, into the villages of the remote countryside came untrained troops from the industrial towns, to make their camps, of tent and marquee, on grassland at the edges of woods; to tear off branches of trees for camouflage and firing, to take hay and straw from stacks for bedding; to remove doors of stable and granary. Prowling, they scrounged hens and eggs, and generally regarded owners and occupiers of land as being stupid, selfish, and hostile to ordinary people like themselves—a mental attitude derived from newspapers which had helped to form the superficialities of their minds: minor irritations to countrymen, who with firm markets to support their work were hoping to build up their living in the art and mystery of farming once again. Minor irritations, of a temporary kind, because major irruptions were upon them by the following winter, when wide areas of level land, scores of thousands of acres, all in cultivation, many in standing crops, were requisitioned, despite protests by farmers who declared that the rhythm of their organizations would be broken, and who pleaded, in the *clichés* of the time, that since Britain had become an island fortress, the production of food for the besieged nation was of first importance.

Upon those wide forsaken lands where tillage was stopped, the dominant weeds arose yet once again to uphold their fruits prepared within umber capsule, silver floss, and hooked ball, with which to claim the surface of the earth as heath and breck once more. But a power stronger than that of the urge of solar florescence was in motion from the inhibitions and frustrations of industrialized man, even as a language of lewdness and cynical contempt of the racial functions of the human body was supplanting the essential rectitude of the farm-labourer.

Strange new machines appeared upon the weedy wastes; travellers by car and cart lost their way in the blackout, for all signposts at crossroads and forked ways had been removed; lanes were closed to traffic; names of villages on wayside memorials to the dead of the previous war were obliterated; lesser country roads ended abruptly in chaos, beside orchards of young apple trees that had been torn from the ground, or plantations of conifers scraped out of the soil.

Hares, following immemorial runs, stopped in dismay, with black-tipped ears erect, narrow nostrils working; loped on; paused; turned back; ran on in wide circles, aimlessly.

Isolated cottages and farmhouses were demolished, their rubble of brick, flint, and pantile tipped with other rubble brought from bombed towns to fill immense and cruciform channels being gouged in the levelled earth.

Old labourers who had worked three or four or five decades in the fields, never going more than a score of miles from their villages, watched their native soil dying as they arose erect in moments from stooping to knock or top the last crop of sugar-beet upon the requisitioned lands.

Upon one such wide tract adjoining the uplands of the farm to the east and south wandered Chee-kai, as the mist of a winter afternoon dissolved a perspective, desolate and mournful, of great oaks and elms lying thrown upon the waste with heaps of quickset thorns, their brown roots asprawl in air, dragged from vanished hedgerows and piled for burning. Chee-kai had lost Pertris; and he had waited in vain by the edge of the High Wood for the curlew-like whistles of the boy who, hurrying from school, had sometimes walked up the side of the Pightle to strew a few currants and a handful of tail-corn by the hedge at the top side of the Breck. The boy had used his small ration for his absent father's "faysan bird", until currants were no more to be obtained by his mother, or any other village woman, on the ration card, at the village shop. Poachers roamed the woods, some of them amateurs from the airfield under construction beyond the boundary; his mother feared that her son might be shot, or otherwise injured, by the trespassing men; and as time wore on, his visits had ceased.

So Chee-kai had wandered, and often being shot at, had flown afar, hiding by day and feeding only in the early mornings and evenings. Sometimes, hearing the cries of partridges, Chee-kai ran to them, to where they called one to another hesitating upon unfamiliar flats of churned and shapeless land, where brittle ice glistened with the cold sheens of the moon, calling one to another to keep together, these little winged people of the lost arable, calling as the first night bombers began to fly eastwards in the dusk.

Fields of lightest land, of poorest fertility, of a packed stony bareness underlying the thinnest of acid breck or scalt soil, became valuable as gravel pits. Deeming themselves fortunate, the owners let them on a basis of royalty paid for every cubic yard removed by contractors, who with mechanical excavators scooped deeper and wider, loading the gravel into fleets of trucks until the pits extended to craters gnawing away entire fields and what had lain beneath them during thousands of centuries since the sea's recession. Columns of trucks sped through the narrow and winding village roads to one or another of the working sites, each covering two square miles of farmland, now being overlaid with long and wide cruciform tracks enclosed within a lesser oval way, also of concrete, a quarter of a million tons of which was slabbed down upon each of the levelled sites.

The boy who had harrowed-in the barley-seed upon the Breck in the year of Chee-kai's birth had fallen in battle, with some of his village friends, in the African desert; others had died in the jungles of the Far East, or were languishing, pale and weak, in prison camps where dysentery and fever and exhaustion of overwork killed many.

And as active youth died in agony while active age acquired money, the gamebirds of East Anglia, once the unwanted granary of Britain and now becoming the winged arsenal, assumed more importance to human eyes. Shopkeepers of the shabby little market towns, supplying a demand, sold weapons of various patterns and usefulness to civilians, soldiers, and airmen—shotguns small in bore with thin damascene barrels, old pin-fire collectors' guns of Belgian manufacture, walking-stick guns, and even flint-lock horse pistols which could fire a charge of black powder and knock a cock pheasant out of a wayside oak-tree or coppice where no keeper would hear or see. Food was becoming scarce; London, delineated as a black stain on the maps, paid paper-money for food—almost any food for its restaurants and hotels: rooks, seagulls, blackbirds, jays, daws, moorfowl, even owls, hawks, and proletarian starlings, all were embroiled, garnished, and raised *à la carte* to the peerage of game. For few if any poached pheasants got so far as the town on the great tidal sewer called Thames, for the 8th United States Army Air Force was arriving, and combat crews drank whisky to give a kick to the weak pub beer. Cartridges were scarce, only to be purchased from gunsmiths by farmers and other sportsmen genuinely shooting over their own land and coverts; but with the growing demand for whisky, a cartridge costing twopence in peacetime was, in war-time from little dealers like the Flockmaster, worth half a crown to any lorry driver on airfield construction earning eighteen or twenty pounds a week. For half a crown brought down a bird, and a bird could be ex-changed by the little men of the black market, with nods and winks and stealthy movements, for a bottle of whisky:

and a bottle was worth three quid from any American bombardier or waist-gunner returning from subzero heights under the deep sinister blue of the troposphere.

Many weapons had pointed at Chee-kai, as he moved about the countryside, but none of the expended shot had so far struck him; he was a fast runner, he dodged and crouched in concealment, he seldom flew. Curlews passing in the sky always made him look up; for he had not forgotten the hoarse-sweet whistles that had meant the gathering of friends below the High Wood in days long since gone by.

But some of the birds that Chee-kai had known, by sight and by sound, had not escaped human eyes which had pursued them for the money their bodies were worth. Quaquila and his mate, crying liquidly *Wet my lips, Wet my lips*, with the voice of lost quails, with the mirage-cries of the quivering deserts of Africa, had been shot upon the steeply sloping boundary field below the High Wood by the poacher with the ·410 gun. This man, before the shooting, had a market for the skins of the little birds of partridge appearance, having been promised four pounds the pair, if in good condition, from a collector living in the market town. The collector's ambition was to have more rare birds migrant to the district skinned and stuffed and set up behind glass, with artificial grasses and marine vegetation as background, than any other amateur taxidermist in England. He had offered twenty pounds for the bar-tailed pheasant.

The poacher had also netted Turtur, with other doves, selling them for thirty shillings each, to unknowing but kindly people who had given tenderness and care to the shapely birds—and never known why their pets had sat so still and subdued in the cages, why the birds of love had languished and died when the summer was over and the migratory urge could not be fulfilled.

The poacher shot warily in the woods of the farm, usually on Sundays, at dusk and early morning. He sold the pheasants he shot to the Flockmaster, who did the deals in whisky which increased the diameter of his roll of pound notes. The poacher seemed to be animated by more than mere personal gain, however; for when he met Czech or Polish soldiers, who were in camp nearby, and learned they were fishermen, he told them that the stream moving past the Carr was full of trout, and even lent them a large prawning net with which to take them out from the holes under the banks. He justified his actions to himself by thoughts that there ought not to be such things as pheasants in woods or rivers with trout in them unless anyone could take them, as there should not be anyone owning any land more than a smallholding; and his taking of the birds became a self-righteous thing whenever he thought of the farmer as a traitor who had not got all he deserved, while the ordinary decent man was losing his life for a better world. His real motive was the resentment of the man of small capacity against another who through greater energy had become more successful than himself, and in the small man's notion that he had a right to take what others took. If soldiers took trout, he had a right to take birds.

The poacher had shot most of the turkeys, knocking them down, one at a time, out of the top branches of the sycamores near the woodland yard one night just before Christmas; these had been disposed of in the ordinary black market, by way of the Flockmaster's cart.

He had shot the wild cockerel of the woodland yard, and three of the hybrids of that bold bird's mating with a hen pheasant: all four specimens were within a glass case, one of many standing on shelves around the lime-washed walls of the lower rooms of his house made by the collector into a private museum, and shown with pride to visitors. Did not the great Rothschild collection contain a bird believed to be a cross between the autochthonous *tetrao tetrix*, the black grouse, and the immigrant *phasianus colchicus*, usually called Chinese pheasant, found on Halsinger Down near Exmoor in North Devon?

The usual round of the poacher, a man about twenty-five years of age who worked on a farm by day and was thereby in what was called a reserved occupation, which meant that he would not be called up for the fighting services, was from the Carr to the High Wood, stopping about a hundred yards short of the woodland yard. He had shot, altogether, about two hundred birds during the first four years of the war; but at the end of 1943 he had run out of ·410 cartridges, which were by then unobtainable, as none were being made in the country, and he had not been able to buy any. The Flockmaster had tried also, declaring that he would pay one pound for a dozen; but without results. Cartridges were to be got from the R.A.F. station where they were used in practice with clay pigeons, by pilots, to keep their eye in—but these were twelve-bore cartridges, and some were duds by intention, in order to surprise and quicken action. Both men had failed to buy a twelve-bore gun: the village wildfowlers would not part with theirs.

With the last of his small-bore cartridges the poacher had shot the otter, whose skin he had sold for three pounds to an East End furrier who had migrated with some of his co-racials from the bombed Whitechapel Road and set up a flourishing furrier's business in the nearby market town.

The otter had been killed as the poacher had waited in the Carr on a cold clear evening of winter, underneath the pine-tree. He was about to chuck up and go home, as he told the collector later, when suddenly he saw the otter coming towards him out of the low-lying swampy bit where the willows grew all tangled and falling; and he had thought the animal was going to attack him, as it stopped when it saw him, opened his mouth and made a threatening, hissing noise through its teeth. He had fired from a distance of not more than three yards; the animal, hit in the head, had leaped and thrown itself about, and while he had been staring at it, he had heard a swishing noise in the air above, and there was a bird coming down. It had pitched in the dark head of the tree only for a moment, and then, uttering a strangely thin piping sound, had flown away towards the Breck, where a partridge was calling *per-tris, per-tris!* through the low mists of the meadow.

The Flockmaster had done well out of the war. He possessed two rolls of pound notes, one hidden in a space behind a loose brick in the tapering breast of his cottage chimney—built in Queen Elizabeth's reign for wood burning on an open hearth, a space now, as in most other cottages, filled in to hold a small iron coal-burning stove with oven—and the other roll carried in his breast pocket, often to be taken out and fingered lovingly when no one was near. Besides his deals in game birds and liquor the Flockmaster was still buying up golden sovereigns from old cottagers, collecting them for the ex-money-lender (now director of a trading company, and of several property investment companies) who met him periodically in the Turnip Arms, tipped a double rum into his pint of beer, and paid the Flockmaster what he had paid for each coin, four pounds, plus a pound note for himself. He resold them for seven pounds.

Not all the Flockmaster's deals had been profitable, however. There was the occasion when, soon after his mother's death, he had tried to do a deal, in a big way, with cockles. Hearing in the Horn and Corn one evening that cockles were much in demand in London, he had, on impulse, and three double rums in three pints, bought two dozen bushels, in washed chemical fertilizer bags; but he had not known how or where to resell such a quantity in bulk; and when he offered them to the regular dealer, whom he had outbid in the first place, that sardonic individual told him shortly that he would give him a price much below that which the Flockmaster had paid for them. Take it or leave it. The Flockmaster cajoled and wheedled for better terms, but no deal was done; and, heedless of the local saying, *The first loss should be the last loss*, he temporized until the "blues" went bad on him. For a few days afterwards he was greeted as the Cockle King: but the shellfish having been tipped into the river, he soon reverted to the familiar name of Flockmaster, and kept to deals in feather, bottle, and coin.

When the poacher told the collector of the return of the bar-tailed bird, the collector increased the offer of twenty pounds to thirty pounds for its body if in good condition. The poacher told this to the Flockmaster, while the pony cropped the grass of the roadside, the Flockmaster exclaimed, "We don't want no gun, 'bor! I've a-got it!" He meant an idea how to get Chee-kai. The poacher asked questions, but the Flockmaster would not say. Leave it to him, all in good time the other should know. And with a couple of winks and several significant nods, he pulled the reins, growled "Git back, yew!" to the horse, and with a flip of the whip trotted away.

When he stopped next, a few miles along the coast road, it was at the back door of a small inn, called the Wild Fowler, kept by a smallholder who also bred game-

cocks. After some bargaining, he bought a bird that he
had had his eye on for several months. And as the two men
were having a drink together in the kitchen, talking-over
old times, the son of the smallholder came in and said,
"Wilbo's back!"

Chapter Twenty-Three

The farmer's wife had done her best to carry on with the work of the farm, after the farmer had been taken away. Arrested without charge, he had been kept in prison without trial, for both Magna Carta and the Bill of Rights had been suspended. During the years of imprisonment, he had never known, from one moment of vacant day to another, or during the voiceless and self-dissolving nights, whether he would be allowed to live or to die, whether or no he would ever again see his loved ones.

The farmer's wife had filled every moment of the dragging weeks and months and years with work for the hands or mind. She had helped to organize the distribution of orange juice and rose-hip syrup—made from the wild-rose seeds gathered from the hedgerows—for the babies of the village, against malnutrition and rickets; she had taken a leading part in creating a local branch of the Women's Institute, as a centre of social life for women, and of useful, creative work. She was an equal-minded woman, with a power of endurance which was the greater for a limited imagination. Thereby she did not suffer, having friends about her who esteemed her, and never mentioned the absent man. She did not know of any reason for his imprisonment, beyond his association with other Englishmen who had opposed the war on the grounds that its continuance to the bitter end could only end in the destruction of Europe, including Britain, and the dissolution of the Empire.

The farmer's wife had done her best to carry on the farm. At first, the teamsman, the stockman, and the two other men had remained working there. The youth had already gone, having been called up for the army at the age of eighteen.

First of the older men to leave had been one part-crippled from the first war. Complaining that there was nothing but trouble on the farm, he had taken a job as civilian worker in a military camp, where he earned nearly double his previous wages for less than half the work he had done in the fields. Next to leave had been the younger man, who had always resented the authority of the teamsman, leaving father and son responsible for a hundred and forty acres of difficult arable land, and sixty of grazing.

Thereafter difficulties had seldom ceased; work was always behindhand. They had increased when the hydraulic lift of the tractor had been broken, when the machine had been backed by the farmer's son, plowing one Saturday afternoon, into a raised bank; the plow beam thus levered up had cracked part of the aluminium hydraulic housing case. No spare parts had been obtainable; it had gradually become clotted with fowl-droppings in the hovel.

Italian prisoners came to work on the farm, in gangs of thirty and forty brought in buses every day. They did little work, idling about the fields and in the woods, many practising with horsehair springe and snare of brass-wire their habits of taking any wild bird or animal, large or small, to be cooked and eaten in large iron cooking pots they brought with them; for without a long rest and a hot meal in the middle of the day, they refused to continue what slight work they did. They hoed the sugar-beet in

May, helped with the haysel in June, brought in the corn-harvest in August, and began to knock and top the sugar-beet in October. After half a year of this, and a week before Old Michaelmas Day, the teamsman, receiving his pay on Friday from the farmer's wife, told her that he had had enough, and gave notice to leave.

The stockman remained. By this time most of the fertility of the fields had been lost; for by orders of the War Agricultural Committee, corn crop after crop had been taken, with only limited artificial fertilizer (and that had lacked potash) available. Long ago the Redpoll heifers and bullocks had been sold; no straw had been trodden into muck in the yards for years. Weeds had come back in the fields; the woodland yard was overgrown with nettles, thistles, and burdocks; the straw stacks rotted, low and sunken beside overgrown hedges. Reeds choked the dykes once more, the grass of the meadows was water-slain. It was as though three years' intensive reconstruction had never taken place; even the new roads were destroyed, having been broken and churned into mud and potholes when for a few months during a rainy winter the farm had been used as a tank and artillery exercise ground. In that time ten out of the dozen new gates and posts had been splintered and broken; and through it all the stockman had remained, "sarvin' the master's interests" as best he could.

For the first few days after his return the man known as Wilbo had scarcely spoken. Dreading the greater light of day, he had kept to his room, wincing away from all thoughts of activity in a staring, harshening world, and accepting the idea of death as the only refuge of honour and truth.

One morning his son, returning from school at midday, came to tell him something of great importance to the boy; but when, after pausing and summoning up fortitude to knock on the door, he had entered the room, he found himself unable to speak. He was frightened of the figure of his father, who was not what he had imagined during many thoughts during the years, which to the boy had been of ordinary life. Breathlessly, after running down the village street, he had gasped out to his mother what he had heard from another boy at school; and asked her to tell his father the news. The mother had suggested that he go in and tell him himself, adding that they must not let him think he was in any way different from before, but to be just ordinary and natural before him.

The boy was peculiarly sensitive to the feelings of others, and diminished by his father's bleak attitude, could not find his tongue. His father asked him, quietly, what he wanted; and when the boy did not reply, he repeated the question tersely: whereupon the boy felt an unaccountable distress, for standing there with hanging head, he was striving not to cry. "Can't even my own son speak to me?" asked the father, with a bitterness that he could not keep out of his voice. The boy broke in tears; he stood sobbing, unable to move, until the door was opened for him and he was told quietly to go back to his mother.

A few minutes later the mother came in, with the boy, his face having been dipped in water to remove tear-stains, and his wet dark hair combed and brushed flat on his head; and as though the first visit had not happened, she said with a smile that they had heard some good news, and must tell him. Chee-kai had been seen on the farm again. "But only a li'l old boy told me, Dad, so it might not be true, you know!" the boy cried out.

For awhile the standing figure said nothing; but the pathos of the expectant faces of mother and son, both so hopeful and kind on his behalf, so innocent of the reality of the forces convulsing the world, cracked momentarily the petrified consciousness of the years of despair, and tears rolled down his cheek as he embraced both of them.

The stockman's problem was intensified by the return of his master. He had not quit during his absence, because he had not been able to bear the thought of letting-down Wilbo; but when he heard rumours at the Cross that the War Agricultural was likely to take possession of the farm, he gave notice. He was over sixty years of age, and since he had, among other duties, tended the two cows kept for the house, and the horses, he had not had a Sunday off nor a day's holiday for six years. And having had a standing offer of a job with a maltster in the town for more than three of those six years, at last he accepted, telling himself and his wife that now the War Agricultural was to run the farm, he would not stay.

It was known at the Cross that Wilbo had in the meantime bought the shell of a tractor like his own, and was working to replace the broken bell-housing of the hydraulic gear. He managed to strip both machines, his son helping him, and make one whole out of the parts. Then he started to work to reclaim the land again. He had seen Chee-kai upon the Pightle, and knew that if he lost his farm, the bird would die. Its survival during the hazards of the years, and now its return, was to him a miracle; and a portent.

Soon the haggard, seldom-speaking face became a commonplace sight in the village. He was an object of amusement to some: did he not sometimes, after working all day, plow throughout a night of full moon, while others shot the roosting pheasants in the woods almost as they pleased? Was not his voice often heard down by the Cross of an evening, travelling as a series of shouts from as far as the High Wood, as the loungers by the flint walls imagined him leaping off the tractor, and running after trespassing soldier or airman of the adjoining R.A.F. station? "Old Wilbo's mobbin' agen!" Did he not spend his free time with his boy, making dummy "bards" with straw and baling wire, some with very long tails made of willow wands, and fixing them in the tops of trees—objects which deceived no one? Once considered a danger, and feared as the unknown, Wilbo was now regarded as a harmless crank, who would not last very long.

One night, plowing up the steep chalky field, set with great flints, the back axle of the tractor snapped with a loud report; and the machine settled on its side.

A prolonged cry, rising in pitch before dying away, was heard by the stockman coming out of the Horn and Corn; he paused, but after the cucket of a cock pheasant in the Long Wood, nothing more was heard. The stockman went home slowly, and did not speak as he took off his boots and went upstairs to bed.

When the County War Agricultural Executive Committee took over the management of any farm, during that period in the history of British husbandry, it did so only with much reluctance, for the last thing it desired to do was to take the place of any farmer. It existed to offer advice when it was sought and to give help when it was asked. It made analyses of the soils of fields, upon request, free of charge; it made available by lecture and demonstration the conclusions of its experiments in practical farming, all with the aim and purpose of raising the standard of husbandry and so of obtaining for the war effort a greater production of food. Where a farm was being mismanaged or neglected, it would first try to persuade, tactfully, the occupier to use better methods; and only if persuasion failed was direct action taken to dispossess the laggard of his land.

It had been observed for some time that the coastal farm was not being farmed in accordance with the rules and usages of good husbandry, and eventually an official called on the farmer with a suggestion that it might be a relief to him if the farm were let to a tenant, since he was not amenable to the idea of Italian prisoners of war coming on his land. It was pointed out to him, in a friendly manner, that with only his wife, and son still at school, to help him, he was not able to farm one hundred and forty acres of arable land as it should be farmed.

There was another reason, too, which the official, with tact and consideration, did not mention; but he bore it in mind should the farmer prove obdurate. He had heard, from the school-mistress and others, that the small boy was being overworked: late one night, under the moon, the boy had been seen sitting on the corn-drill, jumping off at the headlands to lift the coulters while the horses drew the drill around to start off across the field again. On another occasion, the farmer had been heard shouting wildly at the boy, who apparently had not understood what he had been told, or through weariness, had been falling asleep.

The official did not mention this; he had farmed himself through several bitter years of the depression; he had sympathy for the other man's plight. The farmer understood, too: after a moment's reflection, he said quietly that he must yield to *force majeure*.

But he would not agree to let the farm unless a tenant be found who would take the land only; he wished to reserve the sporting rights.

This raised a problem, for while there were many hundreds in the country only too eager to start farming, there would be no farmhouse available, since the farmer would still be occupying it with his family; and while neighbouring farmers would gladly have rented the extra land, it would be only for the sake of the shooting. Having considered these objections, the W.A.E.C. decided to farm the land themselves; and an order was signed dispossessing the farmer.

Deprived of his work, he shut himself away in the studio he had built during the summer before the war, out of a small semi-ruinous barn standing in the garden of the farmhouse, and did nothing. He saw the destruction of his life and work as inevitable; it was the microcosm of the European macrocosm. His entire body ached, as though the heavy limbs were filled with mercury. He thought of the tractor standing in the hovel, its engine worn out, its back broken—the high-tensile steel crystal-lized through fatigue. Now both of them were fit only for the scrap-heap.

About the rectangular room, with its paved floor, whitewashed walls of flint, and dark beam, purlins, and rafters overhead, stood various objects of past husbandry —a flail with twisting joint of cowhorn and leather thong; a curved sickle with worm-bored handle and rust-thinned iron hook; a scythe with fragile blade and snead of willow; a butter churn with the grain of its wooden hoops and staves standing out with much scrubbing of some dead and gone farmhouse daughter.

He stood in the centre of the room, aimlessly; the sky began to roll with deep sound; he began to pace a narrow area of the floor as he felt the solidification of himself deepening, thickening, as one turning slowly to stone under the unending stalactite drip of tears upon the core of human consciousness.

With the help of a village bricklayer, the semi-ruinous barn had been given a paved floor, a wide window facing north, and an open hearth in one corner. It had been designed, not as a refuge from deteriorating life, but as a temple in service to the spirit to which all artists entrust themselves. But now, as the man paced to and fro, the spirit of life was wan, withheld, made negative; in all that he thought and did and was, in the age which somehow had been encoiled about him, the room's objects had lost their significance. The love and care which were once part of their being was gone. They were but objects, the silver candlesticks on the desk, the case of artificial trout flies, the palette, the slender brushes in a jar, the brass ships' lanterns, the neat piles of old magazines—*The Atlantic Monthly, Salmon and Trout Magazine, The Field*, and *The Connoisseur*, the books on the shelves, the paintings on the walls, all without meaning, relics of a dead world, of a life whose rhythm was gone. There were two armchairs in horsehide, smooth with saddle soap—but "of comfort no man speak"; rush brushes bought in the Tyrol with yellow beeswax tapers and goatskin for wine; a pair of hickory skis from New Hampshire; walking sticks cut from the hedges and thickets, ash, blackthorn, and pliable stem of dog-rose. And on the chimney piece, curled with damp, were reproductions of Albrecht Dürer—grasses in natural colour, of a hare cut in wood, and other water colours and etchings of four and a half centuries ago, and still unsurpassed throughout the world for their clarity and truth.

The bombs had brought all to the dust.

Chapter Twenty-Four

Day after day with coarse diapason the blue upper air of the North Sea was humming. Far above water and earth silver-glinting specks were moving almost imperceptibly in the sky. The entire hemisphere seemed to be vibrating as hundreds of bright wraith-like midges moved slowly into the east, white and seeming transparent, like minute pale waterflies that sometimes were seen in midday nuptial flight beside the river.

Morning after morning of orient sunshine the silver air-fleet flew over earth and water through azure skies, leaving multitudinous vapour trails to drift and spread tenuous long after the aircraft had gone out over the sea. Usually they returned in the early afternoon, but seldom in the serene formations of the upper air. They returned at all heights; some flew in so low over the coast that the blisters of the gun turrets could be seen, and the coloured markings of mascots painted on fuselages—perhaps a ship would circle, a red ball of light curve in slender grace into higher air, to fall with thin wavy thread of smoke as the Fortress or Liberator lowered its wheels to land with a wounded crew among the Beaufighters on the aerodrome built upon level fields across the valley from the High Wood.

Evening after evening incarnadined by the sun setting

under the pine-belts and merlin-haunted sandhills of the western sea-board moved the massive drifts of black Halifax and Lancaster bombers, heavy laden upon the suppurating hues of Europe's dying day. As great blow-flies singly they droned overhead, but twenty, thirty, forty, fifty, sixty, a hundred were to be seen by men standing at rest in gardens or children by cottage windows at any moment of glancing upwards; and as they disappeared over the sombrous sea hundreds of others were coming up out of the lingering light of the west. The earth was in full shadow of the sunless night; and through the darkness of being the steady roar persisted, minute after minute, hour upon hour the beat of thousands of stub-exhaust notes merging into a torrent of sound that filled farmhouse parlour and cottage kitchen where families sat behind drawn black curtains, while the panes of leaded casements trembled and tittered and at moments all the pantiles of the roofs of the villages seemed to be vibrating together.

Flights of grey crows stippled the sky above the sand barriers and shingle tongues of the flat and broken shore, flying low over the dun dishevelled surf and beyond into the mists of the sea wastes, called by a wind redolent of icicles a-drip from sun-glazed crags, odorous of warm spruce and fir and dwindling snow.

Harra the Denchman flapped steadily into the north-east, his head turning now left, now right, in scrutiny of small ships whose rigging gave hope of rest; but always greater than the desire for rest was the instinct for renewal in a high land of mountain and forest glowing with midnight sun and pale in the northern dawn.

As stark twilight of the March day cast a leaden light upon the sea, Harra the Denchman passed over a small inflated rubber dinghy where four survivors of a combat crew of a Fortress lay slumped and feeble with cold. Near the raft was an area of smooth but heaving water upon which the shifting sheens and hues of oil were playing, an area to windward of where the aircraft had sunk. One of the men raised his head as the crow flapped over, and by the steady flap of the bird's wings the wild hope came to him that they could not be far from land, and that the Air-Sea Rescue Service of the Royal Air Force might after all be able to find them.

The young man who had looked up was the pilot of the foundered ship, and he wondered, without curiosity and with indifference, if this was indeed the last of many missions with his Combat Wing of the 8th Air Force. He was from a seaport town of New England; all his life, until the past few weeks, he had felt a passion for birds, and for flight, which was almost a lyric ecstasy within him. The illusions of his youth were now abated; the truth of his experiences had left him quiet, as though empty, for he had come to identify himself with his enemy, and life as a test to destruction, and of spiritual value only; therefore he had no desire to escape from his thoughts by the usual method of getting a jag on by liquor. He was a young man punctilious and high-minded, with ambition to be the poet speaking for his generation as in a previous war Wilfred Owen had spoken for the generation of 1914-18. Before he had flown to Europe he had been too modest, or too involved in youthful dream, to believe that his work was worthy of any regard other than his own. Now, having seen through life as it seemed with an ice-cold clarity, he felt that there was no purpose in form or colour, certainly not for man, and maybe not for God, as far as the planet called the Earth was concerned.

The grey crows were followed by flocks of stock-doves which had picked bare many an acre of clover and thousand-headed kale in the fields of England; and Dufa the native ring-dove, the big solid-seeming white-collared bird, had the woods to itself. On the first warm and sunny day of the year Dufa's croodling was heard from the High Wood, across the meadow and the riverside Carr. *Strong i' th' arm and thick i' th' head* is the proverbial description of the East Anglian labourer, that invader-amalgam of Nordic, Angle, Roman, Saxon, Norman and hated red Dane; and strong in throat and crop and thick in feather—overlaying tightly the purple-red muscles of the breast, a tough wad against shot—might apply to the native ring-dove. The farmer's small son had watched Dufa dragging itself along the walk between the Long Wood and the Home Meadow, its crop weighted down by so many acorns that it could not rise into flight.

The boy was now ten years old, and he loved the land and all things natural upon it. He knew the nesting holes of the green and spotted woodpeckers in branches and boles of decaying pine, ash, and beech-tree; he knew where the kingfishers dug their tunnels in sandpit and lip of chalk quarry; he knew the warblers and white-throats which wove their cradles among nettle stalks and bramble bushes, the reed-sparrows and sedge-warblers which nested in the osiers of the Willow Plot, the rush clumps wherein meadow and tree pipits laid their earth-mottled eggs, sought by the cuckoo who every spring watched from the pine-tree at the corner of the Carr; he knew the nesting places of snipe and moorfowl and mallard, and sandpiper among the forget-me-not, loosestrife, plantain, and cress of the riverside. His friends were the wrens who made their ball-nests of hay in the sides of haystacks, and of moss and leaves in the crannies of flint walls; the tree-creepers who pushed themselves by spread and pointed tail feathers up the barky trunks of trees, seeking grub and spider; the swallows who fled twittering along the sky-reflecting dykes and mortar'd their cup-nests of grey mud and feather under the concrete bridges between the meadows; he knew the mellow bubble-strung cry of the wryneck or jynx bird, which hissed like a snake when he peered into its nest of leaves deep within cleft gatepost or split tree stump; he knew of the haunts and habits of magpies, jays, and hawks which had increased so noticeably, with the weasels and stoats; he knew the nests of pheasants and partridges which were nearly always robbed of their eggs by men. He had made maps, painted in watercolours, marked with the nests; but two items had not been recorded that spring—the nest of Kakkabis and Pertris, and the tracks of Chee-kai, for since the return of Italian prisoners working under the War Agricultural Committee the birds had not been seen.

A habit is hard to break; but when broken, is hard to mend. Others made the seed-beds on the farm, others drilled seed into the arable, others would reap the harvest. The dispossessed farmer, repository of broken habit, did not know what to do with himself any more.

One May morning, a Saturday, being a holiday from school, the boy, prompted by his mother, asked his father if he would like to go for a walk with him. The invitation induced hesitation, because of a deep reluctance to face meaningless space and brightness; but the boy's mother said she would come with them, and somewhat nervously the trio set out to walk upon the farm. Conversation ceased when the ex-farmer saw yet once again the broken, pot-holed condition of the roads, the gates and posts lying broken and overgrown with nettles, the new-laid hedges of a few years back wild and dishevelled once again, with barb-wire coils and trenches on the ungrazed hills, now thick with thistles.

As they came to the crest of the hill and to level ground,

so the fields became visible. Soldiers of a searchlight unit were standing about, their encampment of black hutments and radar equipment occupying several acres of what had been one of the best barley fields. They stared at the gaunt figure with the grey hair, and blank look in eye. Some of them had been babies, or unborn, when he had been fighting as a youth in the infantry, and later as a scout pilot of the Royal Flying Corps. Beyond the hutments the level field was a mass of pale yellow charlock smothering the paler green of barley plants. What a difference from the clean and luxuriant barley which had followed the bare-fallow of the year before the war! But what was happening at the far end of the field?

A tall red-wheeled tractor of unfamiliar pattern, its rubber wheels tearing tracks in the corn plants, was rapidly pulling across the field an iron tank on wheels to which was attached a pipe and nozzles which sprayed a mist of yellow liquid upon corn plants and weed plants alike.

A truck with a thousand-gallon tank was standing near the gateway, and men with yellow faces, hands, and clothes were mixing a drum of oily yellow liquid into the tank, from which the barrel of the spraying machine was filled on its return.

The sprayed liquid withered all life that it covered; weeds with broad leaves perished, but from the drooping leaves of corn the liquid dripped, thus preserving the stems. It was claimed that the yellow chemical stimulated the growth of the corn; but it was an addition of sulphate of ammonia to the spray that gave this stimulation. Men working with the stuff wore no gasmasks but they had been warned to wash their hands before eating their dinners; for two Irishmen had already died, neglecting the warning. The milk they had been given as an antidote to the inhalation of the spray had not saved them;

they had felt queer, sweated coldly, and died after a few days in hospital, for at that time the chemical was a new thing, and the men, as boys, had not been trained to obey orders.

When parents and child returned that way the next day, a Sunday, interested to see what the field would look like, they saw twenty acres of corn that appeared to have been scorched by flame. The leaves of the barley were grey. In a few days the new leaves would be appearing; meanwhile the field was a disturbing sight. It was good to see the charlock shrivelled, the stalks of thistle and dock turned black; but what damage would be done to the bacteria which broke down decaying leaf and stalk into humus which dissolved into plant food, and, more valuable, held the water in the soil? Was such farming helping to make a dustbowl of arable England? Was it part of the general scientific ruin of the world? Several fields away lay the aerodrome which had been fields, trees, hedges, and country lanes a year or two before; now from the long dark runway aircraft, loaded with rockets for the destruction of shipping off the Dutch coast, were taking off.

As the three were crossing the pale field, the boy stopped and pointed to a nest of young larks dead in the corn. His father said nothing, and they walked on towards the pine-wood above the steep field where, four years before, smuts of the burning of the oil-tanks of Rotterdam and Ghent had been falling. He saw again the black threads falling on his sun-browned flesh, the black police car; he entered once more the timelessness of day and night when the 'hours were black monarchs that ruled by torture'.

They sat down on the sward beyond the fence, while below lay the folds of the field rising out of the hollow, flanked by the Long and High Woods, and beyond, over the crest of the Pightle, was the azure sea, with lines of white showing the breakers upon the barriers of sand. It was so warm in the sun that they sat there long after the bombers had gone, and the croodling of doves filled the valley below. The man lay on his back, breathing deeply and slowly, his fingers touching the short grasses, where bees burred to the purple florets of wild thyme growing in the sward with tremulous yellow flowers of ladies' bedstraw, and the tiny white blooms of eyebright. Slowly the dark years receded, as he felt the sun on his face once more, and the dear earth of England bearing his body under the sky which, though flawed momentarily as by trails of fear in the remote blue, would shine true on child once more when truth had cleared the lie from life.

While he lay there, he heard a partridge calling, and a peculiar inflexion of the bird's wheezy note echoed mournfully in his mind; for the bird was saying, *per-tris*, *per-tris*, calling perhaps its companion in splendour of which nothing had been seen for some months; the bird he had believed to be dead, and better so, for to die was to be at rest. *Per-tris*, *per-tris*, the bird was calling.

The boy was sitting up, his eyes open wide, listening. He had recognized the voice of Pertris. He wanted to tell his father, who appeared to be sleeping, but he dared not move, for by the sound of the voice, Pertris was coming nearer. He sat still, trying not to move an eyelash, or breathe audibly. Then he saw the head of the bird looking out from the rough grasses at the edge of a disused trench. It ran over the sward to the hedge. The boy did not move; the woman, sitting near him, did not stir; the man seemed to be sleeping.

Pertris, after inspection with head erect, walked into the hedge, and through to the corn. The boy got silently on his feet, and crept to the hedge. He saw the bird walking, saw it pause, and walk on, half running. It settled in a slight hollow, and crouched down. He could just see its back, above the grey leaves of the barley plants. When he walked over to the hollow, it ran away. Searching, he found a dead red-legged partridge quatting on the ground. It was Kakkabis.

The man and woman walked over to see it. Had the bird a nest of eggs somewhere, perhaps in the hedge? They looked about, but could find nothing, *Per-tris, per-tris* called the iving bird, somewhere beyond the hedge. There was no answer, save the plaintive whistle of a greenfinch in a thorn whose blossoms were falling in the windless air, and the distant cooing of a dove.

One morning, in answer to a telephone call, the doctor called in at the farmhouse. He was a man of a little over forty years of age, and therefore had not suffered physically or mentally in battle, being too young for the first war and too old for the second. He was an intelligent and careful doctor, and much liked in the district. He enjoyed country life, though at that period he was much over-worked. A good shot, he received many invitations; he found the exercise and change beneficial for his work, and a relief, too; for often during the past four years he had been called out, in addition to his routine round of visits to private patients and military camps, by day and by night to attend to air-raid casualties, and wounded airmen descending by parachute. He stopped and locked his car outside the farmhouse on the way home from his visit to a military camp; and after a brief consultation with the woman, who said that her husband was becoming more and more violent in his ranting against the war—such rantings alternating with periods of shutting himself away in the studio—he followed her to that building, wherein the occupant had been sitting in a chair, staring before him. Upon the doctor's entry, however, he rose on his feet, to greet the newcomer with aloof courtesy. Cheerfully the doctor shook hands, noting the infirm clasp of the other, while saying that the war ought to be over that year, with the invasion of Europe coming any day now, and the Russians crushing the German armies in the East, and then things would be getting back to normal; though it would take some time of course, he added.

The other man listened, but made no comment. Whereupon the doctor felt his pulse, looked at his tongue and teeth, and peeling back an eyelid, stared, and ordered coat and shirt off. He tapped and listened; fitted stethoscope to his ears, ordered deep respiration and listened again. "You seem quite sound," he pronounced, and thought that what was needed was straightening out by a psychiatrist. There was one in Norwich he knew of, a refugee Austrian Jew, who was very busy nowadays.

While he was reflecting whether he should suggest this he noticed the pictures turned face to wall; and asked if they had been put like that as protection against blast, or glass splinters, while knowing, or guessing, the real reason as his next question suggested. "Why don't you paint again?" The other tried to reply, but could find no words. "May I see them?" asked the doctor. "Certainly," replied the other, moving politely but formally to a frame which he lifted off its nail, reversing it. While the doctor looked, he reversed the other pictures.

The doctor stared, then turned to his patient and exclaimed that he had had no idea that he could paint like that. Looking more critically, he saw that the detail was true, but there was more than meticulous observation and power of recording natural detail, more than an ability to draw, and to compose a picture; there was a true poetic

266

imagination, the very spirit of the creation of life itself in the work. The doctor was Irish, and responsive to the Celtic lyricism of the work, but there was another quality in the paintings which he could not define to himself, a luminous and indeterminate *something* in the depth and colour that made him turn impulsively to the older man, clasp his hand, and exclaim in terms of warmest regard, "My dear fellow, there is genius in the hand and mind that painted those pictures!"

The older man stood still, his lips slightly quivering, his eyelids lowered; a tear rolled down his cheek, and dropped on a paviour of the floor. He could not speak for several moments, but at last looked up with a smile, and said, "One is only a medium, a trustee, as it were."

The doctor turned to the pictures again, moving from one to another, seeing them now with his own personality freed from the petrified feelings of the other man which had constricted him on first coming into the room. "By Jove, yes! You must paint, do nothing but paint! Forget the farm—you're not the only one who's been messed up by this damned war, you know. We're all in it! You did these some years ago, of course?"

He had heard of the bird with the extraordinarily long brown-barred tail from Harcourt, the farmer who had shot at it as it had crossed over the boundary hedge with a covey of partridges. The doctor had been one of the guns on that occasion, and had heard the discussion at lunch and again at tea with other shooters and their wives around the table of the manor house. One of the older sportsmen had remarked that the bird might have been a stray from the woods of an estate of fourteen thousand acres of heath and pine-wood held by one family from the Middle Ages. It was now a forsaken area, used for battle-practice with live shell. A former head of the family had, in the days of Victorian opulence, reared some

267

of the bar-tailed birds in an aviary, and turned them loose in the woods afterwards, where they had bred wild and flourished, being extremely wary, shy, and difficult to put into high flight. The hens resembling cocks of the Old English and Chinese varieties, had been shot; and so the birds had died out.

"Tell me," said the doctor, "did you paint this bird from direct observation, here on your farm? I've heard it was very wild and shy. How did you manage to get near to it?"

"I had half-won its confidence when I was arrested."

Glancing from one picture to another, the doctor wondered if it would be an encouragement to the artist, who obviously was a man of small means, if he offered to buy at least one of the pictures, which surely could not be dear now, and must increase in value as the artist became better known. Upon further thought he decided not to try and buy just then, not through sensibility that his visit was a professional one, but from caution; after all, he told himself, he was no art critic, and really knew very little about art.

He would like another opinion first, and thought of an American airman-poet with whom he was acquainted in his village, a most intelligent young man whose judgment would be interesting. Why not try and bring them together? It should help his new patient, who was in need of rest and relaxation—and friendship. He was doing himself no good by remaining within the confined space of the studio. He needed occupation to form new habits, to take his mind off himself, and one preferably in sunshine and fresh air. And what more fitting occupation than that of painting the English countryside in the May month? Yes, he must bring the American to visit him; he was then on furlough, after hospital, having been wounded and rescued from the sea, following three days in a rubber dinghy which had been washed on to the Point in the early spring, the sole survivor of the crew of a Fortress.

As he prepared to leave, he decided not to mention the idea just then. Any direct suggestion or scheme to alter the solitude-fixation would inevitably be resisted: it must be managed in more subtle manner. So bidding the other a cheery good-bye, and saying he would call in to see him again in a day or two's time, the doctor went away to his motor-car, as the squadrons of bombers returning from the fragmented European continent were making their thunder up in the sun.

As he drove along the coast road, the doctor passed the small boy, whom he had attended for various little ills, standing by one of the decayed posts which supported a few rusty strands of plain wire as a fence along the grass verge above the river. He drew up, and spoke to the boy, who told him that he was watching a cuckoo which had just glided from the pine-tree in the Carr and alighted by a rush clump in the meadow below. Looking down at the small serious face, with the large dark eyes fixed upon his own, he felt a sudden tenderness for the child, and on impulse asked him if he would care to go with him that afternoon in a motor-boat to see the terns on the Point, a sandy tongue at the mouth of the shallow harbour. When they got to his house in a few minutes' time, he could telephone his mother and say that he was having lunch with the doctor, before going with him in a motor-boat to the Point, and that the doctor would bring him back after tea, on his way to the camp.

The use of small boats had been forbidden during the war, but the doctor visited occasionally a defence detachment in a concrete fort hidden in the sandhills, when he was telephoned for.

The boy's eyes lit up, and saying, "Oh, thank you, sir!" he clambered in beside the doctor.

269

Trying to see all things clearly, with balance, without irony, without bitterness, the man called Wilbo leaned against the southern outside wall of the little barn, near hollyhocks and sunflowers rising tall, feeling the warmth of the worn flints and bricks with which it had been built and patched, rebuilt and repatched by generations of village builders, feeling the care and hope with which the dead and gone craftsmen had worked on the wall; feeling the warmth of the westering sun oozing into his bones; feeling a balance coming like a benison between the two sides of his mind which had been in division, even as the spirit of western man; feeling that the purpose of human life was to bear its part in the eternal struggle between light and darkness, as it had been waged in the soul of every poet and visonary since the creation of mind; feeling that resolution of the struggle within a man could only come through fidelity to the remote inner voice of himself in pure aloneness. He leaned there upon the warm, worn stones and bricks of the wall, feeling as one who, condemned for so long to thoughts of death, was now reprieved to live. He looked up when he heard voices and footfalls, to see approaching his small son accompanied by a tall uniformed young man with blue eyes and fair hair; and moving to greet the stranger of whom his approval and liking was immediate, he heard the boy exclaim, breathless with the immensity of his tidings, "Dad! Dad! We have found the Phasian bird!"

Chapter Twenty-Five

Chee-kai had found sanctuary in the Willow Plot on the Home Meadow, where among the wildling osiers whose wands were interwoven above clumps of coarse grasses and brambles he was never disturbed. The woods and coverts of the farm had been invaded by prisoners in dark brown battledress with the letters ITALY in red on their shoulders denoting that they had changed their minds and become *co-operators* for the United Nations' Cause (the word *collaborators* had an ignoble connotation, since it had been used of those who had espoused the Axis Cause) and were being re-educated in the ways of a financial democracy—which may or may not have had connection with the slothful and indifferent way they worked in gangs; whereas the German prisoners who remained loyal to their beliefs worked hard and with good heart as a team.

The Italian prisoners, as has been chronicled, were snarers of birds both small and large; and brought to work of a morning, to hoe sugar-beet or gather hay, many spent the best part of every fine day roaming the woods and hedges adjacent to their work. There was no one to stop them unless an odd gamekeeper encountered them, but he could not watch one place for ever. So, with various British and American troops roaming in uniform

—all bored by the war, browned off, cheesed off, brassed off, as the current slang went—over the farms of East Anglia, few nests of wild pheasants survived to become nids. These troops were amateurs; the Italian Co-operators were professionals. Hares, rabbits, poults, roblets, hedgehogs, squabs of pigeons, all and any small birds were taken, skinned, and cooked in the large iron pots.

But the meadows of the farm had been left alone for several reasons: they were visible from the road: they were rented as grazing for Friesian cows and heifers by one who had nothing to do with the arable of the farm, and who came there only twice a day to fetch the cows for milking; and they were the realm of Townshend Toussaint the Tenth, a black and white bull weighing three-quarters of a ton and with formidable horns.

During the winter before the war the farmer had cut and trimmed the rough and twisted stubs, burnt the old wood, planted new slips of Canadian willow to replace rotten stocks, and repaired the wire fence around the outside of the oval area of the Willow Plot. He had let the right of cutting osiers to a basket-maker who had cut only selected wands for the limited trade of making bushel skeps for carrying chopped roots and chaffed hay to the feeding bins of bullocks, wintering in yards, and hurdle wind-shields for gardens. The farmer had cut the unwanted wands himself, leaving them to rot under the stocks before the rising of the sap. During the spring clusters of buds had broken out of the stocks, to arise in delicate wands of red, yellow, and green, a pleasing sight to some travellers along the road above the river.

Migrant passerine birds which had nested in sedge and reed had found their habitation removed with the clearing of the dykes, when they had returned in spring from

Africa. Warblers, shapely of body and marked by yellow streak in the short head feathers, which had been wont to weave their nests about the sword-like leaves of flag and reed arising from the deep alluvial soil, found among the osiers an alternative security for their nests. Reed buntings came with the warblers, and whitethroats, and occasionally nightingales; and by day and by night throughout the months of May and early June the green wind-swaying Willow Plot was a-churr and a-jarr with brilliant and excited chatter. And here from corn-sowing to haysel had lived Chee-kai, seldom venturing forth between the clear hours of early morning and the calm golden light of late summer afternoon. Always shy and wary, the voices and noises of human beings in the woods had made him avoid those dangerous places, and when he crept forth from the Willow Plot to his feeding it was only after intent scrutiny and hearkening. He moved with head held low, creeping under the lowest strand of barbed wire, and running swiftly to the dyke where freshwater moved seawards, fed by springs under the distant end of the Long Wood; he sprang across the dyke, crept up the broken bank through the weedy jungle of dock, burr, and umbelliferous plants growing alongside the mossy path under the wood, and, after listening again, moved down the hedge. He never flew, but relied on his speed of running to keep himself at a distance from any suspicious noise, however small and remote.

If a wandering cock of Black Neck, White Ring, or hybrid strain crept among the grass tussocks growing thickly under the osiers of the Plot, Chee-kai would, after assuring himself that the intruder was another pheasant, creep upon the bird and drive it forth. Likewise with any dun hen-bird leading her cheepers; for he claimed the Plot as his own, tolerating only the warblers and buntings whose chatter was as a noise-screen under which he hid and rested.

Sometimes in the early morning, before the cowherd came for his cows and long before the sky began to roar with the eastward passage of the bomber divisions, each of over five hundred aircraft, Chee-kai would hear the call of Pertris on the Breck, or from the adjacent common below that sloping field growing its fifth crop of barley—a diminished crop, thin of stalk and small of leaf and ear —and run towards the cry, replying with his high note, seven or eight times repeated, a simple almost frail cry which a casual listener, not seeing the bird which had uttered the call, might have thought to be that of some small hedgerow passerine.

Time had not changed the attitudes of Chee-kai and Pertris towards one another. They still met gladly, the hybrid pheasant running towards the much smaller partridge as though it were still a chick needing protection and security; the old partridge always assuming vigilance and direction for Chee-kai when they were together. The continuance of their friendship was due, on the one side to the fidelity of the nature of Pertris, and on the other to the fact that the hybrid bird had never mated, so no emotions had modified its nature or outlook. And Chee-kai was a lonely bird, needing companionship, as with all warm-blooded creatures.

The sun of summer poured down its beams upon the Willow Plot; the green bunches of tussock grass, called bull-fronts by countrymen, turned yellow at the tips of their broad ribbon leaves, first premonition of the turn of the year as the solar curve inclined upon swelling seeds and fruits of the western hemisphere. The black soil of the meadow was most warm; the roots of the willows sucked moisture from the layers of peat—strung with shells of cockle and other molluscs laid there when the sea's diurnal tides had covered the saltings and creeks before the reclamation and levelling in a past century—and their slender leaves glistened green in the light airs which eddied through the valley with high noon, when the warblers rested from song and dozed after their labours of searching for caterpillar and water-fly, and the hen-birds spread wings, shields from the burn of the sun, over their young asleep within the deep woven nests. Then Chee-kai, lying amidst glowing yellow flowers of kingcup, spread his wings and lay in contentment, his eyes closing and opening again with every sound, never sleeping but resting himself in the lulling contentment of summer, feeling the heat of the sun which he loved upon the glowing feathers of his back; then Chee-kai yielded himself to the great creator of all living, the warmth of all being, the god of the golden sun.

Chee-kai had been lying in the sun, among the clusters of kingcups, happy in the warmth and stillness, when the small boy, accompanied by a tall young man in khaki uniform bearing upon his shoulders badges in red, blue, and yellow a device of wings and star upon and within an embroidered 8, had come quietly over the meadow, the boy leading and the man following, feeling that he was no longer denied re-entry into a world of innocence which had been his before heaven had become metallic, before the sky became steel beaten by the hammers of the brain, the staring troposphere "blue with all malice like a madman's flash, and thinly drawn with famishing for flesh". The clearness of the mind of the boy, its simple directness and lack of exaggeration and emotionalism which was truth, his plain and factual yet lyrical descriptions of the birds and other country objects which he seemed to know by divination, his ready acceptance of friendship on a basis of equality, without shyness and yet with a perfect natural courtesy, the entire absence of a false bloody-mindedness about the war—so unlike the normal small boy with his demands for chewing gum and glamourizing of the alleged heroics of combat—had moved the young man and touched his tenderness, and made him think gladly of his British ancestry in East Anglia, and with pride that his being came from such a root-stock. Happily the two had walked along the turf of the sheep-walks at the edge of the marsh, which now was widely covered with plants of sea-lavender not yet come into flower. They had turned inland by the hedge of a barley field, and reached the coast road, with the river below and the Carr rising dark green at the end of the meadows; and walking down the drift beside the river, had come to the southern end of the wood, crossing over a bridge and so to the narrow spit of land between river and dyke which enclosed the Carr. Walking over a plank, they had come upon the meadows, with the dark crest of the High Wood rising steeply to the south on their left, had crossed concrete culvert and tracts of rushy grazing below the Breck, and following across the common, had arrived at the beginning of the Long Wood and the Home Meadow on which stood the Willow Plot. Approaching with great caution (for the boy was afraid of Townshend Toussaint the bull, and that was why he had never dared to venture upon the meadow before) with light breezes eddying down the valley in their faces, they had trodden softly and slowly over the close-grazed grass, and so come to the wire fence fixed by staples to posts of cleft oak; and the tall young man, peering between rustling leafy wands of willow, had seen something which, by its radiance, had made his heart beats to feel thickly in his neck. And lifting the boy up, he had held him while he stared at the wondrous thing. Then down again, slowly and gently, and a quiet stealing away, downwind as they had come,

and a wide circuit away from the eastern end of the
Willow Plot, and so home to tell the news.

Thus began a friendship between two men which was to
continue until death, and even beyond the chiaroscuro of
terrestrial living. In the common standards of the con-
temporary world these two men should have been
enemies, since belief in ideas constituting war by which
men and women of both sides were tortured, broken,
slain, drowned and burned—manifestations of the agony
of the split mind of western man in political conflict—was
less than an inner faith they shared. Each gave of himself to
the other, as men tried in battle afterwards share a wisdom
which makes them immemorially wiser than the untried
civilian who fights his enemy with words, and, when the
flowers are growing upon the ruins of cities, hangs him
with the logic of a pavement mind.

These were days of early summer when for hour after
hour the singing of larks above the barley of the Breck
was the only sound from the sky: when only the soft,
sleepy croodling of Dufa the dove came from the woods:
when upon the sea-coast only the wavelets moved, only
the wading birds flew piping over sandhill and mudflat.
The fields were empty of human movement, the corn in
ear and the hoers gone.

On such an afternoon, when the friends were sitting on
the grass at the top of the Breck, the Pightle sloping away
behind them through the line of wind-blown thorns, and
the boy was crouching by a small fire to boil a kettle, his
mother cutting bread and butter for tea, Chee-kai walked
down the sloping bank from the High Wood, and they
saw his full beauty as he began to feed quietly in the
shadow of the trees. As they watched, from the lips of the
boy fell notes of curlew-crying wildness, of otters calling

softly one to another in still and starlit nights; the bird looked up, head upheld on neck, his long tail curving away until the tips of the barred feathers lightly touched the grass. The boy whistled again, and from the upland field came the sound of the rusty key turning the lock, and the answering cry, faint and trilling, of Chee-kai. They sat still, and saw Pertris walk down the bank, and watched him seeking among the grasses for seeds, beside Chee-kai.

The two birds remained there, quietly feeding, until through the trees of the Long Wood came the sound of singing, and the rattle of a bicycle on the hard trodden earth of the causeway as a youth came to fetch the cows off the meadow for the afternoon milking. Then the Pightle was empty once more, yet filled with a happiness that could not be spoken.

But the happiness was momentary, even as the clearness of skies from aircraft, which at that time were being directed south to the Channel coast instead of east to the Rhineland. One evening when the pilot arrived, his face showed the forked ways of his mind. The older man had ever been careful not to speak of the war in any way that might have turned the pilot from his duty: even so, the pilot already had penetrated, with the "enlarged and numerous senses" of the poet, to a wider comprehension of reality which was as yet unknown to his fellows. He had no hatred in him; but he could not find love in the world, beyond his feeling for the older man, whom he thought of as one whose light had not been put out by materialism. For himself, there was no purpose in living; in a world so decaying, so florid with self-interest masked as patriotism, the only honourable thing was to die. Thinking often of friends who had fallen, he had asked to be allowed to fly again.

The death-wish gives to the unhappy flesh a calm that

is but a temporary settlement of the mind. For beyond earth's compost, whence that wish is borne with man's arising to the sun, there is a realm remote from the light-years of the mind's calculation, a realm of impersonal harmony, of poetry. The pilot had yet to come to full vision of the poet; but he glimpsed it that night, when the two ways of his mind came together in full flow of truth.

While it was yet evening, the two men sat in the studio talking, seeing through the open windows the sky dimming to hues of brown and purple after a great flaring sunset of a kind rarely beheld in East Anglia, where the air generally is dry and thereby a clear filter of light. After the sun had gone and colour had faded, when Lyra first shone above the woods, and owls were flying darkly over cottage gardens, from north and south of west came the black streams of aircraft, to burden thought with the hopelessness of hope, the helplessness of love, with a vision of little children clasped by mothers against the terrible brilliance of phosphorus bombs, of the vanity of tears and the pity of prayers, of the mercy of fire ultimately resolving all to carbon, ash, and salt of the flesh's foundation. As darkness bore down with its stupendous weights upon the mind, as the earth in orbit seemed to have broken its bearing and to fall in chaos, the poet began to pace the floor of the room; and the older man went quietly to the radiogram in the corner of the studio and with the weak light of a masked torch began to place records in the holder. He switched on the machine, the first record dropped upon the metal disc. He turned the regulator full on, and waited. Then from the amplifier came sounds that were an immediate challenge to that which had transfixed youth, and life, and gaiety, which had cast its slough upon the young, the beautiful, the brave, which had pretended to the golden fleece of truth, when it was but the outworn vestment of those who sat at the tables within the Temple of Life, come there not to pray, but to thieve.

> Sanctus, sanctus, sanctus,
> Dominus Deus Sabaoth,
> Pleni sunt coeli et terra
> gloria eius.

This was the Mass in B Minor of Johann Sebastian Bach, this was the music of the voices of the six-winged seraphim which did cry one unto another, this was the glory of the true German spirit, the immense power and beauty of the German mind, of the European mind, of three millennia of the thought of Hellas arising above the negation of materialism. Through the continuous rolling reverberation in the darkness the choruses arose in antiphony, massively in two groups of three to a sustained harmony above the basses, above the organ diapason, above the roll of bombers, while the tremulo of trumpets was as a bird of beauty rising in radiant flight through the massed darkness which would destroy it.

> Osanna in excelsis.

Passing up the village street at five minutes after ten o'clock from the Horn and Corn, the stockman paused to listen to music which seemed to shine through the torrent of black noise that was shaking air and earth and water.

> Benedictus qui venit
> in nomine Domini.

At a quarter past ten o'clock the listener crept in the shadow of the hedge, to be nearer the barn that he remembered as a bullock box in the old days.

> Agnus Dei qui tollis
> peccata mundi
> miserere nobis.

280

The stockman tip-toed down the gravelly yard, conceal-
ing himself against the lilac bushes from which came the
scent of blossoms he had known there since boyhood. His
pipe was out, he did not think of lighting it.

When it was over, and the last bombers had gone far
out over the sea, he went away up the village street to his
cottage. The night was quiet, the only sound was the
voice of an evejar singing far away down the valley.

The days grew clear and wide over the green earth,
Persephone casting her light upon fields of corn coming
to full sap with the sun, which, leaving far behind the pastures of the Bull, and the Heavenly Twins, Castor and
Pollux, reached the solstice of midsummer, climax of
light and darkness in the western world; and entering
Cancer, ruled that summer's noon was over, that the days
thenceforward must diminish, that the hues of seed and
harvest replace the colours of resurgence and hope. The
nights were wholly twilight, dim with moths as the two
friends wandered by the woods, or sat upon the high
ground, watching the sea far away glimmering in the
dusk; or they lay in armchairs within the studio, doors
and windows open to the warm airs of the night, while
the stars burned dimly over the valley; they spoke seldom,
they understood one another's thoughts, they shared the
comradeship of peace.

The sun passed from the Crab into the sign of the Lion,
where shone Regulus the royal star of Copernicus, with
Gamma Leonis, most beautiful double star of the northern
heaven, the one the hue of golden wheat, the other of
Pomona's ripening apples; the sun entered Virgo, while
the harvest was being gathered, perhaps the last harvest
of the war: the last corn harvest.

And the corn hung bleached in the heat of summer

shimmering like goldbeater's skin above the valley, the barley hung rotten-ripe in the gold-crinkling heat of summer, through which the hammers beat all day, far into the candent sky, as the heavy-laden bombers flew into the east. The sky was blue glass glittering with flaws as it trundled round the sun; the lens of the sky, the fount of all beauty by which men might find truth, was flawed by grey fear which trailed aimlessly in the vacuum under heaven.

The wooden arms of the power binder drawn by the heavy tractor over the cornfields of the farm rotated over and under and over again, stroking the bleached stalks of the barley, so that the knives might easily cut the corn. The harvest sun shone down and burned a deeper brown the arms and necks of the harvesters. The face of the Mediterranean youth on the tractor was dark with dust and kerosene oil.

The two friends, with the boy, watched the passage of the machine, and the slow prisoner labour that followed to set up the short and weedy sheaves. Here was no jocund harvest scene, no rites of the corn spirit, no contentment. Soon they left a scene which had nearly lost its meaning, walking past a smashed gate and post, left lying where it had fallen in the second year of the war. It was the airman's last leave before he returned again to his basic operational unit. Before he said goodbye, he made a request that was instantly perceived for what indeed it was: a security-wish, a device against death, a charm for survival: that he paint on his new ship an enlargement of the painting the older man had given him, of Chee-kai in flight, as they had watched it arising out of a narrowing area of standing corn left by the binder, climbing rapidly over the trees growing upon the crest of the High Wood, outstripping all other birds by its power and velocity, like an arrow of gold whistling over the green meadow, and, high over the pine at the end of the Carr, by a sudden and complete turn of its body braking with wings and tail extended, dropping downwards into the tree and so from sight.

Chapter Twenty-Six

A large American sedan drew up outside the small flint and brick cottage of the Flockmaster. The driver, clad in long double-breasted broad-cloth overcoat, sat a while in the seat, seeking his platinum and gold cigarette case and lighter.

He had come to buy a couple of bottles of whisky for a poker party that night with some of his business associates known (to one another) as the Boys, and (to some others) as the Wide Boys. Some of the Boys were of the original shooting syndicate, who, remaining to spit together in the same pot, had become partners in a more or less (as they sometimes remarked among themselves) big way. For now they were directors, under the chairmanship of the one-time moneylender and mortgage agent, of several small Companies, all legal, limited in liability, and genuinely inspired by a devotion to the profit motive based on the well-known business maxim *If we don't, somebody else will*. Things had gone well during the past four years, following the initial stagnation of the first year of the war, and the future looked even better—if the war didn't end too soon.

The chairman of the trading company had begun the syndicate's wartime activities by supplying lorries and trucks for work on airfield construction, employing someone, a man exempted from call-up into the Services because he was "engaged in work of national importance", to do the buying and selling for him, Soon he had seen possibilities of bigger money in hiring out the trucks to drivers who in turn sub-let them to contractors making the various airfields, of which over eighty were being built upon the level lands of Norfolk alone. As the opportunities grew he foresaw that both labour and machinery would become scarcer; he persuaded his associates to take a chance and buy up, from car-breakers' dumps and scrap-metal merchants' yards, all trucks that had not, in the course of years of stagnancy, literally rusted away. Engine parts, gear boxes, axles, springs, shafts, were exchanged and refitted, to make a truck, however old, runnable. Driven on trade plates of a small garage the syndicate had acquired, the reconditioned trucks found their way to airfield sites, to be put on transport-hire rosters, at the high rates offered by the companies. There they remained, in use, or rather available if and when required for use in any minor capacity, each truck bringing in, on an average, twenty pounds a week regularly.

This sum, even when multiplied a dozen, and, as more old lorries were acquired at ever-increasing prices, a score of times, was soon perceived to be what the Boys called chicken feed, for in the gravel-contracting business, by means of six-yard modern hydraulic tippers, four-figure and even five-figure sums weekly were coming in to established haulage contractors. Moreover some firms, the value of whose shares had risen astronomically (a favourite phrase of the Boys) since airfield construction had started, were able actually to replace their old equipment with hundreds of new steel-bodied lease-lend trucks, together with bulldozers and other machinery, the exchange being managed as a capital replacement and therefore not subject to income tax. Often the Boys talked about it, with a certain amount of sneering among themselves and using the current nickname by which the envied haulage bosses were known in business circles—The Forty Thieves. Why couldn't they get in like that, while the going was good? For, as they told each other, the war would not last for ever.

The difficulty was, if they did become a haulage company—even if they could get permits for new trucks—the income tax authorities would sooner or later want to know where the capital came from in the first place: which would mean that a return of the trading profits from the hiring-out of trucks on airfield construction would have to be made; and nasty questions might be asked why payments of the original purchase of capital equipment had not been made by cheques passed through a banking account.

So for the leader of the Boys the finest pastime in the world—which he was wont to declare could never become over-rated, like the next best—became spoiled by cross thoughts of envy, fear, and uncertainty, which were only partly assuaged by frequent repetition of the old local saying, *Littles by littles*. If they kept on as they were, the game was foolproof, since before the old trucks had been towed to the air stations (as they were generally miscalled) he had arranged with the drivers to enter them on the contractors' hire roll in their own names, so that the real ownership of them was concealed. To protect the driver in each case, a form of instalment-purchase agreement had been signed by him, by which eighty per cent of the weekly sum received for the hiring was paid over—in pound notes. In return the truck was promised to the driver, to become his own property when the construction jobs were over. If the driver had to quit before, for any reason, he renounced his claim on the truck. The driver was also receiving a weekly pay-packet from the construction company, for being a driver.

Having lit a cigarette, and taken a few reflective puffs,

the owner of the 1940 Packard got out and locked it with the ignition key, as required by law. Standing before the door of the Flockmaster's cottage, he knocked with his boot, his hands being thrust into the velvet-lined pockets of a long ulster coat once the property of a sporting Edwardian peer's valet and acquired in lieu of one month's interest (at sixty per cent) on a small loan. He had to kick again before the door opened slightly, and the bony face of the dealer peered at him, and seeing who it was said, "Come you in, master, and sit you down by the fire." The other man entered, and ignoring the invitation, remained standing, saying he had to go on at once, and had only called for a couple of bottles of Johnnie Walker. Then with a sudden change of tone to between confidential and leering, he said he would take as many more bottles as could be spared.

The Flockmaster pretended to consider this, while he wondered if he could ask another ten bob a bottle, which certainly he could get from any Yankee flier. His dilemma was that he did not want to get upside a big man, and yet in justice to himself he ought to say that the price was gone up. For the moment he did not know which way to speak; so he thought to tell his visitor of the price he had heard was being charged by Scobb, of Great Swaring, for a day's work levelling the mounds thrown up around the local searchlight site at the beginning of the war, and no longer needed now that enemy aircraft seldom came over. "Sixty quid, and not one word'v'a lie, guv'nor! As true as I'm a-standin' here, sixty pun fer six hours' wark! I watched th' bulldozer warkin' wi' my own eyes, on the Scrivensett road. Compensation o' sixty quid was allowed by the Claims Officer to level the humps, and Scobb, o' Great Swaring, come out and met Wilbo at th' Cross, jes' outside my yard, and some on 'm heard'm say's price was sixty pun!"

The chairman of the trading company heard this bit of news about one of the Forty Thieves with a shrug of the shoulders, as though shaking off envy. Shubrede Scobb, who had been born in the village of Great Swaring, honestly owned well over a thousand modern trucks, together with over a hundred bulldozers, scrapers, grabs, and excavators; he possessed ten thousand acres of the best land, with shops and houses, hotels, a grain-drying warehouse which he ran in conjunction with a corn merchant's business, drying and buying and selling hundreds of thousands of quarters of corn off farms which cut with the new combine-harvesters, but had no means of drying the grain if, in a damp harvest, it contained more than fourteen per cent moisture. And young Shubrede Scobb, working on his father's smallholding in Swaring for five bob a week when he was sixteen, had been told to clear out of it, as he wouldn't work and thereby was heading for failure in life. Well, b——r Scobb o' Swaring! And turning his thoughts away, the visitor said, "So that rotten Little Englander, 'Wilbo', is still about."

"Yee-es!" replied Flock. "They chuck 'im out's farm. Some dew say he done ten years' wark' in three, but 'tes goin' back now, so what good's't d'n'm? I reckon he's done wi' farmin', they say he don't do narthin' but walk about now." He added significantly, "Maybe his marster wot he come here for had 'ers mind changed for'n." He spat into the fireplace. "The war won't last much longer. Thenk you farmin' will go back agen?"

"It's hard to say," said the other, and at that moment an idea came to him that he pondered. Seeing him in quietened mood, the Flockmaster deemed it a favourable moment to announce that whisky was up ten bob. "I hev tew pay more now, guv'nor, I can't dew it no cheaper." And to his satisfaction, the other said, "That's okay,

Flock, I'll take half a dozen, or a case if you've got 'em."

"Done," cried Flock, and struck with his hand the sleeve of the other's coat, striking the bargain in the manner of the Michaelmas and Ladyday auctions. "I've a-got several jimmy o'goblins, too, guv'nor, though I've heer'd the price is rised, ain't it?"

"Who's been telling you that, Flock? You be careful, my boy, ask no questions and hear no lies they do say, don't'm? You don't want nobody to know you deals in them yaller coins, do you? You don't want to get pinched, eh, old boy?" he leered.

Having let the half-threat sink in, he changed his expression; he winked in a friendly manner, and spoke in his more normal voice, "Nor do I want my business known, see? It may be your business too. So keep it close, my boy, and hark ye to what I'm going to say. I've heard that farm may be sold, and I'm interested as a prospective purchaser, and prepared to risk a drop in values after the war. I like the idea of farming. Land's the best investment anyway, and it's nice to be able to invite a pal to a bit of shooting on a Saturday. What's it worth, twenty pun' an acre? It's been sucked, white crop after white crop, and was farmed badly before the new man came. Twenty pun an acre, I reckon, what's say?" He knew that farms in the past few weeks, and not of the best land either, had been changing hands for as much as forty pounds an acre—land that, before the war, was not worth eight. He was prepared to go up to thirty for the farm; and his idea was to try and buy it at that price, paying in cash, and making a private arrangement that the declared price, for stamp duty shown on the conveyance, should be twenty. That would mean the farm would cost him roughly seven and a half thousand, of which only half need be revealed. Then if those bloodsuckers of the government, the income tax inspectors, checked up, they would have nothing on him. The only thing was, would "Wilbo" play ball?

And telling the Flockmaster once again to keep his mouth tight, and slipping him an extra quid for luck, he prepared to depart with the cardboard carton of a dozen bottles of whisky, feeling that life was good. So did the Flockmaster, shoving the notes into his breeches pocket, the interior of which was as black as his finger-nails. He hoped the guv'nor would not discover how he had watered the whisky after taking a drink for himself out of each bottle—only a little drink, of course, just for the health of the one who bought it. At the door the man in the Edwardian peer's coaching coat said, confidentially, out of the corner of his mouth, "Tell you what, old cock. There's a hundred for you if you can buy the farm for twenty-five pun' an acre! Good enough?"

The Flockmaster did not understand exactly how it was to be done, but he pretended to the required knowledge by putting an expression of what he deemed to be cunning upon his features. "Yew leave it to me, guv'nor," he said. A hundred quid! Blast, with that, and what was hid up, he could buy a pightle of land, even a smallholding, and grow barley and beet like a good'un, and have a five-yard stack o' hay for the little old pony!

With the vision of himself as a smallholder with a little old boy helping him feed his pigs and bullocks, the Flockmaster a day or two later took a shot of whisky to fortify himself for the ordeal (filling up the bottle with water immediately afterwards, before he forgot) and set out to call on Wilbo. He wore his best roan-coloured breeches, with buskins, jacket, and cap, while around his neck was a bandanna 'kerchief pulled through a silver ring that had been cut by his father off the finger of a drowned Lascar on the

Great Barrier Sand, which lay beyond the cockle flats and had brought to grief many a wooden ship in the old days.

He called first at the kitchen, tapping on the door, and when the boy came, said, "Is he in, Wilbo, I mean yer dad, 'bor? Here, like a penny?" The boy did not want to accept the coin, but he did not want to disappoint the Flockmaster, so he took it, holding it in his hand, saying thank you, turning round and giving way to his mother. After hearing what he had to say, the woman asked him to wait, leaving him talking with the boy, and went along the path to the studio. Wilbo was cleaning some brushes in substitute thinning-liquid, turpentine being unobtainable. "Oh damn, what does he want? I have nothing to give anybody." "I did ask him, dear, but he wouldn't say." With anguished eyes he said, "I don't really want to see him. I don't want to see any of them. As the stockman said, they're all out for something. I suppose we all are. Do you think he wants help? I don't like to refuse—oh, it doesn't matter, I feel I'll never be able to paint again. What European artist could create a work of art in these times? If it's grazing for his pony he wants, I haven't got any. Though there's that bit under the Long Wood. But that's near the Willow Plot." He sighed. "Ask him to come down, but stay with me, won't you? I might start talking—you know, nervously, ranting, for he's not my sort."

Cap in hand, the Flockmaster stepped timidly through the open door, and came face to face with the man of whom he had so many contrary feelings. Wilbo looked into his eyes; and something in the visitor's attitude, simple and elemental, coupled with the comic appearance of the unevenly flat bald head set with outjutting ears, thick and oversize upon the bony smallness of the skull, and the dog-like grin of wide thin lips, touched a genial chord in him, and in relief and reaction, he found himself greeting the visitor with exaggerated joviality. "My dear old fellow, how very nice of you to pay me a visit! How are you? As Disraeli used to say to all and sundry, how's the old complaint? Better, I hope. Would you care for a glass of beer? Have a fag? Do have something? A chair?" He pushed a leather chair forward on its castors, and held out a packet of Player's. "Thank'ee sir, I don't mind if I du du," said Flock, putting out a bony finger and thumb, withdrawing a cigarette, and fitting it between his magenta lips. The artist lit it for him. Flock puffed carefully, for he usually smoked only a pipe. He wondered whatever the words meant, and if Wilbo was out to suck him in. He must go steady. Littles by littles.

The next moment his suspicions were confirmed; for Wilbo, who had been taking a lot of glances at him, said suddenly: "Do you mind if I paint your portrait?" And not waiting for an answer, he went on rapidly, "That's wonderful! Would you mind sitting on this chair, by the light? Carry on smoking, and talk as much as you like. Just a moment, I'll find a canvas." He selected one from several standing in a corner of the room. It was a bull-fighting scene. He held it before the sitting man. "That's a thoroughly bad picture. I did it years ago. When much under the influence of Goya. Apart from that, the bull isn't right. You don't see that kind in England. It was supposed to be one of those wild bulls from Andalusia that have feet like goats and can turn like hares. It's time he was decently buried." He set the canvas on the easel upside down, selected a brush, wiped it, and squeezing paints on the palette, stroked the bristles through a blob of colour, and with sharp glances at the bemused Flock-master, passed stroke after stroke upon the old painted surface, of ochre, lake, umber, madder, cobalt, and their hues mixed and pressed and turned upon spaces of the palette with the knife. "Bless you, my dear man," he cried, as the portrait built itself up. "You'll never know what your appearance at this critical moment has meant to me! D'you know, I've been miserably feeling for weeks that I'd never be able to start painting again, when suddenly you walk in, and I am at once reminded of an agaric, which is one of the glories of nature, and so on and so forth. Forgive my burbling, don't take any notice of what I'm saying, this is a terrific moment for me! You shall graze your pony on the grass under the Long Wood if you like, that's what you came about, isn't it? As you know, the meadows are let-off, so I can't do anything about them. There's some grazing of sorts along by the river, below the road, but it's pretty rank, and fit only for burning, in my opinion, but you can graze your pony under the Long Wood, with pleasure—that's lovely—just a minute, a little cobalt in the madder for the lips—that's right, old boy, smile, that's lovely, bravo! A gentle smile, that's it. D'you know, I've often seen you with your pony and trap trotting along the road, and wondered where you were going to." He talked on as he worked, at intervals, in an intense concentration, as a relief. When the composition had built itself up, and he was adding touches of colour, he became quieter, with change of mood.

"Strange how we know so little about one another—the real inner aspiration, the small light men hide under a bushel—so that we fail to see that we dislike the faults in our neighbours the more intensely because they are part of our own darkness—throw the fag over there, in the hearth, anywhere—how many of us know the truth about our neighbours, the real truth, I mean, not just the surface appearance of physical existence. That's what I try to reveal in paint. Reality is one thing, appearances another, the spirit of truth is apart from both. In you I see an ordinary little man just trying to get along—trying to

293

do the best for himself in a bewildering world, a world of which fear is so sad a despoiler. Fear takes more forms than one. The artist must try and be apart from fear, and from the hidden effects of fear especially. Without arrogance, without pride, without conceit or self-conception as a superior being, the artist must strive for balance. The artist is a medium of the impersonal illumination of the spirit—yet must share the 'toil and sweat, the blood and tears' of common humanity. If he try to save his personal life, he will lose his soul. He must be first in that sense, but last in all others. Arrogance is of the brain, so is technique, but the spirit is beyond mere technique, incalculable and unknowable. I suppose all this sounds nonsense to you—in the values of the world it is nonsense. But look at the world to-day—is that truth, what is happening? You don't understand a word of what I'm saying, do you? Do you know what you are really? Shall I tell you? You are your mother's child who day by day, year by year, has changed a little, got wore-up a little, but have you really altered inside? Something inside you is capable of being a generous and kind person under its mistrust of self, which is the same thing as mistrust of others. So you see, I cannot caricature you, or anyone else, Flockmaster—may I call you Flockmaster—thank you— I've tried to convey you into paint as my inside self sees you, as my spirit approaches you. And one day you will see 'Wilbo' plain, too. That's what they call me, isn't it? It's quite a nice name, considering what they must have thought me to be! I shan't keep you much longer, Flockmaster, then you shall have a bottle of beer. D'you know, few painters can put flesh, as it feels when it's *seen* if you know what I mean, on to canvas, but I can do it, by God I can when I trust myself! Look at this!" he cried to his wife and son, when they came into the room, the boy still holding the penny in his hand. "You come and look, too,

294

Flockmaster! I mustn't touch it—don't let me touch it!" (to the boy). He stood back, suddenly tired, the exuberant feeling gone, and self-distaste for his false garrulity taking its place. The upper air was thundering, the tiles of the building were shaking. "I don't know, perhaps after all this feeling is but a discharge of psychopathic inhibitionism become extravertist exhibitionism as the soul-doctors—on a cash basis—would proclaim. I'll go and get some beer." "Coo, it's super, Dad!" said the boy, staring at it. "It's just like the Flockmaster." He smiled happily at his thoughts of the portrait, then at the Flockmaster, who came to peer beside the boy, chuckling in delight. "They'll know thet for me," he kept exclaiming. "Thet they will, 'bor! They'll knaw thet, ah, won'm tho! They'll knaw the Flockmaster, thet's a fact."

But even as he was looking the thought came to the Flockmaster, now that Wilbo and the lady were out of the room, that perhaps it was all done to suck him in. He could always say it was done without his consent. What was old Wilbo's game? There was sump'n in't, you c'u'd 'pend on't! He turned to the boy. "Du yar father charge a lot fur one'r these, 'bor? Du 'a?" "To buy, d'you mean?" asked the boy. "Who, me, 'bor?" The boy looked puzzled. "I don't know what you mean," he said. "Du yar father charge me fur havin' me partrait done?" "He won't charge you, if that's what you mean." "Then it won't cost me narthin'?" "Naow!" said the boy, suddenly imitative, "not a farden, 'bor! Anyway, yu paid me, di'n't you, 'bor?" He opened his palm and revealed the penny. The Flockmaster roared with laughter at the unexpected change in the boy. "Blast!" he cried, "yew en't no Jarman boy, yar a Norfolkm'n, t'rough and t'rough! Blast, yew be a comic, blast, I laff fit fur bust!" and he slapped his thigh and bent down with laughing.

A few moments later, looking at the pictures on the

walls, at the pheasant with the long sweeping tail barred as with brown arrow-heads along its smoke-grey length, he was wagging his head in wonder, as though he could not believe what he saw. "Look yew at thet, now! I nivver seed aught like thet. Yee-s I did, tho'. I see such a bard fly over th' meadders, 'twere a wunnerful sight, ah, thet were!" He stared at it. "Thet bard should be b'rights in a glass case, ah, 'bor! A wal'able bard! Hev you seen thet faysant bard lately, what say?" to the boy. There was no under motive for the remark, for Flock was in truly happy mood, as happy as he had ever been in his life, though he was not conscious of it. He was borne out of his workaday self, lifted away as by a gossamer, he was a child without oppression of fear. A thought came to him: could only Mum have lived to see him there, his portrait on the stand, set up with all them lovely pictures. He was beyond himself, uncrabbed, as floating spawn before it inhabits the confinement of flesh in a voracious world.

There had been no ulterior motive for his remark, but the boy had stiffened. He knew about the Flockmaster's association with the poacher, because the stockman, whose cottage the boy often visited, had told him. For in his tolerance the stockman did not allow his knowledge of Flock's ways to come into the friendship he shared with him at the Cross and in the Horn and Corn; and in like manner the feeling the stockman had for Wilbo (though he had spoken to him only once since his return) was apart from his feeling for Flock. Being at peace within himself, the stockman had no judgment of others, no urge to alter them or see their ways mended. So he could tell the boy, in a kind of subdued mutter, his eyes held down like those of a dog awaiting surprise movements, about "someone" (making it clear who) selling the "bards" after "someone else" had knocked them over.

"Tell you narthin' to nobody 'bout thet longtail faysan bard," he had said once to the boy, "thar's them's'd hev thet bard soon'z yew'd say knife, ah, would'n'm!"

When Wilbo and his wife returned to the studio, they saw the boy standing silent near the Flockmaster. The moment of happiness *en clair* was passed. The boy was withdrawn into himself, guarded against the other. The Flockmaster was trying to think how he could ask what he had come to ask. The artist was without that which had gone into the picture he had painted. So the beer was drunk in an atmosphere of restraint, before the Flockmaster took his leave.

That afternoon he took his pony and tethered it on the strip of grass under the Long Wood, satisfied at his good fortune, and remembering the saying, *littles by littles*.

For years the Flockmaster had been an early riser, getting up soon after the sun in summer, and with the morning star in winter. He liked silence, and the feeling of aloneness. One morning as the dawn was breaking, while he stood under an oak at the bottom of the Long Wood, and the first lark climbed singing to the dimming stars, he heard a partridge calling in the field above, saw a pale movement by the edge of the Willow Plot, and knew what it was.

Chapter Twenty-Seven

—◆◆◆◆◆—

To the Flockmaster a bird was a bird, and if it were good to eat or to sell someone would get it if he did not. And a man had to look arter hisself these days, if he didn't no one else would. Money was money, and many an old'n he'd seen took away to the wark'us (workhouse, or poorhouse) when they had no one to look arter'm, and no money to pay their way; and no one was going to take the Flockmaster, like that, if he could help it.

The Flockmaster kept within a dilapidated shed of flint and pantile standing in his yard, among empty barrels, odd bits of furniture, an old corn-dressing machine, and various heaps of sacks, a wire run in which was the game-cock he had bought at the Wild Fowler. He called his bird Jago. He had an idea how to use Jago, hoping thereby to earn many times the price he had paid for the bird. The idea was one of his secrets, shared by no other man. In the autumn, they would see what they would see, he and his bu'tiful li'l boy Jago.

Upon the autumn fields, through mellow Michaelmas days, the plows were at work. Over the larger fields crawler tractors hauled five-furrow implements, envied by lesser farmers whose wheeled tractors covered less ground; while upon smallholdings pairs of horses pulled

298

single-furrow plows which had been in use before 1914. Pale fields of stubble and green fields of olland, spread with muck twelve tons to the acre, became brown in sections widening hour by hour, as cumulus clouds drifted over and gulls spiralled in white flakes following men, machines and horses. It was fine weather of the back-end, and farmers got on with the work while they could.

In the dark of early mornings, before men were set off to work by steward or farmer, the Flockmaster strolled down to fetch his pony tethered on the weedy grazing under the Long Wood. He led it on the causeway to the bridge over the river, and so to the road and up the hill to the village street and his cart within the flint shed standing in the Great Yard by the Cross. Having harnessed the pony between the slender black shafts, he lifted a wicker basket into the well of the vehicle, and drove away from the village. Sometimes he went along the coastal road to the west; other mornings he turned inland, crossed over the brick bridge and trotted a couple of miles or so before reining up and getting down stiffly from the driver's seat.

One such morning, as day was breaking in the east, making clear the black outlines of trees and stacks and hedges along the lane to market, he drew up behind a clover stack built near the hedge and by a gate. At once the pony began to crop the grass at the side of the lane. Dropping the reins, he got down from the seat, to walk quietly through the gateway and peer round one corner of the stack.

The field on which it stood had been plowed the day before, ready for winter wheat. Beyond the eastern hedge was a small wood growing on a slight rise, a favourite place of pheasants. The Flockmaster, having seen several birds there recently as he drove past in the daytime on his way to market, expected to see what indeed he did see: three cocks feeding about fifty yards away, near to one another. One of them was Koch-karr.

Quietly he stepped through the long grasses to the cart. He lifted the wicker basket from the well, opened the lid carefully, inserted a hand into the basket, and drew from it a bag made of red cloth which he had found on the marsh, part of a drogue which had been towed behind an aircraft as target for anti-aircraft guns in one of the camps. The bag was warm with the bird within, which clucked liquidly as he carried it in his arms, carefully because of the needle-sharp spurs it wore, behind the haystack. There he knelt down, to wait for the sun to rise.

The Flockmaster loved his bird, and spent much time in his kitchen talking to it, gentling it, and trimming its feathers. He fed it on the best food, on barley and wheat scraped up from where elevators had stood by the stacks at harvest, on cockles which he gave it with fragments of crushed shell, with minced sugar-beet, carrot, and cabbage, as well as dried split peas and beans, which he had taken from various roadside fields in season. Sometimes, when he fried himself a dish of flatfish, called butts, speared by a neighbour in one of the creeks of the marsh, he gave the best pieces of thick white flesh to the bird. He was giving it strength for its work.

Upon a shelf within one of the hearthside cupboards was a pair of steel spurs, kept bright and sharp on a stone-slip given him years before by one of the woodsmen of Marlcaster, who had used it for putting a keen edge on the blade of his seven-pound axe.

That morning, by candlelight behind blackout curtains, the Flockmaster had bound the spurs to the bird's legs with adhesive tape, from a roll he had pinched from the Red Cross point when once, and once only, he had been persuaded by an enthusiastic neighbour of the Great Yard wherein he lived, to act as a dummy air-raid casualty, and have his legs put in splints by practising village women proud of their Red Cross uniforms. The Flockmaster had agreed to be a "case" out of bravado, and also in the hope (it had been before the days of black-market whisky) that, for a "casu-wallity", a dose or two of brandy might have been part of the demonstration. That, so far, had been the Flockmaster's only official contribution to the war effort.

Jago was of a strain once famous in the mains held all over East Anglia. As his owner moved through the gateway to the haystack, Jago's blood swelled in anticipation of what was to come, and he chuttered thickly as he heard the string being untied. He was a black and red bird, slim and masculine, with feathers already showing glossy, as though the sun had risen to shine only upon his nervous wings.

His neck arose out of the bag, snake-like, as if it would stretch upward and seek its prey in an imaginative sphere more terrible than the reality by which its living was ruled. His body followed, compact and muscular; and his long dark blue sinewy legs came forth, determined and powerful. The polished steel spur on each heel, of an inch and a half in length, was secured in the most delicate and neat manner. His large, vigorous beak showed aquiline— eagle-like; and his black dilating eyes took in all around him, and shone brilliant with the intensity of his feeling. His comb was cut close, his neck trimmed, his wings clipped, pointed, and strong. The feathers on his back were of the glossiest red, and appeared to be the only ones which were left untouched, for the tail was docked triangularwise. He was a compressed framework of sedate and savage courage.

The bird, as the Flockmaster knelt on one knee to peer

round the corner of the stack, began to cluck defiance. His master began to smooth him, to croon over him, handling him gently, pampering his courage as he prepared the bird for combat. He held Jago round the corner of the stack to let him get sight of the cock pheasants upon the new-turned furrows, encouraging and feeding his crowning and mantling until Jago was nearly dangerous to hold; and then he loosed him for the fight.

Jago ran forward down a furrow towards Koch-karr, chuttering and swift, his head held low, his foreshortened wings urging on the movement of his legs. Koch-karr uttered a double sqwark, a cucket accompanied by a wing flutter—a challenge that had in it more of surprise than menace, more of alarm than defiance. He stood upon the furrow-slice, his head held high. Jago ran on, low and swift, his slim smoothness gone, his hackle feathers ruffed out, a ragged, angular, uncontrollable power directed by the enlarged stare of the eye which would strike and annihilate before it came to its object.

Koch-karr was an old bird, yet horny and arrogant. He had fought and driven all other cocks from his territory of the wood in the early months of the year. As Jago approached, he recovered from surprise; anger swelled his body, and shuffed out his feathers. The pittering of Jago's feet upon the drying soil of the cracked furrow-slice ceased as he came face to face with the pheasant, and crouched on the earth for instant measure of his opponent. Koch-karr crouched likewise.

The Flockmaster could see all, since it was happening less than a score of yards away. He felt the emotions of the bird moving in his blood, he breathed quickly and thickly. The first terrific dart into attitude was to him strikingly grand and beautiful, and the wary sparring, watching, dodging, shuffling for the first cut held him fixed with curiosity: they were beak-point to beak-point, until they dashed up into one tremendous flirt, with the noise and action of two wet umbrellas suddenly forced open, a mingling of powerful, rustling wings and nervous heels in one furious confused mass. The leap—the fire—the passion of strength—were fierce and loud, and obsessed by it, the Flockmaster began to growl and hurr, as his pulse beat faster and passion stirred in him.

Suddenly the whirling feathered raggedness fell apart. The separation was as flaccid as the clash had been taut; the separation was deathlike. With beak open, tongue palpitating, wings dragging, Koch-karr staggered out of the close, drooping, dismantled, a bead of red blood welling out slowly and thickly from a small hole where the steel spur had struck and pierced the skull under the short green featherlets. Koch-karr staggered along the edge of the furrow-slice towards Jago, in an attempt to press forward, tottering on his breast, sinking on his tail; the eye grew dim, and a sweat broke out upon the feathers of the back.

Jago, full of fire and irritated courage, leapt and gave the finishing stroke, clove the quivering thread of life with a slash of the steel dagger on his heel. The pheasant dropped from its former compact shape to a relaxed, draggled object that sprawled in motionless ruin in the furrow; while Jago seemed to have been made doubly fierce and muscular by the short encounter, to have grown in size, his eyes to be larger, as he drew himself up on the furrow and flapped his stub-wings, while the Flockmaster hastened over to him, his arms held out, his mouth wide in a grin and a little moisture dribbling down over his lower lips from the corner of his mouth, as he crooned, "Jago ma b'uty, Jago my li'l boy, li'l b'uty, as true a tradesman as ever used tools!"

He picked up the quivering bird, now released of its former muscular compression, its head jerking about, the nictitating membrane of its eye flickering, and stroked it; then, with a glance around, for the beams of the October sun were level with the furrows and opening a shining golden tunnel of gossamers across the field, he grabbed the pheasant, and went back to the cart. From a cottage of tarred flint down the lane smoke was rising.

Putting Jago into the straw-laid wicker basket, and covering the pheasant with a sack, he mounted the iron step to the seat, took the reins, pulled up the horse's reluctant head, and jogged off towards the distant market town, where he knew a man who would exchange a bird for a bottle.

A mile along the road he met the first team of horses going to work, and in answer to the remark that he was out early, shouted, "Ah, yew got to be ter live these days, 'bor!" and drove on, coming to the market town as the steely sky was being riveted by the first squadrons of the 8th Air Force, so commonplace a sight that he did not bother to look up.

From below the bombers were discernible in the blue as sun-glints; but to the waist-gunners each ship within visual range had a different figure or slogan painted upon the metal nose to the rear of the perspex dome behind which the pilots sat: each figment expressive of the varied temperaments of the men within the frail metal shells. One had upon it an unusual device: a pheasant with white, black, yellow and russet-brown feathers upon its head and body, with tail feathers extending towards the waist gunner in his oxygen mask and clothing electrically heated against the sub-zero cold of thirty thousand feet. The aircraft were staggered in flight, one element above or below the other, and the squadrons were stepped up and splayed out into groups, and the groups into a wing, an aerial armada flying into the east in the shape of a wide and deep pyramid of power riveted by individual ships, among them the ship, whose captain was, at the moment the Flockmaster was arriving at the market square, looking down at the remote and tiny outline of his friend's farm by the sea coast six miles below him, and thinking of the invitation he had received by post the day before, to spend Christmas Day in the farmhouse, to lie back in the leather armchair before a long fire in the open hearth, and hear on the gramophone the music of Bach, of Delius, of Wagner, of Elgar, of Beethoven and relax, relax, relax . . .

Chapter Twenty-Eight

Chee-kai still lived in the Willow Plot, sleeping there at night, and feeding in the woods and on the verges of the arable in the early mornings and late afternoons. The only workers on the farm, apart from the cowman at the premises and on the Home Meadow, were the tractor drivers employed by the War Agricultural Committee and the brown-uni-formed gangs of Italian Co-operators standing about on the sugar-beet field at the southern end of the farm, next to the yeoman's farm over which rode the genial figure of Dick Turpin on horseback, carrying out the orders of Harcourt, his master.

Wilbo had often thought of a suggestion made by the doctor on a subsequent visit, that he should cease to isolate himself, and enter into the normal life of the country, beginning by shooting his own coverts in con-junction with his neighbour, who was prepared to keeper the woods without charge, and to divide the number of guns and the game on a proportion of one to three. The doctor had called in one afternoon, and over a cup of tea had outlined a proposal from Harcourt, the yeoman farmer.

Of the eight guns, a requisite number, Wilbo could have two. He could invite a guest to every shoot to accompany him, or he could let a gun as he wished. The doctor suggested that twenty to thirty guineas for letting a gun, owing to the food shortage, would be reasonable; and he would have no difficulty in letting a gun at that price for the shooting season of 1944. He would receive in addition one quarter of the game shot upon both farms. Harcourt was quite willing to make this arrangement, declared the doctor, as it would improve the drives and provide some fine stands for high birds, such as the Breck below the High Wood, the Pightle, and the meadow around the Carr. "The Willow Plot, too, must be stiff with birds." He became a little impatient when the other appeared not to respond, though he listened politely.

In the days before the war Harcourt, like most farmers owning their own land, and thereby the sporting rights, had been compelled to make money out of his shooting by organizing it for a syndicate, which he had managed himself, paying keeper's and beaters' wages, and letting each gun for as much as he could get.

On large farms, well-wooded and well-keeper'd, with good stands, ten guineas a gun for every hundred acres was considered a satisfactory price to receive. Thus on a farm of a thousand acres, with no eggs hatched under hens in coops and therefore no birds put down, and where, if neither disease nor bad weather in late spring caused ruin of the nids and coveys, five or six hundred head of pheasants might be recorded in the game book for the season between October and January, together with two hundred or more brace of partridges, the farmer organizing the shoot, with luncheon and tea for his eight guests, would count himself fortunate if he received eight hundred pounds. The outgoings from this sum would be a hundred and ten pounds for the keeper and his dog, and a further fifty pounds to beaters, a score or so of whom would be engaged at six shillings a head for each six to eight shooting days.

307

Then there was the money received for the game, after each gun had, according to custom, been presented with a pair of pheasants, or a brace and a half of partridges, on departure after tea around the farmhouse table: a jovial tea, the table loaded with cakes, mince pies, sandwiches, scones, bowls of cream, stewed fruit, and on the sideboard a black Bradenham ham cured in a pickle of molasses, bay leaves, cane sugar, and a pinch (and no more than a pinch if the pink slices were to remain tender) of saltpetre, and smoked in oak-sawdust smouldering in the local butcher's shed. The remainder of the game was hung in a lead-lined, perforated-zinc window'd game house behind a north wall in shade, until collected by the licensed dealer, who paid current market prices for the pheasants, averaging perhaps three shillings a bird, with two shillings for a brace of over-yeared partridges, and half a crown to three shillings for a brace of young birds—judging age swiftly by colour of legs and softness of toepads among other things. Hares might fetch eighteen pence to two shillings; as for rabbits, fivepence to ninepence, according to how shot.

The arable farmer, totting up his receipts at the roll-top desk, would be satisfied if he found that he had received a hundred pounds for his game, and cleared another six hundred from the guns in his syndicated shoot. Deduct tithe at seven shillings an acre—three hundred and fifty pounds for a thousand acres, paid by law to the Ecclesiastical Commissioners for the stipends of parsons and curates and the overhead expenses of the legal and secular branches of the Established Church of England operating from the great City of London—leaving £350. Deduct land tax at a shilling an acre, and income tax on the Schedule "A" assessment of the land at 6s. 6d. in the pound—and what was left would do little more than provide the educational fees of his son and daughter.

As for the profits from farming, he was fortunate if he had worked and worried three hundred and sixty-five days of the year in order not to lose money, but to break even, with corn, beef, mutton, and vegetables not paying the costs of production. Sugar-beet, yes, that paid, if there had been a good season, good weather for seed beds, careful drilling, rain at the right time, good singling and scoring, rain and sun, sun and rain, to make sugar, good ploughing-out, good knocking and topping, and all off and away to the factory before the frosts came.

But with the coming of the war, all that was changed. Prices were stable, being fixed by law; good farming produced good profits; and yeomen farmers could dispense with their ideas of income from syndication, and enjoy their own shooting, inviting as guests their farmer friends. It was in this spirit that Harcourt had made his offer to the neighbour of whom he had heard only a little, and believed less of that little. The newcomer had good coverts; that was what mattered; not his utopian troubles.

Should he join in with Harcourt? Wilbo was still in two minds about it, one induced by the friendliness of the doctor, who had assured him that he need not feel that there was any prejudice against him because of his political beliefs. Wilbo knew this: had not the parson, within forty-eight hours of his return, taken the trouble to call and tell him that he must not worry: that time would clear him and others like him? And his wife had also told him that there were many people ready to be friendly. Warmed by the thought of kindness and even of friendship with his neighbours Wilbo had mentioned, hesitantly, that he would like to reserve the Carr and the meadows; but the doctor had retorted at once that the best drives of high birds over the woods would be spoiled if the meadows were "knocked out of it". It was perhaps an unfortunate expression, for it made Wilbo silent. In his mind he saw the golden bird falling out of the sky, and then in some way he dared not think to himself, all became blank. He did not hear what the doctor was saying: the words came from beyond his consciousness, words entirely without significance when placed against reality.

Observing the look on the other's face, the doctor had taken advantage of his silence to press home the point of the high birds, and to link it with a near-exhortation to the bemused man to come out of himself, to forget his own feelings and to live outwardly, to think more of others, and to forget what could not be helped.

It was not the doctor speaking, it was the sportsman, impelled by imaginative pictures of high rocketing birds crumpling and falling out of the sky to the precise swinging cracks of his new Churchill twelve-bore with 25-inch barrels, a weapon to which he had recently treated himself.

"I'll think it over," Wilbo had stammered. "I'll think it over, if I may." The envoy was disappointed; he had come with the best of good intentions, and he felt he had, in a manner, been rebuffed. "There isn't much time left, Harcourt wants to shoot next week, you know." The artist gave him a slight smile as he said good-bye at the door. "I will think it over."

Recalling the friendly doctor's suggestion, he prowled aimlessly in his studio, broken pictures of thoughts passing through his mind, images of resurgent hopes that for so long had met with denial, and now were faced by extinction. To submit to the world of men as it was, perhaps was the only way. Beauty never could prevail, nor truth, nor rarity, but only the commonplace and useful, whether of imaginative idea or materialized form. By what strange accident had this Arrow Bird come upon the fields of a small Norfolk farm, by what chance had it found friendship with a common partridge, by what fate

310

had it escaped destruction in a countryside of men uprooted and restless with death? A bird radiant and of the sun, born in an age of darkness and beautiful beyond resurrection, bird of light and pride, bird partnered and upheld by loyalty, bird of genius watched over by the brave, the dun, the lowly English partridge, true spirit of the soil of England. Was not the bird's fate yet in his own hands, would not its betrayal and death be but the mark of his expended will? His own diffident words came on memory's echo to mock him, *I will think it over.*

The air of the room was being shaken by the great thunder of the bombers up in the sun; the glass tiles, lighter than those of earthenware, were clattering in the roof. The Wing that had passed over the Flockmaster as he drove into the market town with the dead pheasant and Jago in its wicker basket, was approaching the coast. In the aircraft that bore the device of a bar-tailed pheasant the thoughts of the pilot were of the man pacing the paved floor below, trying to start with colour and brush to express the emotions that seemed to be pouring through him, using his mind as a medium. O bird of terraces of glinting rocks, of mountain winds writhing with dragon's breath shrivelling petals of azalea and magnolia, of high lands where the eagle soared, where the vulture hung beaked upon the sandy plains, the yellow rivers of scoriated lands, veritable dust of a culture disintegrated by the machines of the west. *Phasianus veneratus* of the true travellers of the Middle Ages, bird of phoenix legend and of resurrection . . . had become *phasianus reevesii* since a Mr. Reeves, consul of trade, had claimed credit for the bird's discovery, basing his title on a mere importation in much the same manner that the delicate Chinese drink of tea had been discovered by the commercial exploiters of an ancient culture and imported into England where its use was generally debased, its quality lost, the acids of its spoliation adding to the enervation of a race gathered white-faced in narrow sunless streets of towns down whose sewers the fertility of the earth was squandered . . . before the inevitable explosion of a civilization based not on health and soil and art, the servants of God, but on usury, the agent of God's dark antagonist.

Now the passage of the aircraft over the sea was shaking the heavier pantiles, and vibrating the very air within the lungs . . . with a cry, he threw down his brush, struck his head with his clenched fists, and stood still, a man devoid of purpose in living.

Nothing came of the doctor's suggestion. The coverts of the farm remained unkeeper'd, and unshot. One morning towards the end of the year, Wilbo set off to ride on his bicycle along the coastal road, to where Harcourt was having a shoot. Nowadays he saw himself as a useless man, whose ideas were misplaced, because they were untimely. Ideas outside material time were homeless ideas; they were thoughts taken for the morrow, but not for the profit of to-day. What could he do, he thought desperately, to come back to the herd—but the herd which was on the slopes that led only downwards. Could he be interested in the farm, when all he had striven to build was despoiled? But there was the new generation arising, and the war generation which afterwards would be leaderless and bewildered; for the old partisan ideas were no good any more, they were based on that which was destroying itself. Should he sell the farm, and go far away, become self-withdrawn entirely, the world renounced?

Some months before, his wife had told him that the Flockmaster had hinted to her that if he wanted to sell the farm, he knew a gentleman who was very interested, and who had plenty of money. Land was now considered the best investment; but farmers were already wondering if, a year or two after the war was ended, their industry (as many now called it, for mechanized farms were run on factory methods of production) would become depressed again, as before the war.

It was cold that frosty day of late December when he set forth on his bicycle; a drift of cold air had crossed the sea from the north-east, from beyond Scandinavia and the Baltic; the annual drift of frozen air from Siberia was moving down upon Europe.

Shots sounded across the misty field, which was plowed deep for sugar-beet; shots came from beyond the next field of barley stubble, where, twenty yards behind a tall trimmed hedge of thorn, men were standing or sitting on shooting sticks, their tweed-clad wives behind them, and dogs leashed and pinned to the ground immediately before their feet. No longer were the sporting syndicates formed of wealthy men from the towns; these guns were all farmers—men outwardly contented, but inwardly uncertain, and even insecure, for their businesses were run on overdrafts from the banks, 95 per cent of their profits being taken in tax levied to pay for the destruction wrought upon the enemy's economy until unconditional surrender. Of the future they seldom thought: they did not believe in the propaganda that the war was being waged solely for the idea of a New World; they lived in the present.

They shot keenly. One stand over, collect the birds, lay them out for the man with the straw-laid game-cart, move on to the next stand. Were it distant more than a few hundred yards, and they not required to walk in line across fields to bring over the birds as part of the plan for the next stands, they climbed upon a trailer bearing a long and low flat platform, together with their wives who acted as loaders, and their animals who picked up their shot birds (*Goo' dorg—goo' dorg—goo' dorg:* and then,

313

Dead—dead—and then perhaps to gently retentive muzzle, white-fanged, purple-flewed, *Leave it*—sharply, *leave it!*) Behind a red tractor issuing kerosene fumes, they were borne away, stocking'd legs and leather- and canvas-anklet'd boots swaying below the side of the platform, to the next stand. Line out, await the birds rocketting and whirring overhead, shoot, seek, pick up, and onwards again, with an interval of half an hour for your sandwiches, and a bottle of beer offered by the host, as you stand about in windy field barn or sit on your burberry on a hedge-bank away from the north-east. Then on again; for if time is not exactly money nowadays, birds are birds and these guns fire each about five thousand cartridges between mid-October and the first week in January, and of them four thousand bring down pheasant, partridge, coot, mallard, woodcock, snipe, waterhen, pigeon, hawk, widgeon, teal, and even, (in one case at least) seagulls following the plow. They were among the best game shots in Norfolk, these yeomen farmers who tested everything by the unspoken formula *Does it pay*, whose entire lives had been governed by that formula, by which alone they had survived on their lands within the borders of the premier arable farming and winged-game-shooting county of England.

Seeing the tractor trailer with its load of dogs, tweed-clad women, and brown-faced farmers with guns held upright coming down the lane, hearing laughter and catching a sight of open faces and animated talk, the solitary watcher pretended to be interested in something on a twig of the thorn hedge; and when it had passed, with a whiff of kerosene, into the distance, he stood and stared after it, thinking that he had missed what was safe and good in life, what was unexceptionable, what was most prized, the ordinary, the natural. He longed to be riding among them, to be one of them, with sketchbook and pencil, to paint the compact scene; but now it seemed that he had, through fatal idiosyncrasy, lost his chance of sharing in such a life.

As he stood there, his cheek was lightly touched, and then his ear. Sleet was wandering down the sky.

Far out over the North Sea the unseen tentacles of the locator system, groping beyond the curve of ocean, had touched the returning scattered squadrons, which were appearing as moving blobs of light upon radar screens. At points upon the earth, watchers of the Observer Corps were at their posts, ready to report by telephone what aircraft passed overhead. On stations up and down the island, upon the level lands of Yorkshire and Lincolnshire to the east, throughout the shires of Bedford, Buckingham, Cambridge, and Nottingham in the Midlands, to Wiltshire and Dorset in the south, ambulances and foambowsers were standing by with teams of fire fighters in asbestos suits, in the frosty mists lying upon airfields and making them invisible above a few feet.

Snow was falling as the thunder of the first returning squadrons filled the air over the Point of Terns. They passed away inland, unseen by the sportsmen in the fields; the deep noise rolled away to the west. Behind the disshapen formations, over the sea and beyond the Point of Terns, stragglers were limping in. One of them, with two engines seized and airscrews feathered, was badly shot up: oxygen bottles shattered; holes torn in fuselage, and rudder; one aileron shot away; co-pilot wounded in shoulders, arms, legs, lying unconscious with sulfa tablets undissolved on his tongue; waist-gunner dead; navigator inert through oxygen-lack; bombardier dead; pilot wounded, numb beyond pain, clothing ripped, but conscious of left-hand inboard motor stuttering, of gas-leak

315

in feedline of last functioning engine. As the ship came over land, with remaining strength he rang the bell for crew to jump.

The leading bomber had its wheels down, and as it turned away from the others a red flare burned a bright arc through the air, falling slowly with wavy thread of white smoke drifting. Other ships flew on, but from the one lagging behind came a noise as though hammers were knocking unrhythmically inside it. Smoke was now issuing from its remaining engines. Then under it an object was turning over and over in the air, an object defined by the sudden swaying of legs and body as a parachute opened. Other figures fell from it, and the clattering aircraft slid away down a steep dive, black smoke pouring from a wing, where a point of fire had appeared. It went down beyond the dark mass of the High Wood, and a moment later there came a prolonged rending crash, ugly and sullen as the thick black column of smoke rising into the dull day.

Beyond the wood, an acre of barley stubble was afire. From the roaring centre of the unburdenable heat of blazing octane spirit cannon-shell and tracer crackled and arose in curve and streak as thin plumes, one within and beside another, the tail-flames of a comet, of a bird of fire, flying beyond pain and endeavour, beyond the terrible elements of life, and so coming to truth. For even as the brains within the skull of the pilot were bubbling, his spirit was away and beyond the coiling breath, the eddies and the spirals, the white confusions of the Siberian air covering Europe from North Cape to the peaks of the Pyrenees; and beholding a golden bird flying to him, bringing upon its breast the sun of far Cathay, the azalea groves and deep rocky ravines noisy with rushing waters, broadening into the wide and reedy valley of the Phasis, a river in Colchis.

Chapter Twenty-Nine

As he was cycling along the coast road, Wilbo heard the crash of the bomber through a rushing wind, which, as it increased, caused his machine to move slower and heavier to the thrust of his legs until it seemed to solidify with dead weight beneath him. It was as much as he could do to drag it into the roadside, to fall with it there, before pulling himself up, to clamber over a barred gate, seeking the shelter of a straw stack. His hair whipped his eyes and sleet stung his ears as the grey blast threshed the thorn hedges, screaming in the telegraph wires, and slashing a briar of wild rose as though to tear off his ear.

He crouched behind the straw stack, while icy drills of air bored into his body, and all was occluded by sleet. As the thickness of the blizzard passed away, from the lee of the stack he saw the white-multi-snaking winds pouring over the earth. Then he saw that the stack was moving across the field, leaving him straw by straw.

Just as an army is made up of so many individuals, so a stack is made up of so many straws; each one little by itself, but cohered and disciplined, a massive thing. An army in final defeat is like a straw stack in a hurricane. He watched straw after straw leaving its place in the stack, pale yellow straws riding away on the wind. One followed another, swifter and swifter, until the entire stack seemed to be rising in wild disintegration. Ten acres of oat straw, possibly ten tons, value forty pounds, had passed away with the blizzard.

A tall and distant hedge of straw gleamed, golden rampart, in the sudden light of the low-shining sun. And across three hundred yards of frozen furrows to that hedge the yellow straw was dispread like a flat and cold shaft of sunlight.

When it was quieter, he got over the gate, groped for his bicycle, and set off through a world modulated in streamline to a flowing white design. Every stone, every swede in a field of roots, every dead thistle and stick, all objects which had lain on or out of the earth, were shaped as though for a journey into space. Everywhere the tempest as it blew itself out, as it weakened from hurricane to gale force, as it subsided to the cold shocks of half a gale and thence to a steady breeze, thereafter settling to a gentle flowing of air before yielding the earth to silence, had left the snow in white streamline behind all ground objects.

Broken and neglected things, which in their untidiness had helped to subdue the spirit when he had passed that way—collapsed and abandoned cart, rusty plow, fallen gatepost, the hideous area where the village trash dump was displayed for all who passed by to see—all were modulated by the white and flowing shadows of the snow. Fluted slopes and smooth glacis streamed from the fields and in places filled the road from hedge top to hedge top. Soon it was impossible to move forward awheel. Throwing his bicycle over the hedge, where it disappeared in a white flurry, he waded through the drifts and continued laboriously upon the way home, feeling very tired.

Remembering the taste of frosty pine needles, Chee-kai flew at twilight to roost in the ivy-mantled pine, and settled to sleep, while the snowflakes as they dropped out of the darkness touched his feathers.

When morning came, the woods were gaunt and still under a rime-ringed sun; while tracks of hares and rabbits and pheasants wandered over the white fields. A blank silence lay over the earth, watched by a solitary grey crow from a branch of one of the elms in the High Wood which had crashed in the blizzard that suddenly swept the land.

The meadows and fields lay under a frozen mist, while hoar frost added to twigs and branches of trees and hedges its crystal patterns which sparkled and spangled when for a brief while the sun shone out over the High Wood. Chee-kai remained in his eyrie throughout the short day, pecking snow when he felt thirsty, and plucking pine needles. He settled to sleep as the mist sett.ed in dense white layers over the meadows, above which the frosted canopies of the riverside trees arose as from out a spectral lake. Above the crest of the pine was clear sky, black and hung with the liquid quiver of stars. The Plow uptilted to the Pole, the strewn and glittering shell fragments of the Pleiades lay forsaken in those celestial fields above which Altair the eagle soared, and the Swan flew low. Orion bore his shining mace on high, Aldebaran the bull's eye was in red glare above the Dogstar running the luminous steppes of the south-east, pursuing what no mortal eye dare see, Sirius the hound of heaven shaking his spectral froths as though with rage at an unknown flicker traversing the cold sea fogs, a dark shape with tail of fire moving straight and fast, chattering with horrible menace as it flew from sea to land, so that every roosting bird lifted its head in terror and from High Wood and Carr, Long Wood and Ash Hanger, Lady Torfreda's Plantation, New Oaks and Whistlecraft, and from all the coverts around the hamlets of Dopperwich, Galthorpe and Penstone, the villages of Vair Dalling, Twytown, Swimwade and Musselcreek, the mediaeval towns of Flambeau, All Saints and Staithsuent, and in the great park of far Marlcaster, the sentinel pheasants sounded their alarums.

Here was the legendary flaming drake and black apparition with craking voice of nightcrow made manifest upon the countryside. It crossed the coast by the Point of Terns, it hurtled little more than a hundred feet above the sea, passing over marsh and salt-gut and freshwater dyke at the speed of a mile in eight seconds, it charkled in flamey chatter directly over the pine-tree where Chee-kai screamed in terror, watching it growing smaller over meadow and wooded hill and field, a diminishing flicker-mutter passing away straightly into the night . . . until, its harsh breath expended, it tipped to earth and plunged down and once more the cock pheasants crowed, as a white-blue flash split the sky and the earth rumbled . . . as it was rumbling over the south-eastern sea, where in the Ardennes a great battle was raging.

The boy's mother had decorated the farmhouse parlour, in happy conspiracy with her son quietly excited as Christmas Eve approached. Sprigs of holly and mistletoe adorned the dark beam that crossed the ceiling to another beam above the open brick fireplace, and home-made paper chains were suspended across from the corners of the room. In the open hearth gnarled thorn logs and lengths of old ship's-timber gateposts nearly three feet long and a foot thick lay together upon the bed of ember and ash. The boy staring at the rows of little flames that broke along the grey-barred lengths thought of them as the spirits of birds which had perched upon them in the fire and light of past summer days, sparrow-hawk and kestrel, bullfinch and turtle-dove, woodpecker, jay, greenfinch and yellow wagtail; for the red, blue, and green colours of flames were made by metals driven in the trunks for wire-fencing supports long ago, iron and zinc, and copper trenail of the ship's timber.

A pallid snow-light reflected from the garden made clearer the dark branches of lilac and honeysuckle growing by tiled shed, seen through the leaded panes of the casement windows. The boy sat there, happy that Christmas was coming, and that their friend the Fort pilot was coming to stay. His father had waxed his hickory skis, and made a sledge with barrel-hoop iron nailed on the runners, and promised him a lot of fun on the hills, and of course they would build a snow man. And for the feast on Christmas Day Mum had made mincepies, and there was a honeycomb, a goose to be stuffed and roasted with peeled chestnuts, sage, and thyme, and eaten with apple sauce, leeks and potatoes. There was half a Stilton cheese, and a plum pudding with trinkets hidden in it, including threepenny bits, trouser buttons, and rings all of silver; a bowl of scald cream with thick yellow crust covering it, home-baked wheat scones which he liked better than baker's bread, and a cake with rare currants and sultanas in it, and lots of other lovely things. There was a surprise for the guest, too, for his father had painted a special picture for him, of the Phasian bird flying up into the sun.

He was startled out of his reverie by the thrilling shock of a bell ringing in the room. With fast-beating heart he got up and crossed the floor to lift the telephone from the ledge by the casement window, swallowed the saliva in his mouth, and uttered a careful and subdued "Hullo" to hear a voice asking for his father. Asking the caller to hold on, he ran to the studio, where his father was touching up a painting of Chee-kai sunning itself with spread wings on the snow-crusted top of the pine-tree. The boy behind him, he hurried to the farmhouse parlour, and listened

321

gravely with the instrument to his ear. At length he said, "Thank you, I understand. I am so sorry. Yes, I heard them coming in, and wondered. . . ." He put down the receiver quietly, turned to the boy, patted his head, hesitated as if to speak, then returned to the studio.

The stockman went neither to church nor chapel, but it was his custom on Sunday mornings and on Christmas about noon to stroll down to the Cross, and be among those whom he had known all his life, to lean on the wall and smoke a pipe and talk. Something he heard and saw there before he went to the Horn and Corn for a drink of beer after the people had come out of church—the pubs would not open until after the morning service was over —made him return there shortly after he had eaten his dinner, as though for a stroll, or maybe to visit his brother's cottage at the other end of the village. He wore his best cap and overcoat, both black, and walked with his work-thickened hands in his pockets, pipe in mouth, a man who had earned his holiday. But this sauntering casualness concealed a vague anxiety, and a sense of watchfulness based on a feeling of protection.

The long American saloon car, all chromium and sweeping black, stood in the Great Yard, and his senses quickened as he saw it. Since he had left the farm some time before, the stockman had found himself often thinking of the man who had done so much for his land, a man who, he had once remarked to his son, was "too good", a criticism implying a fault, but—"There harn't another like Wilbo in a hunner thousand. They're all out fer theirselves, but he ain't." And in a sudden divination he had exclaimed. "Thet's true English, thet is." His son had demurred, declaring that to be too good was to be upsetting, like drilling too much seed corn in a field. "Thet ain't no sense in it, it's a silly thing, and he du du silly things, at

times, thet's what I mean, Father." The older man had
agreed, but had added, "What he du du is thet he don't
look arter hisself. He du spend half the night waiting fer
poachers, arter thet thar longtail faysan bard." The stockman knew what no other living person knew: that his old
master, who had gone bankrupt and killed himself, and to
whom he had been deeply attached, had put four eggs in
a pheasant's nest under the pine-tree in the Carr. He had
told the stockman that as a boy he had seen the birds on
a great estate in the Brecklands, famous for its many
thousands of wild pheasants shot every year, and their flight
had so deeply impressed him that he had dreamed of one
day having them on his land, when he became a farmer.
Always in his life he had been too busy to get hold of a
pair of stock birds; but towards the end, he had gone speci-
ally to a game farm and bought four eggs. It had been almost
the last act of the old man's life; and Chee-kai had materialized from that faraway excitement of a young mind.

Now, thinking of his other late master, and convinced
that "some on'm" were out to do Wilbo, he strolled past
the Great Yard, and hearing sounds of loud voices inside
the Flockmaster's shed, he stopped and listened.

A few days before some American soldiers had come to
fire a course on the anti-aircraft range, and like many
others before them, had been contacted by the Flockmaster after closing time in the Turnip Arms, with sug-
gestions that he knew where something stronger than
beer could be gotten.

Inside the little flint barn of the Flockmaster several men
were sitting on boxes and tubs, smoking, talking, drinking, and chewing. The air was thick with the smoke of
Chesterfield and Camel cigarettes; the two soldiers in
khaki were well supplied and generous, feeling themselves
to be in the role of saviours of Old England. They were

dark, plump young men, with olive complexions, wide faces, and dark hair, of emigrant Eastern stock, probably Levantine. Each had bought from the Flockmaster a bottle of whisky, from which he was taking and offering swigs to all present, including four of the partners of the trading company.

The Boys, hearing that duck were in from over the sea, driven by hard weather, had come out for an afternoon's shooting on the marshes, which were free to all. They wore rubber boots, and their guns were in the back of the car. They had to pass the village on their way to the marshes, so they had called in to inquire if any progress had been made about the offer to buy the farm, and had found the soldiers with the open bottles sitting around. At once they had been invited to take a drink. They had had a drink, not meaning to stay: now it was a party, one bottle was already empty, and a second on the way. At the moment the stockman paused outside, hearing loud voices and laughter, the Flockmaster was showing them the gamecock Jago, boasting of its skill and courage. "He's got me three score bards a'ready!" he lied. "Pitter pitter pitter, crock—craw! slish, slosh, slup—and thet's all over wi' goldy longtail!"

The quietest man of the party was the poacher. He was interested in the tommy-guns the young soldiers had with them, and was trying to scheme how, without too much risk, he could get hold of one, hide it up for a year or two, then have the shells altered—the bullets removed —to take shot. He had a number of twelve-bore cartridges, from the R.A.F. station, which he could break up. The tommy-gun would be handier and quicker for the woods, if the lock could be altered to fire single shots.

"Well, you know, boys, we really ought to get cracking," said the man with the round, fleshy face, and reddish hair. "I want to try out my Purdey on the widgeon.

324

Light goes quickly these short days. The last war Christmas, I reckon. Then you boys"—to the soldiers—"will be getting home. And none too soon for you, eh? England's a lousy dump nowadays—still, we mustn't grumble," he added, looking round to find approval for what he considered was an honest admission. But the Boys, like himself a little tight, were lighting cigarettes offered by the soldiers.

The bottle was passed round again. When it was empty, a third bottle was bought and paid for by one of the soldiers. "How about giving Jago a drink?" suggested one of the Boys, pointing at the game cock. "He's earned you a nice little wad, eh Flock my old cock sparrer? Give old Jago some with corn soaked in it. Give 'im a break for once. You work 'im 'ard enough."

But the Flockmaster wouldn't have it. "My li'l old Jago's match fer any bard stone sober," he declared, sententiously. "I won't hev'n led astray, he's too wal'able, thet he is!"

"Oh, wring 'is —— neck, and put 'im feathers an' all in the bloody pot," retorted the other, continuing his line of humour. "Ah, would I?" replied the Flockmaster, looking up at the other with a squint. "There ain't a bard from here to Lunnon this cock wouldn't strike down afore you could say knife!"

"Let's see him doing his stuff, then! Ain't there another cock to match with it? Come on, it's Christmas Day, and we're all out for a bit of sport, ain't we?" He looked at the soldiers.

"Sure we are!" cried one, suddenly animate, as he put a bottle to his lips and gulped. The melancholy returned to his voice as he said in a sing-song tone, after wiping his lips with the back of one podgy hand, "Aw gee, I wanna get me a kraut before I go way back to Detroit."

"Flock here will sell you one, soldier," said the money-

325

lender, pointing with his eyebrows, as he poured a drink into a bakelite cup. "The old bastard'll sell anything from ponking cockles and screwy culls to old rope, won't you, eh?" "Sure he will," said the other soldier, with indifference. "Say, when'r we going to see this goddam cock fight? I sure would like to see that feathered slicker throw those can-openers around. Can't you fix a fight, Pop?" to the Flockmaster.

"I wanna get me a kraut," repeated his companion, in melancholy sing song, as he stared at the floor. "Aw gee, I come forty-five hundred miles, and I go home forty-five hundred miles, an' I never seen one goddam, heiling, goose-steppin' kraut."

"What's a kraut, son?"

"A kraut is about the lowest thing on Gard's earth, I guess," said the soldier, lolling loose like a sack as he perched on the empty hogshead, and speaking with quiet solemnity, "unless it's that all-time low of humanity temporarily crawling about on atolls way over the Pacific, cracking like a yellow all-teeth louse in its fox-hole when the heat is turned on it. I guess a kraut ain't no lower, whichever way a man looks at it." The soldier did not really believe what he was saying: he was trying to talk like the tough, ox-necked hero of one of the strip cartoon series issued in books of gaudy colours to the troops for their mind's contentment. Having delivered himself of his literary eloquence, he leaned forward on his perch upon the seventy-two gallon barrel, the brown boots on the small feet of the heavy legs kicking hollowly on the staves.

The moneylender exchanged a significant glance with one of his pals. The same idea had come to both, with the thought of its danger, and need for caution. The moneylender flicked an eyelid twice at the other, conveying that he would take care of it. He laughed, his eyes became easy.

326

"You'll have to be content with the Japs in the Pacific, son, I guess. There won't be any Nazis left soon, way things are going on." Mouth and eyes were hard as he glanced at his partner. "The only good German is a dead German, eh, Flock?"

"Thar's a Jarman livin' in this place," remarked the Flockmaster. "A Jarman, they say he is, Wilbo."

"Wilbo's no German!" exclaimed the moneylender, with assumed emphasis. "But I'd perhaps agree with you if you called him a fifth-columnist, a phoney farmer living on the fat of the land, while our boys and yours"—looking at the Americans—"are dying out there. In any other country but this he'd have been put up against a wall and shot, with others of his kidney locked up with 'im until recently."

"Thet's it," said Flock, not realising, as he stroked Jago. "Wilbo's no Jarman. What thengs they do say, don't'm? His li'l ole boy's a Norfolkm'n, ain't 'e tho! Fit ter bust, I wor, arter hearin' of'm one marnin!"

The Boys exchanged glances, the moneylender slightly shaking his head, and warning with his eyes, as at an auction sale when deciding to bid no further. Both he and the other two were relieved that the idea behind his words had not gone any further. And, as they repeated to one another several times that evening, after looking round to make sure they were not likely to be overheard, they had their faults, but when all was said and done, they were Englishmen.

Meanwhile the subjects of the talk within the barn had gone out, gloved and mufflered, to enjoy the snow on the hills and sloping fields of the farm. Wilbo carried skis and sticks, his son pulled his new sledge down the village street, meaning to cross over the bridge and reach the upland fields by the lane, and so to avoid the premises and the broken tractor and other implements covered with dust and fowl droppings in the hovel.

On the way down the village street they met the stockman, and exchanged seasonal greetings with him. The stockman hesitated, as though he would say something, but with a wave of his hand Wilbo passed on, as a large American car, with chains on its wheels, drove towards him. Wilbo did not look at it, but the four men within noted that he carried skis, a fact which, as they drove along the coast road, made them give up the idea of going on the marshes for duck shooting, and instead, to leave the car down a cart track not far from the Carr. Getting out, with their guns, and with trepidant anticipation of trying their luck in the Carr, they started to walk down the drift beside the river. Almost at once a pheasant scratching in snow and leaves flew up before them with whirr of wings. They were both startled and elated. They gripped their guns and moved forward. This was fun!

Their whispered remarks revealed the immature consciousness that prompted excuse for what they were doing, half-joking as they were. "Bloody shame when you come to think of it, all these birds going to waste because that —— owns the land." Another time, "Everywhere short of food, at a time like this, and not allowing shooting on his land, he ought to be bloody well shot." And then the inevitable, "Helping Hitler by keeping good food off the market, that's what he's doing." They were now halfway down the drift, in a near-tunnel made of trees growing out of the steep boundary bank on their left, and of branches overhanging the river from the Carr. They pressed through snow covering a wrack of nettles and hemlock stalks. Another pheasant rose up, two shots detonated loud in the enclosed space: the bird fell. Hide it by the base of a sycamore tree, cover it with snow; and afterwards don't forget to look down the barrels of your guns, boys, a little snow down them is enough to cause a burst. "Come on, what's to stop us. Blast, I haven't enjoyed myself so much for a long time, and the hell with Wilbo!"

Others had noticed the tall figure with skis carried on shoulder, the sticks with bamboo circles above the spikes, the boy beside him hauling a sledge. One of the soldiers called to the Flockmaster, to ask who it was. The old fellow peered, and after hesitation, whispered, "Thet's Wilbo." "Who, the goddam fifth-columnist?" "Well, 'tes only what'm said," replied Flock. "Thet little old totty boy wi'm's a Norfolkm'n, t'rough and t'rough. Laugh? I laffed fit to bust." They stared at the figures going over the bridge.

"Now's our chance," said a voice behind the Flockmaster. It was the poacher speaking. He had a peculiar grin on his face. "Wha'jer mean?" asked the soldier. The poacher said that now was their chance to try Jago in the woods. The Flockmaster had told him that he had seen the yellow bird by the Long Wood. The poacher had assumed that Wilbo and the "little old boy" were going on the Common Hills behind the Horn and Corn, where village youths and children usually went to slide when there was snow.

But father and son had continued on past the turning to the Common Hills, and passing the beer-house, had gone on up the lane in the opposite direction, and so to the higher fields of the farm.

Within his barn the Flockmaster was standing indecisive before the suggestion of the poacher, backed up by the soldiers, to take Jago in a sack (the wicker basket being too obvious) and try him on the farm.

"Goo wan! Wilbo ain't no cop! And who's ter know, Flock?"

"I dursen't!"

The Flockmaster hesitated because he did not want to be found there, having a dart at a pheasant. He did not want to lose the grazing for the pony. No considerations of taking game troubled him, because like many another peasant he considered that what was wild ought to be free, and was not so only because there was one law for the rich and another for the poor. He did not know or think that sporting rights were a property to be bought and sold, like his pony or his cart or his cottage. As for the yellow pheasant, that ought by rights to be in a glass case, being a "wal'able bard". But with the further urging of the poacher that he had a right, having been given the grazing, to take a cockerel there to give it a bit of green stuff, the Flockmaster gave way. Jago was put in a sugar-beet pulp bag, and with bridle and head collar over the Flockmaster's arm, they set out ostensibly to visit his pony.

The soldiers went with them, carrying their short weapons slung on their shoulders. It was a local order that they carried them, since the breaking of the Allied front in the Ardennes, and the possibility of a paratroop landing in Britain.

They entered the farm by the gate beyond the river bridge, and walked along the straight road leading to the Corn Barn in the distance. Nobody saw them, nobody stopped them; and once past the hovel, a long tiled shed with its dozen bays separated by oak posts resting on stone blocks, the soldiers unslung their guns, feeling that they were hunters, of the kind they had read about in magazines. But the poacher, who wanted to get the long-tailed pheasant, urged them not to shoot until they had had a chance of trying Jago at it.

They walked to the beginning of the Long Wood, and then the poacher put his finger to his lips, and went ahead cautiously. The Flockmaster and the soldiers followed. After a while the poacher stopped, and held up his hand. From in front, through the frosty air, had come the call of a partridge.

They went on again, walking carefully through the snow. Ahead the shaggy bay pony was to be seen standing with its back to the old ash-tree that leaned over the dyke. Beyond was the Willow Plot. The poacher motioned them to stop. With a finger he pointed to the sky. They listened. Far up in the air there came the sound as of instruments of a brass band being tuned before playing. The cronkling, honkling cries came from a wide and uneven chevron of birds flying inland. "Them's geese, I loves to hear'm," whispered the Flockmaster to the soldiers.

The poacher signed to them to go slowly and quietly. They passed by a great oak-tree, under which were scattered many buff-coloured spangles, which a pair of nuthatches had been knocking from the branches, for the grubs within. Some had been wedged in crevices of the bark, and prised open by the birds. Tracks of a pheasant's feet led away along the ride, beside those of a partridge.

The poacher stopped, as somewhere in front of them came the call, more distinctly, through the bare trunks of the trees—*per-tris*, *per-tris*. A high, frail cry, made up of a series of slight notes, came afterwards. The poacher's upheld hand shook with the urgency of warning to stand still. For him, thirty quid was at stake.

The cronkling of the geese passed away, as the four men came to where the grass narrowed to a border between ride and dyke. Here was the gateway which led steeply up through the trees to the Pightle. When they came to the gateway, the poacher caught a glimpse of the tip of a long tail sticking out behind the trunk of a tree in the wood.

331

The men remained quiet, crouching down on the slope to the gateway. *Per-tris, per-tris*, came the wheezy call of the partridge, quite near in the field. They could see the dark shape on the snow.

The Flockmaster waited behind the thick trunk of the elm by which stood the post on which the gate was hung. He untied the string of the pulp bag, and drew out Jago, to stroke his neck and head with the back of a finger. Jago knew why he had been taken out of the bag, and his head, on the long neck, peered up and down, large-eyed. The two soldiers crouched on their heels below. They passed a bottle between them, taking wet gulps. One drained the bottle, tossed it into a snowdrift, where it disappeared noiselessly, and stared before him, a dull glaze on his eyes.

The poacher knelt by the clapping post of the gate, watching, his hand held out beside him, ready to signal to the Flockmaster. He knew the pheasant was somewhere near, and would run to join the partridge on the Pightle if neither was alarmed. He knew also that the partridge would be tired, after running in the snow. The sound of a key turning in rusty lock came again; nearer. *Per-tris, per-tris.*

The poacher's hand was still upheld. The Flockmaster pressed the gamecock hard against his coat.

Again, and startlingly near, the scrupetting call sounded within half a gunshot of the gate. The frail, rather sweet cry answered. The poacher had heard it before. He knew it was the answering note of the pheasant. He knew that the partridge had been its protector, and that a cock partridge never yielded its duty. So he signalled to the Flockmaster to loose Jago.

Turning round slowly, before sinking to his knees, the Flockmaster put the head of the game-cock through the space between hanging post and tree trunk. The poacher pointed with his finger, stabbing the air. The Flock-master understood, and released Jago.

The game-cock went forward over the snow in a low running crouch. Pertris, who had been standing, head up-held, a dozen feet away from the edge of the wood, let out a screech of alarm *zett-zett-zackle-sitt!* as he saw Jago. He crouched, and as the game-cock came near, he ran at it, to meet it beak to beak and to leap fluttering into the air, matching the leap of the cock. Once he leapt, twice he leapt, thrice he leapt and then a steel spur, glancing by the side of his head, struck out his eye. Pertris gave a cry, which was answered by a swishing of feathers dispread around the base of a beech-tree as Chee-kai, uttering a whistling scream of defiance, ran to where Jago had jumped upon Pertris spread-winged and quivering upon the snow.

Jago, his feathers in a loose ruff round his neck, leapt away from Pertris, and turned to meet Chee-kai. For an instant they circled and wove, beak to beak, Chee-kai with sweep and counter sweep of long barred tail, Jago the taller bird, on longer, stronger legs, his tail little more than a quirt, his wings clipped for swift buffet and stroke, his feet large, with heavy toes of horn, his natural spurs replaced by steel stilettos which in a downward slash in air could pierce the muscle between a man's thumb and forefinger.

Beak to beak, throats near the snow, the two birds wove up, to side, then down, to side, up again, elbow-winged, hackled, eyes dilated, beaks open for greater breath, for greater power—Jago leapt and slashed, Chee-kai leapt and dodged, leapt, avoided, feinted, leapt, bril-liant yellow-cloaked, head cowled in black and white—he jumped six feet in the air, Jago misjudged the height and leapt to drive both stilettos into the cinnamon bars of the tail, to fall back, and before he could recover and

333

crouch again, Chee-kai was on him and a grey spur of horn, curved and tapering to a sharp point, was driven through Jago's neck and his windpipe was pierced, as well as the big vein which lay behind the throat.

It had happened in little more than a minute. Neither bird had seen the men by the gate, as the branches of a thorn overgrown from the hedge along the woodland verge were directly between them and the circling fight upon the snow. Neither birds nor men had seen movement at the edge of the High Wood across the Pightle where Wilbo, having left his son by the woodland yard, about to make an effigy of Santa Claus out of a big drift of snow, had come on skis down the southern side of the High Wood, to the corner where suddenly he saw the yellow and brown leaping birds and a row of faces above the top bar of the gate. There he stemmed, and waited, watching, almost incapable of movement.

At the corner he stood, breathing deeply, for he had imagined that ultimate scene many times, but never known its details. As in a dream he was conscious of several faces of men above the top bar of the gate, of a staccato noise, loud and immediate, of snow spirting around Chee-kai. He began to shout, and then dream enclosed him once more as he pushed off on skis down the slope, the keen air murmuring in his ears as he flew over the snow, seeing a golden rocket arise before him, its barred tail quivering and undulating to the blur of wings carrying it into the air . . . and star-like flashes replaced the faces by the gateway.

The stockman, following four sets of footsteps in the snow under the Long Wood, heard the stutter of a sub-machine-gun before him, heard the echo of the burst followed by another burst, and after a pause and a few seconds, a man shouting, and there was a third prolonged burst. "Oh my dear soul," he cried, and began to run forward, for what had been an unresolved dread in his mind was now reality.

At the eastern end of the farm, where the hedge growing steeply above drift and river was the boundary, the four trespassers had been enjoying themselves. The moneylender was particularly pleased with his Purdey gun, which represented less than one per cent of the great bulk of paper money in his safe, and tucked away in sundry hiding places about his house. The gun had cost two hundred pounds; the Packard car had cost another fifteen hundred, and was the more satisfactory because there was no record of its purchase, and it was likely to increase in value. The Purdey gun was so balanced that it felt light as a feather, coming to the shoulder without conscious weight. Walking down the drift he had killed a pigeon clean with one barrel, and a woodcock with the other, very nearly a left and right. Two more hen pheasants had been shot, but a kestrel had been missed—because, he had claimed, it had flown slowly, too slow for the gun. They had also killed a hare, and "rattled the shins" of a heron that, with apparent laziness (the bird was weak with hunger), had arisen from the frozen dyke.

They had walked across the meadow under the dark and towering High Wood, their rubber boots crunching and purring in the crisp snow. One had gone up through the wood, to drive out any birds. The remaining three were halfway along the meadow side of the hedge under the Breck when they stopped suddenly. The rapid stutter of a sub-machine-gun had come to them over the white, black-wooded landscape. They listened, looking at one another. The stutter came again. Then a double stuttering.

A few moments later the moneylender looked up into

335

the sky and saw a sight that made him give a shout of
'Christ!" for rising above the gap between the Long and
the High Wood was an object that at first did not seem to
be a bird, it was climbing at so steep an angle and drawing
behind it a waving tail of unbelievable length. As it
climbed the beat of its wings was rippling in its spread
tail, then it turned and started to fly level, making for the
High Wood. They watched it flying with amazement,
the tail now compact and in a straight line like the shaft of
an arrow behind the barb of whirring wings. With mor-
tification they saw it was not coming their way, the most
marvellous high bird ever dreamed of; though it was
higher than the effective killing range of forty yards. Even
so, the Boys would have had a smack at it, or a sporting
chance of winging it and bringing it down. Then
abruptly the bird tumbled, with sweep of dispread and
bended tail following its half-roll and dive, and falling to
a lower level, it flew towards the Carr. Chee-kai had been
shot at, and missed, by the fourth man in the High Wood.

Seeing two soldiers moving away slowly along the
path under the Long Wood in front of him, the stockman
hurried forward resolutely, passing the pony tethered
beside the dyke. He did not see the Flockmaster cowering
behind the trunk of an oak-tree, nor the poacher running
up the Pightle to the Breck along the upper edge of the
wood.

He came to the gate, and saw upon the trodden snow
two score and more of small brass shells scattered about,
and recognized the kind left on the meadows in the past
by troops who sometimes had come on the farm for
battle-practice with live ammunition. Looking over the
gate, he saw a partridge lying on the snow, and near it a
gamecock. Going through the gateway, he stared at the
birds awhile, before looking round for further sight of

the soldiers who apparently had shot the birds. Then he saw the body of a man lying in the snow halfway down the slope.

The stockman ran through the snow, seeing that it was Wilbo lying there with one leg and a splintered ski twisted under him, and that he was not moving. With a shock that stopped his breathing for a moment he realized that Wilbo had been shot. He stood there with a dull and helpless thought that it never ought to be, that it was wrong, that it was not justice. Then with full realization of what had happened, he stared at the eyes fixed in the grey face, at the slight movements of the jaw, and knew that Wilbo was trying to say something. He knelt beside him, and began to stroke the forehead with his hand, saying that it would be all right. "Keep yew still, sir, don't yew worry, yew'v had a fall, that's all"; but to himself he thought, O dear Lord, he's a-go.

The stricken man was trying to speak, his eyes were trying to find the stockman's face. Bending his head low, his ear close to the open mouth, the stockman thought he heard the words, in hardly more than a whisper, *don't leave me*. He took the hand lying in the snow, held it between his own, while saying earnestly, "I'm wi' ya, 'bor, ya'll be all right," as he pressed the hand for reassurance. "Lor' bless us, what'm I a-thinkin' of," he muttered, and kneeling up, he took off his overcoat, to lay it tenderly upon Wilbo, lifting the arms outside; and kneeling once more, he took the hand again, and held it between his own.

After a while, he saw that Wilbo was again trying to say something. He bent his head to catch the slow words that were now weaker than a whisper, that strove to find utterance, with the least movement of tongue and jaw. The stockman listened, while sweat broke out on his brow. "Yee-s, yee-s," he said, nodding his head. "I know

337

what ya sayin', I've a-got it," to the eyes that stared fixedly, and were suddenly open wide. "Ya lie still, sir, and rest yerself'." Wilbo began to shudder, to breathe harshly, the breath coming raspingly before the eyes lost their sight, the head settled sideways, the jaw dropped; and with a sigh it was over.

The stockman bent his head, his tears dripping; he remained unmoving for some time, before raising his head, and pushing the back of his hand across his eyes, then to draw up the coat to cover the face, thinking that it were the second master he had found like that in seven year.

When he had risen to his feet again, his feelings resigned once more, he saw the boy on the skyline by the edge of the High Wood, where it joined the upland field. The poacher, coming upon him by the Woodland Yard, had pointed in the direction of the Willow Plot, telling him that Yanks were down there firing at his father's pheasants, and the boy had crept down to look. The stockman went to him, and holding him by the hand, led him home by way of the hedge and the new road down the side of the hill.

Flying strongly for the marshes, Chee-kai approached the three men staring upwards from the meadow below. He was beyond normal range, fully sixty yards over their heads, but they fired, hardly knowing what they were doing in their excitement, as the bird whistled in fast flight over their heads, its long tail held straight and thin behind it. Bang!—bang, bang! the bird flew on—bang! bang!—the bird flew on—bang! the bird checked almost imperceptibly, but flew on. They watched it going straight away in strong level flight, watched it rising as it beat its wings quicker, climbing into the air over the northern end of the Carr. Yet it seemed to be staying in the same high place, its wings to be beating without power. It hovered with humming-bird-like fluttering, it was towering, the last visible sunward flight of a dying bird.

Chee-kai knew not what he was doing as a bright red berry grew on the white feathers of his head, as his flutters became feebler. Chee-kai was faltering, his wings were loosening, the air alone was moving them. Chee-kai was dropping through space—he fell asprawl into the top of the pine tree growing at the northern end of the Carr.

Chee-kai lay across the frozen crest of the tree, his wings spread as though the body lightly was come to rest there. His head lay on a mat of needles silvered with rime. Slowly the blood dripped from the hole made by a single pellet which had pierced throat and palate, and paralysed the motors of the brain.

Under the tree the snow was stained by seven crimson drops. An aged moorcock, Gallinule, approached with mincing steps, sought about the stained snow, and finding nothing, went away again. Huddled upon a lower branch of the pine, Harra the Denchman waited for night to fall.

On the ivy leaves free of snow upon the crest of the pine the drifting wind made minute scratching noises, as of infinitesimal particles of dust beating invisible upon each hollow veined tissue: a dust pouring against each stalk and twig and stretched dark green and glossy skin held by its web and filigree: laying an enamelled surface upon all parts of the trees it touched, each snake-headed bud of beech, each cloven-footed bud of ash, each spangle of oak and seed-cone of fir. And so it was upon all things of the land. Ice-glass coated trunk of tree and stem of grass, wire of fence and telegraph, roosting bird and old nest, pantile of woodshed and iron roof of airfield-hangar, dead thistle-stalks in field, tall poles girdling airfields with lights, and burnt-out aircraft: each was increased many times in weight and thickness by the clear enamellings of the drifting ice-airs; and when the earth turned out of shadow to the light again, men, women and children marvelled at a new world made of crystal.

As the sun shone all these objects flashed and coruscated with the colours of the spectrum, evanescent gleams lancing from a thousand facets. But none saw the colours of Chee-kai lying upon the crest of the pine, every filament and featherlet clear and magnified under a thick casing of ice. The bird in splendour rested there until towards midnight of the day before the thaw, and with a tearing crash, the weight of the ice-crown upon the head of the pine broke the branches and in falling sheared or tore the under branches, themselves already overladen. The bole stood bereft, a splintered mass of its members heaped upon its roots, among them the body of Harra the Denchman, who had died in icy sleep and so found the earth with the body of Chee-kai.

So the chronicle of a hybrid pheasant upon a small farm of East Anglia draws to its close, a tale of those years when endurance seemed to many to be without avail; but endure they did, each man according to the light revealed to him between the time of coming from the earth and inhabiting the envelope that the earth in her generosity gives to him, and the time of returning that envelope to the earth, mother of all living. Dust to dust—the old words, as true and simple as the rising of the sun, the coming of rain, the crumbling of clods under the harrow stroke when the land is timely, when the lark sings over the plowed field and hares run wild upon ley and furrow. Dust to dust—the old words spoken beside the coffin, covered by a Union Jack as befitted an old soldier who,

340

the parson declared to the stockman, the teamsman, the dealer, the innkeepers, the doctor, the woman with her son standing beside her, and others who had come in curiosity or to pay their last respects to the dead, in his own way and according to his own conscience had lived for his country; and who was to say that he had not died for it, he whose last words, spoken through great pain, had striven to lay the blame for what had happened, by a sudden appearance which had taken others unawares, upon himself, and not upon those others. As he put away his life, as he yielded up his spirit from a body so grievously hurt, he had been thinking only of others, in the consciousness of that magnanimity, or greater love, which must be shown to all men, to friends and to enemies alike, if mankind was truly to inherit the earth as the Kingdom of God. Amen.

In the sky wild geese were passing, flying for the Great Barrier Sand where they rested by day, flying with slow flaps of wings one beside and above the other, crying their music of ice-pack and midnight-sun, of seas where the great whales blew, of summer upon the flowery coast of far Spitzbergen.